THE GLORY OF THEIR DEEDS

BENJAMIN WHITE-PATARINO

The Glory of Their Deeds
Published by Benjamin White-Patarino, 2020

Cover Design and Layout by Ellie Bockert Augsburger
www.creativedigitalstudios.com
Copyright ©2020 by Benjamin White-Patarino
All Rights Reserved

ISBN: 978-1-7360879-2-3

ACKNOWLEDGMENTS

My interest in the First World War began when I was eight years old and watched *The Young Indiana Jones Chronicles* for the first time on VHS. Within a short time, I was reading everything I could find about the topic and dreaming up the earliest versions of what would eventually become this novel. In the many years that have passed since then, so many people have supported me along the way that I could write a complete novel just about their efforts. I extend my deepest gratitude and appreciation to all those friends, family, and colleagues who made this novel possible:

Nathalie Mollet and Cathérine Génie, my French aunts, for indulging my desire to visit every First World War monument and cemetery in Picardie. Nathalie single-handedly makes the French language assistant program in Friville-Escarbotin a delight, and acts as mentor and tireless advocate for countless generations of teaching assistants. When I started this book in November 2015, the hard kitchen chair I had in my little French apartment was giving me back problems. Cathérine bought me a cushion for my birthday that made all the difference. She is no longer with us, but the cushion saves my back to this day. Je ne t'oublierai jamais.

Pierre Néri, for his friendship and for helping me get to know France in general and Paris in particular. There never was a kinder, more generous soul than he.

My fellow teaching assistants Marta Sanz Rodriguez de la Flor, Brittany Mabee, Alys Robinson, Sabrina Danler, Chloé Williams, and Cyrille LeJeune. There are few times in my life when I have felt as supported and surrounded by friendship as I did when we were all wandering around northern France.

My teachers and mentors over the years, including Robert Scott Peoples, Robert A. Pois, Daniel Niedringhaus, and Martha Hanna. It's not many teachers or professors who would take the time to indulge a nine-year-old wearing a French infantry helmet with an hours-long history conversation, or allow one of their students to take over teaching a lesson about trench warfare during the class unit about World War I, but these people did exactly that.

Dr. Susan Wei, for challenging me to write clean, efficient prose. I improved more in one year in her IB English class than during any other period of my formal education.

My brother Alec, for sharing my interest and passion in military history over the years. It is a treasured common ground for us, one that becomes even more valuable as work and family constraints tighten with adulthood and age.

My colleague W.P. Brothers, for patiently granting me time to complete this novel while our mutual projects waited for me.

My friends, Chris Wu, Benjamin Collins, Leanne Glenn, and Jackie Turner, who have supported and encouraged my writing in innumerable ways. One cannot overestimate the value to authors of the proofreading, encouragement, and advice of friends such as these.

Aunt Michelle, for being the first one to read and edit this novel. Your Christmas visits always rank among the best family times. My grandparents, Rachel and Vincent, who did not live to see me complete this work, and Bob and Mary, who thankfully did, and my uncles and aunts, Christina, Bob Jr., David, and Michael. Your love and support makes life worthwhile at its darkest points.

My parents, Vincent and Pamela, who always taught me to love writing and history. They encouraged me when I dressed as a World War I soldier for Halloween rather than a character from *Pirates of the Caribbean,* like my contemporaries. They motivated me to keep working on this book when I despaired of having the time to devote to it or finding readers who would care enough about the Great War to pick it up. They supported me to dive headfirst into studying World War I, learning French, and leaving twice to teach English in France (which was really an excuse to research battlefields and monuments in person). I would not have started this work or even had the opportunity to do so had it not been for them.

Finally, Courtney, my fearless, intelligent, beautiful fiancée. I can't imagine her life plans ever included talking about World War I this much, but her support in the final stages of this book has made its completion possible. She is my sunshine.

I dedicate this novel to the generation that endured the Great War, and especially to those who never returned home and lie beneath endless rows of headstones, or in places unknown. May this work continue their legacy and grant them immortality in our memory.

PROLOGUE

May 28, 1918
Cantigny, France
4:45 pm

"Don't bunch up! Spread out! Keep moving!"

Private James Garrison sprinted forward, following the shouted commands of Major Roosevelt through the thick, acrid air. He swallowed hard, strained to breathe, his feet and calves burning from the effort, his arms held out in front of him, pointing his rifle and bayonet ahead of him. He stumbled on the uneven, shell-blasted ground, recovered his footing, tried to quicken his pace, the weight of his equipment pulling him down, making every movement sluggish.

Come on. Keep up.

James raised his head, looked up the slight incline that rose toward the village of Cantigny, just a few hundred yards ahead. Blackened, jagged ruins and scorched tree trunks jutted up from the ground, silhouetted against an afternoon sky splotched and smeared by columns of thick, black smoke.

"That's it! Just a bit farther!" Roosevelt's shout sounded distant and faint over the rumble of artillery and the rapid pops of rifle and machine gun fire. James looked for the major, found him just ahead in the small crowd of men in drab khaki who were rushing toward the village. He was waving a pistol in the air, looking over his shoulder every few steps.

James stumbled again, caught himself from pitching headfirst into a shell crater, turned slightly, ran around its edge, the rotten-eggs odor of spent explosives making him gag. An image entered his mind, of tripping and falling ass over bayonet on the training course near Verdun. He could almost hear William's laughter again.

"That's showing the enemy."

James caught himself smiling and looked to the side, expecting to see his friend there.

A bolt of panic lanced through him. Corporal Rodriguez was running beside him, but William was... Where was he?

They'd been side by side in the jump-off trenches, had waited together until the order had come to move to the front and reinforce the 28th Infantry in their positions east of Cantigny.

"Do you think they're alright up there?" William had asked, his eyes wide.

James had smiled, excitement filling him. "You wouldn't want them finishing the Boche off without us, would you?"

Almost every soldier of the 26th Infantry Regiment had been jealous when they'd learned that the 28th would be the first over the top, the first American unit to launch an offensive in the War since they'd arrived in France more than a year ago. They'd listened with awe in the predawn darkness to the blast of the artillery pounding the German positions, and had borrowed Lieutenant Robinson's field glasses to get a view of the French tanks leading the attack. As the morning had crept on, they had thrilled at the positive news that had come in occasional bursts, held in the hands of breathless runners.

The 28th had entered the village along with French flamethrower teams, secured it with minimal casualties, and then pressed on and taken positions just beyond the town.

But in the afternoon, the tone of the news had shifted, and James had seen the moods of Lieutenant Robinson and Sergeant Stokley change with each message. The Germans had opened a barrage on the American position, had counter-attacked in force.

Then Robinson had shouted the order, repeated and amplified by the sergeants down the line. "Fix bayonets!"

William had been right beside James as he'd slid the bayonet onto the end of his Springfield, fear and excitement coiling together inside of him, igniting into something unbearable. Their first battle, their first time in combat, everything they'd waited and trained for. Then they'd clambered out of the trench and rushed forward together.

But now?

James kept up his pace, looked again for any sign of his friend.

You damned baby!

He shook his head, turned his eyes forward. William was fine, just mixed in with the rest of the company somewhere. James cursed under his breath, felt suddenly embarrassed. He was a man, a soldier. He didn't need his friend with him at every moment.

He focused on pumping his legs, driving himself up the slope and toward the wrecked town, his entrenching tool slapping him on the leg with each step. The boom of the artillery was louder now, and he could see jets of smoke and fire leaping up here and there in the village, rattling the ground under his pounding feet.

"They're shelling the village!" The voice was Sergeant Stokley's, and James looked to his right, saw the man, tall and angular, running a few yards away. "Don't stop when you reach the houses! Move straight through!"

The ground began to level off, and James slowed his pace, closing the gap between him and the tangled mass of rubble that marked the edge of the village. He followed closely behind Stokley and Private Walker as they picked their way around what was left of a house, lifting his feet high to avoid tripping on the charred wood beams and cracked bricks.

"Sarge, what direction are the—?"

A thunderclap from somewhere on the other side of the building cut off James's question. The ground vibrated, and dirt and small chips of masonry fell out of the sky, clinking off the rough steel surface of his helmet. Another boom, another explosion. James gripped the brim of his helmet instinctively, squinted his eyes.

CRACK!

Another shell, then another.

James leapt into the cover of a high pile of bricks, put his back against a crumbling wall. He shut his eyes against the noise of the bombardment, then opened them, his mouth dry.

A few feet beyond him were a pair of bodies in khaki. They were Americans, blood soaking their uniforms, their eyes vacant, their limbs bent at awkward angles. The smell hit him, the odor of burnt flesh, and he turned, looked into the ruins of the house, and saw smoke rising from a small staircase into what must be the cellar. At the top of the stairs was a blackened, charred crust, barely recognizable as a human body except for the German helmet that was lying a few feet from it.

The work of the French flamethrowers.

He looked away, winced as another shell hit nearby.

Some of his fellow soldiers were sprinting past him, and then Stokley was there, shouting, waving.

"Come on, move!"

James swallowed, left the wall, running after the sergeant, his fear mixing with another wave of embarrassment. The sergeant had said to keep moving, to not stop, and James had stopped at the first sign of cover.

You damned idiot.

BOOM!

The shell blast rattled James's teeth, pounded in his chest. He heard someone scream, and kept running. They were passing the toppled church now, its ruined, skeletal steeple jutting up into the sky. To James's right and left, the Americans were emerging from between the wrecked houses and running across the town's central street before disappearing again among the buildings on the other side. He tried to pick out William's lanky form, couldn't find him. A fresh jolt of fear hit him, but he pushed it aside. More shell bursts, more screams. He followed Stokley, Walker, and a few others up a narrow street, stepped over a body, tried not to look at it, and kept running.

The rubble and broken frames of houses gave way to walled gardens and then open country, and the ground sloped gently downward. Far ahead, thick woods sprawled, a heavy, dark wall. Just ahead, the ground, pockmarked by more shell holes, dropped away toward a long, thin line cut into the earth, stretching across the bare field before disappearing into woods on the right.

The American lines.

"Spread out! Spread out!" Major Roosevelt was shouting again, and James looked right and left, moving to the side to distance himself from Rodriguez and Walker. They'd practiced this for months. Keep apart, don't bunch up and make it any easier for the Boche artillery.

The air sizzled, an odd sound, and James realized with a jolt that they were being shot at, the crackle and pop of small arms faint compared to the explosion of shells that threw up dirt in front of them, behind them, breaking in among the American trenches below. Bullets thwacked into the ground in front of him, tossing up puffs of soil, filling the air with a deadly hum. James squinted at the forest, saw the sparkle of muzzle flashes.

A hundred more feet until the American trenches. A man directly in front of James toppled sideways, screamed.

James jumped over him and kept running, clamping his rifle tight in his hands.

Fifty.

Another soldier to James's left stopped in his tracks as suddenly as if he'd hit a wall before falling face-first to the ground.

Twenty.

James jumped down into the trench and collapsed against its side wall, breathing hard. He closed his eyes, flinched at the sound of rifles firing right next to him, and tried to steady his breathing, regain his focus. He smelled the sweet, dry smell of bare earth, tinged by the odors of smoke and gunfire.

"Down the trench, to the right!" Stokley's voice brought James's eyes back open again, and he turned, saw Rodriguez and Walker squeezing past, tromping down the trench, tilting their shoulders to fit past the men of the 28th regiment, who were leaned against the parapet, pointing their rifles out toward the enemy from between sandbags.

James tilted his rifle to point upward and merged into the flow of soldiers from his company moving down the trench, careful to not trip over the legs of the men on the parapet or run into the man in front of him.

James cursed under his breath as another shell exploded somewhere outside the trench. He bent low, keeping his head down. The trench was shallow, clearly the result of hurried work, connecting shell craters together with nothing more than a narrow, snaking ditch. The men of the 28th had dug it after taking the village, and by the looks of it, the enemy hadn't let them take their time. James felt the weight of his entrenching tool on his belt, thought again of Lieutenant Robinson's explanation for all the heavy gear. They needed everything—extra rifle ammunition, hand grenades, rifle grenades, four sandbags, an extra canteen, additional rations —to hold the position for up to two days.

James heard Major Roosevelt's voice, and almost ran into the man in front of him as the company came to a sudden stop.

"Lieutenant, spread your men out along this section. Have some of them fill up the sandbags and shore up this parapet before the enemy attacks again."

"Yes, sir."

The line started forward, and James's stomach worked itself into a hard knot.

Before they attack again?

He shook his head, annoyed at his reaction.

What the hell do you think you're here for?

They continued down the trench a hundred yards or so, James hunching his body forward. They passed a machine gun, one of the French Hotchkiss guns, spraying fire toward the enemy in a staccato rhythm from its emplacement up on the parapet, deafeningly loud in the close confines of the trench. James looked up at the men operating it, feeding strips of ammo into one side, brass spraying out the other like a hot, golden rain. One of the gunners had a bandage on his arm, blood staining through the white cotton.

James tripped forward over a pair of legs, muttered an apology, looked for their owner, then came to a stop. A soldier, an American soldier, was leaning against the back wall of the trench, his arms folded in his lap as if he were simply resting, his head blasted apart, cracked down the center. James stared at the man's face, so much like an empty egg shell, a ruined wall standing in front of the gaping void of his brain cavity. Next to him was a German, facedown, his uniform stained red from a hole in his back, what looked like a bayonet wound. James's stomach churned.

"Garrison! Move!"

James heard the sergeant's barked command and someone shoved him from behind. He willed his feet to move, to catch up with Rodriguez in front of him. He stumbled again, didn't bother looking for what had tripped him, and ducked his head as another shell burst nearby, showering them all with dirt. After a couple dozen more yards, the line stopped.

"Sergeant, get these men in fighting order." Robinson's voice carried back from just ahead.

"On the parapets, men! Stand to!" Stokley squeezed past James, shouting at the troops. "You and you!" He pointed at Walker and another private, Bird. "Start filling sandbags! The rest of you, up!"

The men crawled up the sloped dirt wall of the trench's parapet. In front of James, Walker was shaking his head.

"Christ!" He leaned his rifle against the side of the trench, met James's gaze. "I finally get a chance to bag me some

Boche, and they want me digging holes. How about that, Jimmy?"

James didn't know what to say, so he dug into his musette bag and tossed his empty sandbags to Walker.

"You'll get your chance." Rodriguez was on the parapet now, poking his rifle out between a few sandbags.

"Up! On the parapet!" Stokley was returning down the trench now, pushing past the few soldiers who were still standing at the bottom of the trench or who had dropped down to begin filling the sandbags with the dark, chalk-flecked soil. "Garrison! Get up there! We need every rifle on the firestep."

"What firestep?" Rodriguez hissed so that only James could hear. "This thing's just a ditch."

James ignored him, pulled himself up the side of the trench, the grenades in his musette bag and the clips in his cartridge belt digging into his torso. He stopped, adjusted the rifle in his hands to avoid getting dirt in the action, and kept scooting up. He poked his head over the edge of the parapet, aware that the sighing and whizzing sounds in the air above meant it was still thick with bullets. He scanned the horizon. The woods were much closer now. He could see the individual flashes of rifles and machine guns firing toward the Americans, hear the weapons' distant pops.

The world in front of him dissolved into dirt as a shell exploded a few dozen yards ahead. James buried his face into the earth, slid slightly down the trench, heard more explosions, the pace of the bursts suddenly increasing.

"They're hitting us again!" Stokley's voice sounded small against the bang and boom of the shells. "They'll be coming any minute! Stay sharp!"

The explosions were everywhere, all around, filling every space in James's head. His chest vibrated with the unbearable noise, the ground beneath him shaking. He heard someone cry out as more dirt rained down on him.

"Son of a bitch!"

James looked toward Rodriguez, saw him pulling a small, thin sliver of metal out of his shoulder, a dark stain seeping through his khaki uniform. Shrapnel.

Another boom, more screams, someone down the trench yelling.

"First aid! First aid! Where's the medic?"

He thought of William again, hoped to hell he was still alive, and looked down the trench to either side.

Another explosion, this one closer.

James realized he was looking at the dirt again, raised his head, and realized with a hard knock that the shells had stopped, the sharp crack of rifles firing quiet by comparison.

A shrill, unearthly sound carried through the air, barely audible.

A trench whistle.

He looked ahead again, and could see small gray dots emerging from the woods far ahead, rushing toward him.

"Here they come!" he shouted to no one in particular, feeling suddenly energetic, his training kicking in. A shell couldn't be seen, couldn't be anticipated or fought. But he'd spent more than enough time learning how to deal with enemy soldiers. He ran his gaze over his rifle, brushed away the dirt that had been thrown onto the action. He flipped the safety lever at the back of the rifle, raised the weapon to his shoulder, and rested its stock on the parapet.

"Hey."

Someone tapped James's leg. He looked down, saw Walker holding up a set of sandbags. He reached down, grabbed them one at a time, stacking them in front of him. Walker moved on, and James saw Rodriguez do the same, still cussing as he moved his wounded shoulder. James turned back to his rifle's sights, focused on the thin blade of the front sight, glinting slightly in the late afternoon sunshine. He waited, itching, resting his finger lightly on the trigger, listening for Stokley to give the order to fire. He slowed his breathing, trying to control it.

Just like tin cans. Hold it with your bones.

"Open fire! Let them have—"

The Americans drowned out the rest of Lieutenant Robinson's sentence as they fired, their rifles spitting at the oncoming wave of gray.

James leveled his front sight on a gray dot, hesitated.

It's just a target, like any other.

He pulled the trigger.

The rifle kicked into his shoulder, his ears rang, and, a split second later, the German toppled over. James swallowed, his pulse pounding in his neck. It was so odd, like something out of a dream.

Had he killed the man? Or only wounded him?

"That's it! Keep firing!" Robinson called.

James worked the bolt, found another target, fired. The Germans were closer now, some of them dropping as they ran, while the others sprinted on. He searched for another target, found one, and knocked it down with his volley. He thought of the man down the trench, the man with the broken face, his fear gone, replaced by anger.

His bolt caught, and he realized his rifle was empty. He reached for a clip from his belt, his fingers fumbling with one of the flaps. Ahead, the gray wave was coming apart, melting under the fire from the American trench. But behind it, another wave was dashing from the woods, pressing forward.

He fired, reloaded, and fired again. He lost count of the targets, shooting methodically, automatically. The closest

Germans were just a hundred yards away now, stopping, firing back.

A bullet sizzled past his ear, followed a second later by a grunt and a soft moan. He glanced to his left, saw a soldier sliding down the trench, limp as a rag doll.

"Rifle grenades! Shit!" Rodriguez's curse brought James's attention snapping back to the front. A few of the Germans were kneeling, pointing their rifles skyward, a dull thumping sound and a small flash announcing that they had fired. Heavy black dots arced through the air, some landing out behind the American trench, others falling inside. One landed off to James's right, just around a slight zigzag in the trench line. He heard muffled shouts, then a loud bang, screams. The Americans' rifle fire hesitated, seemed to slow. Then another grenade arced in the trench, again to the right. James covered his head, waited for the explosion, anticipating the pain of shrapnel shards.

BOOM.

He sighed with relief, looked down toward where the explosion had been, and saw several soldiers lying still on the parapet. There was Sergeant Stokley, eyes vacant, helmet missing, face washed with blood. Another soldier was crawling along the bottom of the trench, screaming, blood spattering his legs.

Walker.

James's brain buzzed, and he turned back to his rifle, aiming for any of the Germans kneeling down to fire their deadly grenades. But they were close now, only a few more yards to the trench. James fired, didn't need to bother aiming. His bolt caught again, just as a German dashed right in front of him.

"Dammit!" James punched his bayonet up and forward without thinking, catching his opponent in the midsection. The German screamed, and James pitched backward, carried by the momentum of the running man. They fell together back down the trench, and James felt his helmet roll free, something knocking him in the face.

He pulled himself up, struggling and kicking against the squirming German. He got to his feet and saw his rifle sticking up out of his enemy, who was writhing in the dirt. James reached out, pulled his rifle free, then plunged it back down, once, twice. The German choked and was still.

James looked around, saw Rodriguez pounding the butt of his rifle down onto an enemy's head. The trench was a swarm of activity, gunshots and bayonets, flailing arms, tumbling bodies, some soldiers still up on the parapet, firing toward the remaining Germans outside the trench. Robinson had drawn his .45 pistol and was gunning down Germans as they appeared at the top of the parapet.

"We hold this trench! Push them back!"

James saw motion out of the corner of his eye and jumped to the side, the blade of a bayonet thrusting past him. He swung the butt of his rifle forward, contacted wood, and pushed the German rifle away. He turned, faced his adversary, saw the man's hard eyes, the determined, set line of his mouth. The German thrust again, and James deflected his enemy's blade, pushing forward with his own. The man stepped back, then lunged forward again. Their rifles met, the dull crack of wood and steel, and James slid backward in the soft dirt, the cross of the rifles in front of him the only barrier between him and his opponent. His arms ached, and he felt the German gaining ground, pushing him in.

You fight fair, you die. Boche don't know what fair means.

James let his arms collapse toward him, and the German stumbled forward. At the same time, James brought up his knee and caught his enemy in the groin. The German yelped, and James pushed him back, sending him into the wall of the trench. He locked eyes with the German again, saw they were wide, terrified white orbs in his sweating face.

"*Nein! Nein!*"

James thrust his bayonet forward into his opponent's chest. The man's eyes squeezed shut, and he screamed, or tried to scream, a kind of raspy gurgle escaping his mouth instead. James heard a sob, realized it had come from his own mouth as he twisted the bayonet, pulled back, and thrust forward again and again.

"They're running! Get back on the parapet!"

James pulled his bayonet free and stumbled backward, shaking. He looked for the source of the order. Lieutenant Robinson was still alive, jabbing his pistol in the air, waving.

"Come on, up to the parapet! Shoot them as they run!"

James stepped back, turned to face the parapet, a dull ache splitting his face. He reached up and touched blood.

"James!" The voice, wonderful and familiar, carried down the trench.

"William?"

"James, are you hurt?" William was standing in front of him now, looking at him, concern on his face.

"Where have you been?" The question sounded stupid, childish, and James instantly regretted it.

James shook his head, relief at the sight of his friend rushing through him, making him shake harder.

"Just a bit down there." William pointed a thumb over his shoulder. "I saw they reached the line here, and I wanted to—"

"Garrison! Culver!" Robinson's shouts cut William short. "This is not the time for 'how do you do'! Get up on the firestep, now!"

"Yes, sir!"

They crawled together up the parapet and rested their

rifles on the scattered sandbags. James reached for a new clip and pushed the rounds into his weapon.

"Are you sure you're not hurt badly, James?"

He glanced over, saw the concern on William's face. "Just shoot."

They turned to their rifles, fired, spitting lead at the tattered wave of Germans who were rushing back to the safety of the trees.

CHAPTER 1

August 16, 1919
Saint Vrain, Colorado

"What do you think I should do, Em? Emily? Are you listening?"

Emily Culver woke from her thoughts, looked over at Alice's questioning face, and tried to remember what her friend had been talking about.

"Pardon?" Emily waved her hand, fanning her face with the paper she held—an invitation to the suffrage rally at the end of the month—to disperse the heat of the mid-day sun.

"You weren't listening." Alice's face fell, her green eyes narrowing, her mouth taking a pouty shape.

"I was, too," Emily lied, trying to think quickly of a response. Of course, she truly *hadn't* been paying attention, hadn't heard a word in at least five minutes, not since they'd left Marion's house and started toward 6th Street. It was something about Thomas Webb, no doubt. For the past two weeks, all Alice had been able to talk about was Thomas, his return from overseas, his flirtatious advances. Apparently, despite both war and disease, nothing had changed for Alice at all since high school.

Emily glanced at the suffrage rally invitation, a small event on the University of Colorado campus. She doubted Marion even knew about it, and felt safe assuming that Alice did not. So many other things were different now.

How could her friends have remained the same? Where had they been for the past two years?

Alice raised an eyebrow. "Well, then, what do you think?"

"I…" she began, tucking the invitation into her skirt pocket. "I don't think I'm much help with this sort of thing, sorry."

The response sounded half-hearted, even to Emily's ears. She looked down, expecting to see dirt and dust. Instead, she saw her own black shoes on fresh, black pavement, the dark blue hem of her morning dress swishing as she moved.

Pavement in Saint Vrain. Who would have imagined it?

"Oh, you're so dismal!" Alice giggled. "You know, Marion, Emily spent all that time with the Army and didn't once find herself a man. Think about it! All those soldiers."

"I expect she had other things to do." Marion's voice was soft. "Isn't that right, Emily?"

Emily didn't bother responding, as Alice had immediately launched into her story again.

"Well, I slapped him." Alice giggled again. "Can you imagine?"

"You slapped him?" Marion laughed, too. "For saying he'd kiss you?"

"Of course! He said he'd come back tonight and give me a *real* kiss. I don't want him getting the wrong idea. Do you think he'll still come?"

Emily shook her head. "Probably not."

"Oh, I hope he does!" Alice skipped a couple steps, her excitement grating on Emily's nerves.

Emily rolled her eyes. "You two really don't have to go all this way for me."

"We don't mind," Marion replied. "I…We haven't seen Walt since he got back." Emily heard the hopeful note in Marion's voice, the vulnerability. Marion and Walter had dated for a while before the War, had stayed in touch while Walt had been in France. They'd been the talk of the senior class, the couple everyone knew would someday get married. While Marion didn't talk about it often, Emily had assumed they'd ended things after Walter's injury.

"Don't be silly." Alice waved a hand at Marion. "We aren't going to see him until he's done with his treatments and fit to go out again. But we'll walk you there, Em, and then let you go on your way."

A spark of annoyance skittered through Emily. There were no treatments at this point, and there wouldn't be. Did Alice truly not understand what had happened to the man, the boy who had been their friend?

Emily kept her eyes on the ground. It had been like this ever since she'd returned from France two weeks ago, her patience for her friends' company always thin, always fragile. To make matters worse, it seemed to Emily that they often insisted on doing everything together. Walks down to the market, luncheons and teas, dinner parties. They simply never left her alone.

Today, Emily had been certain she would get some quiet by visiting Walter Gould. After all, her friends had steered clear of him, like many of the neighbors had, ever since he'd been released from the Army hospital and come home. But then Marion had surprised her, offering to keep her company on the walk over. And whatever Marion did, Alice was sure to do. They came as a set.

Then again, it had been like this during high school. Except for the times Emily had spent with William, or his best friend, James, she had almost always been with Marion and Alice. It hadn't annoyed her then, but neither had so many other things in Saint Vrain, a city only one university away from being a dirty little mining-supply town. Most of the same people were there, save the conspicuous absence of soldiers killed or people lost to the flu. The buildings, houses, and streets were all mostly the same, and, if Alice was any indication, the topics of conversation were all the same, too. Nothing had changed at all since before the War, and at times, it seemed to Emily that the War had never happened.

She glared down at the pavement.

Almost nothing had changed.

For the first few days, she had woken up in her own bed, strange and familiar at the same time, and caught herself sleepily wondering if everything had been a dream.

But then, she would always think about William.

She sighed, completely oblivious to Alice's happy chatter as they reached 6th Street and turned left. She'd learned William was missing from her parents when she'd been in Germany, providing for the occupying American armies there, but she hadn't wanted to believe it. Missing in Action in the Meuse. They'd all hung on to hope for as long as they could, especially her younger brother, Julius, and her little sister, Brianna, who seemed convinced that "missing in action" meant William had simply got lost in France while he was fighting the Germans, and that he would come home as soon as possible.

Emily had been the first to give up, the first to decide that her brother must be dead. It was better to face that gaping void rather than pretend it wasn't there. Her mind flashed to the casualty clearing station, to the bodies torn and broken by shellfire, seared by gas, such a sharp contrast to the cheerful babble still flowing from Alice's mouth.

Emily shivered, her mind shifting to a memory of the

coffee line, saw James standing in front of her, his face dirty, his overseas cap gripped tightly in his hands.

"The worst part is the shells. If they don't rip you to pieces, they skewer you with shrapnel, or collapse the trench and bury you alive."

She fought down the wave of emotion that rose inside her at hearing his voice again in her head.

James.

Another person who'd never come home. As a matter of fact, Emily hadn't heard a thing about him since the last time she'd seen him in France.

When she'd still been overseas, Emily had thought many times of visiting the Garrisons and asking them about their son. When she'd come home and begun her visits with Walter, she'd assumed she would eventually stop by—the Garrisons lived right near Walter, after all—but she had been too busy so far.

That was an excuse.

She was too afraid, more like, wondering what his parents would think of her if they knew what James had meant to her, what they'd almost done together. She was afraid she'd discover he'd met the same horrible end he'd described, buried alive in terror and pain somewhere in French dirt. Somewhere with William.

She closed her eyes, fought to return to the present. It was painfully clear. William had died somewhere, his body lost or impossible to identify. They would never know where, they would never know how. Emily had seen too much of the War to believe anything else. Her parents would accept it eventually. They would have to.

The fact that they still hadn't faced reality meant they were the only people Emily couldn't stand being around more than her friends.

"Oh, my goodness!" Alice's shocked voice snapped Emily's attention to the present.

She looked up, her eyes taking a moment to register the scene before her.

Standing in the middle of the street was Walter Gould, a packet of mail in one hand, a cane in the other, dressed in black pants, a white shirt, and a gray tie and vest. His face was brightly lit by a shaft of sun coming through the trees lining the street.

Emily was still not used to it. Shrapnel had done it, shearing off his nose, leaving a skeletal hollow and mangling the right side of his face, crushing in his brow. The surgeons had managed to form what was left into something vaguely resembling a face, but it was a twisted, mutilated version of the handsome features he'd once had. The rest of his body had mostly been spared, though shrapnel wounds along the right side of his body had left their own scars and forced him to walk with a cane.

Emily stared at the uninjured half of his face and saw his anguished expression, his good eye looking toward the ground.

A small crowd of people, the neighbors mostly, had gathered to watch. A policeman, Officer Westlake, stood in front of Walter, his ticket book in hand, sweating in his heavy, dark blue uniform, his face ruddy from the heat.

"I'm sorry to be giving this to you, Mr. Gould. I know you don't mean any harm."

"Walt? What's going on?" Emily stepped forward, saw the neighbors look her way and then quickly avert their eyes.

Walt didn't say anything, but kept staring at the ground.

Emily took another step forward. "Well? Is anyone going to tell me what is happening? Officer?"

"Don't bother, Em," Walter muttered, barely audible. "Just go home."

Emily shook her head and looked at the policeman, who finally glanced at her before turning back to his ticket book.

"Mr. Gould was outside, Miss Culver."

"I can see he's outside. Is that illegal now?" Emily put her hands on her hips, her irritation with Westlake rising.

Walt still suffered pain from his injuries and ought not to be outside in the heat.

"We got complaints," Westlake continued, without looking up.

"Complaints?" Emily repeated the word, anger rising in her throat. "Because he got the mail?"

"Because he went outside." Westlake sighed, turned to face Emily. "I didn't invent the law, miss, but I'm going to enforce it if people complain."

"Em, let's go," Alice whispered.

"Oh no," Marion said.

"What? What law are you talking about?" Emily could hear the volume of her voice rising and ignored the stares of the neighbors. She shook off one of her friend's hands at her elbow.

"Being ugly in the public way, miss. That's the rule now." Westlake turned back to his ticket book, kept writing. "If he wants to go outside with that face, he has to wear a hood or a mask. Like I said, I didn't make the law, but I can't ignore complaints."

Emily gaped, the anger that simmered behind her breastbone flaring into a full boil. Her fists clenched at her side. "Who complained? Who?"

She looked at the neighbors one at a time, though they refused to meet her gaze.

"Emily, it's okay." Walt looked at her, his good brow furrowed. "I don't want you to see this. And Marion..." He glanced at her, his frown deepening. "Just go home, all three of you."

Emily shook her head and strode forward until she stood right next to Westlake.

"Do you know how this man got injured, officer? He was fighting overseas for his country, for democracy!" Her voice was shaking now, her temper barely under control. "Are you going to punish him for serving his country?"

"Miss Culver, I want this to be a respectable town, and—"

"Respectable? Do you think he chose to be injured? And what were you doing while this man was overseas, fighting, risking his life? Would you prefer that he didn't come back?"

Emily heard the catch in her own voice. Her eyes burned, though they remained dry, as they had since France.

Crying had never solved anything overseas, and it wouldn't help now.

"That's enough out of you!" Westlake turned, met Emily's gaze. His eyes were fixed, hard. But in them, Emily could see the smallest glint of doubt.

"Please." Emily spoke quietly now, though her voice still shook. "This is not right."

Westlake stared back at Emily for a long moment, turned, and looked at the neighbors. Walt kept his eyes on his feet, sweat beading on his forehead. Finally, the policeman sighed and folded away his ticket book.

"In recognition of your service, I'm giving you a warning this time." Westlake crossed his arms. "But don't be breaking the law again. Next time you leave your house, take the appropriate precautions."

Emily let out a breath she hadn't known she was holding. Better than nothing, but no soldier should have to wear a mask, ever. She opened her mouth to say this, but the policeman cut her off, facing her again.

"And you, Miss Culver, are lucky I don't charge you for disturbing the peace. I'll be letting your parents know how you acted today."

"Thank you, officer." Marion appeared next to Emily and grabbed hold of her arm. "We appreciate your leniency."

Emily bit back her response, nodded.

Westlake stared at her for a second longer and then glanced around one last time at the neighbors, who had begun to disperse to their homes. He grunted a farewell to Walt and started down the street.

Emily waited for Westlake to disappear around the corner before closing the distance between her and Walt, who still seemed to be examining his shoes, though his good eye was curiously bright.

"Oh my," Alice said breathlessly. "That was a scene! Emily Culver, what got into you?"

Emily ignored Alice and touched a hand to Walt's shoulder. "Let's go inside, okay?"

Walt nodded, turned, and shuffled up the small flagstone path that led to his front porch.

Emily peered over her shoulder, saw her two friends standing together, looking at her. "I'll see you both later, okay?"

"Okay." Marion put on a smile as she looked past Emily at Walter. "I'll call again, Walt?"

He met her eyes, nodded.

Marion hooked elbows with Alice. "Now what were you going to say to Tommy, again?"

Emily watched her friends head down the street, then turned to follow Walt, her gaze raking over the Garrison house, two houses down and across the street.

She froze.

A quick movement, then the swirl of a curtain falling shut.

Her pulse quickened, and she stood rooted to the spot. She must be seeing things.

"Emily?" Walt's voice called out from behind her. "Is something wrong?"

"N-no." Emily said, watching the curtain. "No."

She turned and walked up the steps to Walt's house, annoyed at herself for being so skittish. She was allowing her imagination to get carried away. But, for just a moment, she'd thought she'd seen James Garrison looking out at her.

~

JAMES DROPPED the curtain and stepped back from the window, his heart in his throat.

"Dammit!" He peered through the slit between the curtains, watching as Emily stared back at him, a surprised expression on her face. "Dammit!" he cursed again, shaking his head.

That's what you get for being curious.

He'd heard a commotion outside and had seen Walt standing with the policeman—probably because of that idiotic ugly-in-public law. He had been about to step outside himself when she'd appeared.

Emily.

She'd looked different than the last time he'd seen her, overworked and exhausted, at the casualty clearing station in France. He'd been unable to look away from her now, in a dark blue morning dress and white blouse, her blonde hair drawn up and in a loose bun at the nape of her neck. James had been almost mesmerized as she'd stood up to Officer Westlake and shouted him down. Then she'd turned around, and for a split second, she'd met his gaze.

"Dammit," he whispered one more time.

"James? What's the matter?" His mother's voice carried down the stairs, a series of thumps announcing her approach. "James?"

He watched as Emily turned and walked up the steps and into Walter's house, the door shutting behind her. James exhaled and turned to face the parlor. He winced, the pain in his leg flaring up. He bit his lip and walked across the wooden floor toward one of the burgundy settees.

"Is something the matter?" James's mother rounded the corner into the parlor, and he saw her studying him out of the corner of his eye. "Let me help you."

"No, Mother, thank you." He reached the settee, eased himself down. He felt his mother's hands on his shoulder and held back the sharp words that entered his mind. It was bad enough that his wounds were still sore and stiff at times, but to be treated like an invalid was just too much. He didn't deserve that sort of kindness. "I'm fine. Truly."

James looked up at his mother, saw concern etched on her face. She stepped back and stood awkwardly for a second. "What was happening outside?" She walked to the window and parted the curtain with her hand. James could see her hesitating, could tell she wanted to open them all the way, let in the sunlight. "I heard shouting."

"Walter Gould was in trouble." James leaned back into the settee, folded his arms in his lap. "He went outside without a mask."

"And someone told the police?" His mother turned, crossed her arms over her chest. "Who?"

"I don't know. One of the neighbors. I think Officer Westlake must have been walking his beat, and someone complained to him."

His mother shook her head. "That poor young man. If he were one of their children…"

She trailed off, looked at James, and he knew without asking what she was doing, equating him with Walter Gould, both of them poor, wounded boys.

Except James was nothing like Walter, who couldn't go

outside for fear of the law. Walter had given up so much of himself for his country, a selfless act. James, on the other hand, was afraid to go outside for his own reasons, and he knew his wounds weren't selfless or noble.

You don't deserve to be compared to him.

"Why didn't you go out and help him?" his mother persisted.

James held her gaze for a moment, and she pursed her lips.

"Or call for me? I would have given them all a piece of my mind."

James drummed his fingers on the tops of his thighs. "I was going to go out, but I didn't have to."

"Oh?"

"No." He hesitated. "Someone else did. Walt didn't get a citation."

Her eyebrows rose. "Oh. I see. Who, then?"

It was James who looked at the floor this time. "Emily Culver."

"Oh! Miss Emily?" The joy in his mother's voice was obvious and brought James's gaze back up to hers. "Bravo for her! How did she look?"

Like everything good and beautiful.

"Fine, I suppose."

His mother sat down next to him. "You know, James, I don't understand why you don't go see her. You used to spend quite a lot of time with her and William before the War. She's a nice girl."

James flinched at the sound of his friend's name, pressure building in his chest. He tried to keep his voice even. "Let it go, Mother. I don't want to see her."

That wasn't entirely true. When James had first found out that William had been marked missing, he'd been recovering from his injury at a convalescence station. He'd been filled with guilt, then anger at what had happened, at what he'd done. The news about William had brought two opposite desires within him into conflict.

The first was to never see Emily Culver again, to never have to face her reaction to what he'd done. He didn't want to inflict that pain on her. The second was to return home as soon as the Army discharged him and give her the courtesy of the truth. It was the very least he owed her, given what they had been through together.

He'd been unable to write to her, unable to put words to what he'd seen. The only option had been to tell her in person. In the end, his desire to see her and tell her the truth had won out, and after recovering from his wounds and spending a few months on occupation duty, he'd come home to Saint Vrain in July, only to discover Emily wasn't back yet. He'd held off on visiting the Culvers, as he wanted to wait until Emily's return to share with them what he knew.

The weeks of waiting must have sapped his resolve. By the time he'd finally heard the rumor that Emily was home, he'd been unable to make himself go see her. Better that she never knew William's real fate, that she thought James had died in Europe.

He'd hidden at home the past few weeks and insisted on keeping the curtains closed, terrified someone would see him and tell Emily he was back.

You irrational, cowardly bastard.

His mother hadn't let go of the issue. "But why won't you see her? You know what her family has suffered. Whatever it is you're feeling, they'll understand, surely."

James looked away, pretending to examine the contents of the end table. "No." He closed his eyes. "Though I may have to. She saw me looking."

"She saw you?"

"Yes, through the curtain."

There was a moment's pause. James heard his mother sigh. "You talk as if you were a spy, or a criminal on the run. I wish you'd tell me why you don't want anyone to see you. Or if you can't tell me, tell your father."

A criminal on the run.

Not far from the truth.

His mother pressed on, wringing her hands. "Or tell your cousin Henri in France. He's written you a few times, you know."

Cousin Henri, Major Henri DeLisle, *did* know, was the *only* one who knew.

"You will have to face this one way or another," he'd said, his face grim. "Far better to get it over with and live as best you can now."

James didn't have the heart to reply to his cousin and tell him all the reasons he hadn't taken his good advice.

The door opened, and in stepped James's father, dressed in a tan jacket and trousers, hat in one hand, a bundle of mail and newspapers in the other, his face sweaty and red.

"Howard!" His mother stood, walked to her husband, and gave him a kiss on the cheek. "Will you help me talk sense into our son?"

"Any reason beyond the normal, Elizabeth?"

James rolled his eyes while his mother explained the scene in front of the Gould house, recounting what James had told her. His father, an English professor at the university, was always playing with words, carrying on a clever game with the world. Normally, James liked his father's unique sense of humor. He appreciated it less in moments like this.

"I think it doesn't matter so much that she saw you, son." James's father walked over to him, held out a piece of paper. "Not after this."

James took it, recognized the official War Department

letterhead. He read the letter, read it again, his stomach twisting as he gaped at the final sentence.

In recognition of this courageous act, we are honored to confer to you the Distinguished Service Cross.

"Let me see that." James's mother took the paper from his hands and read it, her eyebrows slowly rising. "My son!" She beamed down at him. "My son, a war hero! Have you telephoned Uncle Chester?"

His father began to open his mouth, but James couldn't stand it anymore. "That's a load of—" He interrupted himself, took a deep breath, tried to stay calm. He clenched his fists, unclenched them. The irony of hearing his parents, of all people, praising his military service was bad enough. But to have the Army reward him for what he'd done…

James raised his chin, kept his voice even. "That's not me."

His parents stared back at him.

"What do you mean?" His father took the paper back from his wife. "Did you not really do what it says here?"

"I…" James searched for words. He would have to tell them. But if they knew what really happened … A wave of fear crept through him.

They'll probably want to disown you.

"Excuse me." James pushed past his parents, walked toward the hallway, seeking the safety of his bedroom.

"But you didn't see the best part!" His father's voice stopped James in his tracks.

"The best part?"

His father crossed the room, rocked on the balls of his feet. "You see, I actually received this notice yesterday—"

His mother glared at her husband. "And you didn't tell me?"

His father continued, seemingly unaware of his wife's scathing expression. "I went and told the fellows down at the store. And Mr. Adler from the *Camera* was there."

James shook his head, already anticipating where his father's anecdote was going.

"He loved the story." His father fumbled with the newspaper, opening it to a page in the middle. "Take a look. Not the front page, but there it is. Sorry I didn't tell either of you, but I wanted it to be a surprise."

James took the paper, no longer hearing his parents' exclamations, his hands shaking as he read his name in the headline.

Hometown War Hero! James Garrison Returns Home.

CHAPTER 2

June 3, 1916

William and James climbed on the back of a passing farm truck, handing the driver fifty cents for his trouble. As the vehicle bumped and splashed over soggy, rutted roads, they chatted happily, holding the newspaper between them like something sacred, as if they might break it. It was the solution, their ticket out. They wouldn't have to give up their friendship.

They hopped off the truck at a muddy intersection, their sack of tin cans jangling. They turned and walked toward the foothills, which were still green from the spring rains. They came to a wide, gently sloping canyon and turned right, following a small gulley that climbed gradually upward, opening onto a broad valley. Uncle Chester was waiting at the gate, the rifle over his shoulder, a couple boxes of ammunition in his free hand.

"I think you boys are ready for the big stuff," he grinned, held out a rifle. "This is a Krag. It's what I used when I was in the service. Got it from the DCM a couple weeks ago."

"Krag?" James pronounced the funny name, shared an excited glance with William.

A real Army rifle!

James took it first, his arms sagging as Chester transferred its unexpected weight into his hands. "It's a lot bigger than the twenty-two."

Uncle Chester chuckled. "Try carrying it a few miles."

Heat rose to James's cheeks. "I would like to." He didn't want to appear weak in front of Chester.

William let out a low whistle. "How far does it shoot?"

Chester stuck his hands in his pockets. "We trained out to 500 yards." He grinned. "I'll start you boys out on the southwest pasture. You can get up to a hundred there."

Chester led them farther up the valley, showing them how to load and handle the rifle. He pointed them toward their destination, up a long slope toward a high, sweeping ridge. They left Chester at the bottom of the hill, climbed steadily upward along a rocky, two-track road, and stopped partway to rest in the shade of a clump of ponderosa pines.

"It's not too heavy." James looked down at the rifle in his hands. It was beautiful, all gleaming, smooth wood and shiny metal. Never mind that his arms really were aching from carrying it.

William wiped sweat off his forehead. "Can I take it for a while?"

James hesitated, pushed the rifle toward his friend.

William took it, his eyes going wide for a second as its full weight came into his hands. "Yeah, it's not too heavy at all."

They got back to their feet and pushed on up the road. Finally, they reached a wide, grassy meadow with a set of humpbacked hills marching along its western side, the taller mountains behind them. They found a toppled tree trunk, set the cans on its side, then trudged to the other side of the meadow.

"I'll go first." James took the rifle from William, loaded it the way Chester had showed them. He put the rifle up to his shoulder, took aim and fired.

"Christ!" James's ears rang, his shoulder stinging.

"Looks like you missed." William held his hands to his ears. "Did that hurt?"

"No." James lied. "Want to try?"

William took the rifle, loaded it, and snugged it into his shoulder. This time, James covered his ears, bracing himself for the weapon's thumping boom.

William fired, lowered the rifle, and massaged the spot on his shoulder where it had kicked him. "Did I get it?"

James squinted across the meadow. "Don't think so."

After they each made a few more unsuccessful attempts to hit the cans, William pointed across the meadow at them. "I tell you, they're mocking us."

They agreed the other side of the meadow was, perhaps, too far for anybody to hit a can and walked part of the way back toward the log, carefully laying the folded newspaper on the ground beside them.

James raised the rifle to his shoulder. "Besides, Chester was shooting at people, and they're bigger than a can." He pulled the trigger, grit his teeth as the weapon kicked him. He looked over the weapon's sights, saw the defiant cans still standing.

It was William's turn again.

"Slow and steady there." James watched his friend concentrate on the sights. "Slow and steady."

"Shhh! Let me think."

"Slow and stea—"

William's gunshot reverberated off the surrounding hills, his bullet smacking the can into the air and backward over the log.

"Nice shot." James tapped William's foot with his own, excitement and jealousy mixing in him.

He couldn't let William beat him. What would he tell Chester?

"Want to go back to the pop gun?" William rolled over on his side, handed James the rifle, grinning.

"Maybe." James smiled back. "I don't know if I can see the cans from here. You mind going down there and holding them up?"

James took the weapon, helped William to his feet, and then dropped down to the ground, settling himself in the wiry, short grass. He shifted the rifle, putting the butt stock carefully into the pocket of his shoulder. He moved his arms to the proper position, remembering Uncle Chester's advice.

"Muscles get tired and shake you all over. Bones don't. Get your supporting arm under the rifle, not out to the side. That's it. Hold it with your bones."

They'd shot the .22 for years, coming up to High Valley Ranch, Uncle Chester's property, every summer and around the year as the weather permitted, any time William's parents weren't aware of what he was doing. At first, they'd shot with Chester there to guide them, then enjoyed refreshments with Aunt Maggie. As they'd gotten older, Chester had sometimes left them to shoot alone while he dealt with the concerns of the ranch. Both James and William had long since become precise and comfortable with the little .22, able to outshoot Chester himself.

Shooting the Krag was no different, or at least that's what James told himself. He worked to control his breathing, focused his eyes on the front sight, and adjusted his body to bring it down over the tiny, gray shape of the distant can. He exhaled, the seconds stretching out, his heart beating against the grass. Sweat trickled down the side of his face, his back burning from the heat of the sun. He tensed his finger, felt the trigger pivoting backward…. Nothing.

"You… forgot to load it."

James bit his lip, warmth that had nothing to do with the sun rising to his cheeks. "I was just feeling the trigger pull."

"Oh." William's voice held a hint of laughter. "I see. Sorry to intrude on your, um, test."

James reached for the bolt, cycled it in the action, ejecting William's last spent shell and chambering a fresh cartridge. It was so unfamiliar compared to the simple motion of the .22's pump. He shouldered the rifle again and put the sights on target, repeating the steps, sweating on the ground. He slowed his breathing, exhaled—

CRACK.

The rifle jumped in his shoulder, his ears rang—and the cans remained untouched on the trunk.

"Let me try again." James cycled the bolt.

"You had your chance!"

They bickered for a couple moments, William finally agreeing to let James take another shot if he also got two shots on his next turn. Their treaty made, James got back into position, taking his time, trying to make every step perfect.

"You don't have to hit it today, you know," William said. "This is only our first time with the Kroog, Krug… whatever it's called."

"Krag," James said, shifting his body. "*You* hit it."

"Well…." William trailed off. "We're about to get plenty of practice, aren't we?"

James couldn't help but smile. "I expect this is most of what we'll do."

He thought of Chester's stories of the Army, the many hours spent on the practice ranges, the competition among the ranks for the highest qualification ratings, the men who could hit any target they could see.

The tin can.

He brought his attention back to the present, back to his target. His focus narrowed down to the rifle's sights, which moved back and forth with his heartbeat, dropping down and coming to rest in front of the can as he exhaled.

BAM.

The can jumped, flipped over in the air, and disappeared behind the log.

William clapped his hands. "Nice shot!"

James got to his hands and knees, handed the Krag to William. "One and one. We're even."

William accepted the rifle, shook his head. "For the moment."

James wiped the sweat off his forehead, pulled himself to his feet, and made way for his friend to lie down in the grass where he had been.

They continued like this for an hour, alternating shots, punching the cans off the log with their rounds. Soon they were hitting more than they were missing, leaving the rifle in the grass to run across the meadow, prop the cans back up, and inspect the ragged bullet holes.

James held one of the cans up to his chest. "Can you imagine? Right through!"

William held another perforated can up to his head, stuck his tongue out to one side, made an exaggerated groaning sound. They laughed, set the cans up, trudged back to the Krag, and continued shooting. Later, they noticed that the boxes of ammunition were almost empty.

"Two more cartridges." James held up the rounds, the brass glinting in the sunlight. "And I believe we are tied."

William gestured toward the ground. "You first."

James lay down, positioned himself, following the now-familiar routine. He aimed at the can, controlled his breathing, and squeezed the trigger.

"It figures I'd find you two doing something silly like this!"

James jumped, the rifle going off a split second later. He looked over the barrel of the rifle and groaned to see his target still sitting on the log.

He stood up, looking for the source of the voice, already knowing who it was. "What are you doing here?"

Emily Culver walked toward them from behind their shooting position, her hands hiking her pastel blue afternoon dress up slightly, showing a glimpse of her black boots and stockings.

"Emily?" William gaped at his sister. "How did you find us?"

"I know where you two like to go." She stopped, breathing hard, and pointed at James. "And your uncle gave me directions."

James rolled his eyes. How like Emily to break up their fun. James didn't blame William for being close to his sister. They were twins, after all, and when they'd all been little, all three of them had played together. Things had changed as they'd grown up, the boys drifting toward their sphere, while Emily moved toward hers. It was the natural way of things. But somehow, Emily had always found a way to intrude on the time James and William spent together. It wasn't right to always have a girl tagging along. That explained why James always felt so out of sorts when she was around, why he was always so aware of her, why he felt embarrassed no matter what he said to her.

"Chester would never betray us like that." James propped the rifle on its butt. "Or was it Aunt Maggie?"

Emily ignored James, put her hands on her hips. "William,

Mom and Dad sent a telegram. They are coming home early today."

"What?" William's eyes widened. "When?"

"Before dinner. They weren't specific, but we need to go. They'll want a report from you."

"A report?" James snorted.

William's parents had given him the task of reading a healthy selection from among the great works of literature and history, all with the goal of preparing the boy for the start of college in the fall. They'd also imposed a strict summer routine, one that didn't include James. It was even worse than normal. William was one of Saint Vrain High School's best athletes, among the top-performing students, and generally regarded by all the teachers as The Most Talented Student They'd Ever Met. James had always hated that reputation, not so much because he was jealous, which he was, a little—his grades were good, too—but because he knew what his friend suffered to earn that title, how much his rigid parents had tortured him.

"Yes, a report." Emily cocked her head to the side, narrowed her eyes at James, before tapping William on the chest with her finger. "And if you don't get home on time, you know they're going to be angry."

"This is ridiculous!" James turned to William. "How can you go along with something so unfair?"

"You poor infant." Emily raised her eyebrows, fixed James with an expression of exaggerated pity. "*Unfair* is what is happening in France right now, while our country keeps its head in the sand. You have relatives there, yes? *Unfair* is the fact that I can't vote in a third of the country. *Unfair* is getting your friend in trouble when you know his parents *will* be unfair."

James scowled. The same old self-righteous talk, turning any odd moment into a time to show off her interest in politics. The problem with Emily was that she was like her brother—too smart for her own good. Unlike William, she wasn't afraid to show off her intelligence. James knew that she had her fair share of issues with the Culver parents, too.

William had told James on several occasions about how much Emily wanted to go to college like her brother. He knew it wasn't typical for a woman to go to school, but Emily was always so involved in world events and so eager to learn that sending her to college seemed a natural choice—and it would be a good strategy.

At least then she would leave James and William alone.

William stared at Emily for a moment, then shrugged. "Well, let's go."

James sighed. Even in the summer, William's parents knew how to ruin a fun day.

"You aren't going to take your last shot?" James pushed the rifle toward his friend.

William reached for the rifle, but Emily cut him off. "You aren't much of a friend, bothering him with something silly like that when he could be in trouble. I suppose coming out here was your idea, as usual?"

James and William looked at each other, then back at Emily.

She pursed her lips. "I thought so. Come on, Will. Forget about the stupid gun."

Emily started down the hill, William trudging behind. James smacked the butt of the rifle on the ground, shouted after them.

"You only say stupid because you've never done it."

Emily looked over her shoulder, but kept walking. "Don't be an idiot."

James looked for whatever words would annoy her the most, found them. "You can't understand a *man's* sport."

Emily turned around now, crossed her arms. "I understand plenty. You like knocking things over. So do dogs, cats, and monkeys."

"At least we can hit the target." James thrust his thumb over his shoulder toward the log.

"Not from what I saw." Emily smiled sweetly.

William's eyes darted between his sister and his friend, a mixture of fear and amusement on his face.

"That's because you ruined the shot." James leaned on the rifle, returned Emily's smile. "I bet you couldn't hit a single one, even if we were standing right next to them."

James stared into Emily's blue eyes as she raised her chin, her golden hair catching the sunlight, a few strands having come loose from her pompadour, a slight sheen of sweat on her face from the heat and the exertion of climbing the hill. He felt an odd tension in his chest, ignored it.

He saw the moment she made up her mind. Something in her eyes snapped, and she walked toward him, her mouth set in a hard line.

"Alright. I'll shoot it. You said you had one more bullet left?"

William raised a hand. "But didn't you just say—"

"Yes." James cut his friend off, worked the bolt, leaving it open. Then he stepped aside and handed Emily the rifle. She took it, a surprised expression flashing across her face as the full weight transferred into her hands.

James pointed at the ground. "Lie down."

She looked at the ground, then at her dress, then at James.

"Or do it standing. It will be harder."

"I don't care." She brought the rifle up to the level of her waist, facing the targets across the meadow.

"Bring it up higher, to your shoulder." James suppressed a laugh as Emily raised the rifle to the height of her shoulder, holding it out in front of her like a fishing pole, her arms wobbling slightly from the strain of holding the heavy weapon so far from her body. "No, no. Like this."

~

Emily bit back a gasp, startled by the contact as James's chest pressed against her back. She felt his arms brushing hers, his hands closing around her hands.

"Y-you could just tell me how to do it!" She looked over her shoulder and up at him, saw the faint stubble on his jaw.

James ignored her, moved her hands on the rifle with his, and pulled her arms backward until the butt end of the rifle was planted in her shoulder.

"Spread your feet apart."

She felt James's foot tapping her own. She moved, the rifle's weight more manageable now that she was holding it closer to her center.

"Now see this notch?" James's right hand let go of hers, and he pointed toward a small metal piece partway down the barrel, his voice vibrating in his chest and against her back. "This is your rear sight. The blade at the tip is the front sight."

Emily nodded, irritated at the difficulty she was having following James's explanations, her concentration rattled by the shock of having a man in such close contact with her.

A man.

You're thinking about James, you fool.

James was her brother's childish friend, a boy.

She blinked, pulled away from him slightly, her irritation with herself growing.

"To aim the rifle," he was saying, "put the blade in the notch. Now center the front sight on that can while keeping that arrangement."

Emily aligned the sights, saw them moving and shaking over the target.

This was harder than it looked.

"Now what?"

He set the cartridge in the open rifle. "Push that handle forward, and lock it down."

Emily reached for the bolt, followed the motion of James's hand. "And?"

"Aim, and when you're going to fire, exhale. Then pull the trigger."

Emily shifted her body slightly, sweat trickling down her neck and under her corset. She fought to keep the sights from moving around, but couldn't get them to stay still. They moved over the can. She exhaled, squeezed the trigger.

CRACK.

She jumped, caught off guard by the incredible loudness of the weapon, and found herself pressed back against James's body.

She set the butt of the weapon on the ground and looked around at him. She felt a shiver of awareness pass between them, then saw an odd look she'd never seen before cross James's face, a strange expression in his blue-gray eyes.

Was he attracted to her?

Good gracious!

Was she attracted to him?

The thought horrified her, but the moment passed.

"Tut-tut," James clucked. "What did I tell you?"

She looked back toward the log. A small cloud of dust was diffusing into the air, the cans untouched.

"Where did I—"

"You hit the dirt out in front." James took the rifle, hoisted it onto his shoulder. "Didn't I tell you that you couldn't hit with a single shot?"

"Hey, now." William stepped forward, hands in his pockets. "That was alright, especially for standing. We didn't hit with our first shots either."

Emily smiled at her brother, enjoying the annoyed look James shot toward William.

"Well then, marksmen." Emily picked up her skirts. "Shall we get going?"

She waited for William to pick up a newspaper that was sitting in the grass next to their shooting area, then she started down the hill, the boys a few steps behind her.

THIS WAS WORSE than Emily had thought it would be.

"William Culver Junior, you are almost a college man. How can you still be such a child?"

Their father stood in front of William in the parlor, their mother a step behind.

Emily and William had left James on Arapahoe Avenue and returned home to find their parents already waiting for them, still dressed in their travel clothes.

William looked at the floor. "I don't know, sir."

Their father shook his head. "You've done a lot of hard work in high school. Do you want to throw it away?"

"No, sir."

"And it's bad enough for you to waste your own time, but to drag your sister into it, too..." He shook his head.

"It's not his fault I was there. I chose to go get him." Emily felt the old irritation flare, the same feeling that came every time her brother took all the blame and suffered all the pressure while her parents either ignored her or acted as if she were incapable of making her own mistakes, a child who followed her brother around.

Her father looked at her, his face changing into a smile. "It's sweet of you to defend your brother, Emmy, but if he'd been responsible, you wouldn't have needed to go out and find him."

Her mother shook her head, clicking her tongue. "A young lady out alone, hitchhiking on farm trucks."

"I didn't ride a farm truck. Walter Gould's family was driving that way. They dropped me off."

But her parents had turned back to William.

"*De Oratore* is waiting for you in your bedroom." Her father pointed toward the staircase. "Start reading now. You can come down for dinner when you've finished."

"Yes, sir." William plodded out of the room and up the stairs, his head still low, the newspaper he and James had been reading hanging down at his side.

"Emmy, get changed for dinner."

"I should eat when William eats. It's not his fault I went out after him."

Her mother widened her eyes and held her in place with her gaze. "Emmy. Change."

Emily stared back, then looked at the floor. She clenched her fists, let a sigh out between her teeth, trying to decide if she should say more, but when she looked up, her mother had already turned into the kitchen to supervise Mrs. Rawlins with dinner, and her father was striding up the stairs.

She followed her father, walked to the entrance of her room, the first one on the right, and stopped. She watched her father enter her parents' bedroom at the end of the hall, past the closed doors to Julius's and Brianna's bedrooms, and waited for a couple seconds. She crept forward, careful to not make the wooden floor creak, until she was next to the closed door of her brother's room. She glanced back toward her parents' room, then eased open her brother's door and stepped inside.

William was seated cross-legged on his bed, a book

propped open on his lap. The room was immaculate, as always, every book in its place on the single, tall bookshelf, the bed sheets crisp and perfect, the small desk bare. Only the various trophies and medals from the athletic events William had won in school prevented the space from looking totally spartan.

William looked up as Emily shut the door behind her. The edges of his mouth curled up slightly.

"I'd say that you'll get in trouble being in here, but somehow I know they'll blame me."

Emily fidgeted with her hands, the truth of William's words summoning a surge of guilt inside her. She wanted to run forward and throw her arms around him and tell him how sorry she was for everything their parents had said.

William must have noticed her expression, because he chuckled. "It's alright. I don't blame you, Em. Thanks for trying."

"But this is why you shouldn't be so sad to go." Emily stepped forward. "College will get you away from here. You'll see."

William was to head to the East Coast in the fall, to Harvard University, their father's *alma mater*. It had not been William's first choice. He'd wanted to go the University of Colorado, right here in Saint Vrain, where James and many of Emily's classmates were going. As usual, William's desires had not mattered, and their parents had officially accepted Harvard's offer of admission in the winter. William had hidden his reaction, but Emily knew her brother well enough to know he'd been crushed. That fact had made the joy she'd felt at the idea of her brother escaping home the source of unbearable guilt.

"Yes, I'll be away from here, from everyone I care about." William looked back down at his book. "You, James. Everyone."

Emily's throat tightened. She had her own reasons to want William to stay, too. Except for the times when he stole off with James, William had been her closest companion for as long as she could remember. She put a hand on his shoulder. "Forget about that idiot. Think about what's best for you."

"For me?" He chuckled. "Going to Harvard has nothing to do with what I want."

The absurdity of the situation made Emily want to laugh. Here William was trying to escape from a world-class education, something Emily wanted desperately—and could probably never have.

She sat down on the bed next to him. "You can see James and me during the summer, and when you've got your degree. You'll be glad you have a career, then."

"Now you sound like them."

Emily ignored him. "And it will get you farther away from all this."

"It won't matter. They'll just find a way to get into everything from long distance." He twisted his face into an exaggerated impression of their father's disapproving frown. "'William, these grades are not acceptable. You need to apply yourself.' Can you imagine, Em? They won't leave me alone."

Emily searched for something to negate her brother's pessimism, but couldn't find it. "Well, you'll still be out of here."

He sighed. "It's okay. Go and get changed before you cause any trouble."

Emily nodded, looked down at the book in her brother's lap. "What's this?"

She pointed toward a piece of paper lying on top of the book, a cut-out rectangle of newsprint. He hadn't been reading *De Oratore* after all.

Did he never want to eat dinner?

William's face changed, breaking into a wide grin. "Just thinking of my future."

Emily took the paper, read the headline across the top.

President Wilson Approves National Defense Act. Regular Army Calls for 10,000 Recruits.

She met William's gaze, took in his satisfied grin. Since when had William taken such an interest in politics? Emily had followed the news of the American Punitive Expedition in Mexico ever since the rebel Pancho Villa had attacked a town in the US a few months ago. President Wilson had since deployed troops to bring Villa to justice—without any success so far. The need for troops in Mexico and the public's ongoing concerns with the War in Europe had made the word "preparedness" a public obsession. Emily had supported the idea of expanding the Regular Army, had thought it a reasonable response to—

The realization hit her, and she bolted to her feet, shaking her head. "You can't be serious!"

"James and I are going together. But don't tell anyone. Promise, Em?"

She shook her head, anger rising in her throat. "You're joining the Army? But why?"

"We've planned it all. I'm eighteen, so Mom and Dad can't stop me. We'll serve a couple years, and when we're done soldiering, we'll have our own money. Then we'll be able to decide what we want to do, and Mom and Dad won't have anything to say about it."

Emily wanted to slap him. Was he so naïve?

"Didn't you just say you wanted to stay here? This means leaving, Will. It'll mean going to Mexico, if not somewhere else."

"It's different. I'll be doing what *I* want. And James will be with me."

"But you'll still be gone!" Emily struggled to keep her

voice from rising and alerting her parents to her presence. "And you could be in danger. How is that better?"

"Anything is better than being their puppet." William jerked his thumb in the direction of the door, toward their parents' room.

"Even getting killed?"

William raised his chin, his jaw tensing. "I'm doing it. I've made up my mind."

They looked at each other for a few moments in silence.

William leaned his head on his hand. "Are you going to tell?"

Yes!

Emily didn't care if it meant Mom and Dad coming down on him again, she wasn't going to just watch her brother run off to God only knew where to do God only knew what. She saw the defiance in William's eyes—and behind it, the pleading, desperate fear.

She closed her eyes, took a deep breath. "No, I won't tell."

Relief blossomed on his face.

Emily turned her back to him, walked to the door. "I'll leave that to you."

"I'm not going to. We're sneaking off to Denver to enlist. I don't want to give anyone time to stop us."

"When?"

There was a moment's pause, and Emily imagined he was weighing whether or not he could trust her. "Later this summer. You'll see."

Tears stung Emily's eyes.

You were ready to see him go to college. Why stop him from going where he wants?

"You better get to your reading if you want to eat." She didn't wait for a reply, but carefully opened the door, and seeing that the hallway was empty, left William alone.

CHAPTER 3

August 17, 1919

"I'm sorry, Walt. What was that?" Emily shook her head, set down her cup of tea, trying to hide her embarrassment with a smile. Walt had been in the middle of saying something and she'd allowed her thoughts to wander off for at least the third time.

James was in Saint Vrain. In the house across the street. She'd arrived home the previous day after her visit with Walt, still furious at Officer Westlake and irritated at herself for having let her mind play tricks on her and imagining James in the window only to find her parents in an excited state. She'd assumed they were reacting to a telephone call from Westlake about her bold behavior earlier, but instead they'd rushed over to her and stuffed a newspaper in her hands.

"Emily, look! I don't believe it!" Her father had tapped the headline with his finger.

"Isn't it wonderful news?" Her mother had been beaming, her eyes bright.

Emily had read the words on the page, her head spinning. She'd sat down on the closest chair, reading and rereading the article, oblivious to her parents as they'd excitedly recounted the contents of the story.

James was alive.

More than that, he was decorated, a war hero, as the article proclaimed.

But on the heels of the great balloon of happiness and relief that had filled her on reading the paper had come a surge of red-hot anger.

She'd thrown the paper on the couch, startling her parents. "Why didn't he tell us?"

"We can call the Garrisons up right now and make some plans if you'd like."

But Emily had run from the parlor, shut herself upstairs in her bedroom and stared out the window, too angry even to speak.

To her mortification, her father had done exactly as he'd suggested, and they'd made plans to meet James and his family for dinner the following night—tonight. Emily had protested, but her parents' minds had been made up.

"I don't see why you're acting like this, Emmy," her father had said, waving his finger at her.

She hadn't bothered to explain. James Garrison was alive, and he hadn't told her, hadn't written a word since last October. How long had he been in France without writing to her to let her know he was still living? How long had he been home, in Saint Vrain, but not telephoned or sent a card? After everything they'd meant to each other...

More like everything you thought *you meant to each other.*

The thought had made it almost impossible to breathe.

Emily had been in the middle of explaining to her father why he absolutely must cancel the meal when her mother had interrupted her.

"He and William were in the same unit. I wonder if he knows...." She hadn't finished, hadn't needed to. They'd all understood.

Maybe he knew what had happened to William.

James had let her think he was dead, subjected her to more grief on top of what she already felt for William, and if he did know what had become of her brother, he hadn't thought to let her family know.

She never wanted to see him again.

She needed to see him again, if only to ask about William. Whatever she'd felt for James, whatever happiness she'd felt at the discovery that he was alive, had been obliterated by the way he'd behaved.

Believe that if you must.

Emily brought herself back to the present, folded her hands in her lap. "Truly, I'm sorry, Walt. I'm not very good company today."

He frowned, keeping the maimed side of his face turned away from her as usual, a habit he maintained despite Emily's efforts to make it very clear she didn't mind his appearance. She saw the sadness in his eyes and knew he probably thought she was tired of him.

"If I'm boring you..." Walt trailed off, a slight rasp in his voice, another symptom of a mangled face and partially mutilated mouth.

"Please," she said, holding his gaze with her own. "Go on."

"I was talking about the pharmacy."

Pharmacy?

Emily searched her mind, trying to remember what he meant. "Right."

"I think Mr. Carlin may take me on." The slightest hint of a grin showed at the corner of the good side of his mouth.

The pharmacy!

Walt had been trying to find work ever since he'd come

home, but his injuries and the attitude of many people toward his appearance had made that a tall order. One restaurant owner had gone so far as to say that Walter's face would make his patrons sick if he were their waiter. Walt had kept looking, and Carlin's pharmacy seemed to be the best choice. After all, before the War, Walt had been studying medicine. It would be a natural fit.

"That's wonderful!" Emily smiled now, picking up her tea again. "When do you start?"

Walt took up his own cup and sipped, a small dribble escaping the crumpled half of his mouth.

Emily pretended not to see.

"It's not certain yet," he said. "But Mr. Carlin says he could use a good man in back."

"Not behind the counter?" Emily heard the sharp tone in her voice and regretted it instantly. Walt was excited about the prospect of working anywhere, and she didn't want to taint that with her own disappointment. Mr. Carlin was yet another neighbor who had fallen in her estimation.

Walt looked at his feet. "No, but it's good work."

"Of course, it is." It would be a huge help to Walt's self-esteem to work again, though the idea that he would have to walk to the pharmacy in a mask...

Emily put on a smile. "So, has Marion contacted you yet?"

"No, not yet." The disappointment in Walter's voice was obvious.

"I'm sure she will. You two were always..." Emily trailed off, not sure if what she was saying was helpful or not.

"We were." His voice was flat, matter-of-fact. "But I think that changed when she knew what happened to me."

"Give her time, Walt." Emily knew how much Marion had cared for Walter. She refused to believe those feelings had completely disappeared.

"Walter?" His mother's voice sounded from elsewhere in

the house. "Are you boring that nice young lady?"

"No, ma'am," Emily replied. "We're fine."

The sound of footsteps on the wooden floor announced Mrs. Gould's entrance a second before she appeared. She was a small woman with a slight build, but there was a quality to her, a solidness that made her seem like a much larger person. Emily had always liked her, ever since she'd been a little girl and Walt had been the occasional playmate of her brother and James.

"Can I get you anything else, Miss Emily? More tea? Some cookies?" Mrs. Gould came to stand next to Emily and put a hand on her shoulder, beaming down at her. She pushed a small plate of little round shortbread cookies toward her.

Emily took one, returned Mrs. Gould's smile. "The cookies will do, thank you."

"It's the least I can offer you." A shadow passed across Mrs. Gould's expression, and Emily didn't need to ask what it was for. "You're family to us."

Heat rose into Emily's cheeks. After all, the time she spent with Walt had started as a mistake. When Emily had come home from the War, everyone, including Mr. and Mrs. Gould, had assumed that she'd worked as a nurse. The Goulds had asked her to come check in on their son and see to the occasional care he might require now that he'd been discharged from the military hospitals. Emily had hesitated. Her few experiences with combat medicine during the War had been beyond difficult. She'd been afraid that seeing Walt would bring her back to that place, to the sights, sounds, and smells of death. Worse, she hadn't wanted to see what had happened to her friend, to witness Walt's suffering when she was overwhelmed with her own loss.

Fortunately, the idea of saying no to Mrs. Gould had filled Emily with such a deep shame that she'd consented to see Walt. It had been clear to everyone very quickly that Emily had no real medical knowledge, but their social meetings had continued over the past weeks, every other day, though sometimes more. Tea, coffee, and one or two times, when Mr. and Mrs. Gould had insisted, even dinner. Facing Walt's pain *had* been difficult, despite the fact that the man had never really shared his feelings or described how his injury had happened, but their time together had been gratifying also.

Emily could tell that Walter's mood lifted whenever she visited him, and that felt like a small victory against the War, against everything it had done to her and her family. But it was more than just altruism that kept Emily there. She'd discovered she needed these visits as much as Walt did. Someone to talk to, someone who understood without needing an explanation.

Someone who had been there.

"That's very kind of you, ma'am." Emily bit into the cookie, enjoying its dry, crumbly sweetness.

"I'm being sincere, especially after what you did yesterday." Mrs. Gould shook her head, pursed her lips. "Had I not been at the grocer's, I'd have..." She trailed off, closed her eyes. "I'd probably be in jail now for murder. Thank you."

Emily almost choked on her cookie, couldn't help but laugh. "I don't doubt it, ma'am."

Walt smiled, his eyes bright. "Yes, thank you, Emily."

She wasn't sure what to say. "Anyone would have done the same."

Mrs. Gould shook her head and sat down in the settee opposite her son, on the other side of the coffee table. "I think we know that's not true. Most of the town supported that law." She sighed. "We'll talk about something less enraging, I think. Did you hear?" She leaned forward, tapped a newspaper folded on the table.

Emily glanced at it, saw the headline. "Yes." The word came out much more harshly than she'd intended.

Mrs. Gould raised an eyebrow. "I had no idea he was home. I haven't seen him around. Have you, Walter?"

He set his empty cup on the table. "No, I don't think so."

"He didn't tell anyone," Emily said. "I suppose he didn't think it was important." She chewed the rest of the cookie, avoiding Mrs. Gould's gaze, which was fixed on her face.

"We're going to head over there soon, see if he'd like a visit."

"Hmm." Emily pretended to examine her teacup, tried to keep her anger out of her voice. "My parents want us to do the same. We're having the Garrisons over for dinner tonight."

"Good." Walt's voice held a note of warning that brought Emily's gaze back up to him. He, too, was studying her, a slight frown on his face. "That's the right thing to do, Em."

She wasn't going to accept this, not from anyone else. Her parents had already found her anger at James incomprehensible, and she didn't need to argue about it with someone else.

"Well, then." Emily set her tea on the table. "I suppose I've taken enough of your time. I ought to be getting home anyway to prepare for dinner."

She stood up, saw the surprised look on Mrs. Gould's face.

"Oh, are you sure? If you wait a few more minutes, my husband will be home. I'm sure he'd like to say hello again after what you—"

"No, thank you." Emily immediately regretted interrupting Mrs. Gould, looked at her shoes. "I'm sorry for my manners."

She looked up, saw that both of her hosts were watching her, expecting her to say more.

She searched for the words. "I'm not much looking forward to this. I thought he was dead."

"And you're disappointed he's not?" Walt crossed his arms over his chest, wincing at the motion.

"No, I…" Emily clenched her skirt with both hands. "He *let* me think he was dead. Why didn't he write to me, or you, or someone?"

"Maybe he didn't have the time." Mrs. Gould gestured toward the front door, in the direction of the Garrison house. "He's probably only just come home!"

"When they were working out our dinner, Mrs. Garrison told my mother he'd been back for a month. He didn't care enough about m—" She interrupted herself, hoped neither of her hosts had noticed. "He didn't care that his friends would think him dead and would grieve for him."

They all stood in silence for a minute.

Emily took a deep breath. "I've gone and been bad company again. I'm sorry. See you in a couple days?"

"Of course, Miss Emily. Any time." Mrs. Gould smiled, though Emily could see in her eyes that she was concerned. She thrust the plate of cookies toward Emily again.

"No, thank you." Emily smiled despite the tumult of her emotions. "See you then, Walt."

Walt nodded, though his gaze was still fixed on her, his mouth in a hard line. "Yes."

Mrs. Gould escorted Emily out of the parlor and into the foyer, and Emily was about to step outside when Walt's voice brought her to a stop.

"When I heard you were going to visit me regularly, I was against the idea."

She turned around, saw him limping around the corner, grunting softly with each step.

"Walter! What a thing to say!" Mrs. Gould put her hands on her hips.

He halted in front of her, wobbling slightly as he stood. "To tell you the truth, there are times I wish you all thought I was dead."

Mrs. Gould opened her mouth, closed it.

"Why?" Emily fought the temptation to run forward and hug Walter, the desolate look on his broken face cutting through her own emotions.

"Because sometimes I wish…" He trailed off, looked at the floor for a second, then met her gaze. "I was worried what you would think. I didn't want you all to know me like this."

"But I don't think James was hurt—"

"Do you know that for sure?" He grimaced, shifted his weight.

Emily stared back at him, felt the edge of her anger twisting into something worse. Guilt. She *didn't* know for sure that he hadn't been wounded. The article hadn't mentioned any injuries that she could remember, but it had been very short. She had only gotten a glimpse of him through the window—and only for a split second. She hadn't been able to note his physical condition. What if he had been injured?

And what if he's maimed, like Walt?

"Walter, dear, you should sit." Mrs. Gould put an arm on her son's shoulder, started steering him back toward the parlor. "Emily, I'll be back in a minute to show you out properly."

"No need." She wanted to get away from the accusing look in Walt's eyes, from the guilt and the fear that had replaced her outrage.

She turned, stepped out into the hot afternoon air, and, just before she closed the door, she heard Walt calling after her.

"Tell James hello, and I'll be seeing him soon."

CHAPTER 4

October 1, 1916
Fort Riley, Kansas

James peered over his rifle, watching as his target dipped below the berm, then slowly rose back up. He relaxed, let his body rest where he lay in the grass, and raised his head.

A long, thin stick with an orange dot on the end appeared from behind the berm and came to rest in front of the target at a point in the seven ring.

"Damn."

How had he thrown the shot that badly? He opened the breech block, his frustration mounting.

"You won't get that kind of shit past me, Garrison. Is that clear?"

James jumped. He hadn't realized First Sergeant Minor was behind him.

"Yes, First Sergeant."

"Get back to it, mister"

"Yes, First Sergeant."

James waited, tried to make out the sounds of Minor walking away over the deafening boom of the rifles firing up and down the line.

"Don't let him rattle you."

James followed the source of the voice, saw William looking over at him from the adjacent firing lane.

He raised his voice, trying to speak over the thunder of the rifle fire. "I don't see him ragging anyone else so hard."

William grinned. "It's because he knows we can shoot."

"So?" James raised an eyebrow, irritated at William's ability to view Minor's combative behavior as anything but an annoyance.

"So, shoot. Prove him right."

"I'd rather sock him on the jaw."

William rolled his eyes. "Shoot."

James grumbled, adjusted his body position, the sweet scent of earth and mown grass rising up from the ground. He and William had consistently outshot most of the other trainees from the moment they'd picked up the so-called "trapdoor" rifles, antiques from before the Spanish-American war. James had hoped that after weeks of being yelled at during physical exercises, being yelled at in close-order drill, and being yelled at while standing in formation, his skill with a rifle would earn him some praise.

Not so.

Minor had conveniently raised his expectations, demanding that William and James score nothing less than a nine with each shot. It was damned infuriating.

James slipped a cartridge into the breech of his rifle, closed the block, cocked the hammer, and watched as William did the same and then aimed and fired. William's target dipped down, and James imagined the recruits running pit duty hurriedly searching for the new hole, marking it, and running the heavy, counter-weighted target stand back up.

The stick appeared and hovered the orange marker in front of the target.

James whistled. "A nine at five o'clock. Good shot." He ignored the twinge of jealousy he felt at his friend's success. James was a good shot. But William had been outshooting him by a narrow margin since their first range instruction at Riley.

"Thanks." William opened the breech block and ejected the spent casing. "Stop stalling and shoot."

"I'm not stalling." James sighted down his rifle. "I just want to see the score I have to beat."

He heard William chuckle as he focused on getting his body positioning perfect, controlling his breathing. He exhaled and pulled the trigger.

THE RECRUITS STOOD TOGETHER in a long line, barefoot and stripped down to their underwear, shuffling through the quartermaster's office and emerging on the other side with new, perfectly folded bundles of drab khaki.

James shivered in the cool air, grateful for the sunshine. Discomfort had become a daily condition since arriving at Riley, and this time, it was well worth it. After weeks of marching around and training in whatever clothes they had brought with them, they would be receiving uniforms.

He ducked his head, stepped into the office, his eyes adjusting to the relative darkness of the room. A long counter was against one wall, and behind it were shelves stacked full of folded uniforms. Three privates were dashing back and forth between the counter and the shelves, taking pieces of paper from the soldiers and returning with arms full of khaki cloth, a pair of brown leather boots perched on top. A lieutenant stood, cross-armed, occasionally giving orders to the frantic privates.

"Step over here, soldier."

James turned, saw a sergeant brandishing a measuring tape at him. There were several of them there, each measuring a soldier's waist, chest, arms.

James stepped out of line, wrinkled his nose at the odor of the room, an odd mixture of fresh woolen cloth, new leather, and the sharp odor of stale sweat. The sergeant ran the tape along James body, making James gasp as the cold strip touched his bare skin.

The sergeant jotted down numbers on a piece of paper. When he had finished, he pushed the paper into James's hands.

"Right. Next! Move it along!"

James stepped back into the line, shuffled behind the man in front of him until he was next to the counter. One of the privates grabbed his piece of paper, looked up at him.

"What shoe size?"

"Eleven."

The man nodded, turned around, hunted among the shelves, grabbing trousers here, a shirt there, a tunic farther down. After a minute or so, the private returned, thrust the bundle across the counter and into James's arms.

James nodded a thank you at the private, then walked outside, where some of the men were milling around, slipping on their uniforms. James spotted William, who was buttoning up his shirt, and walked over to him.

"Does it fit alright?" James set his bundle down, searched for socks.

"A little tight in the neck. The arms aren't long enough." William looked down at himself, stretched his arms out, a good inch of wrist showing beyond the cuff.

James chuckled. "A hose wouldn't be long enough." Ever since freshman year of high school, William had always been one of the taller boys around. Next to some of the little fellows in the company—some energetic Italians from Kansas City—he seemed truly gigantic.

"I think I'll get a photo taken on our next liberty." William smoothed his tunic. "Send it home to Emily."

"How has she stood up to being alone with your parents?" James asked the question in his best, most casual tone. He wouldn't admit it to anyone, especially William, but he'd found himself missing Emily since he and William had left Saint Vrain. He'd told himself it was just habit. He'd never gone more than a couple days without seeing her since he could remember.

"Pretty well, actually. They've finally agreed to let her go to college."

"Maybe you taught your folks a lesson by leaving. Did Emily a favor." James slipped into the drab brown socks, pulled on the trousers. They had an odd shape to them, generous in the hips and tight around the knee and the calf. He flexed his leg, grimaced. How was he supposed to run in something that pinched his knee so much?

He hopped a little as he pushed his feet into the boots, laced them up. "Harvard?"

"No, CU."

James couldn't help but grin. Emily had done it. She was going to attend college.

He pulled the mustard-brown collared shirt from the shrinking pile of khaki, threaded his arms through the sleeves, buttoned it closed, and tucked it into his trousers.

"You should write to her yourself." There was something in the tone of William's voice.

James glanced up at his friend, saw that he was smiling. "What's that supposed to mean?"

"Oh, nothing. You just seem to ask about her a lot. And I'm sure she'd appreciate it."

"I'm just being polite."

Next was the tunic, thick and coarse in his hands. James fastened it closed, felt the scratch of wool against his neck from the tight standing collar. He looked around him, saw some of the men pulling the material of their shirt collars up under the tunic collar, and did the same. "Besides, your sister blames me for getting you into this, remember? I'm just your idiot friend to her."

William's grin widened. "If you say so."

"I do." James picked up the pair of khaki canvas gaiters, resisted the urge to toss them at William. How could anyone in his right mind imagine that he and Emily were romantically interested in each other? It was beyond absurd. A memory flickered through James's mind, of being pressed close against her, smelling the rose scent of her hair as he guided the Krag rifle into her shoulder and moved her hands into position...

He blinked, bringing his focus back to the gaiters. He spent a few minutes figuring them out, putting them on wrong, taking them back off, then lacing them on again, this time the correct way.

James stood up, his uniform fully in place. "What do you think?"

William put his hands on his hips. "I think we'll make soldiers yet." His eyes lit up. "Say, why don't we *both* get our pictures taken for Em? She'll like that."

James punched his friend in the arm. "Shut up." He spread his arms to either side. "Honestly, though. How do I look?"

August 17, 1919

JAMES STARED at himself in the mirror, his hands fumbling with the black silk bow tie around his neck. The white collared shirt and black dinner jacket seemed alien to him, stiff and strange. It had been a long time since he'd dressed for dinner. In the Army, he'd worn what he'd been told to wear, and since he'd only been around his parents since he'd returned from France, he hadn't needed to wear anything as formal as what he'd put on now. That made it, what—three years?

"Let me help you."

James saw the reflection of his mother behind his own. She'd done up her hair into an elaborate pompadour and had put on a nice black evening dress.

He turned, let her take over. "Thanks."

She frowned, knotting her brow as she went to work.

"You look good, son."

"What does it matter?"

"This is for the best, James. You can't lock yourself away forever. I wish you'd tell me why this bothers you so much."

He didn't respond, didn't know what to say that wouldn't be saying too much.

"There." She finished with the tie, put her hands on his shoulders, and turned him to face the mirror, a smile on her face. "Pressed and ready for the party."

James's father entered the room from the hallway, already dressed in a black dinner jacket and tie that matched the ones James wore, his driving cap on his head, a light gray duster folded over his arm. "How's our war hero?"

James turned his back to them. "I wish you wouldn't call me that."

He could almost hear the shouts of his parents the night he'd told them he was going to the Army, how they'd threatened to disown him, how they'd pleaded with him, how his father had hardly talked to him up until the day he'd left, preferring a brooding silence to actual verbal interaction. William had done it correctly, sneaking out without telling anyone, leaving only a written note behind him, and thus avoiding the spectacle of a family dispute.

Now, to hear his father talking, it was as if his parents had planned James's military career from the start, with the full knowledge that their son would go on to save France and the civilized world from the clutches of Prussian autocracy. If the truth weren't so bitterly different, it would be funny.

James's mother put a hand on his shoulder. "He's ready. Shall we?"

They walked out to the little carriage house, and his parents climbed into the Hupmobile. James stayed outside and helped his father back the vehicle down the gravel path to the street, grateful that the sun had gone behind the mountains.

He glanced over at the Gould house, saw light glowing through the curtains. Not for the first time, he wished he were honoring the invitation from Walter rather than the one from the Culvers. Mrs. Gould had come earlier that day to invite James to visit, and he'd had to decline, setting a date later in the week.

His father chuckled. "Hop in, soldier."

James saluted his father, an exaggerated gesture, and climbed into the vehicle's back seat. The car grumbled off into the gathering darkness, trundling downhill through narrow streets that seemed both familiar and completely alien. He'd walked this way so many times. To school, to meet William for some adventure, to go to the general store, to drop off a package at the post office. Unfortunately, in all the times he'd come this way, the journey had never seemed to pass as quickly as it did that evening. It seemed like no time at all before the car was pulling up in front of the Culver house and lurching to a halt.

James's stomach knotted as he stepped out of the car. He stood, rooted to the spot. The house was exactly like he remembered it, a red brick house with a white portico that ran the entire length of the building's front. Small flower beds lined the walkway to the door, and a little garage stood separately from the house, at the end of a wide gravel driveway.

James stared at the second floor, the two windows facing the street, William's and Emily's old rooms. Emily's was lit, a soft golden glow escaping the white lace curtains. William's room was dark. Memories assailed him, memories of standing there on the lawn, waving up to William, of hoarse whispers late at night, of glimpsing Emily in her chemise through the curtains and trying to avert his eyes, but looking back. It was all there, vivid and yet detached, unreachable.

Another time. Another life.

He fought the impulse to kick his father out of the driver's seat and speed back home.

"Now you will remember your manners, won't you?"

James realized his mother was talking to him. He looked down at her and tried to let the memories go.

She frowned, the corners of her mouth wrinkling. "I didn't realize… If this is too difficult—"

"Well don't just sit there on the street!" Mr. Culver's voice boomed from the front door.

Dammit.

James saw Mr. and Mrs. Culver standing on the portico, just outside the door, their dark dinner clothes fluttering slightly in the cool evening breeze that had begun to blow from the mountains. They were smiling as they exchanged greetings with his parents, though James could tell their cheerfulness was forced, or at least exaggerated, and their smiles didn't fully reach their eyes. He required no explanation.

His mother gave Mr. Culver her hand, then stood in front of Mrs. Culver. The two women were silent for a moment, then embraced.

"We should always have been this way," his mother murmured.

Mrs. Culver's voice quavered. "Now we will be."

James's throat tightened. There was nothing for it now. He squared his shoulders and started up the stairs, aware of the stiffness in his leg, his slight limp.

"Welcome back." Mr. Culver held out a hand. "To your country, and to our home."

James took it, returned the man's firm grip. "Thank you, sir."

It seemed so strange. How many times had Mr. Culver told him off, or been the source of his and William's mutual complaints? Now he looked at James with something that looked an awful lot like warmth, or even affection.

James fought the odd impulse to laugh.

He felt a hand on his shoulder and turned to face Mrs. Culver, whose eyes were still bright. He hoped no one noticed his intake of breath when she pulled him into a hug.

Her voice was gentle, so low that James wondered if anyone else heard. "You were always a good friend. We know that."

His insides twisted. In the end, he'd been anything but a good friend. "Thank you, ma'am."

"I mean it. We know you were important to him."

James's throat closed, and he wanted to tell her again and again that he was sorry, so sorry, but he didn't dare speak for fear he would lose his composure in front of everyone. He only managed to choke out a quiet thank you.

They pulled apart, and James looked behind Mrs. Culver and into the house, searching for—

"Emily is upstairs," Mr. Culver said. "She's… taking her time."

James caught the quick glance that Mr. Culver cast at his wife.

Did she not want to see him either?

He followed Mr. and Mrs. Culver into the foyer, his parents trailing behind him. Oblivious to the conversation of the others, James's mind flashed briefly to the last time he'd seen her. Her blood-spattered dress. The exhaustion and strain in her blue eyes.

She'd been shocked when she'd seen him through the curtains yesterday, her expression one of complete surprise. And why wouldn't she be? After he'd stopped writing to her, how could she possibly have known anything about him or his whereabouts? He wouldn't be surprised if she'd thought he was dead or missing.

He fought the guilt slithering in his guts. He hadn't meant to keep her out, hadn't wanted to hurt her.

A poor excuse if ever there was one.

He'd chosen to leave her in the dark because the alternative was unthinkable.

How would you react if someone had treated you that way?

James didn't like the answer to that question.

He almost fell over as a small pair of arms closed around his waist. He looked down, saw that Brianna had appeared out of nowhere, dressed in a little gray evening dress. And there was Julius, walking toward him in a jacket and tie, holding out a hand to shake, his face the image of serious masculinity.

"Hello, Jimmy!" Brianna looked up at him, her eyes so much like her older sister's.

"Brianna, you're…" James found himself smiling and forgot for a moment about Emily. "You're so big!"

Brianna had been five when he'd left, and Julius had been

eight. They'd both grown so much. He and William had spent no small amount of time trying to keep them from intruding in their fun. He was surprised they were so happy to see him.

James shook Julius's hand, his heart lurching at the boy's close resemblance to William.

"Welcome to our home, James," Julius said. "Mr. and Mrs. Garrison." He shook their hands in turn.

James's mother laughed. "Thank you, young sir."

"Brianna, dear." Mrs. Culver pried the girl from James's side. "Run upstairs and grab your sister."

Brianna nodded and scampered out of the room, her skirts swishing behind her.

The Culvers led them through the parlor and into the dining room, showing them to their assigned places at the table. James sat, the seat beside his and the one across empty. He'd been put in the middle of the Culver kids. But which would be Emily's seat, and which would Brianna fill?

The rich smell of beef and red wine sauce wafted into the room from the kitchen, but James's stomach was already too filled with knots to feel any hunger.

"We had Mrs. Rawlins prepare a beef bourguignon. We know you must miss the French cuisine."

"What?" James found Mrs. Culver looking at him, waiting for an answer. "Oh, yes. Very much. Thank you."

It was a lie. He'd eaten more French food at home before the War than in France, where he'd been lucky to get canned mystery meat and slumgullion soup—the greasy, improvised stew the Army cooks had thrown together out of whatever they could find.

"Good." Mr. Culver smiled. "Then you're in for a treat. We got a good French red for tonight. Might as well enjoy things like this while we can."

A dismal expression passed over his face, and James knew the reason why.

Back in January, the Eighteenth Amendment, which made alcohol illegal in the United States, had been ratified, a fact that many of the doughboys in France had learned with no small amount of disdain. What would they do with the bottles of a rough red wine, the stuff the French troops called *pinard*, tucked away in their foot lockers?

The new amendment would come into effect next January. Based on the stories his father shared from his friends at the general store, James knew that not a few people were spending the intervening time consuming as much alcohol as they could.

"Ah!" His father stood up, looking toward the entrance to the dining room. "Miss Emily."

James turned, and his mind went blank.

She stood, unmoving, holding Brianna's hand, her gaze meeting his, her expression unreadable. She wore a dark blue dress, her hair done up, a silver necklace around her slender neck. He couldn't remember having ever seen someone so beautiful in his life, the sight of her planting an ache inside his chest.

Don't stare, idiot!

"Sit over there, my dear." Mrs. Culver's voice broke his trance, and he followed where her finger was pointing—to the seat right next to his.

Tonight was going to be far more difficult than he'd imagined.

CHAPTER 5

Emily willed her legs to move as she rounded the table and walked toward her chair, the one next to James.

"Miss Emily." Mrs. Garrison rose from her chair as Emily passed. "Look at you! When did you become such a beautiful young woman?"

Emily wasn't sure how to respond to a question like that, but forced a smile. "Thank you."

Mr. Garrison ducked his head in deference. "How are you, Emily?"

Aware of James's gaze on her, she extended her hand, and Mr. Garrison shook it gently.

"As well as I can be, thank you." She took a few more steps, stood next to her chair, looking at James again.

He was different, older somehow, and she could swear that his jawline had become harder, squarer, and his shoulders wider. Maybe that was normal. They'd all been so young —the soldiers, her brother, and his friend. Boys. This was a man. It was strange to see him clean-shaven and groomed, his brown hair neatly combed. An image of him in mud-caked khaki flashed through her mind.

Anger flared inside her. He was not like Walt, not disfigured. What excuse could he possibly have for not telling her he'd come home?

James held her gaze for a moment, then stood up, his chair scraping the floor. The sharpest edge of her anger blunted itself as he put weight on his left leg, winced, stood slowly to his full height, a few inches taller than she.

"Emily." He held her gaze, his face neutral, his eyes filled with some emotion she couldn't decipher.

She realized everyone was waiting for her to respond and held out her hand. "Good to see you again, James."

He took her hand, his gaze locked with hers as he held it, shook it lightly, the contact rattling her thoughts.

"Right." Mr. Culver cleared his throat. "Shall we eat?"

EMILY HAD NEVER KNOWN a meal to drag on so long. They had passed through the entrées and the salad, were now working their way through the main course—and every minute with James sitting silently beside her seemed to last a full hour.

Mr. Garrison leaned over his plate, catching Emily's eye. "I understand you served as a nurse in France."

"No, sir. I worked with the Red Cross, but not as a nurse."

"Oh." Mr. Garrison turned back to his food.

"I helped with a canteen." Emily took a bite, chewed, swallowed. "We gave the soldiers little things—stationery, hot chocolate, coffee, cigarettes, sweaters that people knit and sent to us."

"A bit of home," Mrs. Garrison offered, smiling.

"Yes. It wasn't much." Emily had felt so proud to join the Red Cross, proud to go to France to do something, anything to contribute to the War that had pulled her brother and so many of the boys she knew from school into danger. She'd felt a great satisfaction thinking of the happiness she'd bring to all those soldiers—until the first time a unit returning from the front had passed through the station. Then it had been only too clear how inconsequential her efforts really were.

"Oh, but you mustn't say that!" Her mother shook her head. "I'm sure it meant the world to those boys."

"I don't think they were worried about hot chocolate, mother."

"You'd be surprised." James's voice was so quiet that Emily thought for a moment she had imagined it.

She avoided looking at him, focused on her dinner.

Her father smiled. "You see, right from the mouth of a war hero."

She thought she heard James mutter something under his breath.

Mrs. Garrison sipped her wine. "Then you stayed back from the lines? Good. I would hate to think of a young girl in the middle of all that."

"Actually, we were close to the lines, and one time..." Emily put down her utensils, her appetite vanishing at the flood of memories.

"And how was that? Maybe you *should* have stuck with nursing."

Emily nodded, her pulse quickening.

Blood, so much blood. On her hands, wiped down the front of her skirt, coloring the mud, soaking the stretchers, trickling from wounds, from the stumps of mangled limbs. She closed her eyes, shook her head, looked across the table at Julius and Brianna, who were occupied with their plates.

Not now, not in front of everyone.

She sucked in a breath as warm fingers touched her arm. Emily looked down, saw James's hand resting lightly on her arm. She met his gaze, saw the concern written there, the understanding. His eyebrows rose, as if he were asking a question.

She nodded, her anger at him forgotten for a moment.

Her father's cutlery clinked on the porcelain. "How much longer does your freedom last, Howard?"

James shook his head, his eyes darting to Mr. Culver then back to her, a look of annoyance passing across his features as he returned his attention to his food. Emily picked up her fork, knew exactly what he meant.

It had been this way since she'd come home. Someone would ask her about France, would listen politely for a short time, but would inevitably lose interest before the subject could be discussed beyond the most superficial details. It was as if people thought she were describing a trip to summer camp, the happenings of a weekend, or a day at school. She'd answer the questions, be made to recall things she wished she'd never seen in the first place, and then be left with her own emotional turmoil as people lost interest in the topic, seeming not to notice what the conversation had cost her. It was almost as if they didn't *want* to notice.

Clearly, James had had the same experience.

"Classes start again at the end of the month." Mr. Garrison dabbed his mouth with his napkin.

"Are you going to school, James?"

"No, Mrs. Culver."

"But why?" Emily's mother held her fork in the air, halfway to her mouth.

"I... I haven't decided if I want to."

Mr. Garrison let out a grunt. "Good luck reasoning with him. We've tried. He only wants to sit around and mope all day."

So James had been moping all this time instead of contacting her? Emily didn't know what was stronger, the anger she felt at him for ignoring her when he was doing nothing more productive, or the concern that filled her at the idea that he must be suffering.

"Howard." Mrs. Garrison's sharp tone brought a momentary silence to the table.

"Well, I'm sure that will pass." Emily's father set down his fork, his plate empty. "I'm sure you'll be plenty motivated with time. You did take that machine gun post, after all."

Emily saw James jerk as if he'd been struck.

"Say," Emily's mother said. "Why don't you tell us something about the War?"

"Yes, please!" Julius chimed in, bringing the gaze of all the adults to him. "I'd like very much to hear about your medal, Mr. Garrison."

"I... I don't think..."

"Yes," Emily's father raised his glass. "We'd like to hear about your exploits."

"I'd rather not." James was staring at the plate in front of him.

"Good luck with this one, too." Mr. Garrison chuckled. "He still hasn't told us the story, or anything about France, really."

Apparently, Emily wasn't the only one James had shut out. She looked him over again, searching for some kind of wound. What had happened to him?

There was a long silence, and Emily saw her parents share a glance. She realized what was about to happen right before her mother spoke again.

"James, you must understand. When we invited you here tonight, we were hoping you could help us." Emily's mother paused, seemed to gather her emotions. "The day our William went missing was the same day you won your award, the seventh of November. We know you two were in the same unit, and you were always so close. We were hoping…" Her voice caught and she trailed off, looking at her husband.

Emily's father finished his wife's sentence. "We were hoping you might know more about what happened that day."

Emily's heart seemed to stop. She saw James's jaw tighten and his hands clench shut in his lap, his knuckles turning white. She knew what he was feeling, even if she didn't know why. Hadn't she had the same reaction just moments ago?

The room fell silent again, Emily's emotions at war while she waited for James to reply. She wanted him to speak, to buck up and face whatever it was so he could tell her about her brother. At the same time, she wanted everyone to stop staring at him, to leave him alone. She wanted to pull him against her and take that awful, wrenched look off his face. She'd seen that look before, in the rest camps, at the clearing station.

Yes, she wanted to know about William.

But not like this.

She moved her hand to rest over his. She searched for her voice, found it. "Mother, Father—maybe we should leave this for another time."

James jerked his head up suddenly. His face was pale, small beads of sweat appearing on his forehead. His eyes were hollow, dead, looked almost bored. "You want to know about that day?"

Mrs. Garrison's brow furrowed. "James, are you—"

He cut her off, his voice even, calm, matter-of-fact. "I ran into a bunker. There were five Germans there manning the machine gun. I shot two instantly. The other three reached for their weapons. I shot one more, and was out of cartridges."

"James," Mr. Garrison reached across Emily for his son's hand. "I think that's enough."

James stared ahead of him at nothing. "I didn't have time to reload and ran at the other two. I bayoneted the first as he pulled a pistol. The other one turned and ran down the trench. I knocked him down and stabbed him through the back."

Chills ran down Emily's spine, her emotions reflected in the horrified expressions on the faces around her.

James let out a harsh laugh that descended into a sob, his face crumpling. "Hours later, our regiment left the line for good. And they gave me a medal for that. They gave me a goddamned medal."

The Garrisons flinched at their son's profanity, looked helplessly at each other, clearly unsure what to do.

Tears gathered in James's eyes, and Emily glared at her parents, a new anger uncoiling inside her. "Why did you push him?"

Her mother ignored her, her voice desperate, pleading. "But William? Where was William?"

James shot to his feet so quickly that Emily gasped. In a second, he was around the table and out of the room, the front door crashing open and closed again a moment later.

"James!" Mrs. Garrison shouted after her son. "James?"

"I'm sorry." Emily's father reached for his wine. "I didn't realize he was so upset."

Emily scooted her chair back, threw her napkin on the table. "Didn't you?"

She dashed out of the room, ignoring the calls of her parents as she hurried toward the front door.

"SON OF A BITCH." James staggered up the darkened street, running his hands through his hair. He stopped, bent over, and placed his hands on his knees, his breathing coming in hard, jagged gasps.

"Garrison, stop! Stop!"

"James, what the hell are you doing?"

He squeezed his eyes shut and tried to slow his breathing, pushing away the memory, the smell of smoke and rotting bodies, the cold squish of wet grass beneath his soggy feet.

"James?"

He jerked around, saw Emily following him in her high-heeled shoes.

He couldn't let her see him like this, couldn't take the risk she would pick up questioning him where her mother had left off. He backed away, turned, and started walking down the street, tears streaming from his eyes.

"James, wait!"

He heard her steps behind him, quickened his pace.

Run. Just keep running.

"I'm sorry! Please stop."

He heard the note of concern in her voice, felt himself slowing, coming to a stop. A second later, she was there, and he felt her hand on his arm.

"James, I'm sorry. I..." She trailed off. "They were wrong to push you."

He clenched his jaw, blinked furiously, guilt making him nearly sick. She had no idea how little he deserved her kindness.

"Hey, you're right here." She tugged him, pulled him around, and turned him to face her.

He looked down at her, saw the worry etched on her face.

"It's alright." Her voice was soothing, like a mother talking to a child. "You're alright."

The urge to hold onto her, onto anything, overwhelmed him. He reached out, pulling her against him, wrapping an arm around her.

She gasped at the sudden contact, but held on. "It's okay."

His breathing slowed, and his muscles relaxed. Emily was still whispering to him, reassuring him, the sound of her voice chasing away the last strangling ropes of his panic.

You don't deserve this from her.

He pulled away, stepped backward, wiped his eyes. "I, uh. I'm sorry. I'm afraid I made a fool of myself."

"Someone certainly did, but not you." She cast an irritated look back at the house. "They don't understand. To them, the War was sitting at the table reading newspapers about how our boys were winning all the time. I doubt it was even real to them, until… well, you know."

"I can't blame them. I knew this was going to happen. I didn't want to come here." He regretted the words as soon as he'd said them.

"Would you have told me you were home?" Emily put her hands on her hips, her voice taking on a sharper edge. "Eventually, would you have told me you were still alive? I would have thought you and I meant more to each other…" She trailed off, color rising to her cheeks.

James clenched his teeth, not sure how to respond, the vulnerability in her voice more painful than any shout or accusation could be.

"I was over there, too." She reached out for his hand again. "I know what you must have gone through. Couldn't you at least have talked to me? Me, if no one else?"

For your own damned sake, no. You of all people.

"Emily, I didn't mean…" Anything he thought to say sounded ridiculous and artificial.

"Do you know what I thought, James? I thought you were dead—or missing like William." She bit her lip, and he could tell she was fighting to hold back her emotions.

"I'm sorry." It sounded like a stupid, weak response even to his ears.

He wanted to pull her into his embrace again, to explain everything, to beg her for her forgiveness.

She dropped her hand from her face, her eyes hardening as they looked up at him. "Why are you here?"

"I was invited."

She sighed. "No, why are you here in *Saint Vrain*? If you didn't want to bother seeing me again, why did you come back? You had to know we'd see you eventually."

"Because…"

Just tell her!

Her eyebrows rose, and she frowned, waiting for him to finish.

He couldn't make himself tell her, couldn't form the words.

"Good night, James." She turned, started walking back toward the house.

"Emily, please." He lurched after her, stopped. "I came because I owed it to you." The words were out of his mouth before he could stop them.

"What?" She turned around, shook her head. "You just implied you would never have communicated with me. What did I have to do with it?"

"James, Emily?" Mr. and Mrs. Culver appeared at the door, followed by James's parents, Julius, and Brianna.

"Are you two alright?" James's father peered at them from the comparative brightness of the lit porch. "Won't you come back inside?"

James looked back at Emily, at the question in her eyes.

They were all here. He'd already made a scene. The damage was done.

He took a deep breath, kept his gaze on Emily.

"I owed you, because I know. I know what happened to William."

On the porch, Mrs. Culver gasped, and Emily raised a hand to her mouth, took a step backward.

Tears returned to James's eyes, and he didn't bother to wipe them. "I'm so sorry, Emily. I'm so sorry."

Tell her all *of it.*

She shook her head, stepped backward again.

"William is dead. I saw him die." He could hear again the rattle of that machine gun, the sudden blast from the shell, the image of horror floating in front of him.

"My God," Mr. Culver groaned.

Mrs. Culver let out a sob.

"I wanted to tell you. Please believe me. I just couldn't. I didn't want…"

What? To hurt Emily, or for her to know the truth, the whole truth, the truth she still didn't know?

You selfish bastard.

Emily was still shaking her head. "But the Army said—"

"I saw it happen."

"Why? Why didn't you tell us?"

"Because I…"

Because she meant more to him than anyone. Because he'd rather die than leave her with that image of her brother. Because he didn't want her to hate him.

Too late for that one, pal.

"I'm so sorry." He stepped toward her, reached for her. "God, Emily, I'm so sorry."

He stumbled as her hand hit his face, the slap catching him off guard. He rubbed his stinging skin as Emily turned around and ran up the stairs. She stumbled, kicked her shoes off, and kept running, pushing past her parents, who were holding each other in an embrace, Julius and Brianna pulled against them.

James's father coughed. "My deepest condolences. I… uh, suppose we'll be going."

Mr. Culver nodded silently, offered his hand. They shook, and James's mother put her arms briefly around Mrs. Culver, hugging her from behind. They separated, and James's parents started down the steps. But he didn't wait for them to climb into the car. He was already running home, trying to chase away the chasm that had opened inside him with the burn in his legs, the ache in his lungs.

It was over. He'd done it. He could be at peace.

Another lie?

It wasn't over by half.

He ran harder.

CHAPTER 6

April 6, 1917

Emily bolted up the front steps, the newspaper clutched in her hand, her heart in her throat. She threw open the front door and ran into the parlor, looking for her parents.

"Emmy!" Brianna jumped up from where she was sitting on the settee, dashed over to her, picture book in hand, and threw her arms around Emily's waist.

Emily stopped a minute to pat her sister's head, trying and failing to remain calm. "Brie, where's Mom? Is Dad home yet?"

The little girl shook her head. "Mommy's upstairs."

Emily bent down, gave Brianna a hug, then took the stairs as fast as her long, light green afternoon dress would allow her. She strode down the hall, reached her parents' room, knocked. She stood there a moment, tapping her toe on the wooden floor.

"Yes?"

She opened the door, stepped inside.

"Emmy?" Her mother turned from where she was folding some of her husband's shirts next to the armoire. "Emmy, what's the matter? You look ill."

She'd been like this ever since William had snuck off—prone to worrying, quick to react.

Emily held up the massive newspaper headline for her mother to read. "Congress has declared war on Germany."

"Oh." The color drained from her mother's face. She took a couple slow steps, then sat down on the bed.

Emily sat down beside her, offered the newspaper. "There's more in here. The news just came through."

Her mother took the paper, held it in her lap. After a moment, she cleared her throat. "Dear, there are some letters on the table for you. I think you'd better open them."

A FEW HOURS LATER, Emily sat on the settee, leaning back against the firm cushion, the letters from James and William folded in her lap. Brianna and Julius had gone outside to play with the neighbor kids, leaving Emily alone with her parents.

She glanced at them, the anger rolling off her father where he sat, his newspaper held out in front of him like a shield, her mother focused on her knitting needles, her motions erratic. Emily would have to pick her moment. Her parents would not like what she had to say.

She took a deep breath, opened her mouth to speak, and closed it, drumming her fingers on the opened envelopes in her lap. She'd hoped the letters would contain information about what the boys would be doing now that America was at war. William had always been the one with whom she'd discussed major happenings, and she wanted to know how he felt.

Was he excited, like so many of the other people in town? Did he support the War? Was he afraid?

She'd realized as soon as she'd opened the letter how silly this idea was, the high emotions of the moment getting the better of her. William had posted the letter days ago. He did not mention Germany at all. He merely talked about the boredom he and the other troops were tolerating at the moment. They'd finished their training in the winter, joined their regiment, the 26th Infantry, and started toward the border, certain that they'd finally get to have adventures in Mexico—only to be ordered back in February. Since then, they'd been in garrison, passing their days doing fatigue duty and drill.

It had almost made her want to laugh. How many boys talked about soldiering with hushed awe, recounting stories of adventure? The truth of military service seemed incredibly dull, more working and waiting than fighting.

"I don't expect we'll have anything to worry about." Her mother didn't lift her gaze from the growing garment in front of her. "I don't expect they'll send the troops from the border, will they?"

Emily glanced at her father, who was buried in his newspaper, the pages about the War removed from the stack and folded on the end table next to him.

"I'm not sure." Emily held up William's letter. "He says they're not at the border anymore. The paper said the Army would likely send all the trained troops over to France soon, within the month, and send more once they are ready."

Some of the boys had already left for Denver to enlist. Walter Gould had even borrowed his parents' car to drive a gaggle of his eager friends, William and James's old school buddies, to the capital. She'd seen them when she'd walked downtown to find out if anyone had more news, only to watch them drive away.

It had left her feeling utterly helpless. How long had she followed the news of this war and wished the United States would intervene and protect the Western democracies? Now, it was finally happening, and she was left standing on a curb, useless.

The decision that she had made then had been a very easy one.

Her mother fumbled with her knitting, stopped. "But I can't imagine they'd send them over so quickly. They only just finished their training."

"I can't say." It was maddening, this lack of information, nothing but the speculation of the town.

Her father folded his paper to a new page, his face hidden from view. "None of that is our concern. William made his choice, and it's not for us to wonder about it."

Emily didn't bother concealing the scowl spreading across her face. "It's your country at war, too, regardless of how you feel about your son."

He didn't respond.

"I expect we'll know more in William's next letter." Her mother resumed her needlework. "Or maybe James Garrison will learn something."

Emily was about to respond, but her father interrupted her, dropping his newspaper and fixing his wife with an ugly glare.

"I don't want that boy's name mentioned in this house, do you understand? If it weren't for him, William would be at Harvard now, and I wouldn't have to hear all this whining about his whereabouts." He turned, pointed at Emily. "I have half a mind to take away anything he writes to you. I don't much like the idea of a malcontent fool like that being in contact with my daughter."

"Dear, I—" Her mother started to speak, but her father had already barricaded himself behind his newspaper again.

She looked back at Emily. "If he learns something, you will tell me, won't you? And make sure he knows to watch out for our William."

Emily ignored the loud *humph* from her father. "I will."

James had begun writing to her all of a sudden a few months ago. His unexpected correspondence had surprised her and she hadn't responded to the first two or three letters, still suspecting that James's influence had been to blame for her brother's choice to throw away a perfectly good college education.

William's letters had helped change her mind. She'd read a new confidence in her brother's words, a difference in his attitude. She'd noticed a difference in James, too, who seemed like an entirely different person in his letters from the one she'd known in person. Still a boy, eager to get into the action and make a name for himself in the military, but more serious now than she'd ever remembered him being, thoughtful, intelligent. She couldn't figure out whether his changed character was another positive effect of the Army, or whether it had not changed at all, and she had simply never seen him clearly.

One short paragraph in particular had instantly and finally changed her opinion of him.

I heard you are going to CU next year. Good work winning that battle! I think it will be a good fit for you, and you will be happier there than locked away at home with those parents of yours. You are too smart not to go.

She'd never considered James particularly supportive of women's liberation—he'd always seemed so annoyed to have a *girl* intrude on his time with her brother—but his appreciation for her success against her parents had earned him a return letter from her. Since then, they'd corresponded almost as frequently as she and William had.

Emily wouldn't admit it to anyone, especially not her

mother and father, but she had even begun looking forward to James's letters, felt a rush of excitement when she saw his name on the envelope.

Today, that excitement had been tempered by the knowledge that he, too, would now be in harm's way should his and William's regiment be sent to France. He was yet another person for her to worry about.

That was why she had to make this choice, the only choice that made sense.

She studied her parents in silence for a few more minutes, mesmerized for a moment by the motions of her mother's knitting.

There will never be a perfect time.

She cleared her throat.

"I heard the Red Cross is calling for volunteers. The Salvation Army and the YMCA, too." She watched her parents' reactions carefully. They continued as before, seeming not to notice her.

"I heard they would take women for service."

Her mother looked up and stared at her as if to measure her. Her father rattled his paper, shifting in his seat.

"I've decided to go."

"But Emmy, dear, why?" Her mother set down her knitting again. "They'll have plenty of men to deal with this war. Surely you don't need to go as well."

"But that's the issue, Mother. The men are doing their part. I'd like to do mine. You've read the papers, haven't you? Don't you remember what the Germans did in Belgium in Fourteen, the plans the Kaiser made with Mexico?"

No one in town could have forgotten the news about the so-called Zimmerman Telegraph—an offer from Germany to give the Mexicans their former territories in the US in exchange for supporting the Central Powers in case America should join the Allies. Even many of the isolationists in town had uttered strong words for the Germans' diplomatic machinations when the news had broken several weeks ago.

Her mother was shaking her head silently now, as if she did not understand.

Emily pressed on. "And it's about time the United States entered this war. We can't ignore our duty to democracy. I need to be part of that."

"But why *you*?" Her mother leaned forward, something desperate in her voice.

Emily raised her chin. "Because William may end up in France, and I don't want to be sitting around here doing nothing if he does."

The newspaper collapsed onto her father's lap. He glared at her, his face turning red as he rose to his feet.

"How long did I endure you whining to me about college?"

Hot anger boiled in Emily's chest. "Things are different now."

He threw his paper onto the chair and came to stand before her. "Oh, yes, things are different. All because our idiot son did an idiotic thing and snuck away to the Army like a thief in the night."

"He only snuck away because y—"

"You want to go join him?" Her father jabbed a finger at her face. "That's perfectly acceptable to me. No one in this family gives a damn what I think."

Before Emily could respond, he stormed out of the room and up the stairs, leaving her alone with her mother, who had started crying softly into her handkerchief.

Emily's anger at her father gave way to a harder emotion to face. Guilt. She had expected both of her parents to be furious, but she hadn't known her mother would react this way.

She took her letters in hand, stood up, and walked over to

her mother. She put a hand on her shoulder, wasn't sure what to say.

"It's alright." Her words seemed ridiculous, inadequate.

"You won't be going to France, will you? Not to the fighting?"

"I...I don't know. I don't think so." Emily wasn't exactly sure *what* she would be doing in the Red Cross, had only needed to know that she would be doing *something*.

Her mother looked up at her, her eyes rimmed with tears. "Promise me you will be safe. That you won't put yourself in some foolish situation to prove you're as brave as the boys."

"I promise." Emily knew it was an absurd thing to promise, that her location and activities would likely be totally out of her control, but the slight relief on her mother's face made it worth the trouble.

"I won't lose one of my children in this war. The Kaiser can do what he likes, but not with my children."

Emily didn't know how to reply. She could only stand there, her hand still on her mother's shoulder.

James hunched down as he ran, pointing his bayonet ahead of him. The air hummed around his head, thick with bullets. He strained to make out the enemy position through the fog, to locate the muzzle flash of the machine guns, but he could only see William running a few yards ahead of him.

"William!" James strained to catch up with him, his lungs bursting. The ground was so steep, sloping upwards into the mist. No matter how hard James pumped his legs, he couldn't close the distance between him and his friend. "Slow down!"

William didn't hear him over the terrible noise of the German guns that seemed to come surround them, firing at them from every direction.

Had they fallen behind enemy lines?

Where was the rest of the platoon?

Had only he and William survived?

James swiveled his head around as he ran, but couldn't see the others. The fog hid everything, closed in around him like a huge white fist. Ahead, William was farther away, sliding into the haze. If he vanished, James would be alone. How would he find him again?

James stretched his arm out, but he was too far behind. William's dark outline broke apart, split into a hundred pieces that melted into the fog.

"No!" James ran on, completely enclosed by the murk now.

Panic seized him, choking the breath from his lungs. He stopped running, unable to take another step. He swung out, trying to ward off the whiteness surrounding him. Where had his rifle gone? And why had he halted? He had to keep moving, or the Germans would find him. He had to catch up with William.

His lungs burned from his uphill sprint, or... Could it be gas?

James fumbled for his gas mask, his fingers reaching, searching without finding, helpless as the cloud swirled around him, choking him, smothering him until everything was white oblivion.

JAMES BOLTED UPRIGHT. It was all black now. He was dying, dead already. The gas was choking him, making his eyes water. He jumped to his feet, ran a few steps, and dropped to the ground. He clutched at something soft and gripped it hard with his fingers, cold sweat dripping down his forehead.

If he was dead, how could he still feel?

He lay still, breathing hard, the odor of dust in his nose. Gradually, his surroundings took shape. A gray line—the crack under a wooden door a foot or so in front of him. The carpet. The sound of crickets.

His room. He was in his bedroom, at home in Saint Vrain.

He let out a long breath, trying to dispel his lingering sense of dread.

"James?" His mother's voice sounded in the hallway outside, light spilling through the crack under his door, making him blink. "James, are you alright in there?"

"Y-yes." James swallowed, found his voice. "Yes, I'm fine."

"It sounded like you fell over."

"I…" James looked for an excuse. "I dropped something." He didn't want to worry his parents. What would they think if they found him there, prostrate on the floor? What kind of man would act in such a way?

"Oh." His mother didn't sound convinced. "You will tell me if you need anything?"

"Yes."

There was a pause, and James saw the silhouette of his mother's feet under the door. Some part of him wished she would turn the knob and come inside.

"Good night." She turned, and a second later the light in the hall went out.

James got to his feet and walked to his bed. His bedding was in disarray, a pale mess of tangled white sheets and scattered pillows. Lacking the energy to tidy up, he eased himself onto his mattress, took a deep breath, and shut his eyes, doing his best to forget the image of William breaking apart in front of him.

Still, sleep did not come.

Emily woke up, turned over in her bed, and glanced toward the window, at the light filtering through the drawn curtains. She could just glimpse of the day outside through a slit in the drapes.

It was late. Maybe ten, or eleven.

She rolled over, her limbs heavy, and stared at the fibers of her pillow case, her mind numb. She didn't know how long she stayed like that, her own breathing so loud, the beat of her heart against the mattress like a drum banging in her head. Her eyes ached, but she would not cry, or could not. It wouldn't solve anything, and how would it affect her family to see her tears?

They didn't need her pain. They had plenty of their own. She'd heard her parents sobbing in the night, the sound waking her. She'd lain under her sheets, not knowing what to do, drifting in and out of a fitful sleep.

William was dead. No more doubts. No more slivers of hope.

Hadn't she already accepted this? Hadn't she known it?

She'd thought she had, and had felt irritated at her parents' insistent hopefulness, their impossible, absurd illusions. She hadn't realized how much she'd been clinging to those same illusions until James had ripped them from her.

She thought of him, the anguish in his eyes as he'd told her, the look of surprise on his face when she'd struck him.

Telling her about William had caused him pain.

She felt no anger toward him now, felt nothing besides the grief that seemed to be in every part of her body, sitting on top of her like a lead blanket.

She started, her eyes jerking back open. Had she nodded off again? Her stomach growled, protesting its empty state. A small flicker of irritation fluttered through her. She huffed, annoyed that the functioning of her body should continue no matter how she felt. She threw back her covers, saw last night's evening dress thrown over the chair beside her small writing desk. She worked herself into it, not bothering to put up her hair, which was loose and messy about her shoulders, and walked out into the hallway. Her parents' door was shut, but she could hear voices from downstairs.

Emily rubbed her eyes and trudged down the stairs, her mind in a numb fog, a dull ache in her chest. Brianna and Julius were sitting on the settee, Mrs. Rawlins between them, reading from a book. *Tom Sawyer,* from the sound of it.

"Good morning, Miss Emily." Mrs. Rawlins smiled faintly, her round cheeks rosy, her eyes red. "Can I make you some breakfast?"

Emily nodded, touched by the obvious grief on the woman's face. She'd been their cook for as long as Emily could remember and had known both her and William since they were tiny.

Mrs. Rawlins stood and straightened her white apron over her simple gray blouse and skirts. She stopped in front of Emily, pulled her into a hug.

Emily fought the urge to lean against Mrs. Rawlins and let the older woman hold her like a child. She couldn't be weak now, and she didn't want to upset her siblings more than they already were.

"Thank you," she whispered.

Mrs. Rawlins let go of her and shuffled off toward the kitchen. Emily picked up the book the cook had set down and eased herself onto the settee between her brother and sister. Brianna scooted close to her and put her head on Emily's shoulder. Julius sat with his back ramrod-straight, his expression blank, only the puffy red of his eyes betraying his grief.

Trying to be the little man.

Emily moved herself next to her brother, taking the choice away, tugging Brianna along with her. For a moment, they all sat together silently, Emily feeling the contact of her sister's head on her shoulder, her brother's arm pressing against hers. Then she opened the book, and started reading.

After a few minutes, the delicious scent of eggs and bacon began to filter out into the parlor. Emily kept reading, ignoring the persistent growl of her stomach, trying to keep her mind on Tom and Huck's exploits rather than the tired wanderings of her brain.

"Breakfast is ready, children, Miss Emily!" Mrs. Rawlins called from the dining room. Emily stood, let Julius pass in front of her, and followed behind, Brianna attached to her side. They entered the dining room, took seats in front of three plates that had been put next to each other on one side of the table, each with a small cup of orange juice, a small mug of coffee in front of the middle plate. Mrs. Rawlins passed by, a tray of food clanking softly as she walked out and up the stairs toward their parents' room.

Emily stared at her food, picked up a piece of toast, scraped butter across it. She took a bite, then another. Soon, she was eating with as much gusto as the children, who were silent except for the scrape and clink of their utensils.

Emily looked across the table to where James had sat the night before and found herself thinking that maybe it *would* have been better if he'd never told them about William or they'd never known James was alive.

No, this was better.

At least they knew now, and could begin telling the rest of the family, writing the difficult letters, speaking to friends and colleagues, everyone who had known or loved William. Emily thought of Alice and Marion, of trying to explain it to them. She felt the absurd impulse to hide, to never see them again if it meant not having to say those awful words and admit the truth to anyone.

Just like James.

"I wanted to tell you. Please believe me. I just couldn't."

James's words from the night before filtered back into her mind. She felt again the raw, animal rage that had roared to life inside her in that moment, the sensation of her hand smacking his face. Guilt coiled around her heart and up into her throat.

She couldn't remember a day of her life when James had not been William's friend. Surely he'd known what the news would do to her, to her parents, to the children. Could she blame him for not wanting to bring that grief to them, to be the one to give them that news?

She shivered, heard again the casual, dead tone of his voice as he'd described killing those Germans. She remembered his sudden descent into tears, the erratic violence of his emotions. When she'd caught him outside in the street and held him against her, she'd felt his heart racing, his rapid breathing. He was a man in pain, and telling her about William had only added to it.

She couldn't be mad at him—at least, she shouldn't be. He should have told them earlier, yes, but she couldn't hate him for delaying, not now that she knew, and not now that she'd seen him and how the War had marked him. It was even worse than the last time she'd seen him in France at the canteen near Vavincourt.

She sipped her coffee, the hot liquid moving down to her numb center. She thought of James standing in front of her in the street, remembered the tears he'd been trying to hide. She could almost feel her arms go around his neck again. In that moment, it had just been the two of them, like before, and it had felt right holding him. It had brought out a feeling in her that she'd spent the last few months trying to bury. She'd wanted for all the world to take away his pain, to make him act like his old self.

It made her next decision all the more painful.

James had answered her most important question about William—and raised a hundred more. Those questions now tugged at her. How had her brother died? Had James been right beside him? Had William suffered? Had it been quick, painless? Had he lingered for hours in an aid station? She pressed her eyes shut, pushing away the image of her brother lying in one of those awful places, surrounded by the smells and sounds of death and misery.

She believed James that her brother was dead—it only made sense now that William had remained missing for so long, and James's emotions had made it clear that he was either telling the truth or should take up acting—but there were still so many missing pieces, so many unanswered questions. Theories and ideas swarmed inside her mind and coalesced around one, insoluble riddle.

Why had the Army declared William missing if James had seen him die?

She glanced over at Julius, the concentrated, deliberate way in which he ate. Brianna, was resting her head on the table beside her empty plate. Emily heard muffled voices upstairs, the unmistakable note of emotion in them.

It would be hard, but it was the only thing Emily could do.

Regardless of how hurt James was, and regardless of her feelings for him, she had to know what had happened to William, and she would not give up until she did.

She would make James tell her everything.

CHAPTER 7

August 19, 1919

James walked along the side of the road, his eyes facing front, the sun heating his skin. Sweat beaded on his forehead, trickling down his temples. The foothills rose up from the plains, their grassy sides golden brown, and the smell of dried, cured grasses filled his nose, the occasional clump of pine trees offering the temptation of shade. Irritated at his limp, he squared his shoulders, opening up his chest, walking in the way the Army had taught him out of habit.

His mind flicked back to a muddy road, water squishing in his boots, and he was suddenly grateful to be dry, to not have the weight of the pack on his back, the cartridges and canteen on his belt, the sling of his rifle biting one shoulder, the incessant plinking of raindrops on his steel helmet.

He heard the grumble of a motor, stopped, and stuck out his thumb. The truck lurched to a halt. James offered fifty cents, and the man accepted. James sat in the back, looking at his feet so as not to see the other side of the empty bed. This had always been his and William's preferred way to get to High Valley Ranch, and this was the first time James had made the trip alone.

Uncle Chester had telephoned that morning to ask if James could come up to the ranch for a day or two.

"I could use the help," he'd said, his voice scratchy over the telephone speaker.

James doubted that. Chester had more than enough hands on the ranch. He had never asked James to do any kind of work there. Instead, Chester had brought him to see cattle getting roped and branded, a fascinating thing for a boy obsessed with cowboys and adventure to witness.

James suspected his parents had talked to Chester about James's behavior with the Culvers, and his uncle had decided to help in the only way he could. It was just as well, because staying at home had become unbearable.

In the two days since the dinner with the Culvers, James's parents hadn't spoken more than a few sentences to him, nothing outside of the most basic pleasantries, asking if he'd like coffee or tea, if he could please pass the butter. They didn't seem angry at him—when he did catch them looking, all he could see in their expressions was concern, fear even.

They were worried about him and didn't have a clue what to do about it.

For some reason, that made being around them worse. He'd hoped that now they knew at least part of what had happened, his parents would offer some wisdom, some perspective on life he lacked. The fact that they were as overwhelmed as he was made him angry. How could they be so useless when he needed them to have answers?

It was irrational, he knew.

He also felt sorry for them, sad that they were so obviously lost. Their son was clearly not what they wanted him to be anymore. After the scene he'd made the other night and the manner in which he'd finally told the Culvers about William, he wouldn't be surprised if they were as glad to have him out of the house as he was to be gone.

The truck slowed to a stop, and James hopped out, thanking the driver. He followed the familiar road into the foothills, up the shallow canyon, the valley spreading out in front of him, framed on either side by hog-backed ridges. He stopped, looking around. It had been a very long time, and yet it all looked the same. He continued up the road, spied Chester standing up ahead at the gate, all tanned leanness and angular lines, the same old salt-and-pepper mustache on his face, his blue eyes, the trait that looked the most like his sister—James's mother—watching him carefully.

"Welcome back." Chester offered his hand and James took it.

They shook, and held the contact for a moment before letting go.

James looked around, half expecting to see the .22 or the Krag leaned on a post.

"I don't think I want to shoot today."

Hell, James wasn't sure he wanted to look down the sights of a rifle ever again.

Chester nodded. "Good, because I asked you here to work."

He held James's gaze, and an understanding passed between them.

Of course. He fought the Spanish. He understands.

"I'm ready."

"Good." Chester moved aside as James walked through the gate and swung it shut. "I got a fence over on the south side that's down. Had to go chase a couple cows all over creation. They're getting out into Forest Service land. We're going to fix it. You know anything about barbed wire fences?"

An image flashed through James's mind, of a man falling forward into the spirals of wire, screaming, trying to free himself, jerking as the machine gun bullets caught him.

Chester must have noticed James's reaction because he put a hand on his shoulder. "We'll start with some H-braces anyway. We need some new ones."

~

"SHE SLAPPED YOU, HUH?" Chester whistled. "Can't say I blame her. In a moment like that, I wouldn't blame her for doing just about anything.

"I suppose I don't, either." James drove the iron digging bar into the growing hole in the ground, gnawing away at the tough Colorado dirt. He'd heard Chester jest about the soil conditions at the ranch before, his old joke that he should just call the whole property High Valley Rock. "I should have told her sooner."

"I think that's a given."

"I really meant to." James paused, a good pile of loosened soil and rock in the bottom of the hole. "It was my whole reason to come home. I just didn't want to see what the news would do to her."

It was true, but not the *whole* truth. James had considered staying in France, living with his cousin Henri, someone who had experienced the same war as he, someone who might forgive him for what had happened. But when he'd learned that William had been marked missing, he'd known he had to tell Emily otherwise, even if it meant she might find out the full story.

"Hmmm." Chester thrust his shovel down into the hole, removing the debris James had loosened. "Looks like a few more inches."

James waited for Chester to finish and then struck down

with the digging bar, enjoying the physical labor, the strain in his muscles. It was better this way, outside, in the fresh air. They continued for a while in silence, alternating their jobs, shade from a stand of ponderosas shielding them from the afternoon sunshine.

"Did I ever tell you about my friend Marlow?" Chester said at last.

James searched his memory, sifting through his uncle's many stories. "No, I don't think so." He stepped out of the way for Chester to work the shovel.

"He was a buddy of mine in the Army. We were in the Philippines, both of us in a little line of trench we'd dug to defend our outpost." Chester's shovel strokes grew more violent as he stabbed and attacked the loose dirt. "We hadn't seen any fighting for a while. Then he looked over the trench. I saw movement and was a bit too slow telling Marlow to get his damned head down. He got a bullet right in the face."

Chester stopped, breathing hard from the exertion. He fixed James with a look that held the shadows of pain, old ghosts. "I blamed myself for that for a long time. Still do. Doesn't make any sense, who lives and who dies in a war."

"No, it doesn't." James averted his gaze from Chester, fighting to hide his reaction as he plunged the digging bar back into the hole. His uncle's words struck too close to the truth, touching some savage despair in him.

"Maggie spent a long time trying to get me to accept Marlow's death. It's pretty easy to feel guilty for being the one who made it home."

"Yeah." But what had happened to William was worse than that, so much worse. "You think that's deep enough?"

"Let me scoop it out." Chester did just that, then gave a few jabs at the hole for good measure. "Perfect."

James set down the digging bar and picked up the log

Chester had already prepared, its bottom end charred to protect it from rot. He winced, his leg protesting the extra weight. Chester grabbed the other end of the log, and heat that had nothing to do with exertion rushed into James's cheeks.

He hated being weak.

The two men tilted the log into the hole, and James laid the digging bar across its mouth to see where it fell in relation to a notch they'd cut in the wood.

"Close enough." Chester picked his shovel back up and began scooping dirt back into the hole from the small pile beside it.

James hoisted the digging bar up, turned it around, and pounded the tamping end into the ground, packing the dirt that Chester sprinkled into the hole and around the post.

"Is Emily special to you?"

The question caught James off guard. "How do you mean?"

Chester raised an eyebrow. "You put yourself through all kinds of misery to come back to Saint Vrain just to tell her about William, then you torture yourself some more because you realize what that news will do to her. Seems to me she means a lot to you."

James stopped tamping with the bar, feeling exposed. "It was just the right thing to do. That's all."

Chester rolled his eyes. "Keep tamping."

James started at the dirt again. "Right."

"I think you should see her again."

James laughed. "Yeah? Turn the other cheek?"

"I'm serious."

"I doubt she wants to see me." The pain and outrage on Emily's face when she had struck him had been obvious. "She probably hates my guts."

If she knew everything, she absolutely would.

Chester finished shoveling dirt in the hole and watched as James continued tamping. "Are you so sure?"

James stopped, gave the post a firm wiggle. "Nice and solid."

"You three were close before the War. You, Emily, and William. And you were the last one with William when he died, the only one who can tell her and her family what his life was like in the War, what his experiences were." Chester paced a few feet from the post, stopped, and kicked the dirt to mark the spot where the next upright for the H-brace would go. "Like it or not, that's going to mean something to her one day."

"I suppose you're going to tell me that I need her, too." James heard the anger in his voice, didn't care. "That her forgiveness will make me feel right again."

As if either were possible.

"No, James," Chester said, his eyes sad, his mouth a hard line. "I don't think that's her job at all."

JAMES STEPPED out of Chester's dented Dodge car and closed the door behind him.

"Thanks for the ride."

"Thanks for the help."

They exchanged promises for another visit soon. There was always more work that needed to get done at the ranch. Then James watched Chester's car putter off down the street, all the muscles in his body aching now, the sedentary ride home enough for them to become sore and stiff. The fence project had been exactly what he'd needed, something to occupy his body and his mind, the accomplishment of the completed labor a small buoy for his mood. He'd even come to enjoy the task of stretching the barbed wire, the perfect, straight cords of steel a rebuttal to the tangled loops he remembered from the War. Most of all, he'd appreciated the time with his uncle. If the conversation had become hard at times, he still preferred Chester's directness to his parents' silence and veiled conversations.

"There he is, there's the soldier."

A whispered voice and movement to the side caught his gaze, and he saw Mrs. Carrol and her little boy, Gilbert, who'd been just a baby when he'd left for the War, standing and looking at him, the woman's parasol cocked to one side.

James waved, tried to smile.

Mrs. Carrol waved back, and so did the little boy, a bright smile on his little face.

This had happened a couple times since that idiot news article had come out, the awkward attention from people who seemed to admire him for doing something they couldn't imagine and gaining a medal he didn't deserve. He waved again, then walked up the front steps to his house, eager to get inside.

He opened the door and stopped in his tracks. His parents were both seated in the parlor, facing the door, their gaze on him.

James eased the door shut, their serious expressions making him wary. "Good afternoon."

His mother gave him a tight smile. "Hello, James. How was Chester?"

"Fine." He stepped forward, leaned against the back of an empty chair. "Is everything okay?"

"Mrs. Gould visited while you were gone." His father frowned. "She wants to move your visit with Walter up to tomorrow."

"Good." James would be glad to see Walter, spend some time catching up with his old friend. He hadn't talked to him since before the War. He started walking for the stairs, then noticed that the gaze of his parents was still on him. "Is there something else?"

"Emily Culver telephoned," his mother said. "She'd like to see you again."

James froze, his pulse quickening. "Oh."

"I told her you would be happy to see her, James." His mother's posture was perfect in her chair, her head tilted up, her features set.

James closed his eyes, massaged his temple, the buzz of irritation building there. "You didn't think you needed to ask me first?"

His parents glanced at each other, and his father pointed at James's chest. "Son, we're sorry for whatever you are feeling. Truly, we are. We wish we knew what to say to help you, but you have a responsibility here."

His mother nodded. "You gave the Culvers quite a hard shock the other night."

"And Emily returned the favor." James put a hand to his cheek. "I don't think seeing me again is going to help her."

"She apologized for slapping you. She just wants to talk. That's all." His mother's eyes held an almost pleading look in them.

James thought of what Chester had said only a few hours earlier, annoyed at how quickly his uncle had proved him wrong. "When did she say she wants to meet?"

"We told her you'd see her tomorrow."

"And again, you didn't think to ask me first? I am *not* going back to their house." He'd rather face German Maxims again than be in the Culver house, surrounded by their pain.

"She suggested meeting you when you see Walter Gould. She goes over there all the time." His father grinned. "Kill two birds with one stone, we thought."

James frowned at his father's attempt at levity.

His father's grin vanished, his face falling into hard,

determined lines. "It's time for you to get out there, James. Get a job, get an education. This has gone on long enough."

"Capital." James stepped toward the stairs. "Anything else you've decided for me while I was gone?"

His parents looked at each other, and James's stomach sank.

"What?"

His mother pursed her lips. "We received a letter from the mayor. Now that everyone—" she paused, looked at her feet for a second. "—Or almost everyone is home from France, he'd like to celebrate their return."

James shook his head, already anticipating her next words. "Oh, no."

"The town is planning a parade, and you're going to be in it."

CHAPTER 8

July 20, 1917
Near Verdun, France

Captain Henri DeLisle peeked out the flap of his tent at the group of men in khaki assembling into formation on the parade ground next to the flagpole, their uniforms disheveled, their motions awkward, unpracticed.

Americans. His mother's people. They were finally here, and by the look of it, they weren't prepared to do a single thing.

He turned, retreating to the comparative dim of his tent, irritation prickling at his temples. He sat down on the edge of his cot, rested his head on his hand. On the day the United States had entered the War, he'd been overjoyed. Like all the other soldiers, he'd been caught in a spell of despair after another failed offensive at the Chemin des Dames in April had yielded hundreds of thousands of casualties without any significant gains.

He'd been naïve to expect anything there but failure. He had seen more than his share of death since 1914, and still the War continued, both sides fighting for the same ground they'd occupied for years. The image of himself, his blue-and-red uniform perfect, hand waving a sword in the air, advancing with his troops in a line across an open field, settled in his mind—and he almost laughed. Things had changed since then, the war of soldiers in bright uniforms with gleaming bayonets giving way to the war of mud and trenches.

There weren't many of the others from his class left, the fresh batch of officers from Saint Cyr who'd been at the front lines when the War had broken out. At the Marne, in Champagne, at Verdun, and the Somme, most of the old faces in the regiment had disappeared, buried alive in bombardments, cut down by machine guns, suffocated by gas, and burned by flamethrowers.

Then, there had been hope. Joffre, the old commanding general of the French army, had been replaced by Nivelle, who had spoken of decisive victory, promising that things would be different this time, circulating words of encouragement and confidence.

On les a, the sheet had said. We have them. No more of the old ways.

But the Chemin des Dames had gone exactly as so many offensives before. Henri pressed his eyes shut, putting aside the images that flooded his mind. The charge across the marshy, soggy ground, the mud sucking at their boots. The long push up the scraggy, broken hill. The German Maxims that shot at them from concealed bunkers. Reaching the top of the ridge, his men exhausted, his unit whittled down by half—only to be thrown back by fresh German reserves, whose lines had been untouched by the bombardment.

More foolish, lazy planning, more senseless death.

Then, men had suddenly refused to attack again, sitting in their trenches, or refusing to move up to the front lines. A single word had passed among the officers, spoken in hushed voices.

Mutiny.

Even men in Henri's company had taken part, their rebellion tearing him in two. This war was necessary. Every time he looked out on the mutilated countryside of his homeland, he knew France was fighting to save herself, her culture, her language. Everyone knew what the *Boche* had done in Belgium and in the swathe of France they still occupied and plundered. Yet he'd shared the disgust of his soldiers with their generals, the old men who sat behind the lines and launched pointless attacks, continuing the bloodshed even after it was clear to every soldier in the field that the offensive had failed. He hadn't taken part in the "collective indiscipline," as the top brass had called it, but he hadn't done much to stop them either, and he certainly hadn't taken up arms against his own soldiers.

Nivelle had resigned, replaced by Pétain, perhaps the one general in the army every soldier respected. Already, there had been improvements. An end to the Chemin des Dames attacks. Promises of reforms in the army. Better food, better pay, even guaranteed leave. These things had done much to buoy the mood of his soldiers, help them regain their confidence, their acceptance of the fight and their duty. But it was America's entry into the War that had lifted Henri's spirits the most.

He heard again the excited words of his mother in her letters from home, her satisfaction that her native country had finally done the right thing and joined this war for civilization. Never mind that, despite three years of conflict, none of her relations had come to France with the other American volunteers. Never mind that they had showed no sign that they cared about what was happening to a country with which they had blood ties.

The Americans were coming—perhaps even his cousin, who was supposedly in the US Army now—and the possibilities raised by their entry into the War had filled Henri with new energy. He'd never been able to make the long journey to the United States, though some of his cousins had visited him in France on occasion, but he knew it was a huge country with a great population. The idea that millions of fresh troops would soon be pouring into France had once again given him hope.

When his colonel had told him he'd been selected to assist with training the new American units because of his fluent English, he'd been reluctant to leave his troops but excited to participate in something great, to contribute something that would do more than his leadership in the trenches could.

Then he'd seen the troops of this so-called First Division, and he'd tasted disappointment yet again. These were not first-class, experienced soldiers—many of them were hardly better than recruits, while others had never seen combat of any kind. One of their own officers, a Lieutenant Robinson, had explained it best.

"The US Army has been a small force since our Civil War," he'd said. "We had to scrape together just about every raw soldier in the States to get the First Division here on time."

Henri's hope had plummeted, the full weight of the situation hitting him. "But what of the experienced men, the regulars?"

"We've still got a few, but the Army passed a lot of them out to help form new units in the US. They'll be over eventually, but with new divisions."

The great American war machine, the millions of men waiting to flood the Allied lines and deliver a swift victory over the Germans, was yet another illusion. If the situation was truly as bad as the Lieutenant said, it could be months, years even, before the Americans were ready to fight. This First Division was here to boost morale, nothing more.

"Captain?" Corporal Desmoulins poked his head into DeLisle's tent, snapped a quick salute. "They've assembled for you, sir."

"Very well." Henri stood, walked over the packed dirt floor of his tent to his folding chair, picked his helmet off it, and put it on his head, its weight familiar.

Sitting in this tent and bemoaning the sorry state of the US Army wouldn't help anyone, his people least of all. There was much work to do, and he would see it done. These Americans would become fighting men. He would make sure of it.

He bent low, stepped out of his tent and into the sunshine. The parade ground was a large, square clearing amid the neat rows of tents. The nightly rains and heavy foot traffic had stirred up the mud, mixing with the grass in a soggy mess. In the distance were dotted thick stands of wood, the hills rolling gently as they marched toward the Meuse river.

He saw the eyes of all the American troops turn toward him, the curiosity on their faces. His gaze passed over Major Roosevelt, the company's commander, who stood next to his own Lieutenant Salesse, the Frenchman's sky-blue uniform a sharp contrast to the drab uniforms of the Americans. It impressed Henri that the son of a former president should be in France—almost as much as it impressed him to see a major standing in the mud with his troops. Many of the officers in the American regiment, including its commander, Colonel Hamilton Smith, whom he had met the previous day, were competent, professional. Their men, on the other hand...

He reached into his pocket and took out several sheets of

paper, the copies he'd prepared of this company's training schedule for the week.

"See to it that this gets to the American platoon leaders."

"Yes, Captain."

Desmoulins accepted the papers, stepped backward.

Henri walked toward the assembled ranks, his boots squishing in the muddy grass, and Major Roosevelt moved forward to meet him.

Henri saluted, switched to English. "Good morning, sir."

"Good morning, Captain." Roosevelt returned the salute. "They're all yours."

Henri passed Roosevelt, walking in front of the silent ranks of Americans.

So young.

Many of them looked like boys, no stubble on their chins, their cheeks full.

Henri took a few steps back, faced the company, meeting their eyes. He took a breath.

"Not far from here is Verdun. You may already know the name." He crossed his arms behind his back. "For ten months last year, the Germans attacked that city. For ten months, they sustained enormous casualties to take our forts, push us toward the Meuse River, and seize Verdun itself. We suffered just as much holding them back." He paused, controlling the desperate, bloody memories that returned to him at the mention of the name Verdun, both the pride and the agony of the French army. He'd been rotated through there more than once, had seen the worst of the fighting on *Mort Homme*, the Dead Man's Hill.

He lifted his chin. "The enemy you will face is determined, and he has been in battle for three years. He will have no mercy for inexperience or foolishness. If you do not learn how to fight him, he will kill you without hesitation."

The Americans shifted uncomfortably, exchanged

glances, no doubt taken aback by Henri's frank talk.

Good.

He watched Desmoulins for a second as he walked along the outside of the formation, handing the papers to the American officers one by one.

"Your instructors here," Henri continued, "will teach you everything we have learned about how to fight the Germans and how to survive modern war. I expect you will survive and put forward your best effort. More than one million of my people have already died fighting this war." He swallowed the lump that formed in his throat.

Not a single family in France had gone untouched, and so many of the men he'd known and grown up with were gone.

"But rest assured—if we fail, far more will die, and America's shores will also suffer the brutality of German aggression. We have a common purpose. We stop them here, throw them back, and make them pay for what they have done." He spat the final words, his anger getting the best of him.

You've said enough.

Henri looked over his shoulder, feeling embarrassed at his obvious show of emotion, and nodded at Major Roosevelt.

Roosevelt took a step forward. "Company, attention!"

The Americans moved into the familiar position, though a little too slowly for Henri's taste. That, too, would change. If a man was going to be a soldier, he must look and act like one, too.

"Follow your platoon leaders to your training stations." Roosevelt crossed his arms. "Dismissed!"

The company broke into a buzz of activity as the different platoons assembled, their officers calling out orders.

"I expect your words will give them the proper motivation."

Henri turned, saw Major Roosevelt smiling at him. "They are very young. I don't know if what I said will mean anything until they see action themselves."

How true that was. He remembered a certain Henri DeLisle once caring far too much about shoe polish and clean uniforms, disregarding the machine gun as an unsoldierly contraption.

"Lieutenant Salesse, see to it that the instructors are ready."

"Yes, sir." Salesse saluted and hurried off, leaving Henri standing with Roosevelt, who was watching as the American soldiers began to file out, one company at a time.

Roosevelt noticed Henri looking, and met his gaze. "If you have a moment, I'd like to meet and discuss your plans for our training. I'd like to make sure we use our time as efficiently as possible."

"Very good."

"And I have certain directives from my own superiors regarding the kind of training we must incorporate into your instruction."

"As you wish." He gestured at his tent. He was already starting to like Roosevelt, the man radiating confidence and professional bearing. Here was an officer who knew what it was to lead, no pen-pusher in a castle somewhere leaving all the work to his subordinates.

Henri followed Roosevelt toward his tent and was about to duck inside when he heard someone call out.

"Henri?"

He turned, surprised to hear his given name. And then he saw him.

His cousin, James Garrison, was waving at him, marching with the American soldiers.

~

"NOW POINT with your other arm and throw."

"Like this?" James pointed his left arm up at a 45-degree angle, his right hand gripping the heavy dummy grenade, right arm cocked at his side, his body bladed toward the parapet. All along the training trench, other Americans were doing the same, paired off with French soldiers and NCOs, a flurry of throws and awkward poses frozen for correction and approval. He glanced down the trench, saw William and Lieutenant Robinson both preparing to throw, the blue French helmets they'd all been made to wear a funny contrast with their drab brown uniforms.

Sergeant Fournier, the French instructor, nodded, inspecting James's positioning from beneath the brim of his helmet. "Yes. This is it exactly. Remember the grenade goes where your arm points. Now throw."

James took a deep breath and brought his right arm up and forward, tossing the grenade up and out of the training trench and into the grassy field before it. It bounced, rolled to a stop.

Fournier raised his eyebrows. "Very good."

"Thank you, sergeant."

Fournier turned around, caught the gaze of Corporal Girard, his assistant. "Je pense que c'est grâce au baseball qu'ils sont tous si forts avec les grenades."

James understood, of course, the benefit of having relatives in France.

I think it's thanks to baseball that they're all so good with grenades.

"Evidemment." Girard grinned. "Ça se voit." *Obviously. It shows.*

James cleared his throat. "Merci, vous êtes gentils."

Girard and Fournier turned and gaped at him, no doubt surprised to hear an American speak French—especially with a decent accent. Unfortunately, most of the other doughboys in James's company didn't speak a word of French beyond the handful of phrases they'd learned from a little booklet the Army had given them on the boat from America. Worse, their Yankee accents were so bad that, when they tried to speak, the French looked at them with a mixture of confusion and amusement, and seemed not to understand a word.

"We're not here for a social engagement, sergeant."

James looked up out of the trench and saw his cousin Henri pacing along the top of the trench, looking down at the activity of the company.

James met his gaze, grinned.

Henri nodded, his face neutral, and kept walking.

James's grin drooped into a frown. Henri had been like that since he'd seen James here, formal, correct—and not very warm. Henri was a few years older than he was, but he could remember long days spent together before the War when he had visited his aunt and uncle's family in Chartres. They'd had a wonderful time, had exchanged letters in French off and on for several years after. The War had put an end to all that, and the only news about Henri that James had heard for a long time had come from his Aunt Ethyl's letters to his father. He hadn't expected to run into his cousin during his military service—the probability seemed too small —but he had always thought that, if he had a chance to see Henri during an overlapping leave or a chance encounter, it would be a happy reunion. It was beyond James why Henri should treat him with such coldness, as if there were some great anger between them.

James watched his cousin, whose expression oscillated between scorn and irritation as he strode along the top of the trench, shaking his head, pointing and shouting corrections to the American soldiers. Irritation prickled the back of James's neck. Who was Henri to be so snobbish to his own people?

This was the 26th Infantry, the Blue Spaders. Every man in the regiment knew this was the best unit in the First Division. Hell, the entire American Expeditionary Force.

He thought of Colonel Smith standing in front of him and the other soldiers holding the regiment's insignia, a blue arrowhead over an argent shield, trimmed with gold.

"This arrowhead comes from the Mohawk people. It represents a spirit of courage, of resourceful daring, and the relentless pursuit of the enemy." Hamilton had pointed at the arrowhead, meeting the gaze of each soldier and officer around him. "These are the values I expect out of each man in this unit."

The arrowhead looked so much like a spade from a deck of cards that the men had soon begun to refer to themselves accordingly.

The Blue Spaders.

James swelled with pride thinking of the insignia, the lethal force he and his comrades would bring to this war when they were ready. That Henri could look down on them now, could disdain even his own cousin…

Maybe he was just acting that way. It wasn't unusual for officers or NCOs to be harsh toward the men under their command.

Or maybe rank has given him a big head.

"Practice again." Fournier waved to get James's attention and pointed to the bucket of training grenades at the bottom of the trench between them.

"Okay." James set aside thoughts of his cousin, picked up the grenade, and assumed the position once again.

An hour later, the Americans clambered out of the trench, grabbed their rifles from where they had stacked them together in neat tipis, and followed their instructors across the grassy field and over a small rise to a wide, flat area, backed by a thick, shaggy stand of trees. Staggered lines of posts jutted out of the ground, big burlap sacks made to look like enemy soldiers. Beyond, another, shallower trench ran across the field, the tops of more posts barely visible within it.

The French gestured for the Americans to sit down, and Henri stepped forward to explain the drill. Nothing complicated. An assault course to simulate actual combat.

"With your bayonets fixed, you will charge forward, kill your target in the first line, withdraw your blade, run on to the second target, and attack again." Henri turned, pointed toward the trench. "Your final objective is the trench. You will attack the target in the trench, climb out the other side and continue through to the trees. Speed and aggression are your goal."

James tried to catch Henri's eye, but his cousin seemed to be looking at everyone in the platoon but him.

"Once you are at the end of the field," Henri was saying, "You will run around the outside and return to this position to begin again."

"On your feet!" Lieutenant Robinson stood and turned to face the assembled platoon. "Form lines by squad."

James pushed himself up with the butt of his rifle, followed Sergeant Stokley's shouted commands, got in line next to William, resting his rifle beside him at order arms, his right hand on the forestock, the butt on the ground by his right foot. The Americans adjusted themselves as Fournier walked along the formation, giving orders to increase the distance between men.

"Fix… bayonets!" Robinson's voice carried from somewhere behind James.

James reached to his belt, pulled the blade from its scabbard, and fit it on the muzzle of his Springfield. A hell of a rifle it was, far beyond the trapdoor antiques they'd used in training, beyond Chester's Krag even. James felt the smooth wood of the rifle's stock beneath his hand, his heart pounding in his chest as he returned the weapon to order arms.

This is just training, you idiot!

"Port… arms!"

James hoisted the rifle up, holding it across his body with his hands, the bayonet blade pointing up and to the left.

Through the line of men in front of him, James saw Henri step forward.

"We will not begin until you can execute your lieutenant's orders properly."

A ripple of whispers passed through the ranks.

William shook his head. "What's wrong with your cousin?"

"Beats me."

"That's your cousin?" Another soldier in James's squad, Walker, leaned forward to look at him past William, his expression incredulous.

"Quiet there," Stokley growled.

Robinson ordered them back to order arms, then repeated the command for port arms.

Henri folded his arms across his chest. "Again."

The whispers were groans now.

The Americans repeated the routine two more times before Henri nodded his approval to Robinson.

One of the soldiers in the front line snorted. Henri's gaze snapped onto the American ranks, and he smiled.

"You think I am too worried by silly formalities, *non?*" Henri's smile disappeared. "When you are muddy in your trenches, when you are covered with lice and you cannot sleep or eat because the shells are raining and the mess parties cannot reach you, when you must sit beside the friend that has died as the rats eat him, you will be grateful for discipline. Discipline will be your only tool then, your only means to survive."

Henri stopped, seemed to be wrestling with some kind of emotion.

A note of concern mingled with James's irritation. Had his cousin seen and done all those things? He shivered, the answer obvious.

Henri waved at Robinson and stepped out of the way of the American line. A minute later, the first line took off across the field. The other soldiers watched as their comrades speared the bags and kept running, one soldier stumbling. As soon as the first line disappeared into the trench, Robinson turned, faced the next line, James's line.

"Charge your...bayonets!"

On the word *bayonets*, James brought the rifle down, the wrist of the stock in his right hand at waist level, his left arm straightened out in front of him, hand on the forestock, his bayonet pointing forward.

"Charge!"

The line surged forward, dashing across the field as one. James pushed himself, tried to keep pace with William, knew he would fail against the best athlete of Saint Vrain High School. In a few seconds, he reached the first bag. He slowed, jabbed his bayonet point forward, heard Henri shouting behind him.

"Aggression! Kill him!"

James withdrew the bayonet, ran to the next target, stabbed it, and sprinted on toward the trench. He plunged down into the trench, went too fast, and fell over, tumbling to the ground.

He heard William laugh. "That's showing the enemy."

"Get up, Garrison!" Lieutenant Robinson shouted from the starting line.

James picked himself up, grabbed his rifle, and impaled

the last bag. Breathing hard, he climbed out of the trench and ran on toward the trees. He followed William, Walker, and Corporal Rodriguez around the edge of the field and back toward the starting point, watching as the other squads in the platoon ran the course, acutely aware of the occasional glances of the other men his way.

Great way to make a good impression.

"Come on! These Boche want to kill you! Don't tickle the bastard!" Henri's voice was almost hoarse as he shouted at the line of soldiers who had just started.

"Reform the line!" Stokley held an arm out, and James took position at the end of the line, next to Walker, still catching his breath. Robinson brought them through the drill again—port arms, charge bayonets—and James launched himself forward for the second time. He reached the first bag, thrust his bayonet into it, and was withdrawing his blade when a shout stopped him cold.

"No!"

James looked behind him, saw Henri striding toward him, Lieutenant Robinson and Sergeant Fournier in tow.

"Everyone stop!" Henri reached James, pointed at the bag. "This bastard would slit your throat while you slept. Don't play with him. Kill him!"

James thrust again, not sure what he was doing wrong.

"Put your whole body into it. This Boche just killed your friend." Henri pointed at William, who stood nearby, gaping at the spectacle with the rest of the squad. "Stab him!"

James tried again, felt the rifle being ripped out of his hands.

"You cannot fight like this. You will die, do you understand?"

James stammered, looking for words, his own temper flaring.

"Move." Henri pushed him back with the rifle's stock.

"Kill him!" Henri punched the bayonet forward, pivoting his body, all of his strength put into the thrust, a yell erupting from his mouth, raising the hair on the back of James's neck.

Instantly, Henri snapped back, withdrew the blade, ready for another strike. "Kill him!" He didn't hand the rifle back to James, but thrust again, his yell becoming a scream, jagged with emotion. James saw the burn in his cousin's eyes, a look of undisguised hatred as he drove the blade into the bag, withdrew, struck again and again.

Robinson and Fournier shared startled looks, the on-looking Americans, the whole platoon now, shifting awkwardly, sharing whispers, confused glances.

Henri stepped back, his face and eyes red, his breathing rapid. He pushed the rifle back into James's hands.

For a moment, no one spoke. Then Henri straightened, looked around for Robinson.

"Train these men properly, Lieutenant."

"Yes, sir." Robinson nodded. "Company, reform your lines!"

"Hurry it up!" Stokley added.

Without another word, Henri started away across the field, heading back toward the parade ground. The soldiers trudged to the starting line, talking in low voices, some of them looking at James.

William was next to James now, his hand on James's shoulder. "How are you doing?"

"You'd almost think he didn't like me." James managed a grin, still looking after his cousin as he and William plodded with the rest of the company, rifles held down at their sides.

"I think he likes you a lot."

James spun around. "Really? And he shows it by throwing me in hot water in front of everyone."

William shook his head. "No. I just don't think he wants you to get killed."

"He didn't have to act that way." James searched for words, his feeling of rejection at his cousin's behavior growing with each second. "He didn't have to be mean about it."

They reached the starting point, arranged themselves into a line.

"No?" William's brow furrowed. "What do you think we're training for here? Poking holes in bags?"

"One more time," Robinson was saying. "Charge your… bayonets!"

James assumed the position.

"Now we'll keep Captain DeLisle's words in mind," Stokley shouted. "Those aren't burlap sacks out there. They're goddamned Boche, and don't you forget it. You kill them however you can. Hurt them, knock them down, gut them. You fight fair, you die. Boche don't know what fair means."

James stared across the field at the sack, thought of his cousin's anger, the pain so obvious in his behavior. What had happened to him since those days before the War? It was easy to see now how much he had changed. What had the damned Germans done to him?

From behind his irritation at Henri's temper emerged a worse emotion, sadness. And hot on its heels, fear. What would it be like to face them, these *Boche?*

On Robinson's command, the line charged forward again, but this time, when James reached the bag and he ran his blade through the course fabric, the tangle of emotions in his chest coalesced into a bright, burning rage. He put his whole body into the thrust, withdrew his blade, punched it through the burlap once more, pulled back, and smacked across the bag with his buttstock, a shout escaping his mouth.

"Good!" Stokley called after James as he ran to the next bag. "We'll make a killer of you yet."

CHAPTER 9

August 20, 1919

E mily looked ahead at the intersection with 6th Street and stopped in her tracks. She stood there, sweating under her wide hat, the reflection of the sun off her white afternoon dress almost blinding. It took Alice and Marion a moment to notice that Emily wasn't next to them. They turned, concern written on their faces.

Marion frowned, walked back to Emily, and reached out with her hand. "Em? What's the matter?"

"I'm not sure if this is a good idea."

"Would you like to go home?"

"Go home?" Alice shifted her parasol, shook her head. "We're almost there already!"

Emily took Marion's hand, gave her a small smile. This whole plan had made so much more sense this morning. She'd telephoned Walt the previous day to tell him she would have to cancel her time with him to see James instead. To her surprise, Walt had told her that he, too, had plans to see James that day.

"Why not kill two birds with one stone?" he'd asked. "It will be just like before."

Nothing would ever be the same again, not with William dead, Walt disfigured, and James a different person than the one she remembered. Nonetheless, Emily had liked the idea. It was to be her first day outside the house since the dinner with the Garrisons, and while she'd been determined to talk to James and learn more about what had happened to William, the idea of being face-to-face with him had suddenly seemed frightening. Having Walt there somehow made her feel safer.

That's when Alice and Marion had become involved. About a half hour before it was time to leave for Walt's house, they'd showed up unannounced on her doorstep. They'd been worried about Emily and her family and had brought some fruit pies to share. Emily had explained that she would be leaving soon, but she had felt bad at the idea of turning away her friends' kindness. Instead, she'd found herself inviting them to join her at Walt's house.

Her friends would be yet another shield against... what?

Against whatever it is he has to tell you.

She shook off the idea that she needed a shield. This was James, her brother's best friend, a man for whom she had cared, not some insane murderer.

Alice and Marion had agreed to her proposal immediately, without any mention of Walter's ruined face or their own potential discomfort at seeing it. Perhaps there was hope for Saint Vrain after all.

The walk over had been pleasant enough. It was good to be outside again, to be in the light, surrounded by fresh air and the activity of the town, away from the pall that hung over her own home. She'd even been glad for the absurd chatter of her friends. Alice was suspiciously silent about Tommy, though, talking in almost awed terms about James's medal and the vague account in the newspaper about how he'd won it. Emily had been torn between laughter and horror, remembering James's expression and his numb voice as he'd recounted killing those Germans.

One part of her had been glad that her friend would soon get a taste of the War, something to make her see, make her understand, to blunt the oblivious happiness which Emily could no longer share. But another part of her, growing stronger with each step, wanted to shield Marion and Alice, protect them from the conflict that had changed James so much, mutilated Walter's face, and killed William.

Standing there now, James and Walter's street up ahead, Emily could see how much of a mistake this whole visit was. It seemed impossible that they could just sit down to tea and have a civilized discussion without shocking her friends.

"We can turn around if you like." Marion squeezed her hand. "It's very soon to be seeing him again."

Emily's mind sprang back to all the questions she'd thought to ask James, everything she wanted to know about William's life in the Army and his death. A few days ago, she'd wanted more than anything to know what had become of her brother. Now, she knew. Learning the truth had been… difficult. Terrible. Were there even appropriate words for it?

Would answering these last questions bring her peace, or would it hurt her again?

Emily squeezed back and focused on the feel of her friend's hand.

No. If she turned back now, she would never stop wondering.

"I have to go." Emily took a deep breath, and started walking again, her friends beside her.

"Good for you." Alice looked over at her from under her wide white straw hat, twirling her parasol in her hands. "If you didn't go, I think you would be mad at yourself later. You like to finish things you start."

Emily shared a surprised glance with Marion.

Had Alice just said that?

"Besides," Alice giggled. "I'd like to see our war hero."

Our war hero?

That explained the sudden lack of interest in Tommy.

An odd irritation prickled along Emily's nerves, and she was torn between laughing at her friend's sudden change of heart and—was that jealousy?

They reached the intersection, turned left.

Why on Earth should she be jealous? Hadn't James made it clear that he didn't have feelings for her anymore by leaving her in the dark so long?

Emily ignored the ache in her chest that emerged at that thought. She didn't have time for those kinds of feelings. Her brother was dead. Nothing else mattered anymore.

"It looks like you have a reputation, my dear." Alice inclined her head in the direction of one of the houses along the street. A man was on his porch, newspaper in hand, staring at Emily as she came up the street. It had been like this since her confrontation with Westlake the other day.

"Good." Emily met the man's gaze and smiled. "Hopefully they'll keep that in mind before they decide to be cruel."

They reached Walt's house and walked up the front steps. Heart in her throat, Emily reached for the knocker, tapped it three times.

The door opened, revealing Mrs. Gould. Without saying a word, she reached for Emily and pulled her into a hug.

"I'm so sorry, my dear." Mrs. Gould rocked them both gently on the spot. "I think we all hoped that it wouldn't end this way."

Emily's throat constricted. "Thank you. After such a long time, we should have expected this."

Mrs. Gould pulled away, put a hand on Emily's cheek, a shadow passing over her face. "No one ever expects it."

Of course. She'd know better than most.

"Mrs. Gould." Emily coughed, forcing the emotion out of her voice. "These are my friends. Marion Carithers. Alice Munroe."

"Yes, I remember you girls from the other day." Mrs. Gould smiled, extending a hand to each girl in turn.

"Pleased to meet you."

"Glad to make your acquaintance."

"Didn't you ladies go to school with Walter's class?"

Alice nodded. "Yes, ma'am."

Mrs. Gould's eyes narrowed as she stared at Marion. "And you… I remember you. Didn't you and Walt…?"

Marion looked at the ground. "We saw each other before the war."

Mrs. Gould's jaw worked, and Emily thought for a moment she was going to say something stern.

Mrs. Gould's smile returned and she stepped backward into the foyer. "That's good. It will be like old times, then."

Emily could tell from the note of irony in the woman's voice that she didn't entirely believe that any more than she did.

Alice folded her parasol, and they all stepped inside, shutting the door behind them. There was a gentle commotion as the three young women took off their hats and hung them on the rack just inside the entryway. Then they followed Mrs. Gould into the parlor.

James.

He was sitting across from Walter, wearing a white shirt, gray trousers, a gray vest, and a black tie, a mug in his hand and a smile on his face. Emily's pulse quickened slightly. He looked so much like his old self—save his eyes, which his smile didn't seem to reach.

He turned, and she knew the second he laid eyes on her. His smile faded, his mouth turning into a hard line. He stood, looked between Emily, Alice, and Marion, his expression becoming one of surprise.

"James Garrison." Alice stepped forward, held out her hand. "I don't suppose you remember me, do you?"

"Miss Alice, yes." He took her hand, gave it a gentle shake, smiling slightly. "I think we had a mathematics class together."

"Oh!" Alice took her hand back, put it over her mouth, an exaggerated, girlish gesture. "How wonderful of you not to forget."

While Alice exchanged pleasantries with James—the hot weather, what Alice had been doing since high school—Emily stood with Mrs. Gould. Marion walked over to Walt, who was trying to push himself to his feet with a cane.

"No, you sit down." Marion sat next to him and offered her hand. "How are you, Walt?"

He closed his hand over hers, held it. "I haven't seen you in a long time."

No one could miss the hard edge to his voice, though the look on his face held no anger. His good eye shone with an intensity of emotion that Emily was almost afraid to name.

For a split second, she could see the young man she'd known walking with Marion before the War, confident, kissing Marion when he'd boarded the train to basic training in Denver. They'd all been there to see him off. So much of the town had shown up that day when so many young men had left. Now that he was back...

"I'm sorry." Marion's voice caught, and she reached over with her other hand to hold Walt's with both of hers. "I'm here now."

Mrs. Gould cleared her throat. "Tea, coffee? I made some muffins."

The young people expressed their beverage preferences one at a time and assumed their seats around the room. Alice took the spot right beside James on one of the settees, leaving Emily one of the chairs at the end of the coffee table. Emily eased herself into the chair and looked at her friends. How she had thought she would ever have a substantive conversation with James with so many other people in the room, she couldn't say. It was clear now that this would be a wholly social visit.

Well done, Em.

She'd protected herself from James so completely that she doubted she'd get to share a word with him. Judging by the steady flow of verbiage from her mouth, Alice was clearly determined to keep James's attention on her.

Emily's breath caught in her throat. James was looking past Alice and right at her, his face holding a look of concern. She held his gaze, nodded her head slightly.

The moment passed, and James returned his attention to Alice. Marion and Walt were still talking, discussing what they'd both been doing since they'd last written, around the time when Walt had been wounded.

Emily sat silently, folded her hands in her lap, suddenly feeling very alone.

"Emily, dear, could you help me?"

She looked up and saw Mrs. Gould holding a platter of tea cups and a tea pot by the entrance to the kitchen.

"Of course." She stood and walked over to her.

"Are you holding up?" Mrs. Gould asked under her breath. "Can I do anything for you?"

Emily shook her head. "I'll manage."

"I heard James and Walt talking before you arrived. I know the point of this little get-together."

Emily looked over her shoulder at her friends, who were still deep in conversation. "I'm not sure Alice and

Marion do. But it's no trouble. Really. I think it was a bad idea, anyway." She shrugged, grabbed hold of the platter. "Here."

Mrs. Gould disappeared back into the kitchen. Emily turned and walked around the coffee table, offering the cups to her friends. A second later, Mrs. Gould reappeared, carrying a small basket full of muffins, a red cloth folded over them.

Mrs. Gould laid the basket on the table. "You've caused quite the stir in Saint Vrain, Mr. Garrison." She made to sit down in the space between Alice and James, who scooted aside to make room. The look of undisguised annoyance on Alice's face nearly made Emily laugh. "I'd like to hear your part of it."

James rotated the cup in his hands, staring at it as he seemed to weigh his response. Mrs. Gould winked at Emily, and Emily wasn't sure what to do. She was touched that Mrs. Gould wanted to help her bridge the subject of William's time in the War, but she was afraid of James's reaction and didn't want to see him in the same agony he'd experienced last time.

"I'm sorry, ma'am," James said, finally. "I'd rather not discuss that day." He smiled at Mrs. Gould and met Emily's gaze. "It was horrible, and I don't want to be bad company."

"Oh, please do tell!" Alice leaned forward, looking past Mrs. Gould. "I think we'd all like to know how you earned that medal of yours."

"If not that, then at least share something about the War." Mrs. Gould looked between James and Walt. "You know, none of us ever went to France."

She gestured at Emily, "Save for our Miss Culver here."

James and Walt shared grim glances, but didn't say anything.

"You can't imagine how many of us stayed here and

worried, preoccupied with imagined horrors. I would like to know the real ones. Walt has never talked about it."

"Please," Emily added, surprised by her own voice. "I'd like to know, too." She closed her eyes, steeling herself. "And I'd like to know what it was like for William. He never truly told me."

It was true that William hadn't talked candidly about all the horrors he'd seen in the Army. His letters had always been vague, and the one time she had seen him in France, he'd been tight-lipped about the subject. Emily had seen plenty of sights that she wished she hadn't, had been in range of the bigger German guns more than a few times, but she'd never been to the front lines, in the trenches.

Marion set her cup on the coffee table. "I'd like to know, too."

Emily saw the moment James made his decision. He nodded silently and took a sip of his tea, his jaw set in a hard line. "Alright. We'll talk about the War."

~

October 21, 1917
South of Verdun
Luneville Sector

JAMES GAGGED, fighting not to vomit. He focused on the soaked khaki haversack of the man in front of him as the company slogged along the trench, no sound but the patter of rain and the sucking, slurping noise of boots in mud. He tried and failed to ignore the smell.

It was unreal, the odor overwhelming, penetrating through him, driving away every thought. The rotting, soggy wood of the trench revetting and duckboards. Human waste, urine, and the sharp smell of lime. Some awful, sickly chemical scent rising from the churning, liquid mud. A horrid, putrid stench that James didn't care to name.

The trench zigzagged lazily forward, little waterfalls of rainwater trickling down its sides, filling it with more muck. The column stopped, waited for a minute, then kept moving, every yard of ground seeming to take forever to traverse, James's feet heavy from the sucking mud that clumped on his boots.

It's just the zigzags.

He thought back to Henri's description, his explanation for the shape of the trenches. Each zigzag described what they called a fire bay, and the zigzags protected people in the trenches from enfilading fire and the effect of shell strikes.

"If a shell lands in the trench, it may destroy one fire bay and every man in it," Henri had said, his voice flat, devoid of emotion. "But the walls of the trench will prevent the detonation from carrying into the next fire bay. Similarly, one man cannot shoot down the length of the trench and kill everyone in it. The cost of this protection is the difficulty of transporting men and supplies through the trenches. For each mile of ground as the crow flies, a man must walk through fifteen miles of trenches."

The French instructors had passed out aerial photographs, and James had almost laughed when he'd seen the grainy picture of the trenches from above. They were not at all what he'd expected. The trench lines looked like the battlements at the top of a castle wall, neat crenellations traced across the French countryside. There was a fire trench in front, little D-shaped saps thrust out beyond the line and into No Man's Land, and multiple reserve trenches spaced a few hundred yards back from the front, all connected by the rough communication trenches running between them. Just like the one the Spaders were in now.

No more photographs, no more clean mockups dug into

parade grounds, no more lectures. They were seeing the real thing now. A stay at the front, an opportunity to gain experience, as Major Roosevelt had explained to them all, to prepare the doughboys to eventually take their place in the Allied line.

"Dammit." James stumbled, his feet splashing in the mud. He cursed under his breath as water dripped off the brim of his helmet and down the back of his tunic. He reached up and pushed the helmet back on his head, then adjusted the weight of his Springfield on his shoulder.

The man in front of him, Walker, looked over his shoulder. "Step down, pass it back."

James looked over his shoulder at Corporal Rodriguez. "Step down, pass it back."

A few yards further along, the trench reached a T-junction and grew deeper, the floor sloping down slightly.

The fire trench.

James slipped on the wet duckboard that ramped down, regained his footing, and stepped into the gray-black pool of water. It was deeper than he thought, coming halfway up to his knee, soaking the odd woolen wraps that had replaced their gaiters—puttees, as the Brits called them. The line turned to the left, splashing down the trench in single file.

French soldiers, scattered here and there along the parapet, looked over to watch the Spaders pass. A few of them nodded in acknowledgement, their light blue uniforms dripping water, spattered with mud. Some of them were curled up beneath rain sheets in holes scooped out of the sides of the trench, their eyes staring ahead of them, hollow, their legs jutting out into the trench, submerged in the water.

James looked back at them, returning their silent nods with his own.

The air split with a deafening roar, and James lurched to the side, flattening himself against the wall of the trench and covering his head. Then another explosion, further away, and another. Rifles fired up and down the trench, a peppering of shots out toward No Man's Land, the staccato thump of a machine gun somewhere.

Then there was silence, and the metallic drip-drop of rain pattering on James's helmet, his own breathing.

The French had warned them about this, too, the sporadic shellfire.

And you handled that like a real veteran, Garrison.

James shook off the lingering panic in his blood, ignoring the soft chuckle of one of the Frenchmen.

"Come on, Jimmy." Walker was waving at him, his wide eyes betraying his own fear.

James plodded back into line, moved on down the trench, angling his body to squeeze past the French soldiers. The space was narrow, cluttered with men, equipment hanging off the revetting.

The sky overhead shrieked, a different sound now, a rushing noise, the distant boom of a cannon. It was outgoing artillery, the French response to the German shells, the casual exchange of fire.

Quiet sector, my foot.

If this is what a quiet area was like, what was it like during a real battle? The question hung in his mind as he trudged down the trench. A few minutes later, they stopped, and Sergeant Stokley yelled out orders to settle in. They'd be staying here overnight.

"Settle in and have a look," Stokley slipped past the line of men. "Don't stick anything over the top that you don't want shot off. We'll be handing out work details in a few minutes."

"In this weather, Sarge?" Rodriguez unclipped his haversack from his cartridge belt.

"Who in hell do you think keeps this thing from

collapsing in on itself? Unless you want to float away, we have work to do on the drainage system."

James wriggled his haversack off, looked for somewhere dry to put it. He saw William a few yards down the trench, slipping his pack into an empty dugout.

"Here." James walked down the trench, pulled his waxed canvas tent section from his haversack. They took Walker, Rodriguez, and Collins's haversacks, wrapped them together with their own in the heavy cloth, and placed the bundle inside the dugout.

"Anyone want to look?" William sniffed, his voice thick with a stuffy nose. He pointed to the firestep and the parapet above, steel loopholes—metal plates with slots cut in them—surrounded and topped by sandbags.

James nodded and clambered up on the parapet, grateful to have his legs out of the muddy water. Careful to keep their heads below the top of the sandbags, they poked their rifles out of the loopholes, and James sighted his weapon, peering out at the expanse beyond.

No Man's Land. They'd heard the endless stories, the fantastic reports in newspapers.

The weak, gray light reflected out of an endless expanse of water-filled craters, their lips overlapping, all manner of debris cast here and there—a rusty sheet of corrugated metal, what looked like a broken wagon wheel, and—was that a chimney out there? A ruined house? A few dozen yards from the trenches was the tangled, looped mass of the French wire, held up by curly metal stakes, water dripping from the many barbs, catching the light like dew. Small bits of cloth, caught on the sharp barbs, fluttered in the damp air. A heavy, gray shape was hung over the wire.

James stared at it, realized what it was.

A corpse, the arms held in a strange pose by the wire, hung in the tangled nest of steel, looked as though it would suddenly jump up and walk. James's stomach turned, and he looked at something, anything else.

Where the hell were the Germans? James traversed his rifle around, searching for any sign of the enemy.

They're all below ground level, like you.

Looking at No Man's Land now, James found it odd. A war with an empty battlefield. Was there a German out there somewhere, looking for him, hidden out beyond that mess of craters, the grizzly wire?

James yelled as a shell exploded in front of the trenches, out in the wire. Then another, closer, off to the right somewhere. The routine repeated again—odd rifle shots up and down the trench, the French response, a few shells sizzling through the dismal sky, distant explosions, jets of dirt and fire thrown out a few hundred yards away.

Get hold of yourself.

He looked at William and saw the same startled expression on his friend's face that he imagined was on his own. William grinned, stuck his hand out, his palm turned up, catching the rain.

"Great accommodations," James offered.

"The best."

Later, Stokley returned, and their squad sloshed off together, heading farther down the trench, rifles slung, entrenching tools and bayonets bouncing on their belts. The water rose as they walked, up at their knees now, this section of trench lower.

"Right." Stokley stopped and turned to face them, pointing at the trench wall beside him. "Our Frenchie friends say there are a set of deep craters about ten yards through the dirt here, back toward the reserve trench. If we can dig a sap through here, we can create a drain for some of this water."

One man, Private Caldwell, stepped forward. "Shouldn't we be worrying more about the Boche, Sarge?"

"You don't like mud, Caldwell?" Stokley sneered. "Listen up, all of you. This war's as much about digging as it is about shooting. If we keep our trench together and in good order, we stand a better chance against the Hun." He pointed at Caldwell. "It's what protects your empty heads."

A large clump of mud sloughed off the trench wall and tumbled into the water with a slimy splash. James fought the absurd impulse to laugh. In this kind of climate, keeping the damned trench from simply eroding away would be a constant task.

The men worked their entrenching tools—short, T-handled shovels—off their belts and attacked the trench wall, first removing the soggy woven wattle revetting, then pushing their shovels into the soaked earth. They worked in a relay, some men excavating the wall and tossing the dirt backward into a small pile that poked above the top of the smelly water while the rest took shovelfuls of dirt from the pile and heaved it up and over the parapet, flinging it toward the German lines and spattering themselves with mud in the process. They rotated every fifteen minutes, working mostly in silence, broken occasionally by the odd shell and random crack of rifle fire, the short stutter of a machine gun.

James drove his shovel into the trench wall, wrinkling his nose at the rank smell that rose from it. All the terrible odors had managed to soak into the ground, poisoning it.

"Don't throw those shovels up too high," Walker said, behind James. "I heard a sniper took one guy's thumb off when he was digging like we are now."

"Don't be an idiot, Dave," Rodriguez scoffed, though James could tell from his tone of voice that the idea bothered him.

"It's true. They'll shoot whatever gets exposed above the trench."

James imagined the empty, cratered wasteland he'd seen, the German searching for him on the other side of No Man's Land. Before, he'd imagined an infantryman like him, some fellow peeking through a loophole. He'd forgotten to think of the snipers.

Henri had mentioned them, too, the men who hid in ruins and piles of debris in No Man's Land, or fabricated fake tree trunks or other clever places to hide, their scopes always searching the opposing line, delivering death with shocking suddenness.

How the hell was a man supposed to sleep knowing that such efficient killers could be stalking him out in No Man's Land? Or that some German raiding party might drop into the trench at any moment with knives and pistols drawn?

Don't worry about it. Control yourself.

James tightened his grip on the shovel, matching the rhythm of William, who was working next to him. If Cousin Henri had survived, he would, too. He wasn't about to disappoint everyone, let them down by being a coward.

His shovel hit something solid, a rock. He moved the spade around the object, tried to find its edge. He reached his foot up, kicked the shovel into the ground, and felt the spade break past the obstacle. He withdrew the dirt—and gagged. The faint smell grew suddenly strong, unbearable, stinging his eyes.

"Oh, Jesus!" Walker was right behind James, his voice odd and nasal, as if his nose were pinched shut.

William stepped back. "Good God."

James stared at the hole from which he'd just pulled dirt, saw two pale sticks protruding from the ground.

Not sticks. Human bones.

They looked like pieces of an arm, their ends splintered by James's shovel.

"What the hell are you standing around for?" Stokley pushed past James and scraped his shovel over the dirt next to the bones. The earth fell away, revealing the rest of the arm, small scraps of cloth still wrapped around it here and there, little spots of flesh clinging to the bones, tissue still connecting the bones and fingers together.

James noticed that the dirt seemed to move, small white pebbles twitching.

Maggots.

He stepped back, bumping into Walker, and bent over. He put his hands on his knees, resisting his desire to run, anything to escape that smell.

Stokley stepped back from the grizzly sight. "Looks like someone already lives here. We'll have to re-bury him elsewhere."

"You want us to keep digging through that?" William pointed at the bones, gaping.

"We need to drain this water. You want trench foot?"

None of the men responded, everyone looking anywhere but at the arm.

"That's what I thought. Keep working." Stokley picked up the arm with the end of the shovel and tossed it back onto the dirt pile.

Walker clapped James on the back. "Go ahead."

Don't be a coward!

James stood up straight and walked forward between Stokley and William, who had resumed digging, muttering something beneath his breath. James swallowed, his mouth dry, and thrust his shovel into the dirt. He felt it hit something hard again and stopped working, trying to take a deep breath.

"James," William put a hand on his shoulder. "Maybe you should—"

James didn't wait for his friend to finish, but turned, ran a short distance down the trench, and vomited, spilling the contents of his guts into the filthy water.

CHAPTER 10

August 20, 1919

The room fell suddenly quiet as James finished his story, leaving a faint queasy feeling in Emily's stomach. She stared at James, his face lit by the late-afternoon sun that slashed through the windows and across the floors and furniture in broad, yellow beams. His gaze was hard, his jawline tight, his expression strangely detached. She looked at the partially finished muffin on the little plate in her hands, frowned, her appetite gone. She set the plate down, her mind filled with the images of horror James had described, the smells, the sounds, and, above all, the mud.

She remembered her fair share of mud as well, had smelled death herself. She closed her eyes, trying to shut out the memories that flooded her brain.

"Leave that one, Miss Culver. He's gone."

Marion was the first to speak. "I… had no idea."

Emily opened her eyes, looked across the coffee table at her friend's concerned face. Marion looked between James and Walter, her face pale, her brow furrowed.

Alice had one hand at her throat, looked as if she were going to be sick "Neither did I."

Mrs. Gould chuckled. "I remember a photo that ran in the paper in Eighteen. It showed some of our boys with nurses. Clean beds, clean bandages. I remember it shocked Mrs. Carrol because the men were unconscious and weren't sitting there with banjoes or some such thing." She laughed again. "No, Miss Alice, I don't expect any of us knew."

Emily caught James's gaze. "Did it get worse that night? Did you manage to sleep at all? Did William?" The answers seemed obvious, but Emily couldn't help asking for them. She hated picturing William confronted with all that misery —the snipers, the raiders, the random, indifferent death brought by the shells.

James shrugged. "It was… pretty tough digging the rest of that drainage ditch. We were all tired that night. I don't think we slept, though. You never sleep well in a trench."

Emily recalled the long lines of men shuffling past the canteen table, the exhaustion written on their faces. It made more sense now.

"The thirst was the worst part." Walt picked up his tea cup, sipped. "Sometimes we wouldn't get water for days. You couldn't drink the stuff in the trench, not if you didn't want to turn your guts to liquid."

James nodded. "The mess parties had a hard time making it up to the line, especially during a bombardment."

Walt took a bite of his muffin, made a snorting sound. "Banjoes."

The phone rang, and Mrs. Gould rushed out of the parlor. A second later, she called from the other room. "Walter, it's for you!"

Walter grabbed hold of his cane, pushed himself to his feet.

Marion stood up, too. "Would you like some—"

"I'll manage."

"Oh." Marion sat back down, and Emily could tell Walt's sharp tone had stung her.

Walter grimaced as he started toward the door to the kitchen. "Excuse me."

Emily's gaze followed him out of the room. It couldn't be easy for a young man to be so weakened.

A moment after Walter had disappeared into the next room, James spoke. "Let him do things on his own."

Marion nodded. "I don't mean to insult him. I suppose I ought not to offer."

"You didn't, and you should keep right on offering. Just let him be angry sometimes."

They all sat in silence for a minute.

Alice cleared her throat, slid back next to James on the settee. "Well, James. You told quite the story. But I'd still like to know how you won that medal. Was it really in the last days of the War?"

James looked down at his cup. "Yes. Less than a week before the end. Hours before they pulled us from the line."

A tingle ran up Emily's spine. Is that when William had died? Only a few days from safety and life? She thought of the awful, distant, dead look on James's face as he'd talked about the trench. This would be painful for him to talk about, too, but there wouldn't be a better moment.

She opened her mouth to speak—

"Walter? What's the matter?" Marion's voice interrupted Emily.

She swiveled her head around, saw Walter limping into the room, rage written on his face. Mrs. Gould followed a couple steps behind him, wringing her hands.

Walt walked all the way to his seat without speaking, then eased himself back into the chair and stared across the room and out the window.

Marion looked over at Mrs. Gould, who sat back between Alice and James, parting them once more.

"Mr. Carlin just called." Mrs. Gould shook her head, and Emily could tell she was fighting tears. "The pharmacy doesn't want Walt."

"What?" Hot anger flushed Emily's cheeks. "Why?"

"Carlin heard what happened with Officer Westlake." Walt leaned forward and poured himself some more tea, his attempt to hide his emotions betrayed by the slight shake in his hands, the tinge of emotion in his voice. "He's worried I'll cause a scene if anyone spots me from the front counter."

Marion's eyes narrowed, her own outrage obvious. "A scene?"

"But you said the job would have been in the back, away from people." Emily heard her own voice rising, balled her fists to keep from shouting.

It wouldn't help Walter now if she exploded, even if it were on his behalf.

"That's what he said. I suppose he can't risk even that." Walter tried to sip, stopped, the cup midway to his mouth. His lips trembled, and his voice was barely more than a whisper. "I wish I'd died. My life is over anyway."

Mrs. Gould reached across the coffee table, put a hand on her son's knee.

"I'm so sorry." Marion reached for his hand, but he withdrew it.

"Don't pity me."

Tears came to Marion's eyes, and she folded her hands in her lap.

Emily stared at Walt, not knowing what to say. In the past couple of days, she'd found herself wishing so many times that William had come home, even if he'd been maimed like Walt. Looking at her friend now, his broken features, the despair on the good half of his face, she couldn't help but wonder if that was a selfish wish.

How would William have reacted to being shunned by their neighbors, made to stay indoors, without a job, without any independence? She remembered him sitting on his bed, a look of defiance on his face at the idea of their parents controlling his life indefinitely.

How would he have felt about the War following him forever, choosing his destiny?

Maybe it was a mercy that he didn't have to live like this. Emily hated herself for thinking that, felt like a traitor to her brother and Walter.

"Sorry to disappoint you, Walt, but you're stuck living." James leaned back in his seat. "And that bastard isn't worth what you're doing to yourself right now. We'll find something else." He glanced at Alice and Marion's shocked expressions and rolled his eyes. "Sorry for my profanity, ladies."

We'll find something else? Since when had James cared about Walt so much? And who was he to talk so bluntly to Walter?

"James, I don't think you can talk like that—"

Walter waved a hand at her. "It's alright, Emily, Mother. I appreciate that, James."

Emily gaped. Perhaps this *was* the way to talk to Walt, the harsh, direct words of soldiers, no coddling.

"Fix bayonets?" James offered his tea cup across the table.

Walt grinned. "Fix bayonets."

They clinked the china together.

It was Emily's turn to roll her eyes.

Men!

Walter seemed to relax, and he turned to Marion, gave her a slight grin. He offered his hand and she took it, returning his smile.

Walter looked back at James. "But that doesn't get me a job. Do you have any ideas?"

James poured himself more tea. "Just one."

~

August 23, 1919

JAMES CLIMBED up and eased himself into the seat of Mr. Gould's Ford Model T. He stared for a moment at the controls, trying to remember everything his dad had taught him before the War. It'd been a long time since he'd driven a car, and James now regretted his assurances that taking the vehicle himself would be no problem.

Mr. Gould had agreed to lend the vehicle the other day at tea when he'd come home and heard James's idea for Walt's employment. Walt stood now with Mrs. Gould on the front steps, watching, his wide smile and kind features reminding James so much of what Walt had looked like before going to France.

Emily, standing on the other side of the vehicle beside Marion, cleared her throat. "If you're unsure of how to drive the vehicle, I'm sure Mr. Gould can take us."

"It really wouldn't be a problem." Walt shrugged, his face partially concealed by some light gray cloth fashioned into a sort of hood, a concession to the idiot sensibilities of the neighbors.

"I think I have it." James wasn't going to let the car defeat him, not in front of Emily.

Trying to impress her, are you?

No. Not at all. Why should he care what Emily thought?

Right.

He checked that the key was switched to *off*, put the throttle lever part way down, and pushed the spark lever all the way up. He made sure the handbrake lever was fully to the rear, then drummed on the steering wheel with his fingers for a second before remembering. "Fuel."

He climbed back out of the car, walked around to where Emily was standing and lifted up the front bench seat, revealing the fuel tank. He pulled the long, white dipstick out from where it was stowed, and unscrewed the fuel cap. The odor of gasoline stung his nose as he pushed the end of the dipstick inside, then withdrew it.

Five gallons. Plenty.

"Get in." He gestured at his friends, who looked at him with obvious skepticism.

He opened the hood, turned the fuel switch, and opened the lower petcock at the rear of the engine, satisfied when a small dribble of oil flowed out. He tightened the petcock and closed the hood before rounding the fender to stand in front of the vehicle and grab hold of the crank with his right hand. He made to turn it.

"Don't forget the choke!" Mrs. Gould called from the front steps.

"Oh. Thanks." Heat rose to James's face. He pulled out the choke with his left hand, cranked the engine three more times. He looked up, saw Emily watching him from the front seat. "Emily, turn the key."

"Magneto?"

"Yeah."

James put the choke cable back in, readied himself. He placed his right hand on the car's left fender and took hold of the crank with his left hand, careful to keep his hand open. He'd heard more than a few stories of fellows who'd broken their wrists when their cars had kicked back. He pulled hard, cranking the handle clockwise. The car sputtered, started.

James walked to the driver's side, hauled himself up and into the seat next to Emily. He advanced the spark lever until the sputters in the engine smoothed out to a nice hum. In another minute, they were off, the car grumbling down the street.

For God's sake, don't crash the damned thing!

It was so odd to drive a motorcar along the familiar streets rather than walking or hoping for a lift from his parents or a passing farm or ranch truck.

William would have loved it.

A lump formed in his throat, but he ignored it.

"Does your uncle know about my, uh, abilities?" Walt shouted from the back seat over the hum of the engine.

"He knows everything." James cranked the wheel to turn onto Broadway. "Don't worry about it."

Chester had instantly accepted James's proposal to give Walter some work at the ranch.

"Lord knows there's more than enough to do around here," he'd said, his voice slightly fuzzy from the static of the telephone line.

They'd made plans for the coming weekend, something simple to see how Walter took to the work and whether or not he truly was fit enough.

The paved streets of downtown gave way to hard-packed dirt and then the rutted roads of the countryside as they drove north. Soon, they were in open country, the early morning sunshine casting a reddish hue on the yellow grasses of the foothills, which shimmered in the slight breeze. James smelled something delicious wafting from the back seat. He glanced over his shoulder, saw Marion peeking inside a basket.

"I hope some of that is for us." Walter's voice held a note of humor, the happiest he'd sounded since James had first visited him. His face was uncovered now, the hood folded up in his lap.

"Of course." Marion giggled. "It's for all of us, silly. Mom and I made it last night."

James couldn't help but smile. He hadn't been surprised that Emily had wanted to come along. He knew from Mrs. Gould that she'd already done so much to help Walter and keep him company over the past few weeks. However, he had expected Marion to do the same as Alice and decline the trip to High Valley Ranch.

When she'd instead insisted on coming along, James had at first worried that including her would make it impossible to fully enjoy the day. He didn't want to worry about whether everyone was comfortable being outside for hours on end. Walt's obvious delight at having Marion with them had changed his mind.

Anyone could see that those two still had feelings for each other, even if they had yet to say so themselves. The idea that they might be able to continue as they had before the War lifted James's mood. His eyes darted over to Emily. She was wearing a sturdy chocolate brown morning dress with a white blouse and matching white hat with blue trim, her hair in a bun, a few stray strands blowing in the wind that came through the opened windows.

Eyes on the road, idiot.

There was no point in even considering it. She probably still hated him for keeping her in the dark, being the bearer of bad news. And if she didn't, she *would* hate him if she knew everything.

How long will it be before the truth comes out?

James had never wanted to talk about the War again, but he'd found himself going on the other day about that first time in the trench, drudging up every painful, disgusting sight from that place. One way or another, the truth would get out.

James tightened his grip on the steering wheel, slowed the

car, turned onto the road that ran up into the canyon. In a few minutes, they were bumping up to the gate, which Chester had already pulled open. He was standing with Aunt Maggie, who waved. Emily waved back while James brought the car to a bumpy stop and switched it off.

"You've finally got your own wheels, then?" Chester appeared at the door next to James. "Not bad for a Lizzie."

"No, just borrowing." James double-checked that the handbrake was locked up before climbing out of the cabin, the wounds in his leg stiff and sore—though not as bad as they had been. Perhaps his parents were right and getting out and about was truly the best way to move forward and regain his strength.

"Right." Chester crossed his arms. "Let's get right to work."

"Oh nonsense, Chester." Maggie, a tall, willowy woman with red hair and blue eyes, gave James a hug and kissed him on the cheek. "We're civilized people. You all come inside and have something to drink before working on that fence of his." She released James, looked into the car. "Well hello, Miss Emily! I haven't seen you in ages. You're quite the beautiful young lady now."

"Thank you, Mrs. Jones." Emily smiled, and something tugged in James's chest.

Yes, she certainly was beautiful, and completely beyond his reach now.

Marion stepped down from the car, straightened her hat, and turned around, ready to support Walter as he untucked himself from the seat and stepped down. The request for help never came. James watched the reactions of his aunt and uncle, hoping they wouldn't cause his friend any embarrassment. He wasn't disappointed.

"Oh, don't bother with that thing!" Maggie waved her

hand at Walter as he started wrapping himself up in his hood. "If it's fit for God to see, it's more than fit for me."

Maggie stepped forward, hooked arms with Walter and Marion, and gently pulled them along with her up the road, heading in the direction of the house.

"I don't think I've met you two before, but you're friends of our James, so I'm determined that you'll be my friends, too."

Chester shook his head as his wife passed, a grin betraying his supposed annoyance. "That wife of mine knows just how to waste time. Maggie, there's work to do!"

"Oh, never mind him." Maggie beamed.

James watched his aunt trudge up the road with Marion and Walter and couldn't help but chuckle. Emily was next to him and Chester now, and he could see she was smiling, too.

Emily reached a hand out to Chester, who took it. "Thank you for this."

"I'm happy to oblige. My, you really have grown up, haven't you? Hasn't she, James?"

James caught his uncle's pointed look and wanted to punch the old man in the face.

Leave it alone.

"Yes, very beautiful."

Had he just said that out loud?

Emily blushed. "You're very kind."

They started up the road, which climbed gently upward, following a creek bed around a sharp curve. The Jones house was just ahead, set in a large grassy valley between two rocky, steep hills. Beyond, James could see the path that wound its way up the hills toward the high meadow, where he and William had shot the Krag all those years ago.

The house itself was large, with a porch running along its north side. Its wood paneling was painted a cheerful yellow color, the beams, trim, and shutters a clean white. James could barely remember when the house had gone up, replacing the tiny, one-room cabin that had stood there before it, the old Jones homestead.

There was a barn just behind the house, the usual red and white, and a few small garden beds separated by low stone walls, made with the same gray-black granite scattered everywhere on the ranch. Farther up the valley, the bunkhouse for the ranch hands, also painted yellow, was tucked among a few clumps of ponderosa pines.

"It's so lovely," Emily murmured. "I'd forgotten."

"You're always welcome," Chester replied.

They met Walter, Marion, and Maggie in the front parlor, and spent the next few minutes fussing over who would drink what, before being herded out onto the north porch to sit around a small white table while Maggie brought out glasses of iced tea and coffee cake. They enjoyed their refreshments and looked out onto the valley, James relishing the view from the shade and grateful that the conversation remained light.

Chester didn't let them sit there for long.

He stood, clapped his hands together. "We've got at least one more H-brace to put in, and I'm not letting you go home until it's finished."

Maggie smiled. "You really are impossible."

It took a few more minutes to escape the house, Maggie insisting that, in addition to the tools, James and Chester should haul a couple small folding chairs for the ladies to sit on, along with some extra canteens of water in Chester's rucksack.

"Are you sure you girls wouldn't rather stay here?"

Emily shook her head. "No, thank you, ma'am. I think we'd like to watch."

"Yes, we would," Marion added. "At least for a while."

James knew that the real reason the women wanted to

come was to help Walter in case he had trouble, but he didn't share that fact.

They left the lunch Marion had brought at the house and promised Maggie they'd return to eat at a reasonable time. Soon, they were all hiking up to the fence line, Walter leading the group. After a half hour, they arrived, all of them breathing hard and sweating in the growing heat of the day. They were a hundred yards farther along the line than when James had last been there, near where the fence disappeared into a patch of woods.

Emily and Marion took the chairs and set them up in the shade while the boys got to work. The posts were already laid nearby and ready to be put in the ground, their ends blackened with soot to ward off rot.

"Right about here." Chester kicked the dirt and handed Walter the iron digging bar.

Walter wobbled a little on the spot, and James was afraid he would fall over. Walter set his face, tossed his cane aside, and started digging, his motions awkward and slower than those of an uninjured man, but strong. The spade end of the digging bar broke the earth, drove into it. Walter stopped, noticing everyone watching him.

"Did you boys come here to work or spectate with the ladies?"

James smiled, scooped away the dirt Walter had chopped loose. "We just wanted you to get a head start. I'm here to work, of course."

"I'll spectate." Chester strolled over to where Emily and Marion were seated and plopped himself down on the pine needles.

James fought not to grin, put on a frown instead. "Isn't this your fence?"

"Hell, you boys need to pay me back for the iced tea." He

looked over his shoulder at the ladies. "Excuse my damned language."

Emily shook her head, laughing. "We won't tell if you won't."

⌁

EMILY TOOK a sip of water from the canteen, watching as James and Walter switched tools again.

She'd been afraid that Walter would struggle, need help and encouragement. Instead, he'd worked for a full hour now. While his pace had slowed, and his expression showed that he felt some discomfort, he hadn't complained, and he hadn't asked James for a break. Emily could tell James had been watching Walter, too, subtly timing the moments when they switched jobs for when Walter's motions started to slow.

He had taken to this work better than she could have hoped. Unfortunately—or, rather, fortunately—that meant her presence here was extraneous.

This whole excursion had turned out to be much less interesting than she had imagined. That was a good thing, for Walter's sake, but she had half a mind to ask the boys to give her a chance to dig. Everyone would no doubt find that behavior unladylike. God forbid she risk dirtying her clothes.

She thought of her long, light blue Red Cross skirt, the bottom inch of its hem spattered in mud, her boots and stockings filthy, a bloody handprint on her sleeve. How silly it seemed now, after the War, to spend so much time worrying about clothes.

She sighed, supposed it was better to be bored here, in the fresh air and sunshine, than at home. A small knot of guilt uncoiled inside her. Her parents probably needed her right now, but she didn't know what to do for them. They had emerged from their room but were almost totally silent now, polite and formal to an extreme as they went about their day, her father leaving for work and coming home again in the evening with the same empty expression. Emily had her own pain, the same pain, but she wasn't going to lock herself at home with it. Seeing her parents like that was its own injury, and she couldn't bring herself to be around it any longer.

"What will you ladies be doing for the fall?" Chester's voice interrupted Emily's thoughts.

James and Walter both stopped, said something to each other, and unbuttoned their vests and shirts, revealing their white undershirts. They folded the shirts and set them on a patch of grass. James took the digging bar and struck down into the hole, the muscles of his back shifting as he worked.

Maybe this wasn't so boring.

Emily Culver!

She diverted her gaze to look at Chester and Marion, color rising into her cheeks.

"I haven't thought much about it." Marion shrugged. "I may apply to school."

"Oh, Marion, that's wonderful!" Emily reached over and touched her friend's hand.

Marion smiled. "I figure, why not? You got accepted, didn't you, Em?"

Chester looked at Emily. "I hadn't heard this. Are you going to CU?"

"Yes. Well…" Emily trailed off. "I was accepted to enter in the fall of Seventeen, but I put it off to volunteer in France. I'd like to reapply."

She wasn't certain if her parents would have changed their minds. They'd been so unwilling to let her attend, then so angry when she'd regretted her offer of admission to work for the Red Cross. Would they support her if she tried again?

"You must." Marion squeezed her hand. "You inspired me, you know."

"I did?" That was news.

"You've done so many things." Marion looked over at Walter. "All the boys left for France, and then you were gone, too, and I was alone with Alice. It was strange. Everything here just continued like it had, except I was missing Walt and missing you and didn't know what was happening to either of you between your letters. It was horrible, not knowing. When Walt…"

Emily followed Marion's gaze and looked at Walter, who was laughing at something James had said.

Marion cleared her throat and continued. "Now, I suppose we're both becoming old maids. I'd rather do something than wait around for something that may never happen."

Emily understood that only too well.

Marion turned, looked at Emily again. "You will apply again, won't you? It would be so wonderful to go together."

Emily grinned. "I will try. And if I can't… I think I'll move to Denver, get a job."

"On your own?" Marion's eyes widened.

"I've read about all kinds of young ladies doing it. I won't stay here drifting between tea parties all day. I've worked before, and I liked it. I want to do it again."

Chester smiled. "Quite the suffragette, are you?"

She raised her chin. "Well?"

He laughed. "Nothing. Listen: Maggie and I both do plenty to work this ranch. I couldn't make do without her. I can't say I always like her choices, but I have no doubt Maggie can make decisions and have a say in what goes on. That's just how it's been here. I remember how some folks said society would fall apart when Colorado passed suffrage in Ninety-Three. Minus this new law about alcohol, it seems to me that society has continued just fine. Though maybe I should want things to be a bit more backward." He grinned, winked at her. "It would give me some more peace around the house."

Emily laughed. She couldn't imagine Maggie ever being the silent, obedient housewife—and she knew without asking that Chester didn't really want her to be that.

"I don't know what nonsense he's telling you, but you must go back to school," James shouted over at her, wiping sweat off his forehead as he leaned against the digging bar. "You wanted to so much."

Emily couldn't stop herself from smiling like an idiot at him.

"Keep working over there!" Chester tossed a water canteen out to James.

James laughed, snatched up the canteen, and handed it to Walter.

"I think I'd rather work than go to school," Walt said. "Professors are too much like officers."

"You two are awful." Marion laughed. "Now get that brace in!"

James and Walter both chuckled and resumed their work.

"I'm glad you came with him today." Chester's voice was so low that Emily thought for a second she'd imagined it.

She realized she was still smiling at James and pressed her mouth into a hard line. "What do you mean?"

"I know what he told you must have been hard to hear. But I know it was hard for him to tell. He and William were very close."

"Yes." Emily swallowed, all the better to keep down the sudden surge of emotion that followed hearing her brother's name.

"And I don't think William was the only Culver James cared about."

Emily looked over at him, surprised and embarrassed to hear Chester talk like that in front of Marion. Had James told his uncle about what had happened in France? "What do you—"

"Oh, the old man's gone and said too much." Chester raised a hand, cutting Emily off mid-sentence. "But I do hope you'll be back, and I hope James will be with you."

Emily tried to change the subject. "I expect Walter certainly will be."

"Both of you were part of that war, and that's something you'll always share." Chester picked up a dried pine needle, rolled it between his fingers. "More than that, you both cared quite a bit for William. That's one heck of a bond, and a loss you'll both need to face."

Emily scoffed, her old anger flaring. "I have faced it. And if James and I had such a bond, why did he take so long to tell me?"

Chester thought for a moment. "Have you ever seen someone in pain? Real emotional pain?"

Emily thought of her parents. "Yes."

"Was it easy to deal with? And what would you do if you were the one who had to bring it to someone?"

Emily opened her mouth to speak, then stopped.

You'd hide from it, like you're hiding from your parents right now.

Chester raised his eyebrows. Then he looked over at the boys, stood. "Alright, let's get that post in. You kids look like you need a man's help."

CHAPTER 11

May 31, 1918
Near Mory, France

"Wake up, ladies!"

A woman's voice jarred Emily from her sleep. She blinked, opened her eyes, disoriented, forgetting for a moment where she was. She stared at the back of the girl on the cot next to hers, long black hair spilling out from under an olive-green wool blanket.

Gertrude. The Red Cross Canteen. France.

"Up!" That had to be Mrs. Wolfe. Who else would be shouting this early in the morning? "Time is wasting, and there's work to do!"

The bang of a wooden spoon on a metal pot split the air.

Definitely Mrs. Wolfe.

Emily sat up, her loose hair brushing her bare arms. She clutched her rough blanket against her chest, not wanting to pull herself from the warmth of her cot. She looked over at Mrs. Wolfe, whose short stature and pointy nose always reminded Emily more of a mouse than a fierce predator. She smacked the cooking pot with the spoon one more time, her light blue skirt and white apron swishing with her motions.

No, "fierce predator" described her perfectly.

"You've got ten minutes to wash up and make yourselves decent." She turned, opened the heavy canvas flap of the tent, and walked outside into the blue-black predawn light.

Gertrude yawned. "I'd give money to hit *her* with that spoon for once."

Emily couldn't help but laugh. She peeled back her blanket and shivered, her white cotton drawers and chemise no defense against the heavy, chill morning air. She stood, her bare feet touching the tent's cold, hard-packed dirt floor, and trudged after Gertrude, toward the end of the tent opposite the entrance, rubbing the sleep out of her eyes. The other girls—eight, including Gertrude—vanished one at a time into a little room divided from the rest of the tent by a canvas sheet hanging from the roof supports.

Emily stood behind Gertrude and Lilly, waiting her turn. She shivered as she watched each of the other women went behind the sheet and emerged a few minutes later, their skin pink from the cold.

Hurry up!

At last, it was her turn. She pulled the sheet aside and walked over to the small folding table where a few basins of water had been laid out with a folded pile of gray washcloths. She reached for a cloth, dunked it into the lukewarm water, squeezed it out, and started scrubbing her skin. She worked over her arms, her neck and face, her legs below her bloomers, periodically dipping her cloth back into the basin and wringing out the dirt. She saved her armpits for last, trying to wash away the odors of her own body, to feel clean again. What she would give for a real bath with real soap! There simply wasn't enough time, space, or hot water for nine girls to be totally naked and in a tub one at a time. With any luck, they'd be billeted in a village again soon and could pay to use one of the *bains douches,* the public bathhouses that seemed to be in every little French town.

Working in the field afforded no such luxuries, but the front did have one comfort the women hadn't known at home.

Emily eyed the small box set to the side of the basin and the little white packages inside it. One of the women had heard the story from a nearby group of nurses and acquired a case of the cellucotton bandages, the kind normally used to dress soldiers' wounds, for the girls to use during their monthlies. Emily had doubted that the small pads would truly be as useful as the stories claimed, but after trying them for herself, she'd come to trust the bandages as much as anyone. How strange that such a useful thing had never been available at home, and that she should find it here, a place where a simple thing like a bath was so hard to come by.

Then again, so many things were not what she had expected. No wiping the brows of handsome soldiers like in some Civil War novel, no exciting battles or heroic speeches —the men took those for themselves, she supposed. To her, war seemed to be about work and mud, and both in ample supply. Even France itself was not at all what she'd imagined, the glamour and sophistication of Paris only one facet of the country, the vast, rolling countryside and quiet little villages another. There, robust people with strong hands still followed horses and oxen with their plows, used few tractors, and owned few motorcars. Most vehicles were part of the constant military traffic. Even little Saint Vrain seemed more modern than many of these French villages.

Emily squeezed out her washcloth one last time, left it beside the basin of water—now a light brownish gray color— and walked back to her cot. She bent over, slid out the black foot locker beneath her cot, and opened it. She moved aside the small pile of letters from home, from William and James, pulled out her clothes, and placed them on the bed, shivering again, her damp skin rising into goosebumps.

"Lace me up?" Gertrude was fastening the front busk of her corset.

Emily turned, her hands clumsy with the cold, taking longer than usual to pull the cords tight and tie them off. Then she wrapped her own corset around her waist and fastened the eyelets of the busk while Gertrude worked the laces.

"Thanks." Emily slipped into her stockings and her light blue skirt, fastened the matching light blue blouse with its wide, white collar, and then pulled on a gray sweater. Grateful for the extra fabric between her and the cold, her hands moved to her hair, twisting and tying it into a simple bun at the nape of her neck. Then she put the white apron over her head and tied it behind her waist.

"There." She noticed a small stain on the front, yesterday's coffee, and spat on her fingers. She rubbed the stain, hoped Mrs. Wolfe wouldn't see it. She sighed, placing the white hat with its small red cross and white hood on top of her hair.

She pushed her foot locker back under her cot and saw that some of the other girls were already walking out of the tent. She rushed through tying her boot laces and dashed after them, ducking as she pushed past the flap, one hand on her hat to keep it from falling off.

She looked around the little camp, the sounds of the outside world no longer muffled by the thick canvas.

A horse somewhere, the squeak of a wagon wheel.

She sniffed, took a deep breath, the clean scent of rain filling her lungs. It had rained last night, like almost every night. Many small puddles shimmered in the growing light, and the road off to the left was a mess of muddy ruts. The ground between the half-dozen structures that made up the camp was just as bad. A network of wide wooden planks, a makeshift boardwalk, connected the tents together and offered a path out of the filth. Across the road, the broad, grassy plain—where regiments coming back from the front were supposed to stay—sparkled, the raindrops silver in the unbelievably green grass. It was so much different from Colorado, the cured browns and golds of her home. A few shell craters dotted the field, a reminder that they were still within range of the bigger German guns.

Emily spied Gertrude vanishing into the galley tent, directly across the camp from the girls' barracks. She strode across the boardwalk, careful not to slip on the soggy wood. Inside, the other girls had already started their work.

"Miss Culver, hurry up." Mrs. Wolfe frowned at her. "We may be getting a large number of soldiers today, and we can't be held up by lollygagging."

A large group? That was something different. So far, they'd only served small numbers of American troops, and most of those had been on their way from one area to another, busy with training. Was it true, then, about the battle? They'd heard the cannons for days, had assumed it was just another battle between the Germans and the French, another chaotic fight in the series of offensives the Germans had launched this spring.

Some of the girls had been terrified, worried that the Allied lines would break and the camp would be overrun by murdering, raping Huns. Emily had instead been preoccupied with the rumor that it was American soldiers attacking this time, for the *first* time. If Americans were at Cantigny, it could mean William and James had been in battle. They hadn't mentioned anything about it in their letters, but of course, there were probably restrictions on what they could and could not write, and the letters she had now were already many days old. If her boys were there, had they made it through alive?

What if they were already dead?

A little bolt of fear shot through her.

"Sorry, ma'am." Emily stood still, not wanting to risk Mrs. Wolfe's growing irritation.

Mrs. Wolfe crossed her arms. "Well?"

"Is it true then about Cantigny? Are American soldiers there?" Emily tried to keep the tone of her voice casual, didn't want to give the woman any vulnerability to exploit.

The other girls slowed their work, clearly listening.

"Yes, that's what I've heard." She frowned, and Emily thought she saw some softer emotion ripple across the woman's face. Then Mrs. Wolfe looked down and scowled. "Your apron is stained."

"Sorry, Mrs. Wolfe."

Whose idea was it to issue a white apron, anyway?

Emily stood for a moment longer, looking for a task. Gertrude and Florence were both cranking coffee grinders. Ruth was dipping cooking utensils into a vat of boiling water, sterilizing them. Lilly, Grace, and Clara were mixing up batter, while Helen filled the fryer pot with oil. Rose was struggling with an armful of clean coffee pots, trying to carry them over to a small table beside Gertrude.

Emily moved past Mrs. Wolfe. "Rose, let me help." She took a couple of the pots, set them down on the table.

"Thanks, Em."

Emily tapped her foot on the ground, thinking. Gertie and Florence looked like they still needed some time to get the coffee done.

"Mrs. Wolfe," Emily said, turning on her heel. "May Rose and I go set up the booth?"

Mrs. Wolfe nodded, pulled out a set of keys and handed them to Emily. "Make yourselves useful."

"Come on." Emily and Rose stepped back out of the galley tent, turned, and followed the boardwalk down to the canteen booth, the only structure in the camp that wasn't a tent. It made sense to keep the camp as mobile as possible, considering the terrifying gains the Germans had made over the past few months. Little more than a crude wooden shed with a corrugated iron roof, the booth stood right beside the road.

They paused at the closed door, and Emily fumbled with the keys until she found the right one. She opened the padlock, pulled the door open, and stepped inside. It was dark and smelled of musty wood and tobacco. She walked across the small space, her boots tapping on the wood plank flooring. Several large chests were stacked against the far wall, each one locked shut. They'd learned very quickly that soldiers weren't above breaking into the booth to "liberate" whatever supplies they desired. She unlocked the chests, placing the heavy padlocks next to them on the floor.

"I'll get the window." Rose held out a hand.

Emily dropped the keys in her palm and turned to the chests. She opened the one on top, which held neat stacks of sharpened pencils and stationery. This would go to the rest tent, the one with the tables where soldiers could sit. She heard the scrape of wood and the squeaking of hinges as Rose unlocked the shutters and swung them open, light suddenly spilled into the booth.

Emily blinked as she lifted the trunk, set it down, and opened the next one. The sweet, earthy odor of tobacco filled her nose, and she reached in, grabbing a handful of the small white cigarette boxes. She swiveled around, put the boxes in Rose's waiting hands, and reached for more. The women worked for a few minutes in silence, Emily pulling out boxes while Rose organized them in the shelves below the counter.

"That'll do for now." Rose reached for the folded white

cloth tucked under the shelf, and Emily grabbed the other end. They unfolded it, a large white flag with a red cross on the front, and draped it together over the counter, making sure that the cross was out front, facing the road, and that the corners were hooked onto the two nails in the counter top.

Florence stepped up into the booth, set a coffee pot, wrapped in cloth to keep it warm, on the counter. "They're just about ready to start with breakfast."

"Thanks." It was Emily's turn to help.

She returned to the galley tent, where she helped Ruth and Gertrude prepare the simple meal—porridge with some bacon and dried fruit. She set a serving into each of the folding metal mess kits they'd received from the Army, and then poured coffee into the small tin cups. She'd been happy to discover the kits were the same kind with which William and James ate every day. It made her feel like she was sharing their experience in some small way. It made them seem closer.

Her stomach growled, her mouth watering at the scent of the freshly made doughnuts which they laid out on a large tin platter and covered with a cloth. They saved the best things for the soldiers, and Emily knew that was right. Those boys were fighting and enduring the unimaginable, and the least they could get was a doughnut.

A knot tightened in Emily's stomach. She hoped a letter would come today, something from her boys, telling her they were alive and well.

It'll come when it comes.

It wouldn't help anyone to worry too much now.

The girls carried the mess kits, cups, and utensils out and over to the rest tent, where most of the women had now gathered to eat. It took a couple trips to get everything over, but soon Emily was seated in front of her own breakfast.

Mrs. Wolfe picked up her spoon. "Let's not dawdle, ladies."

Emily chewed the bland porridge, sawed apart the pieces of dried apple with her spoon, and mixed them in. It wasn't the best food she had ever tasted, but she was grateful for anything that took the edge off her hunger.

The women ate in silence, the tapping and scraping of their utensils the only noise. The meal was over in a fraction of the time it took to prepare, and then the women dispersed. Clara and Ruth went to the booth to relieve Rose and Florence. Helen and Lilly followed them to retrieve the trunk of supplies for the rest tent, and the others retired to the galley tent to clean the dishes and continue making doughnuts and coffee.

A half hour later, Emily stepped out of the galley tent carrying a platter of doughnuts and walked toward the booth. The sun was fully out now. It had burned off the clouds but done nothing to dry up the mud, which seeped between cracks in the boardwalk. Emily glanced across the road, stopped in her tracks. Little white tents had started to fill the field, groups of men in drab brown uniforms milling about, stacking rifles in tipis.

Soldiers.

Some of them were already lining up at the booth. She looked up and down the growing group of men, saw the mud on their uniforms, the fatigue written on their features. Some of them wore the flat, dishpan-shaped helmets of American and British soldiers, while others held their helmets in their hands. White bandages, blotched with an unmistakable red, stuck out against the muted khaki crowd, wrapped around arms, foreheads, hands, and legs.

These men had fought the enemy. But which unit were they?

Emily quickened her pace, slid on one of the boards and

regained her balance, aware of the men's gaze turning to her. She stepped into the booth, squeezed behind Clara and Ruth, who were filling the men's coffee cups as they shuffled past the window. Emily set the doughnuts on the counter and heard a few groans from the men as the smell of the fresh confections hit them.

Clara paused mid-pour. "Em, could you handle the cigarettes, too?"

Emily nodded, turned to the men, and smiled. "Hello, soldiers. Would you like something to eat?"

It was important to smile, to give the troops a pleasant face, a friendly reminder of home.

Emily put doughnuts out onto the mess kits of the men as they passed and occasionally stopped to sell a package of cigarettes. She hated asking the troops for money, but the Red Cross required it, and Mrs. Wolfe was careful to inventory the booth's merchandise and account for all sales at the end of each day.

"Here you are."

"Thank you, miss."

"Have a doughnut, soldier."

"Thank you."

She tried to meet the eyes of each man as he passed, to say something friendly or encouraging. She ignored the smell of them, the odor of wet wool uniforms, of unwashed bodies. The exhaustion on their dirt-covered faces was obvious—as was their delight to be looking at women. Some of them were so young, even younger than William had looked when he'd left. They returned her smile with their own shy grins, blushed, or even looked down at their cups, too embarrassed to talk to her. Others, usually the older ones, men in their twenties or thirties, met her gaze full-on, seemed to be perusing her, something less innocent on their faces.

One soldier, dark-haired with a Brooklyn accent, took off

his helmet, held it in his hands. "How much for smokes, miss?"

"Ten cents per pack of twenty."

He dug out some change, slid it across the wooden counter, and Emily reached down and handed him one of the packs. "There you are, soldier."

He beamed. "Thanks, miss."

"Say." Emily held out a hand to stop him from walking on. "What unit is this? Where have you been serving?"

"We're the Twenty-Eighth Infantry." The soldier glowed with pride. "We just came from liberating Cantigny."

Her heart skipped a beat. The 28th was in the same division as William and James's unit. Had they been at the battle, too?

"Do you know where the Twenty-Sixth is?"

"No clue. I think they stayed in reserve. Good day, miss."

"Good day." Emily wasn't sure which emotion was stronger, her relief that her brother and James probably hadn't been fighting, or her disappointment that they weren't here with this group of men.

She looked to the next soldier, a lanky fellow with a bandage around his left hand. "Would you like a doughnut?"

It continued like this for some time, some of the other girls arriving occasionally with fresh pots of coffee and replenished platters of doughnuts. The line in front of the booth had simply continued to grow, the men flocking to the canteen in their hundreds. There had to be at least a full regiment here.

"Sorry to cut in." A tall, solidly built man pushed through the line and held out his cup to Ruth. "I have to be at battalion in ten minutes."

Some of the men grumbled, but they stepped aside. Emily noticed the metal rank pins on his epaulettes, the Sam

Browne belt, and the odd, narrow cap on his head, the one they called an overseas cap.

An officer.

Maybe he would know something.

He raised his cup of coffee to his nose. "Smells like heaven! Thank you, miss." He turned to Emily and pointed at the doughnuts. "I hope one of those is for me."

She placed a doughnut on his mess kit. "Sir, are you in charge of all these men?"

He laughed. "I'm a lieutenant, miss. Lieutenant Robinson. I don't have the stars or the moustache to be in charge of so many soldiers."

Some of the men chuckled.

"Do you know where the Twenty-Sixth Infantry is?"

Robinson's eyes lit up. "That's my outfit."

"But I thought these men are from the Twenty-Eighth?"

"They are, mostly." Robinson raised his cup, and the men around him cheered. "But the men in my company were brought up to fill the line against an enemy counter-attack. Some damn—I mean, darn hard fighting."

It seemed so unlikely that James and William would just happen to be in that one company. Could they be?

Emily leaned forward, wanting to ask more, but Robinson was already walking back across the road toward the now busy field.

"Well aren't you the prettiest sight I've seen in a while."

Emily turned and saw another man standing in front of her, shorter than Robinson, with ruddy cheeks, green eyes, and sandy brown hair.

"W—would you like a doughnut, soldier."

"Absolutely, sweetheart." He chuckled and looked to the men around him, who also laughed. "Say, what's your name?"

Emily ignored him, plopping a doughnut onto his mess tin. "There you are."

He picked it up, stuck a finger through the hole in the center, and winked at her. "I'm Louis."

Irritation buzzed at her temples, made her cheeks burn. She glanced at the other girls, who were watching her sideways, uncomfortable expressions on their faces as they continued pouring coffee.

Where was Mrs. Wolfe when you needed her?

"You like me, miss?" He leaned across the counter. He was so close that she could smell him, stale sweat and cigarette smoke.

She raised her chin. "You're blocking the line. Is there anything else you want?"

He winked at her again, twirling the doughnut.

"Very well." She put her hands on her hips, looked at the next man. "Next?"

"Hold on, hold on." Louis set down his doughnut, waved his free hand. "Can I get a pack of smokes?"

"Ten cents, please."

He raised his eyebrows. "You charge for this? After the shit I've been through, you're charging me?"

Emily flinched, surprised by his sudden change of tone. "I'm sorry, soldier, but that's our policy."

"Your policy is crap." Louis worked a greasy smile back on his face. "How about it, honey? Can I have one for free, just one pack?"

"You want cigarettes, you pay." She glanced at Ruth, nodded. Ruth set down the pot and dashed out the booth.

The soldier snorted, sneered at her, looking her up and down. "I bet that's not the only thing you charge for."

Emily gaped at him, unable to prevent the horrified expression that spread across her face.

"Hey, idiot!" Someone shouted, the voice familiar.

She realized who it was a second before he appeared, relief flooding through her.

James!

He pushed through the other men, grabbed Louis by the shoulder, and spun him around. "You watch your mouth when you're talking to a lady."

Louis clenched his fists. "Who's saying?"

"The man who's going to knock your teeth out, that's who."

She watched as James moved forward, a head taller than Louis, rage on his dirty face. He stood right in front of Louis, forcing him to take a step back.

"Get in line." William appeared through the crowd of soldiers. "I get first shot at the bastard."

William!

Despite the situation, Emily couldn't help but smile.

Her brother and James were here, and they were both safe.

Louis looked between James and William, took a step back. "Just being friendly."

"Go be friendly elsewhere, you piece of shit." James put a hand on the soldier's chest, pushed.

Louis glared, and Emily thought for a moment that he would try to fight. Instead, he reached for the doughnuts and grabbed another one, knocking a few off the tray and onto the counter, one rolling off and into the mud.

"You men!" Mrs. Wolfe was in the booth now, her voice so huge and powerful Emily couldn't believe it came from the woman's small body. "You either act civil or get out of here. I'll call the MPs if you like."

Louis scowled at Mrs. Wolfe, took a bite of his doughnut, and walked away.

Mrs. Wolfe waved her hand at James and William. "You, too. Get away from my girls."

"These men helped me." Emily pointed to her brother. "This is my brother, William Culver."

Mrs. Wolfe's expression softened. "Alright, then. You boys get back in line. And the rest of you…" She waved her finger at the other men in line. "You mind your manners if you don't want trouble."

She turned on her heels and walked out, the busy hum and traffic of the booth resuming gradually.

Emily smiled at James and William. "Thank you."

She was so relieved to see them here, alive, in front of her. She looked at them, the glazed, flat look in their eyes, the exhaustion, their filthy uniforms, a strange chemical smell— was that poison gas? —drifting off them, mingling with their more natural odors.

She tried not to wrinkle her nose, didn't want them to feel embarrassed. "How are you? Was there fighting?"

They looked at each other, and Emily saw some other emotion mixed with the fatigue. Was that pride? Sadness? Both?

William reached for her. "It's good to see you, Em."

"I'll be in the rest tent in a few hours." Emily took his hand, squeezed it. "I'll see you there."

"Looking forward to it." James smiled, and Emily's heart tripped.

Stop this girlish nonsense!

She waved goodbye to them and turned back to her work, energized.

"Would you like a doughnut, soldier?"

CHAPTER 12

August 29, 1919

Emily poked at her roast chicken with mashed potatoes, looking down toward the end of the table at her father. He was straight-backed, seeming only to notice what he was eating, his gaze distant, dark circles beneath his eyes. Brianna and Julius were already most of the way through their dinner, chewing quietly. She watched them, Brianna's body bobbing, the result of her swinging her legs under her chair, a habit that her mother normally scolded. The children seemed almost normal again, as if nothing had happened and William was going to walk into the dining room at any moment. Not so with her mother, who shared the same dazed, absent expression as her husband.

Emily couldn't blame them, imagined she was feeling much the same thing, the dull, crushing numbness that followed the early, sharp pain. It was so much worse, just sitting here, surrounded by their grief. It made it harder for her to concentrate on something else, *anything* else.

She set down her utensils, looked at the folded piece of paper in her lap, the bold words announcing the women's suffrage rally on the CU campus. In all the chaos of the past weeks, she'd totally forgotten about the event. She'd only remembered when she'd cleaned her room—a task she'd neglected since the bad news had come—the paper falling out of a pile of her clothes.

She'd ceased asking her parents' permission for things when she'd come home from France. The idea that she, an adult woman, after having worked as she had, should have to ask anyone for permission was beyond ridiculous. Her parents had mostly accepted—or resigned themselves—to the new status quo, offering only sporadic resistance.

But things were different since the news about William, and she wanted to go gently with them, to offer them some sign of respect, of how things used to be. She wanted to talk to them, to break the spell of silence that had descended on the house.

She cleared her throat. "There is a rally for women's suffrage tomorrow on campus." Next to the silence of everyone else, her voice was surprising even to her, seemed incredibly loud.

Brianna and Julius looked up at her father, who kept on eating.

Emily waited a second, then went on. "I'd like to go… if you approve."

Still nothing.

She leaned forward. "May I go?"

Her father stirred, raised his head, and seemed almost to be looking past her at something on the wall.

"You know I don't approve, but I don't suppose that matters to you." He sipped from his wine glass. "You may go and waste your time however you like."

She sat back in her chair, the words like a slap in the face.

Good. Get angry.

So much better than all the silence.

"You really should be thinking about other things, Emmy." Her mother's voice was quiet, tired. "It's time to think about marriage and family. You've got to live the life your brother didn't get to live."

Emily looked over at her mother, her temper flaring. This was good. They were talking for a change, about something besides the weather.

"William would have agreed with me. And having a voice in my own government doesn't prevent me from having a family someday, when I'm ready and have an education."

The college discussion would wait, but Emily figured she ought to slip in a reference earlier to prepare the ground.

"But we can already vote. Why do you even need a rally?"

"In Colorado, yes. But not everywhere, and that has to change. We have to show support for the new amendment." Emily couldn't understand why she needed to explain this to her mother, a woman. It was bad enough fighting the ideas of so many men without needing to convince other women, too. "Things are different than they were, Mother."

"Because of the War?" Her mother raised an eyebrow. "Honestly, Emmy, I don't understand how anything you did over there changes the basic facts of life here. You won't be a young lady much longer. By your age, I was married. Do you want to be a spinster?"

How could they not understand?

"The War changes every—"

"Enough of this." Her father massaged his temple. "I won't have discord in my house. Emily, go to your rally. If you don't have the sense to make the right choices, you're beyond our help."

He returned to his meal, the discussion over.

"At least don't go alone, Emily." Her mother tilted her head, her lips pursed. "I've heard some of those rallies are awfully rough. Wouldn't you agree, dear?"

Her father didn't say anything.

Emily watched her father, unsure whether she wanted to hit him or hug him. "That's alright, Mother. I won't go alone."

The rest of dinner passed by in silence. Brianna and Julius finished first and were excused from the table. Her parents were next, leaving Emily alone as Mrs. Rawlins cleared the dishes.

She finished her meal, wondering who could go with her. Her parents were, obviously, not an option, and she wasn't certain who among her acquaintances would support the rally.

She sighed, took a bite of the lukewarm mashed potatoes. So many people seemed to have no idea and acted as if everything was the same as it had been before Emily left, before the War. How could they think otherwise? They hadn't been there, hadn't seen the women who'd worked beside the men, sharing the mud.

James did.

The thought took her by surprise. She thought through her list of acquaintances once more. Alice wouldn't care. Marion might go, if she were free. Walter might understand, too, but he was working at the ranch now, and appearing in public risked scorn and humiliation.

James.

She saw Chester's face, heard again his words.

"Both of you were part of that war, and that's something you'll always share."

No. It wouldn't work. Being around James always brought up emotions that made her uncomfortable, and she was certain the reverse was true, too. She would ask Marion.

Emily stood. "Thank you, Mrs. Rawlins."

"You're welcome, sweetie." The woman smiled at her.

Emily walked out into the parlor, hoping to find her parents there, reading and knitting as normal. Brianna was there, putting together a puzzle on the floor, and Julius was sitting on the couch, a book propped open on his knee. Her parents had no doubt retreated to their room already.

Brianna looked up at her. "Wanna help?"

Emily smiled at her sister. "In a minute."

She angled for the hallway that led to her father's study and stopped in front of the telephone. She turned the crank, picked up the receiver, and leaned in toward the microphone. "Operator? Saint Vrain three-oh-seven. Thank you."

Marion picked up on the other end, and Emily explained about the rally.

"I'm sorry, Em. I've planned to visit Walter around that time when he comes home from the ranch."

"Oh." Emily couldn't keep the disappointment out of her voice.

"Sorry. Good luck!"

"Thanks. Have a good evening."

"Good evening."

She hung up and tapped her fingers on the phone's wooden case.

James. Would he even support a suffrage rally?

"You must go back to school. You wanted to so much."

She remembered his words, the sight of him standing there in his undershirt, shovel in hand. She picked up the receiver again.

"Operator? Hello again. Saint Vrain four-thirteen, please."

～

JAMES PICKED UP A PEBBLE, tossed it at the green water, and

waited for the satisfying plop as it broke the surface. Ripples rolled past partially submerged rocks, stumps, and the green stalks of cattails, light green algae bobbing at the disturbance. How many times had his father brought him here, to the turtle pond near the auditorium, when he was a small child?

He strolled out onto the wooden footbridge that crossed the pond and looked down, trying to spot a fish. Instead, he saw the dark green-black form of a turtle, its feet paddling back and forth. He watched it for a moment, marveling at how much less clumsy and slow it seemed underwater than on land.

He looked up at the trees framing the pond and the stately architecture of the auditorium. Beyond, people were already filling the grassy quadrangle. Had he not left for the Army, had the War never happened, this would have been his school. He and William would have been starting their senior year soon. Would they have stayed in touch, William at Harvard, and James here at CU? Would they still be friends?

Did it matter? William would still be alive.

It seemed insane now, having turned down this beautiful campus for everything he'd seen and done in France, and he felt guilty standing there. He'd rejected this place, and he had no business being here among civilized people.

But if not for them, what the hell were you fighting for?

The thought surprised him, and, for a moment, he could see Emily in front of him in her stiff Red Cross uniform at the canteen in Vavincourt.

"What you are fighting for here is going to matter to millions of people. It's the most important thing anyone on Earth is doing."

He stared at a pair of students across the pond from him seated next to an ash tree. Was this what victory was supposed to look like? People sitting in peace under trees with books? It looked an awful lot like complacency, like forgetting. Had those boys ever seen a trench? Did they care what had been done for them?

James couldn't decide whether he hated the students, loved them, or felt jealous of them, their contented looks, their relaxed, easy manner. Maybe he felt all three.

He sighed, glanced at his watch. Still a few minutes early.

Still time to back out.

This is a stupid idea.

James needed to avoid Emily, needed to put off the inevitable, the questions she'd eventually ask. He needed to avoid the awful, slithering guilt he felt whenever he was around her.

Then why had he felt such a rush of happiness when she'd called him last night? Something about it had felt so normal, so *right*, as if he'd never been to France and would be walking to high school the next day. Even if he knew that it couldn't possibly last long, the idea that she might still like him, care for him, even, took such a weight off his shoulders.

And when that changes?

James looked for the turtle again, found it climbing onto one of the logs.

No. He was not going to back out on her. After what he'd done, he owed her the respect of keeping his commitments.

"James!"

And now he didn't have a choice.

He turned around and saw Emily walking up the path from Broadway. She wore a light blue afternoon dress with a white hat. She carried a white sign that read "Colorado women stand with their sisters" over one shoulder and waved at him with her free hand.

"Hello." He waved back, feeling suddenly awkward. "How are you?"

She stopped in front of him. "I'm well. You?"

They looked at each other for a second, both seeming

unsure what to do. Emily held out her hand. James took it and gave it a gentle shake.

To think he'd kissed her, nearly made love to her. It all seemed a lifetime ago.

"I think they're about to start." James pointed toward the group assembled on the quadrangle.

"Good timing." She smiled, shook her sign lightly.

They turned and crossed the bridge, their footsteps drumming on the aged wood. Neither of them spoke for a minute, and James searched for something to break the silence.

"Uh, how is the family? Are they alright now that they…?" He trailed off.

Now they know their son is dead.

Emily's expression dimmed for a moment, and James regretted the question.

She looked up at him, sadness in her blue eyes. "They're…. They're doing as well as can be expected."

"I'm sorry. I didn't mean…" He searched for the right words. "I'm sorry I was the bearer of that news."

She stopped, shifting uncomfortably, her hands gripping tightly to her sign. "James, I… I know you didn't want to cause us pain. I don't know if I can blame you for wanting to avoid it."

"You don't?" Surprised, he repeated her words, sounding stupid even to his own ears.

"It's been hard for me to face my own parents' grief." She looked at the ground, emotion stealing into her voice. "I couldn't imagine having to be the one to bring the bad news."

"Emily, I really am so sorry."

For more than you can possibly know.

She looked up at him again, her lips curving in a slight smile. "I know, and I forgive you."

He looked down at her, torn between happiness and a

poisonous wave of guilt. He should tell her, right now, and get it over with.

The moment passed, and they walked on together in silence once more. They walked by the auditorium, heading onto the crowded quadrangle.

"Thanks for coming today." Emily shifted her sign to her other shoulder.

"Oh, you're welcome." James put his hands in his pockets, feeling suddenly exposed. There weren't as many men there as women. "I'm curious, Em. Women can already vote in Colorado. Why are they having this rally?"

He couldn't remember a time when women hadn't voted, remembered learning in school that the state had led the way on the suffrage issue, giving women the vote in 1893—before James had even been born. It was one reason why Emily's activism had never seemed as odd to him as it had to some people.

"Because of the amendment."

"Amendment?" Clearly, James hadn't paid attention to politics.

"Yes, the Nineteenth Amendment. It'll give women across the country the right to vote, if it passes. It's being ratified by all the states."

"Has Colorado ratified?"

She shook her head. "No, not yet. I was still in France when the ratifications started in June."

"I suppose I was here." He'd been glad to escape the hideous boredom of the convalescent hospital and then the Army camps after the end of the fighting, waiting to be released and shipped back overseas, a lead weight resting in his chest. It was then that he'd heard William had been marked missing, and he'd known he had to go home, to tell the truth.

Or at least part of it.

Emily narrowed her eyes. "Until this amendment passes, the vote isn't safe. That's why we have to stand with our sisters elsewhere."

They joined the crowd—mostly women, and many of them college girls, judging by their age—and Emily squeezed through, James tailing behind, until they were right in front of the small stage the rally organizers had put together. Emily lifted her sign off her shoulder and held it up. James looked around at the other signs.

Votes for Women.

Women are Citizens.

Equal Voice in Gov't.

The speeches began a minute later, a solid, middle-aged woman in dark green taking the stage. She spoke for what seemed like a long time, and James did his best to listen, though he found himself looking over at Emily, an expression of happiness and determination on her face.

"We won't let our own freedoms distract us from supporting the common cause, for women who still can't vote." The woman's voice boomed through a metal bullhorn.

Cheers from the crowd.

She held a fist in the air. "Remember Pennsylvania, the Carolinas, Virginia, and all the places where women must follow laws they have no voice in making! Until the Nineteenth Amendment to the Constitution of the United States—"

More cheers, drowning out her voice.

The woman stopped, waited. "Until the amendment passes, we must continue our campaign!"

Emily clapped, and James did the same, buoyed by the energy of the crowd.

The woman climbed down, and another woman followed her to say more of the same. As the second woman got down from the stage, James felt something being pushed into his hands.

"Emily, what—?"

"Hold this." She handed him the sign and stepped around the stage as the second woman climbed down.

James gaped at Emily as she climbed onto the stage, took the bullhorn, and faced the crowd.

"I served in France." Her voice shook slightly, and James could tell she was nervous.

Some of the women in the crowd cheered, called out.

"Me, too."

"I was there."

"I served in France," she continued, seemed not to know what else to say.

"Tell us," James shouted up at her, giving her what he hoped was an encouraging smile.

She smiled back. "And I saw the work we women can do for our country. Our country asked us to share the burden of the War with our men, and we were there. We didn't carry rifles, but we carried supplies that kept our fighting men in good spirits." She paused, seemed to struggle for words. "And sometimes, we carried the wounded and the dying."

He thought of the aid station, remembered her in her Red Cross uniform, sitting on a crate, hands bloody, her face an image of exhaustion and despair.

"I say we've carried enough for all our sisters to have their voices heard."

More cheers from the crowd, and James clapped, couldn't stop himself from smiling like an idiot, mesmerized by her charismatic presence on the stage.

"And we won't stop with the vote. Equal pay. Equal respect. These are the things we must—"

An object sailed through the air and landed near Emily's feet, breaking into pieces.

A glass bottle.

Gasps.

"Get off the stage, trollop!"

James looked for the source of the voice, saw a small group of boys, college students, striding across the quadrangle, bottles in hand, smirks on their faces.

"Go home and iron my shirt!" A different one shouted as he threw another bottle.

This one sailed past Emily's head, landing somewhere beyond with the tinkle of breaking glass.

James's temper flared, and he pushed through the crowd toward the idiots. They were young—too young to have served or seen the work women had done in France. James would enjoy teaching them.

Some of the women had begun to shout back, tossing their own insults.

"Get out of here, children."

"Your mother and sisters are women!"

James exited the crowd, locked eyes with the nearest boy, the one who had tossed the first bottle.

The boy grinned. "Having fun with the hens?"

"I'll have fun knocking your face in a minute." James stepped forward. He flinched as something flew past his head from behind.

The broken bottle!

Or rather the neck and mouth of it. It smacked the boy in his chest, and he staggered backward, a look of shock on his face. James looked over his shoulder and saw Emily standing there, her hand extended from the throw.

James looked back to the boy, who was feeling the front of the dark jacket he wore. "You tore it, you bitch!" He brought his hand away. "I'm bleeding!"

But the crowd was cheering now, the women and men behind James emboldened by Emily's defiance.

The boys stepped backward, made rude gestures at Emily, and started away across the quadrangle.

The crowd roared its approval, and Emily's voice rose above the noise.

"Now, what was I saying?"

CHAPTER 13

"You were magnificent." James smiled down at her as they walked back toward the pond, her sign still in his hands. "Really, you were."

Emily looked down at the handkerchief in her hand. It was stained red with her own blood. The sharp glass had cut her finger when she'd thrown it. She hadn't even realized at first, her anger at the idiot boys crowding out any pain. "I suppose it was very foolish of me. I could have hurt him."

"He'd have deserved it."

Emily couldn't help but share James's smile. "He would have, wouldn't he?"

They both laughed, walked on, in front of the auditorium now. She felt light, blissfully happy on adrenaline and satisfaction. She'd seen James stepping toward the men, had realized that he meant to fight, and her fear for him had mixed with her outrage at the boys' attitude. Before she'd had a moment to think, she'd picked up the remains of the bottle and lobbed the glass with all her strength. The fact that she'd hit her target had surprised her as much as anyone.

She looked at James again, at the way he carried the sign over his shoulder, like a rifle. "I'm glad you came."

He met her gaze, then looked down "I am, too, though I don't know why you asked me."

"Marion wasn't free." The words came out wrong, and Emily wished she could pull them back.

His expression fell. "Oh."

"And I knew you would understand," she added quickly. "You know things aren't the same as they were before the War, don't you?"

He shrugged. "Not for everyone, at least. Some people..."

He didn't finish the sentence, and he didn't need to. Emily nodded.

Some people act like everything is the same.

They rounded the corner of the auditorium and angled toward the pond. They had just entered a small thicket of blue spruces that straddled the path when someone stepped out in front of them.

It was the same boy who'd thrown the bottles.

"Hello again." The boy stepped toward them, fists clenched at his side. "I thought I'd continue our discussion from earlier."

Emily squared herself to him, refused to step back.

"I think there's already been enough said." James stepped in front of her, put a hand on her arm, and dropped the sign on the ground.

The boy laughed, pointed at the sign. "That's where that garbage belongs."

"And that's where you'll be if you don't shut up and leave." James's voice was low, ice cold.

"Honestly, do you boys have to solve everything with violence?" Emily kept her fear out of her voice.

"See?" The boy laughed. "She doesn't need your help. Step aside."

James said nothing, his grip on Emily's arm tightening.

She noticed the boy's eyes flicking at the trees, realized what was going to happen a second before it did.

Another boy burst out from between two of the trees directly behind James, lunged toward him. "Got ya!"

JAMES MOVED down the German trench, searching for movement, his heart pounding in his ears, his rifle pointed forward, his bayonet point leading him. Gunshots and screams carried from elsewhere down the trench, the drum of shells bursting, screeching overhead. They reached the end of the firebay, and James put his back against the wall of the trench. He looked at Sergeant Daniels, Stokley's replacement, waiting for the order to go around the corner.

"Grenades." Sergeant Daniels looked at William and Rodriguez, who slung their rifles over their shoulders and pulled out the dull gray grenades from their webbing.

James flattened himself against the wall of the trench, motioned to Private Cheeney to step next to him. He wanted someone else to go in with him.

Daniels raised an arm, brought it down in a chopping motion. "Now!"

William and Rodriguez threw their grenades around the corner.

A shout. Curses in German. A deafening blast. Screams.

James charged around the corner, coughed as the acrid smell of the grenade stung his nostrils. The Germans, four of them, were heaped against the firestep, blood soaking their uniforms, their helmets knocked askew. One was lying still halfway out of the entrance of a deep dugout, as if he'd been trying to escape. James shouldered his rifle, glanced down the dugout, saw nothing. He moved carefully, ready to stab the first German who moved.

"What the—"

A sharp crack cut Cheeney's cry short. James spun around, saw another German clambering out of the dugout and over the body of his comrade, pistol pointed at Cheeney, who staggered and fell to the ground.

William and the others were rounding the corner. They didn't know.

James didn't think, but ran at the German, who turned to face him. James knocked the pistol aside with his bayonet, pushed the German against the trench wall, screamed as he lifted the man off his feet with his rifle across his neck. The German choked, spluttered. James dropped him, pounded down at him with his rifle, then punched his blade into the man's chest, again and again...

EMILY SAW something snap in James's eyes the second the boy jumped out, gasped as James turned and attacked him. He moved so quickly, crossing the distance in a heartbeat.

The boy yelled and stumbled backward, but James was already on top of him. He punched him once, twice in the face, yanked him forward by the collar, lifted him, and threw him against the tree.

"Hey!" The first boy pushed past Emily as James turned to meet him.

The boy tried to punch James but only managed to clip him, James's attempt to dodge the blow a split second too late. James lowered his head and charged forward, catching the boy around the midsection. They tumbled together to the path. James's fists flew, punching him in the face.

"James, stop!" Emily ran forward, grabbed his shoulder.

He spun around, looked up at her, moved as if to hit her, and she saw something animal and raw in his eyes. She stepped back. "Stop!"

James froze, breathing hard, his gaze locked with hers. He

stood, wiped his nose, and glared down at the young man. "Get out of here."

The boy got slowly to his feet and scampered over to where his friend was still trying to stand up. The two boys ran off together, looking over their shoulders as they staggered away.

James stood there, put his hands on his knees, and something dripped from his nose.

Emily took one step toward him, then another. "James?"

He shook his head. "Sorry. I don't know what came over me."

She looked in her hand and saw she was still holding her handkerchief. "Here."

She put a hand on his back and pushed the handkerchief into his hand.

He straightened up, pressed the cloth to his nose, catching the weak stream of blood that ran from it. He laughed weakly, his eyes red. "The jerk got me."

She remembered him at the dining table at home, the panic, the intense emotion that had rolled off him as he'd recounted the story of how he'd won his medal. Was his burst of violence the result of another memory from the War?

She tried to sound encouraging. "I'd say you gave better than you got."

He nodded, turned his face from her. He sniffed, his breathing rough, and Emily knew he was trying to hide how upset he was.

"Hey, it's alright." She put a hand on his arm, tried to turn him back. He wouldn't move, so she stepped around him and stood right in front of him. "It's okay."

He looked at her hand on his arm and chuckled. "You're bleeding again."

"Oh?" She saw her own blood on James's shirt.

He folded the handkerchief, putting the bloody part inside, and handed it back to her. "Take it, I'm done."

They looked at each other for a moment—and then they laughed, the thought of them both standing there, bleeding, beyond absurd.

"And here it was I told Mother I'd be safe." Emily chuckled, unable to stop the laughter.

"Things were going so well."

She watched his features, the darker emotion that still haunted his eyes, shadows the laughter did not reach, and found herself reaching up with her good hand, touching his cheek.

She heard her own intake of breath as he put his hand over hers. He was so close to her, and she could hear his breath slowing, his other hand sliding around to the small of her back. Her heart jumped into her throat, her every nerve intensely aware of him, his breathing, the warmth of his hand on hers.

She knew he was going to kiss her, so she tilted her face upward to meet him. His lips touched hers, so gently, a feather. She slid her hand out from under his and around the back of his neck, felt her hat sliding back on her head. She kissed him back, pulled him down and against her, suddenly hungry for the feel of him.

"Emily!" Marion's voice broke through her thoughts. "Emily!"

She pulled back, felt James do the same, the intensity in his eyes drawing the breath from her.

"Emily! James!" There was a note of fear in Marion's voice, of panic.

She turned, saw her friend running across the bridge over the turtle pond, one hand on her navy-blue hat, the other lifting her matching skirt. She wore a look of absolute terror, and as she got closer, Emily could see she'd been crying.

"Marion? What's the matter? Are you—"

Her voice was raw with panic. "Emily, it's Walter. He tried to hang himself!"

Emily's heart gave a hard knock, the hard, painful jolt of fear driving away the lingering warmth of the kiss. "What?"

"Come quickly! Mrs. Gould wants you!" She looked at James. "You, too."

Without another word, the three of them ran back down the path, moving as fast as they could toward Sixth Street.

"THANK GOODNESS YOU'RE HERE." Mrs. Gould stepped aside, let James past. "He's in the parlor."

James entered and waited for Emily and Marion, his eyes adjusting to the light. He watched as Emily wordlessly drew Mrs. Gould into an embrace.

"Thank you, dear." Mrs. Gould smiled, then drew back, wiping her eyes.

They walked together into the parlor, where Walt was sitting as normal in his chair, his cane across his lap. He faced the wall, angry red marks on his neck.

Rope burn.

"Oh, Walter." Emily stepped past James and stood in front of Walt. "Why did you do it?"

Walter didn't say anything, but kept staring off into space, the mutilated side of his face turned away from them.

"Please talk to us." Marion sat down next to him. "Please."

"How'd it happen?" James looked around at Mrs. Gould.

"I was getting things ready for Marion's visit. Your Uncle Chester dropped Walter off from working at the ranch, and Walt went upstairs. I heard a bump and thought he'd fallen over. I went to his room and found him." She put a hand over her mouth, started crying.

James put an arm around her.

She sniffed. "I called Marion right away to come get you."

"Did you call the doctor?"

"No." She shook her head. "I was afraid they'd lock him up. But I did call my husband. He's on his way home now. What should I do?"

James didn't have an answer for that, and after seeing how Officer Westlake had treated Walter, he couldn't blame Mrs. Gould for not trusting the authorities.

"Walter, I don't understand," Emily was saying. "Everything has been going well. Did Chester say something?"

James shifted on the spot, but didn't speak. He couldn't imagine Chester ever antagonizing Walter, not when he'd shown the man so much kindness. It just wasn't in his nature.

"One of the ranch hands, maybe?" Marion looked back at James.

"If that happened, tell us." James crossed his arms, resolving to call Chester as soon as he got home. "We can make sure he gets punished."

Walter didn't move, kept his eyes averted from them.

"Well what, then?" Emily threw her hands in the air. "Do you see what you're doing to your mother? To us? It's one thing to feel pain, but it's another to hurt people who care about you. That's selfish, Walter. It doesn't matter what you've been through. It's wrong."

Walter did turn his head then, his eyes red from crying. "Wrong?" His voice was hoarse, ragged. "Do you realize how I feel when I come back from there?"

Emily sat down across from Walter. "How? You seemed to like it before."

"Every one of my wounds hurts. I feel sick from it. I can't work as fast as the other men, or as well."

Marion shook her head. "But you *can* work. Isn't that something?"

"It's just a reminder of all the things I *can't* do like a normal man." His voice rose as he spoke faster and faster. "I will never be able to work a normal job, or be outside, or walk like a real goddamned person. So why live? Why bother? What do I have to lose?"

"Isn't there anything you are happy about?" Marion's voice was so small, so vulnerable. "What about us?" She looked at her friends. "Emily and James and I?"

Walt's expression softened. He pointed at Emily, then James. "I don't think I do you any favors. Look at you all, coming here, worrying about the cripple when you should be out living your lives."

Emily met James's gaze, shook her head. How do you argue with someone who doesn't believe life is worth living?

James took a step forward, rounding the coffee table until he was directly in front of Walter. "No one's saying that things are the same as they were."

An understatement if ever there was one.

Marion nodded. "I'm sure some of the pain will get better as your wounds heal. You just need time."

Walter held up his hands, a gesture of exasperation. "How much time? How do you know that for sure? Are you telling me I should be happy because it could be worse? It can always be worse. Always. That doesn't mean I have to like it."

"No, you don't." James fought the urge to grab Walter by the shoulders and shake him. "But you have a choice. Not everyone got that." He heard his own voice crack and hoped no one else noticed. "William didn't."

And whose fault was that?

Walter opened his mouth, closed it, and looked at Emily.

"If you don't care how your death would hurt us, then think about the other guys who didn't get the chance you have now, to build something with what you've got." Faces, names flashed through James mind, the men he'd seen die, whose final agony he had witnessed. He clenched his hand, trying to drive away the memories. "You owe it to those guys to do the things they couldn't."

Easier said than done. He hoped Walter wouldn't point out that he himself had spent weeks hiding at home, pretending to be dead.

You hypocrite.

Why was it always so much easier to see these things clearly with others than with himself? Maybe because Walter's pain was an honest one, wounds earned serving his country, free of shame.

Walter's eyes narrowed and he pointed at James's closed fists. "What happened to you?"

James looked down and saw the bloodstain on his sleeve where Emily had touched him with her injured hand, the redness of his knuckles.

"Some troublemakers tried to jump us at the suffrage rally," Emily replied. "James… dissuaded them."

"Are you hurt?" Mrs. Gould looked over James and Emily, seemed to be examining them for injury.

Emily flexed her hand. "Just a scratch or two."

James turned back to Walt. "How about it?"

Walter's frown deepened, but he didn't speak.

James crossed his arms. "Do we drag you to a doctor right now? Or are you going to do the best you can with what you have?"

"Those are the only two options?" Walter looked up at them, raised his good eyebrow.

"We won't accept any others." Emily smiled.

"You won't be alone," Marion added.

"You see?" Mrs. Gould wiped her eyes. "It's not just me who wants you alive."

Walter met James's eyes again, nodded, the despair in them still strong. "Fix bayonets?"

"Fix bayonets."

CHAPTER 14

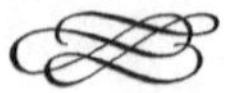

May 31, 1918
Near Mory, France

"Strip it all off, fellows." The young corporal pushed his hand cart alongside the makeshift shower stalls and stopped in front of James. "Time to cook the cooties."

James shivered, stripping off his uniform one item at a time until he was naked, enjoying the feeling of cool, clean air on his skin. They'd all lived in their clothes for many days now—along with a healthy population of lice. James bent over, picking the pile of dirty, stinking khaki from the smooth wood boards that served as a floor, and gathered them in his arms. He reached over the top of his stall—a heavy, white cloth hung from a rickety metal frame—and dropped the heap into the corporal's cart as he passed.

"Take the filthy bastards."

Caldwell looked over at him from a few stalls down. "You're the one who's filthy, Garrison."

William, in the stall between Caldwell and Bird, pulled his

undershirt over his head. "You're just jealous because he stole your lice."

The men laughed and the corporal kept walking, his cart filling with the soldiers' dirty uniforms. The mood of the group faded from bitter exhaustion to something lighter, the tension of the battle and the long march to the rear leaving them in the midday sun.

James watched the corporal roll the cart toward the truck that had parked in the middle of the field, the one with the big cylinder on the back, the pressure cooker to clean and delouse the men's uniforms.

Good riddance!

He bent down, picked up the bar of soap he'd been given, then stood and reached above him to the bucket that was suspended above his stall, a short spout poking out of its bottom. He turned the small lever on the side of the nozzle, freeing a weak stream of water, gasping as the cold liquid hit his skin.

No hot showers in the Army.

It didn't matter. He put his head under the water, let it flow over him.

"Don't take too long!" Sergeant Daniels was passing by now, already clean and in a fresh uniform. "You only get one bucket!"

Daniels was the new sergeant for James's squad, the man they'd brought from another platoon to replace Stokley. A strong-looking fellow with a square jaw and thinning hair, he seemed competent, though he lacked Stokley's booming voice and gruff attitude, two things to which James had become accustomed. James thought of Stokley lying in the trench, his vacant expression staring back at him. The man had been with them since before they'd arrived in France and then... It had all happened so quickly.

No sense obsessing over it now.

Not while the water was running, anyway.

James attacked the dirt and filth that clung to his body, scrubbing with the soap, working as quickly as he could. It was like washing someone else's body. He had so many bruises, small cuts scattered over his skin. Where had they come from? He remembered tumbling backward with the German he'd bayoneted, the one he'd skewered in mid-air as he'd jumped into the American trench. The man's eyes had been enormous, ringed with white, agony on his face.

James clenched his jaw and focused on the chill of the water, the faint, clean smell of the soap. He looked far across the field, toward the road and the Red Cross canteen beyond. It felt strange being naked like this in open air when Emily was so near, even if he knew that he was across a busy field and hidden behind a cloth barrier.

Emily.

When he'd spotted her standing in that booth with her tray of doughnuts, he'd thought she was the prettiest girl he'd ever seen, had filled instantly with joy at the sight of her familiar, beautiful face, even if it was under that awkward Red Cross hood. She'd looked a little older than the last time he'd seen her—had it really been eighteen months? Despite the simple, modest lines of her light blue uniform, it was obvious that her figure was fuller and more feminine now, more young woman than girl. He'd had a hard time looking away from her. He had refrained from cutting the line and walking over to her only because William had thought it would be funny to surprise her by walking up to her casually and asking for a doughnut.

Unfortunately, James hadn't been the only one to notice her looks. That idiot who'd mouthed off at her had been one nasty word away from a beating. James and William had pushed past the others as soon as they'd realized what was going on. Luckily, they hadn't needed to beat the man, and even James's anger at the foulmouthed soldier's words hadn't dimmed the happiness he'd felt at seeing her.

Or the excitement he felt now, knowing he would talk to her again.

He finished scrubbing, let the last trickles of the water rinse away the suds. A minute later, the corporal returned, draping fresh underclothes and uniforms over the barriers. James slipped on the long white drawers and undershirt, stepped into the trousers, buttoned his new tunic shut. He put on one sock, hopped as he slipped that foot into one of the new boots, not wanting to get his foot wet again, then repeated the process with the other foot. He opened up his stall and joined the stream of partially-dressed men strolling over to a stand of trees.

He finished dressing and wrapped the new puttees around his legs, one at a time. Some of the other men were shaving, using a few basins of water to wet their brushes and shaving soap, a small mirror hung on a branch. He pulled out his toiletry kit and joined them but couldn't compete with the crowd for the mirror. Instead, he felt his soap-slicked stubble with his free hand, shaving blind.

"Slow down there." William chuckled, rinsing off his razor. "She won't like it if your face is all cut up."

"Who?" Heat rose into James's cheeks, and he was grateful the shaving soap hid his blush.

"Oh, I don't know." William folded away his toiletry kit. "The girl you've been writing to for more than a year, the one you gaped at just now like an idiot."

A small sliver of fear crept into James's thoughts. Was William serious? Did he not approve of James's interest in Emily? Not that he *was* interested, mind you.

William smiled, winked. "I think we both know who."

The bastard!

James knew he wasn't serious, a fact that annoyed him as much as it relieved him.

"If we're talking about your sister, you'd better stop this mess fast." Caldwell sat on a log nearby, wrapping his puttees. "She can do better."

"Does everyone share this idea that I'm in love with William's sister? Hmm?" James ignored the smiles of the men around him and contorted his face to pull his skin tight for the razor.

"Gee, I don't know." Bird cleared his throat, talked in a high, exaggerated voice. "Hey fellows, I just got this letter from William's sis. Let me read it a hundred times when I don't think anyone is looking!"

They all laughed, except James, who searched for something to say—and failed. He had taken to reading Emily's letters over and over again whenever he received them, had not thought anyone would care to notice.

William stepped away from the basin, sat next to Caldwell. "Leave him alone." He grinned conspiratorially. "He has somewhere to be, you know."

"Yeah, the canteen." Caldwell winked.

"I just want some stationery." James rinsed his face off, felt for any missed patches of stubble. "Emily's being there is a coincidence. I'd go regardless."

He stepped away from the shaving area and folded away his kit.

Bird crossed his arms. "Suit yourself, then. I got a look at her in line. Not too bad. If you don't want her, I'll be happy to—"

"Shut up," William and James said at the same time.

The squad went to work on a few details ordered by Sergeant Daniels—cleaning rifles, organizing and inventorying some of the company equipment—until Lieutenant

Robinson intervened and insisted the work load remain light to allow the soldiers time to rest.

Robinson smiled, his hands on his belt. "Might as well let these boys enjoy the sun while we have it, sergeant."

"Yes, sir."

James could have kissed the lieutenant, and he and William wasted no time before plodding across the flattened grass toward the Red Cross canteen. They weaved between groups of soldiers, men carrying supplies and setting up dog tents.

"I knew it couldn't possibly last long." William frowned as they stepped through the thick mud on the road, the dirty water splashing up onto their boots and puttees. They walked over to the booth, no line now, two of the girls inside.

"Miss, do you know where the rest tent is?" James put his hands on the counter, met the gaze of one of the young women inside, a pretty girl with dark hair and large brown eyes.

She smiled. "Just behind. Keep going straight. Follow the boardwalk." She looked at William, squinted slightly. "You're Emily's brother?"

William nodded. "Yeah."

"I can see the resemblance. She should still be back there." She looked back at James. "You should be James, then."

"Um, yes." James tilted his head to the side. "How would you know that?"

"Oh, nothing. We heard about what you both did earlier." She straightened the hat on her head, her smile growing broader. "And Emily mentions you sometimes, that's all. I'm Gertrude, by the way."

James stared back at the woman's knowing smile and couldn't decide if he was thrilled Emily was talking about him or irritated that everyone seemed to think they were involved in some kind of courtship. "Nice to meet you. Let's go, Will."

They rounded the booth, and James swore he heard Gertrude and the other woman in the booth giggle. He and William kept to the boardwalk, the hobnails on their boots tapping on the warped wood. They spotted a large tent ahead and stepped inside.

James almost ran into a table by the door. It held a large chest, filled with stacks of clean, white envelopes and blank paper. Small, sharpened pencils stood at attention inside a rusty coffee can next to the chest. There were three rows of folding tables and chairs, soldiers scattered here and there, sipping cups of coffee, bent over pieces of paper, or talking in low voices to other men. They all looked like troops from the 28th, none of the fellows from James and William's company.

James scanned the room and found Emily sitting beside a soldier, pencil in hand.

She wrote as the man talked, her brow furrowed in concentration. Her graceful neck was bent forward slightly, the hood of her hat concealing her hair and draping over her shoulders. Something tightened in his chest, and he suddenly felt... nervous? How could that be? It was only Emily, after all.

William nudged James forward. "Come on."

James grabbed a piece of paper and a pencil—it had been a week since he'd written home—and followed his friend, weaving between the tables. They pulled out chairs and sat down silently, William next to her and James on the other side of the table, beside the other soldier.

The soldier, a short, wiry fellow with brown hair and hazel eyes, was still talking, a slight southwestern accent coloring his words. "I'm eating real good, but the food ain't as nice as yours. The nurses here are really nice. It's them that wrote this letter for me."

Emily glanced up, saw James and William, and smiled, her features brightening as she wrote the soldier's words in her flowing cursive. James couldn't help but smile back—like an idiot.

She looked back at the soldier. "Go on, Frank."

Frank leaned back in his chair. "I don't know where I'm gonna go next, but I'll try to write when I can. Don't worry about me too much. Love, Frankie."

Emily finished writing, folded the paper, and tucked it into an envelope. She handed it to Frank, who beamed at her.

"There you go, soldier. You should have no trouble posting this."

"Thank you, miss." Frank blushed. "Thanks for writing. I never saw much use for it."

"I'm glad to help." She set down the pencil, glanced at William.

Frank followed her gaze to James and William, probably thought they needed Emily's help, too. "You boys are lucky. You've got an angel here."

Emily blushed. "Nonsense. Best of luck to you."

Frank stood up, put on his cap, and walked away.

"An angel?" William raised an eyebrow. "Should I tell Mom and Dad that some doughboy will steal you for his wife?"

"Don't be ridiculous." She frowned, arching an eyebrow. Then her face split into a smile again and she leaned forward, laughing as she pulled William into a hug. "How are you? Are you hurt at all?"

"We're alright now." William rocked her back and forth slightly. Growing up as twins, they'd never been very far apart, and James knew that the separation from his sister could not have been easy for William, even if he didn't show it.

The siblings pulled apart, and Emily looked over at James. They held each other's gaze for a second, and James wasn't sure if he should stand up to hug her or stay still. He held out a hand instead.

She grabbed hold of it and squeezed. "Tell me all about it, boys."

James looked at William, who stared back.

What the hell was there to say?

James thought of the dash through Cantigny, the scorched bodies, the fighting in the trench, and looked back at Emily, her delicate features, her mouth pursed in a line. Somehow, it didn't seem right to tell her about it. She was something beautiful and clean. She didn't need to hear about any of what he'd seen—or done.

Emily released James's hand and looked between them, raising her eyebrows. "Is either of you going to say something? I heard you saw action."

"Yes, we did." James raised his chin and tried to keep his voice impassive. "We reinforced the 28th at Cantigny and fought off some enemy counter-attacks."

Just words, a simple sentence that stood for so much horror. He blinked hard, pushing away the memory of the German's expression as he'd stabbed him over and over with his bayonet.

"Nein! Nein!"

"Are you alright?" Emily asked again. "Did any of your soldiers get hurt, or...?"

"It was a hard couple of days." William's voice was flat. He noticed Emily's concerned expression, and he grinned faintly as he put a hand on her arm. "We're fine."

"Good." She leaned back in her chair, but didn't look convinced.

There was some commotion by the door, and James saw an older woman, the one who'd dressed down the rude soldier at the booth earlier, entering with another one of the young women, barking commands.

Emily looked over her shoulder. "I'll probably have to get back to work in a minute."

William chuckled. "Not much time for visiting, I suppose."

"None, really. Mrs. Wolfe is a drill sergeant."

James looked down at the paper he'd grabbed from the chest by the door. An idea came to him, and he slid the paper across the table. "You *are* working."

"Excuse me?" Emily took the paper.

"We're illiterate, remember?"

"Just do what you did with Frankie." William had caught on, winking at James.

Emily shook her head, but started writing something. James watched the older woman glance over at Emily and give a satisfied nod.

Whatever works, works.

"How long do you think you'll be in this area?" Emily's voice was low, and she kept her eyes on the paper.

James shrugged. "No way to know. We'll probably move to Mory soon and then rejoin the regiment."

"Probably not long," William added. "But if we're given a real leave nearby, maybe we can find a way to meet you."

Unlikely, but James didn't say that. In reality, they'd probably be on the move quickly, and would be so far from here by the time they were given rest again that they'd have no way to get back to this spot, wherever this spot really was.

Emily stopped writing, tapped her pencil on the paper a couple times. "They cleaned you up pretty well. Are you comfortable?"

James fought the urge to snort. Comfortable was not the

watchword in the Army. Still, things were nicer here than they'd been in quite a while, with the frantic march to the frontline, the wait near Cantigny, the attack...

"Yes." James flexed his toes in his new boots. "They're taking really good care of us."

William scratched his chin. "I don't like that you're here, Emily."

She looked up sharply at him. "What do you—"

"You're still in range of the bigger guns, and the front's been changing every day." William leaned forward, his expression grave. "Will they be moving you to the rear at all?"

James hadn't thought about that, and now that William mentioned it, he didn't like it either. He'd seen enough of what heavy artillery could do to know he didn't want Emily near it.

She put down her pencil and looked up at them, her jaw set. "This *is* the rear. And I'm happy to share the danger with you men. Besides, with so much fighting going on elsewhere, I can't imagine why the Germans would target this canteen."

James really did snort this time. Since when did Germans need a reason?

He realized Emily was glaring at him. "We just don't want you in danger."

She looked down at her paper again, started scribbling. "Worry about yourselves. I'll be fine."

They all sat in silence for a minute.

James cleared his throat. "Well. How about you, Em? How are they treating—?"

"Culver! Garrison!" Caldwell's voice carried from the entrance of the tent. "Sarge found some more things for us to do."

Apparently, Lieutenant Robinson's idea of what consti-tuted rest and Sergeant Daniels's were two different things.

Emily sighed. "Already?"

"Maybe we can pretend to help you write." William grinned as he stood. "Hopefully we can drop by later."

It was obvious to all of them how unlikely that was.

William and Emily hugged.

"Come on!" Caldwell gestured as he stepped back outside.

William pulled apart from his sister, and James started after him.

"James, wait."

He stopped, turned around, and found Emily standing right behind him.

"Is he…" She folded her hands in front of her stomach, lowered her voice. "Is he handling it well?"

"Yes," James responded, not sure what else to say. William was alive, which was as good as anyone could ask for. "He's a natural."

It sounded nice, and it softened Emily's worried expression. "He was always good at everything. I'm glad he's taking to it well. And I'm glad he has you. You will take care of him, won't you?" She touched his arm. "And you'll tell me how he is when you write?"

"I'll do my best." It was a ridiculous thing to promise, but James didn't want to disappoint her.

"I know it's hardest for you both, being at the front. But you can't know what it's like to wait for your letters, not knowing if another will come." She blinked, her eyes suddenly bright. "Please write as much as you can, even if you haven't got a reply from me yet—and don't spare me any details, okay?"

He looked into her eyes, saw the shadow of worry there, the raw fear for her brother. He reached up and put a hand on her cheek, wanting to do anything to make her smile again. He heard her intake of breath, but she didn't back away.

"James, let's go!" William was shouting from somewhere outside.

They stepped apart, their motions suddenly awkward.

"Take care," she said, hugging her arms across her body.

"I'll see you later." He turned and walked toward the exit, the feel of her skin still tingling on his fingertips.

CHAPTER 15

May 31, 1918
Near Mory, France

"Miss Culver, lock up the booth." Mrs. Wolfe rose from the table, leaving her dinner plate lying there, her cutlery tucked across it. "Let Gertrude know she can come in for her meal. The rest of you, let's get started on this mess while we still have some light."

Emily pushed back her plate and stood, smoothing her skirts, the meal of thick stew warming her. They had put it together with some canned meat, and it had turned out better than she'd expected. Mrs. Wolfe had been stricter since earlier that day, when she'd learned that the troops resting here had indeed come from fighting at Cantigny.

Emily didn't understand why, but she wouldn't tempt the woman's mood.

She walked out of the rest tent and along the boardwalk toward the booth, her fatigue settling onto her shoulders, weighing down her eyelids, dragging at her limbs. She looked toward the west, the sun dipping below a clump of forest, lighting it on fire, the sky smudged orange and red and pink, the underside of clouds painted the same colors. The church spire in Mory was just visible above the trees, black against the bright sunset. She stopped to look at the beautiful scene—only for the distant, muffled thunder of artillery somewhere to roll through the air in faint waves.

How could one world hold so much loveliness and so much ugliness at the same time?

She kept walking and hugged her arms around herself to ward off the damp chill in the evening air. They'd had a lot of soldiers come through today, had sold a lot of the cigarettes. They'd had to make three huge batches of doughnuts to satisfy the demand. She'd personally helped a dozen or so men with their letters home.

She yawned, felt an unfamiliar sense of… satisfaction. She never remembered days at home feeling like this. The work made everything pass so quickly, and yet by the time the evening came, the days felt so long, and she was more than ready to collapse into her indifferent cot.

She missed proper bathing, she wouldn't mind better food, and, most of all, she wished she didn't have to constantly worry about William, James, and the other boys from home. At the same time, she couldn't help but value her work here. She was part of something, a piece of the war effort, an unstoppable, well-oiled machine rolling toward victory and a free, peaceful world. This was how a modern woman should live—a meaningful contributor, proud of her own work, confident in her own abilities. As horrifying and terrible as the War was, joining the Red Cross had been the best choice Emily had ever made.

How Alice and Marion were managing back home, Emily couldn't imagine. She knew from letters that Marion worried about Walt so much that she found it hard to concentrate on anything. If Emily didn't have her job to do, the distraction of her work, she would go insane. She resolved to suggest to Marion that she involve herself with more of the war effort back home—the victory gardens, the bond drives, the wool brigades, collecting peach pits for gas masks, whatever there was to do.

Surely doing *something* was better than doing nothing and worrying.

Emily finally reached the booth and stepped inside. "Gertie, Mrs. Wolfe says you can come eat."

"I've already packed it up." Gertrude was settling the chest with all the stationery supplies on top of the one that held the cigarettes. She grabbed the broom leaning against the wall and handed it to Emily. "You just need to clean up and lock everything."

Emily grabbed it, but when she tried to pull it toward her, Gertrude didn't let go.

"I saw him." Gertie grinned, flicked her eyes over in the direction of the field full of dog tents.

Emily stared at her friend. "Who?"

"You know who. James."

Emily's cheeks burned, irritation sparking through her. "So did a lot of people. He probably sees himself in the mirror, too."

Gertie ignored Emily, her grin spreading into a full smile now. "You didn't say he was so handsome."

"I...I didn't?" Emily hated the stammer in her voice, so much like some foolish school girl.

"And I heard how he stood up for you today." Gertrude giggled. "You never told me he was so smitten with you, either."

Emily raised her chin. "Because he's not. He's my brother's friend. I knew him growing up, so we choose to stay in touch. It's nothing more."

She gave a sharp tug, pulling the broom out of her friend's hands.

"Oh." Gertrude held her hands out, palms forward, a gesture of surrender. "I didn't know."

"Your food's getting cold." Emily turned her back as Gertrude walked out the door, though she was sure she heard another giggle escape her friend's mouth.

How ridiculous!

Emily attacked the floor with her broom, gathering the dirt and clods of drying mud into a pile by the door and sweeping them outside.

James was her friend, and she was not some lovesick girl dreaming of her soldier boy at the front. She'd seen enough of those girls in this war, and she'd seen what happened when they got bad news. She wasn't going to be one.

She remembered James standing in front of her in the rest tent, reaching for her. He'd touched her, put a hand on her cheek. She remembered the sensation, the odd warmth that had filled her. No, that must have been shock. It was incorrect for a man to touch a woman like that, especially in front of the other soldiers and Red Cross girls. She'd been so grateful no one had noticed. No one here knew they were childhood friends. People would interpret the gesture incorrectly.

Or maybe they'd be right.

His obvious concern for her anxiety about William had moved her, even if he'd expressed it in an inappropriate manner.

She realized she was standing still, leaning on the broom, her hand on her cheek where he'd touched it. She sighed and lifted the broom up to brush the crumbs off the counter and outside.

James *had* looked handsome—clean-shaven in a crisp, fresh khaki uniform—but why should that matter? Plenty of men were handsome. And just because he'd stood up for her didn't mean he had romantic feelings for her. She would hope he'd stand up for any woman in a situation like that.

Gertrude was seeing things. That was all there was to it. Besides, Emily had more important things to think about than just James. Now that the Americans had seen action, they'd certainly be in the fighting again. No more training, no more waiting. William's regiment was in the fight, and would be in it from now on.

A ball tightened in her chest, her usual knot of worry. She shook it off, leaned the broom in the corner, and focused on her work. She shuttered the booth's front window, looked around for the padlocks in the near darkness. She saw them on one of the shelves, locked shut to each other in a little knot.

The keys.

She felt her pocket, realized she didn't have them anymore. Mrs. Wolfe had taken them back during the day. Emily shook her head, irritation at her forgetfulness flaring at her temples. She should have gotten them before coming out to the booth. Now Mrs. Wolfe would upbraid her for sure.

Emily walked out of the booth and shut the door behind her—better to pretend it was locked in case a soldier came looking for some smokes—and started across the camp toward the mess tent, where she figured Mrs. Wolfe would probably be, directing the dish cleaning.

She stepped forward, and the world exploded.

JAMES CROUCHED LOW, his knees sinking in the mud of the road. "Son of a bitch!"

He dropped the ammunition cans he'd been carrying,

watched as a flash lit the woods off behind the Red Cross camp.

The Germans were shelling the area. His mind raced to the others—William, Caldwell, Bird, Emily.

There was nothing he could do.

Another explosion cut the air, somewhere off behind him, toward the camp. He looked around in what was left of the dim evening light, searching for cover.

A pair of shells blasted the woods beyond the camp one after the other, vibrating in his chest.

The Germans were throwing shells wide, bracketing the area. Chances were they'd hit toward the middle soon, and James didn't want to be in the open when that happened.

His eyes fixed on the Red Cross booth a few dozen yards ahead.

Another thunderclap, this one closer.

The booth would have to do. It wouldn't do a damned thing against a direct hit or even the bigger shell fragments, but it was better than nothing, and it was close by.

He launched himself into a sprint, leaving the ammo cans behind.

A bright flash knifed through the air a hundred yards down the road, a patch of ground lifted and sprayed out in all directions, fire and mud mixed together, the sound of the blast hitting James like a wall. He dropped to the ground, hugged the dirt, waited, his heart pounding against the mud.

He picked himself up and ran again, his head lowered. He rounded the booth, and his foot caught on something soft. He pitched forward, landing hard on the boardwalk, the breath driven from his lungs. He rolled, saw someone next to him, the white apron, the white-hooded hat lying askew. One of the Red Cross women. Her face was to the ground, her hands pressed over her ears.

Another shell burst somewhere, the flash lighting up the girl's features for an instant.

"Emily?" James shouted over the cacophony.

She peeked above the dirt, and he saw recognition in her wide, terrified eyes.

"Come on!" He got to his feet, his side aching where he'd struck the ground.

She shook her head, didn't move, clearly in a panic.

He took hold of her under the arms. "We can't stay—"

Another shell drowned out his words.

James pulled hard, and Emily stood, her hat tumbling to the side. He pulled her close and dragged her the dozen or so feet to the booth. He reached for the door handle—thank goodness it was open—and he hauled Emily inside.

The booth was almost totally dark, but James drew her down to the ground with him, his arms wrapped around her. They needed to get low, present as small a target as possible for the whizzing shrapnel balls and shell fragments.

He pulled her closer, felt her head against his chest, her soft hair against his face. He closed his eyes, hoped for the unbearable noise of the shells to stop.

James wasn't sure how long they stayed there, but it seemed like hours, the crack and boom of the shells assaulting his ears, making them both flinch, their rapid breathing mixing together, his heartbeat in his mouth.

Then, suddenly, there was silence.

He strained his ringing ears, listening. It wouldn't surprise him if the Germans waited a while before firing again, hoping that people would emerge from their cover and be more vulnerable again. Then he heard a high rushing sound, a distant boom, the unmistakable noise of outbound shells, the French artillery responding to the German bombardment from somewhere to the rear.

He felt Emily pulling away from him. He looked down at

her, his vision adjusted to the darkness now, and saw her pale face in the half-light, her eyes still wide, her hair a gold mess.

"Are you hurt?"

She shook her head, her voice thick. "No. Are you?"

~

EMILY LOOKED UP AT JAMES, her heart still racing.

"I'm fine." He shifted into a sitting position, winced, then chuckled. "That damned boardwalk gave me a good punch, though. So much for a clean uniform."

She glanced down at his tunic, could make out the darker stain of the mud. With a start, she realized she must be dirty, too. She felt down the front of her dress, the heavy, gritty wetness of the mud.

What would Mrs. Wolfe say?

Then another thought hit her.

Was Mrs. Wolfe even alive?

She started shaking, clasped her trembling hands together.

"We're lucky we're toward the rear," James was saying. "They couldn't use all their field guns, and I doubt they were able to observe their fire well."

"Lucky?" Emily didn't know what James meant, but she knew enough to realize how close they had been to getting killed. "What's unlucky?"

James met her gaze, held it. "It's harder in the trenches sometimes, that's all. It could have been worse. It's... You can't imagine, Emily."

She studied the serious, tired expression on his face, the silent anguish in his eyes.

Worse?

Is this what it was like up front? She'd heard the grumble

of distant artillery before, but she'd never known what it was like to be there, under that rain of steel. Was this what James and William endured every day?

Her heart hadn't stopped pounding, her own fear mixing with the unbearable wave of sadness she felt—sadness for her brother, sadness at the resigned, dead expression on James's face.

She reached up, put a hand on his cheek. She needed to touch him, to take away the pain she saw in his eyes. She bent forward and kissed his cheek.

She heard his breath catch, but he didn't move. She scooted closer, kissing his brow, her other arm wrapping around his shoulders. She kissed his other cheek, felt him pulling away until she was looking up at him.

"Emily..." He trailed off, one of his hands threading through her hair at the nape of her neck, the other wrapping around her waist.

She heard a little gasp escape her mouth, her pulse racing painfully. She'd never been touched like this by a man before, was caught between exhilaration and fear, the desire to run away and the need to kiss him again. He pulled her toward him, and she heard herself whimper, her eyes drifting shut as their lips met.

It was so strange, the soft warmth of lips on lips, different than she'd ever imagined. She relaxed against him, crossed her arms behind his neck, and realized he probably had no idea what to do either. The thought was calming somehow.

"Is anyone hurt over here?"

She heard Mrs. Wolfe's words through a fog, but was desperate to keep kissing him.

"Are there any wounded over here?" Mrs. Wolfe was getting closer.

James groaned softly as Emily pulled away.

"I..." She leaned her head back, away from him, but he

stayed with her, trailing soft kisses on her neck. "I can't be found like this."

He stopped, his brow furrowed as he looked down at her. "I'm sorry…I…"

They sat there for a moment, the only noise the sound of their mingled breathing—and footsteps on the boardwalk.

She pulled his hand from her hair, kissed it. "I have to go."

He nodded. "Emily, I…"

She shook her head, put a finger on his lips.

"Hello? Is someone in there?"

Emily stood, her legs shaky and weak, her chest full of some ragged, forceful emotion she didn't recognize.

"I'm here, Mrs. Wolfe. I'm in here."

Emily took one last look at James, then turned, and stepped outside, careful to not open the door too wide.

"Emily?" Mrs. Wolfe was several yards away, approaching from the mess tent, a few of the other girls hanging around her. Emily had expected the camp to be in pieces, but it looked untouched as far as she could tell in the darkness. Shouts were carrying over from the soldiers' camp, a confused disarray.

"Yes, Mrs. Wolfe."

"Oh, thank goodness." Mrs. Wolfe sighed, wiped her forehead. "Are you hurt?"

Emily shook her head, smoothed her skirts, felt the mud on them again, hoped the heat in her face didn't show. "I was closing up and hid when the shells came."

"Never mind that now." Mrs. Wolfe held out a hand.

Emily took it, not used to seeing this kind of concern from the stern woman.

"We haven't found Ruth yet," Mrs. Wolfe said. "Help us look."

Emily nodded and followed after Mrs. Wolfe, glancing back at the booth one last time.

They spent the next ten minutes searching the camp before they finally found Ruth, terrified, under one of the cots in the barracks. They really had been lucky. None of the women had been hit, and save for a few shrapnel holes in the tents, the camp had been spared. Judging by the sputtering ambulance cars that arrived a few minutes later, the soldiers across the road had been less fortunate, though Emily gratefully counted only a few stretchers being loaded.

She knew it was unlikely that William was among them, but the thought that it *could* be him gnawed at her. When Mrs. Wolfe sent her and a couple others to finish closing the booth, she walked toward the group around the ambulance, fists clenched at her side.

She stopped at the edge of the road, Gertrude and Clara in tow. "Is William Culver of the Twenty-Sixth Infantry there?"

The soldiers talked among themselves, and one of them, a sergeant judging by the marks on his sleeve, turned to a man by the side of the ambulance.

"You!"

"Caldwell, sergeant."

"Yeah, Caldwell. You're one of the Twenty-Sixth. Are any of these guys Culver?"

"No, sergeant. I saw him a few minutes ago." He turned, the headlamps of the other ambulance lighting up his grin as he looked at her. "You're his sister, right?"

"Yes. Thank you!"

Emily led Clara and Gertrude toward the booth. She knew James would be long gone and yet was still disappointed to find it empty.

"Looks like someone's been into the stationery." Gertrude pointed toward the chests, which were no longer stacked.

Emily frowned. Had someone come in and robbed it after she and James had left? She noticed a piece of paper folded on the counter, her name written across it, and she snatched it up before the other two noticed. "I wonder what could have happened."

The girls stacked the chests correctly and locked them, then placed the padlocks on the window cover and finally the door, shutting the booth for the night.

It was only when Emily was undressing for bed, folding her muddy skirt beside her cot, that she took out the piece of paper, and read what was written inside, the familiar name in tight cursive.

From this moment forward, I will think only of you.

- *James.*

CHAPTER 16

September 3, 1919

James stopped mid-step, stared up Emily's street, his pulse painful in his neck.

This was a stupid idea. After the way he'd lost his composure at their house, he was a fool to expect Mr. and Mrs. Culver to allow him to see Emily. They probably didn't want him anywhere near their daughter, and James couldn't blame them for feeling that way.

There was no way a romance with Emily could end well. The facts—and his own actions—made it impossible. One day, she would figure out the truth and know exactly what kind of man James was. And what if he did something to hurt her or someone else in the meantime? His reaction with those boys at the suffrage rally had taken him totally by surprise.

He remembered the raw, jagged emotion that had overtaken him when they had jumped him and Emily, how he'd felt again the tight confines of the trench, the fear of combat. He'd wanted to kill those boys with his bare hands.

He shivered, oblivious to the warmth of the sun that filtered through the trees and splashed across his face.

He was dangerous to Emily, for more than one reason, and her parents would realize that.

Even if they didn't, what would she say? In the immediate aftermath of Walt's suicide attempt, he and Emily hadn't had time to discuss what had happened between them. She hadn't seemed upset when he'd kissed her—in fact, she'd kissed him back—but Marion had interrupted them, and Emily hadn't had much time to react. Not that it was the first time they'd kissed, but after he'd cut her off from all communication and allowed her to think he was dead… After that, it was entirely reasonable that she would have lost whatever feelings she'd once had for him.

But the way she had kissed him… Maybe her feelings weren't entirely gone.

He stood still, thrust his hands into his pockets, and rocked on the balls of his feet.

This was Chester's doing. James had visited yesterday evening to see if troubles with the other ranch hands had been behind Walter's desire to kill himself. Even if Walter had denied that such a thing had happened, James had wanted to be sure.

"Any man on this ranch knows he'd be out of work if he was unkind to that boy," Chester had said, crossing his arms. "No one here has treated him with anything but respect."

Then they'd talked about Emily, James eager to share his conflicted feelings about her with someone—though he had left out the fact that he'd kissed her.

Chester had suppressed a grin, fixing James with a knowing look. "I'm too much of a gentleman to brag about how I saw your little romance with Miss Culver from a long way back."

"Chester!" Maggie had slapped her husband lightly on the arm, smiling. "Don't torture your nephew."

Chester had ignored her. "No, I'm not going to brag, even though I was right. But I want you to explain to me how can you tell Walter some damned thing about fixing bayonets if you don't even have the guts to pursue a pretty girl like Emily? Don't you practice what you preach, boy?"

James hadn't known how to respond, but after a half hour or so of his uncle pushing and encouraging him, he'd resolved to talk to Emily's parents about courting her in earnest.

That resolve had bled away over the course of the morning, and by the time he'd rounded the corner and started up Emily's street, it was nowhere to be found.

So much for bayonets, soldier.

He turned on his heel, took a couple steps back down the street, stopped himself. He noticed a woman watching him from the porch of one of the nearby houses, bent over a small rose bush, a pair of shears in her hands.

He stared back at her, tried to smile, and waved, feeling like an idiot. No doubt he looked like one, too, stopping and turning and stopping again, like some animal pacing in a cage.

The woman shook her head and turned back to her rose.

James looked down at his shoes. He could just walk home, forget about the whole idea. That would certainly be easy enough. But then he remembered the way she'd tilted her face to meet his kiss, how he had felt her pulling him down and into the embrace.

She'd wanted that kiss as much as he had.

Think about the other guys who didn't get the chance you have now, to build something with what you've got. You owe it to those guys to do the things they couldn't.

He heard the words he'd spoken to Walter, his resolve

returning. He took a deep breath, turned, and continued up the street.

～

EMILY KNEW this wouldn't be easy.

"But I don't understand, dear." Her mother shook her head, her face the image of concern. "You'll be so much older than the other girls. Won't you be lonely?"

"I should think I'll be busy enough with my studies, Mother." Emily ran her finger around the top of her teacup, suppressing her growing irritation.

It was as if her parents thought college was a social opportunity and not a serious choice.

She pressed her point. "And I imagine there will be plenty of girls my age who did war service."

Her mother picked up her own cup, frowned. "You're not getting any younger, you know. By your age, I'd met your father." She smiled faintly and looked over at her husband, who was leaning back in his armchair, his eyes closed, a hand massaging his temple.

Emily opened her mouth, closed it, and sipped her tea instead. How could she possibly make them understand? It wasn't the nineteenth century anymore, and Emily wasn't her mother. How could she explain what it had meant to her to work at the canteen, to feel useful? How could she make them see how important this was to her?

"Wouldn't you like to have a family?"

"Yes, I think so. But..." Emily searched for the words. "I would like to *do* something, too. To accomplish something of my own."

"But isn't raising a family an accomplishment? Isn't that important?" Her mother raised her eyebrows, a harder edge to her voice.

"It's Nineteen-Nineteen, Mother. Things aren't the same for women now."

"You keep saying that." Her father opened his eyes, sighed. "But I recall having this conversation *before* the War, too."

"When you agreed to let me go." She held his gaze, raised her chin.

He drummed his fingers on the armrest of the chair. "Not very consistent, your women's liberation. You say you want independence and your own accomplishments, and yet you won't simply *go* to college, but want us to send you there and take on the expense."

"All I want is for you to give me the same support you'd have given William."

Both of her parents flinched visibly at the mention of her brother's name. The room was silent for a moment.

Perhaps a truly independent woman would find a way to pay for school herself and wouldn't ask for her parents' help. But why should she have to? Why should she not have the same support a son would have? The same support they'd promised her before she'd left to serve her country?

Emily spoke again, keeping her voice even. "If I have to find my own way to pay for an education, I will, or find work somewhere. But all I want is for you to do what you promised before I went to France. You've said you respected the work I did there. You can hardly punish me for having done it by withholding now the support you agreed to provide before."

Her parents looked at each other for a moment, then her mother sighed.

"I don't understand you anymore, and..." She swallowed, tears gathering in her eyes. "I'm afraid I'm losing you to this new world of yours."

Emily set her cup on the table, reached across it for her mother's hands. "You're not losing me, I—"

"Stop pretending like you care." Her father waved his hand at her, a gesture of annoyance. "If you did, you wouldn't be forcing this issue on us now, in our grief."

Emily leaned back in her chair, shook her head, his words a slap to the face. "Isn't it my grief, too?"

Someone knocked on the door, cutting off her father's reply. He waved off Emily's words again and closed his eyes, his hand back at his temple.

She stood, smoothed the skirt of her morning dress, and rounded the settee. This was far from the right time for someone to visit. She took a deep breath, put a pleasant expression on her face, and pulled open the door.

Her heart hit her breastbone. "James?"

He stood on the front porch, dressed in a khaki three-piece suit, a dark brown tie trailing from the crisp white collar of his shirt. She hadn't seen him since the other day, had spent more than a little time thinking about their last kiss.

"Hello, Emily." He smiled, planting a warmth in her chest. "H-How are you?"

There was uncertainty in his voice and something in his eyes that didn't quite match the smile.

"Oh, I'm well. You?" She glanced down, saw his hands clenched at his side.

He's nervous.

"Fine, thank you." He cocked his head to the side. "May I come inside? Is your father home?"

Emily started to respond, but her mother's voice interrupted her.

"Who is it, Emily?"

"It's James Garrison, Mother." She looked back at James and searched his face, trying to figure out what he had in mind. "He wants to talk to Father."

"Might as well let him in, then." Her father's voice still

held a tone of irritation, and Emily thought for a second she should tell James to come back at another time. It was an excuse to save him from her father's temper, but James had heard her father speak and was stepping forward and over the threshold.

"James, what are you doing?" She kept her voice low so that only he could hear her.

He didn't respond, but she heard her own slight intake of air as he gripped her hand and gave it a gentle squeeze.

She was afraid her father would notice, but the contact lasted only for a moment, and then James was walking over toward the settee.

"How do you do, sir, ma'am?" James stopped next to the settee and looked at Emily's parents with what he hoped was a friendly, unbothered expression.

Mrs. Culver stood. "Sit down, Mr. Garrison. Would you like anything? We were just sharing some tea."

James looked at Mrs. Culver's rigid smile, the strained look on Mr. Culver's face. Clearly, more than tea time had been going on here.

Either that, or they just don't like seeing you.

James shook his head, sat down. "No, thank you, ma'am."

Mrs. Culver took her seat again and looked at her husband, who was drumming his fingers on his armrest.

James realized that everyone was waiting for him to speak. He fidgeted, sweat breaking out on his forehead.

"Rather extraordinary, the weather." James pointed back toward the door. "Hopefully it won't be so hot next month."

"I'd say it's already starting to cool off." Mr. Culver's voice was flat.

James took a deep breath. After all the things he'd seen

and done, this should be easy. He felt Emily sit down beside him, her presence all the encouragement he needed.

"I wanted to apologize to you… for how I acted when you invited me for dinner. I didn't mean to cause a scene."

Neither of Emily's parents said anything, so he continued. "I gave you very painful news, and in the worst possible way. I'm sorry."

It wasn't the only thing he was sorry for, but how could he ever explain it all to them?

Mrs. Culver nodded, a faint—but now genuine—smile on her face. "We appreciate that. Don't we, dear?"

"Hmmm," Mr. Culver replied, his non-reaction more intimidating somehow than a shout.

James clasped his hands in his lap, gripped them hard. "You see, it's important to me that we be on good terms. I think you know William and I were always very close friends, and…"

He faltered, intensely aware of Emily's gaze on the side of his face. "And because of how I feel about your daughter."

He heard her small gasp, saw her mother's eyes widening. He leaned forward, wanting to say his piece before they reacted. "Mr. Culver, I'd like your permission to see Emily… Properly chaperoned, of course."

No one spoke for a moment, and James's mouth went dry. Mr. Culver stared at him, seemed to be measuring him, but Mrs. Culver's expression changed instantly, her surprise chased away by a wide smile. "Emily, you didn't tell us you had an admirer!"

"Indeed." The edge in Emily's voice drew James's gaze to her. Her mouth was set in a firm line, her gaze hard. "This is a surprise to me, too."

James's heart fell. Had he been wrong to think she still had feelings for him? Had the kiss really been unreciprocated on her part? What had he done to make her so angry?

Mr. Culver chuckled. "I think you have your work cut out for you, young man."

James looked back at Emily's father, who had leaned into the chair, his face wearing a satisfied smirk.

"You have my permission," Mr. Culver continued. "I'd be happy to see Emily focusing on more normal things for a girl her age."

Emily sighed in disgust, and James could feel the heat of anger radiating from her.

Not sure what to say, and eager to get away from this strange, hostile scene, he stood. "Thank you, sir."

"You're going already?" Mrs. Culver looked up at him, still smiling. "Won't you stay a little longer?"

James shook his head. "No thank you, ma'am. I…" He searched for a reason. "My parents have some work for me."

Mr. Culver gestured for the door. "Very well. Emily, will you show our guest out?"

She stood now, too, and started toward the front door without saying a word.

"Right…Good day, sir, ma'am."

"Good day, Mr. Garrison."

James followed Emily, tried to meet her gaze as she opened the door and held it for him. Instead, she looked away. His own irritation flared. He'd come here, faced her parents, exposed his feelings, and she was angry at him? If she didn't really have feelings for him, she should just say so, rather than treat him like this. They weren't children, after all.

He stepped out, turned, and spoke in a low voice so that only she could hear. "Emily, if I've misinterpreted your feelings, then I won't pursue this any further. You seem to have made your position very clear."

She took a deep breath and stepped outside with him.

"How can I have made my position clear if you never asked what it was?"

James stared at her, not understanding.

She rolled her eyes, put her hands on her hips. "Why didn't you talk to me first?"

"I… I thought we understood each other. I thought when we—" he interrupted himself and glanced toward the parlor window, worried her parents would still hear him. "I thought we made our feelings clear in France and the other day, after the rally. Was I wrong?"

He hated the vulnerable, weak note in his voice, hated feeling exposed like this.

They held each other's gaze for a moment, and her expression softened.

"Yes… but not about that." She pointed a thumb over her shoulder. "Do you have to defer to your parents' judgement about personal matters?"

James shrugged. "No, not usually. I'm an adult."

"So am I."

He looked at her, realization dawning on him. Why would the woman who had stood on the platform on the CU quadrangle talking about suffrage want James to defer to her father over her own judgment?

His cheeks burned.

What a foolish mistake!

He remembered William's many complaints about how his parents had practiced a strict control over his life, how Emily had fought to go to college before the War.

"Emily, I'm sorry." The apology sounded weak, but what else could he say? She was still looking at him, so he kept searching for words. "It's not that I don't respect your choice. I just thought you'd already made it."

She looked at him for a long moment in silence, and Mrs. Culver's voice drifted out from inside the door.

"Emily? Is anything the matter?"

Emily looked over her shoulder, sighed, then looked back at James. "I'll telephone tonight."

"You'll telephone?" James repeated her words, trying to read her expression. Was she still angry at him? Was this just a way to get him to leave?

She smiled slightly. "To fix a date, of course."

His face split in a stupid grin, a balloon of relief and happiness expanding in his chest. "You will?"

You sound like a damned schoolboy.

Her smile grew, her amusement at his flustered state obvious. "But that doesn't mean you'll get away with something like this again."

He laughed, his relief complete now, though he could tell from the tone of her voice that she was still irritated. "I wouldn't dare."

CHAPTER 17

Emily slipped her arm through James's, acutely aware of her mother's presence behind her. If she didn't like the gesture, that was her own business. Emily was an adult woman now, a woman who'd been on her own and done more than hold hands. It was one thing to have a chaperone, but quite another to pretend it was 1890.

James looked down at her, the corners of his mouth tugging slightly upward. He winked, moved slightly closer to her as they shuffled forward in the short line outside Curran's Opera House.

"True Heart Susie," her mother said suddenly, reading the name of the film they were going to see on the marquee above the front entrance. "How exciting! It's been too long since I saw a picture, and without having to wear a mask! You know they closed all the theaters for so long because of the influenza."

James looked around, nodded. "It looks swell."

Not for the first time that evening, the conversation fell flat, an awkward silence stretching between them. Emily glanced at her mother, noting her curious expression as she craned her neck to look over the small crowd. The edge of her irritation softened. This was the happiest and most animated her mother had seemed in the few weeks since she'd learned of William's death. Perhaps it was worth the inconvenience of having her along if it would distract her from her grief.

Her mother noticed her looking, glanced down at Emily and James's entwined arms. She raised an eyebrow. Emily pretended to not notice the disapproving look that had appeared on her mother's face and turned back around. She almost giggled to herself. If she had her way, she and James would keep her mother plenty busy.

And her mother wouldn't be the only one to benefit. In the week since James had asked her father for permission to date her, Emily had felt different—lighter, filled with excitement as the night of the date approached.

The ache was still there, a dull knot in her chest that could suddenly engulf her at the strangest moments, whenever her mind drifted to thoughts of her brother. But at least now she had something joyful on which to concentrate.

And if that meant setting aside her desire to know the truth about how William died, it was worthwhile—for the time being, anyway. She looked at James as he talked to the man in the booth and purchased three tickets for the film. In time, he would open up.

She had to believe he would.

James took hold of the door from the man ahead of them in line and held it open for Emily and her mother, gesturing for them to enter. They stepped inside, followed the flow of people into the auditorium, James a step behind them. Emily chose a row of seats toward the middle of the room and scooted along the empty chairs. She'd thought her mother would position herself between her and James, but instead she had slid into the row directly behind.

All the better to observe.

Emily sat down, smoothing the skirt of her lavender-colored dress. A second later, James was standing beside her.

"Would you like anything from the concession stand?"

"No, thanks."

He nodded. "I'll be right back, then."

She watched him walk back out of the theater, drumming her fingers on her thighs while she waited for him to return. She felt a tap on her shoulder, and she shifted to look behind her at her mother.

"Just because it will be dark doesn't mean you can get away with whatever you like, missy." Her mother's mouth was in a hard line, one eyebrow raised. "Remember, I'll be giving your father a full report."

It was an empty threat. Her father was so thrilled by the idea that Emily would be pursuing the usual distractions of romance and the potential of future marriage that she imagined he would continue to support her courting James so long as nothing extreme happened.

Emily didn't bother to conceal her scowl. "I hardly expect him to start making love to me in the theater, Mother."

Her mother huffed and leaned back in her chair. "I certainly hope not. Ah, thank you, Mr. Garrison!"

James was back, holding out a red-and-white Cracker Jack box to her mother, another one tucked under his arm. "You're welcome."

He plopped down in his chair and opened the box. Emily shifted in her chair, putting herself as close to him as she could, watching the men in the small chamber orchestra arranging themselves in the pit, tuning their instruments.

"I think this is the first time I've been in a movie house since France," James said.

Emily thought for a second. "I suppose it's mine, too."

She'd been so occupied with other things since returning

from France—worrying about her brother, helping her parents with Brianna and Julius, spending time with Walter —that she hadn't taken the time to go.

James smiled at her. "This is nice."

"It's what civilized people do."

They looked at each other for a moment, and Emily knew he was thinking of the same things she was—the mud and the discomfort of camps and the front, the fear and hopelessness of wondering when the fighting would end.

His smile faded, and he looked forward. "Then I suppose I don't belong here."

"What do you mean by that?"

He didn't answer, but he didn't need to. Emily had known before she'd asked.

"I jumped into a trench. There were five Germans there with the machine gun. I shot two instantly."

She remembered his matter-of-fact description of the way he'd killed the Germans, the pained look on his face. But didn't he understand that it had been a war, that he'd done the right thing, his duty?

She opened her mouth to say something, but then the lights faded to black. Instead, she reached over and put her hand on his. After a second, he took it, and held on.

The screen flickered, and the newsreel played, the usual odd bits of information from around the country. The White Sox and the Reds were doing well, the sort of news William would have loved and Julius still got excited about.

But Emily found it hard to concentrate on the newsreel, her attention instead on James's thumb, which had begun to stroke soft circles over the sensitive skin on the back of her hand. She swallowed, glanced carefully over her shoulder at her mother, whose attention was on the screen. Emily shut her eyes, the contact bringing the memory of kissing him back to her mind, making her heart beat a little faster—and then it stopped.

She opened her eyes and thought for a second that her mother must have noticed and caught James's attention, but then her eyes fixed on the screen.

President Wilson was standing before a crowd, giving a silent speech. The intertitle came a second later.

The President on the campaign trail—for the White House and the League!

Now an image of what looked like Congress was on the screen, a politician talking and waving his arms in pantomime gestures.

The League faces tough opposition in the legislature.

She glanced at James, who was shaking his head. She didn't blame him. The League of Nations, one of President Wilson's Fourteen Points, was a cornerstone of the man's plan to create a peaceful world after the War. Emily had read about the League many times before in France, and after she'd come back to the United States. The idea of an international body whose purpose was to settle disputes peacefully made sense to her, a reasonable way to avoid another Great War. That the League would face such harsh opposition domestically had never occurred to Emily—and it left her feeling angry and hopeless.

"What a load of hooey," a man whispered nearby.

"Those damned Europeans just want us to solve their problems," another replied.

There were murmurs of approval around the theater. Emily felt James's muscles tense.

"Idiots." James frown was just barely visible in the half-light. He looked at Emily, his voice rising. "Don't they know that's what we were fighting for—to stop this from ever happening again? What the hell was it all for, otherwise?"

She squeezed his hand, didn't know what to say. It was

true that the League would be much less powerful without American support. Who then would keep the next great aggressor in check?

"They'll come around." Emily hoped that she sounded reassuring, putting a smile on her face that she didn't feel.

James raised an eyebrow, but said nothing.

"Ahem." Emily's mother cleared her throat.

A second later, Emily felt her mother's hand pushing her aside. She leaned away from James in her chair and let go of his hand as the band began to play and the film's opening credits appeared.

IT DIDN'T TAKE LONG before her mother's attention was completely on the film, and James offered his hand again. Emily pressed close against him, trying to focus on the screen through the excitement of being so near to him.

The film ended, and the screen faded to black, but James stood before the lights came up again.

"Come on."

They squeezed past the other viewers, leaving her mother behind, and made it to the side aisle as the lights turned on. Emily laughed as they ran into the lobby, then out the front door. It was evening now, the heat of the day fading into the pleasant warmth of evening, the hint of the autumn to come. James led her a few steps around the closed box office booth until they were shielded from the door.

He faced her, hesitating, and they stood for a moment, no sound on the quiet street but their breathing. Then his hand cupped her cheek, and she pushed herself up on her tiptoes. Emily's mind went blank as their lips met, every thought driven away by the contact.

But it was only for a moment. James drew back, a smile

on his face, and Emily fought the urge to wrap her hands around his neck and pull him down again, to keep kissing him. People were streaming from the front door now. It would be only a second before her mother appeared.

James winked, then sprinted across the front of the building, tucking himself behind the other ticket booth.

"Emily? Emily, where are you?" Her mother emerged from the building, her voice betraying more than a little frustration.

"Over here!" Emily stepped forward, trying not to look over at James as she met her mother by the door.

What is he up to?

"What got into you?" Her mother stopped in front of her, put her hands on her hips. She looked around and frowned. "Where's James?"

"Um…" Emily looked past her mother, watched as James snuck out from his cover and walked back into the building. "He's inside."

"Inside? Well, then why are you here?"

"I needed the air." It was the only lie that sounded feasible.

Suddenly James pushed the doors open, an exaggerated gesture, swiveling his head around as if looking for someone. "Mrs. Culver? Ah, there you ladies are!"

Emily's mother turned on him. "And where were you, young man?"

His eyes widened, a look of pure innocence on his face. For an instant, Emily could see again the young boy, the one who always got William into trouble. "Didn't Emily tell you? I wanted to ask what other films they will be playing this year."

"Ah." Her mother relaxed and looked between them. "I think it's time we headed home."

They walked down the street to where James had parked his father's Hupmobile, then rode the short distance to

Emily's house, James behind the wheel and Emily's mother in the back seat.

"Thank you for a lovely evening," James said as he parked the car in front of Emily's home.

"I had a splendid time." She grinned, barely containing her happiness. "We will do it again soon?"

"Promise." James returned her smile, winked.

If that meant he'd kiss her again, then she could hardly wait.

He hopped down, walked around the side of the vehicle, and opened the door for Emily and her mother.

"Thank you for your good behavior, Mr. Garrison." Her mother stepped out of the vehicle. "You both acted acceptably, if not perfectly."

Emily ignored her mother and accepted James's hand as she stepped down, an excuse to touch him. She pretended to stumble, thrilled when James caught her around the waist.

"Are you alright there?"

"Sorry." A shiver of delight streaked up her spine. "Lost my balance."

"Time for dinner, I think." Mrs. Culver linked arms with Emily, tugging her away from James. "Good night, Mr. Garrison. Thank you for the evening."

"You're welcome, ma'am."

They walked up the stairs, and her mother leaned in close. "I was young once, you know. You didn't trip."

Emily suppressed a laugh. "Mother, it was a long step down."

She turned around to wave goodbye to James once more at the door, then followed her mother inside, feeling light and blissful—a feeling that followed her through dinner and all the way to her pillow, where she found it difficult to fall asleep.

~

JAMES TRUDGED up the front steps and opened his front door, his emotions at war with each other. Other than the anti-League idiots, the evening had gone well, better than he'd hoped. He burst with excitement at the idea of seeing of Emily again, felt intoxicated by her. That was no surprise—she'd made him feel that way before—but now he felt guilty every second he was with her, hated himself for the information he was withholding.

"How did it go?" His mother set down the book she'd been reading, stood from the settee.

"Fine. It was great." James avoided his mother's gaze, wanted to get upstairs and spend some time alone before dinner.

"Oh. Did she turn you down for another date? Was the picture bad?"

"No, no." James waved a hand as he crossed the room. "We had a good time, the movie was fine. It was all fine."

He reached the stairs—just as his father descended, straightening his dinner jacket.

"Better get dressed for supper, son." He winked. "I know your mother is eager to hear about your night."

"I don't think it went well." The concern in his mother's voice was obvious.

"What happened?" His father was blocking his way up the stairs.

James halted, his internal turmoil boiling over into frustration. Couldn't they just leave him alone?

"James." His mother was behind him now, putting a hand on his shoulder. "What went wrong?"

He took a deep breath and put what he hoped was a convincing smile on his face. "Nothing went wrong. It was a good time."

His mother studied him for a second, then crossed her arms over her chest. "I want this to go well for you, you know that? We both do. We know you like her, and anything that lifts you out of whatever it is you've been going through since you got home is something we support."

James nodded, but didn't say anything, his throat constricting. How he wished he *could* confide in them and tell them what he was feeling. But how could they still love him if they knew?

"Go ahead and get dressed." His father moved past him, patted his arm. "Then you can tell us how it went over dinner."

James stepped up the stairs, walked to his room, and entered, leaving himself in the dark for a moment before turning on the electric light. He changed out of his coat and tie and into his dinner jacket, avoiding his reflection in the mirror by his closet.

He didn't deserve to stand within a mile of Emily, and yet he'd spent the evening next to her, holding her hand. He had even kissed her. He thought of the little scheme he'd used to trick Mrs. Culver. In the moment, it had seemed exciting, fun even. Now, it was another sign of what he already knew. He wasn't worthy of her, and after what he'd done, he had no right to even look at her.

And yet…. He couldn't remember any other moment in a long stretch of time when he'd felt as happy or excited as he'd been tonight when he'd been next to her, when he'd kissed her. How could he walk away from that?

Worse, she'd helped initiate the kiss. It was clear she really did share his feelings. There was no good way forward —he would either hurt her by staying with her, or hurt her by dropping her to conceal the truth.

Which was worse, he couldn't say.

Dinner was quiet enough. James made up something

about his leg hurting—not entirely a lie, though it had been better since he'd been out of the house more often—and invented a concern that maybe Mrs. Culver hadn't liked the film. His parents didn't seem fully satisfied, but at least they stopped asking.

Later, James lay in bed, his thoughts torn between the image of Emily pushing herself up to meet him, her eyes closed as he'd ended the kiss, and of another place, across the Atlantic, a place of mud and pain.

The shriek of a shell. The shock, the numb realization.

That night, sleep was a long time coming.

CHAPTER 18

July 17, 1918
South of Soissons, France

"Wire." James repeated the word, shouting over the grumble of passing motors. He stepped high, could barely make out the line of rusty iron in the total darkness. Something tugged on his leg, and he knew a barb had caught somewhere on his puttee. He twisted his leg to free it and kept walking, following the dark form of Caldwell marching in front of him.

"Wire, watch your step," William piped up behind him, passing the warning down, a chorus of tired, strained voices.

James shifted the weight of his rifle and pack on his shoulder, ignored the dull ache in his legs, the pain in his feet. Surely, they had to be close. He stared at the vehicle traffic pushing the infantrymen to the side of the road. The huge, bulky forms of artillery guns on their rickety carriages, the long line of trucks of every type and size, the civilian horse-drawn carts interspersed with the military traffic. Beyond, faint flashes lit the black horizon, the din of the motor vehicles drowning out the distant booming noise that James knew must follow each flash.

An artillery barrage. The frontline.

"Ten bucks says the Frenchies have no idea where they're taking us." The voice was Bird's, from somewhere up ahead.

Caldwell chuckled. "I'll raise it to twenty."

Someone else, Corporal Rodriguez, huffed. "How about both of you boys give your brains a rest and shut up? I don't think they can handle walking and talking at the same time."

No doubt the man's temper was short on account of his shoulder. He'd come back to the regiment after recuperating from the wound he'd received at Cantigny, but it was obvious it still bothered him.

"Have you seen this goddamned thing?" There was the clunk of a fist knocking on metal. "You want to carry it, Rod?"

James couldn't help but chuckle, imagining the Chauchat, a French automatic rifle the Army had issued to Bird, sitting on the wiry man's shoulder. It was an awkward-looking piece, with a funny, half-moon magazine—and it was heavy. Even with its ammo—the odd, fat cartridges the French used —distributed between Bird and Shoals, his green assistant gunner, it was quite the load.

"Just be grateful for the exercise." William laughed. "It'll make you stronger against the Hun."

Bird groaned. "Wise guy."

"Keep it up, men. Keep up the pace! That's it!" Lieutenant Robinson's voice grew louder, becoming audible over the motors. A second later, he passed by, walking down the line, calling out encouragement to the men.

The lieutenant's shouts grew quieter as he passed back along the platoon, then grew louder again as he quickly walked forward.

"Sir?" James called out into the dark, stumbling on the uneven ground.

"Yes, private." Robinson was there a second later, breathing hard.

"Are we lost, sir?"

Robinson shook his head, his expression hidden by the darkness. "Not lost, but a little late. The French know where we're going."

"And where is that, sir?" William asked.

Robinson kept walking beside James, craning his head to look back at William. "We're going to pass through a village, Coeuvres, then take position somewhere beyond. You'll get another shot at the Germans soon enough."

"Yes, sir," James and William replied at the same moment.

Robinson nodded, then accelerated past James and farther up the line, urging the men on, clearly trying to bolster their confidence.

A shot at the Germans.

James wasn't sure how encouraging that was. It sounded simple enough, harmless, like a sports match. But the whole division was walking toward a battle, and James had heard enough rumors to know it would be a big one, the great counter-attack after the German advances of the past months.

As soon as Robinson was out of earshot, Caldwell snorted. "Does he think he's our nanny?"

James frowned. "Shut up and walk, Graham."

"I'd rather have a nanny than Lieutenant Henderson," Bird called back. There were some low mumbles of agreement, and James found himself nodding even though he knew no one could see. They were lucky to have Robinson. Not every platoon had an officer who bothered to talk directly to the men.

Henderson, the officer for another platoon, seemed never

to know what was happening and left everything to his sergeants. Robinson was always there, and he always knew what to do next. Caldwell might have found Robinson's active leadership annoying, but it had won James's fierce loyalty—and that of most of the platoon.

"Son of a bitch." The voice belonged to Waddill, another man in James's squad.

James wondered what the man was cursing about and received an answer a moment later—the soft, liquid tap of a raindrop striking his helmet.

Did it always have to rain like this in France?

He groaned, heard the same sound repeated up and down the line. The rhythm of the drops increased, until, a minute later, it had become a sizzling roar, joining the noise of the endless convoy of trucks passing by.

James shifted his cartridge belt and his pack again, sending a few drops of water down the back of his raincoat. At least they'd already been dressed for the impending storm, the one they'd hoped wouldn't come after all—but that wouldn't help his other gear, or his rifle. Irritation prickled up the back of his neck—he'd just cleaned and oiled the Springfield, and now he'd have to do it again soon if he didn't want it to rust.

He sighed, kept marching in silence, concentrating on taking the next step, and the next, staying close behind Caldwell. None of the other men spoke, either, no more teasing or sarcastic remarks, just the task of moving forward, of enduring. The ground squelched beneath James's feet. The churned dirt road was soon thick with slippery mud that clumped on his boots, weighing down each step. The passing trucks whined, their tires spinning in the mud then splashing the soldiers as they found purchase and lurched forward.

"Watch your step!"

"Watch your step," Caldwell repeated, moved to the right.

"Watch your step." James stepped high, searching for another wire—and pitched face-first into a huge puddle. He gasped as the cold, filthy water hit him, soaking him entirely. His rifle slipped off his shoulder and fell into the deep puddle with a loud splash. He spat out a mouthful of mud, pushed himself up onto his hands and knees. He felt someone pulling him up until he was on his feet, looking at William.

"Are you hurt?"

"No." James was too angry to say anything else. He straightened his helmet, bent over, felt for his rifle in the water. The puddle was deep, much deeper than any normal pothole, and much wider too. He hauled up the rifle, cursing under his breath.

It would definitely need a cleaning now.

"What's holding you up?" Sergeant Daniels shouted from behind.

James didn't reply, but slung his rifle back over his shoulder, increasing his pace to catch up with Caldwell. He shivered, wet to the skin.

After a few minutes, William spoke up. "At least the rain will wash the mud off."

"Swell." James wasn't in the mood for William's cheerfulness, and the condition of the road demanded his attention. There were many more holes like the other one, some off to the side of the road, the water in them catching the distant flashes of the front, while others broke the road's surface.

James realized what they were with a start. The puddle hadn't been a pothole—these were shell craters, signs of the heavy fighting of spring and early summer.

As the rainstorm and the night ground on, James gave up keeping track of time, all his energy on the next step, mud, cold, and fatigue wearing him down. The column kept marching, the earth rising and falling beneath them as flat ground gave way to gentle, rolling hills. The vehicle traffic had petered out, and the booming of the guns was growing louder, the flashes closer, casting great jagged, tangled forms up ahead into silhouette.

James strained his eyes, trying to figure out what they were marching toward.

Another flash, and he understood.

Ruined buildings.

Coeuvres.

They picked their way through the wreckage of a French village. Not wanting to trip again, James took special care as he stepped over bricks, half-burned wooden beams and fence rails, the debris of a shattered wagon. He glanced at one of the houses, the threshold dark, the door hanging open partially off its hinges. His boot struck something with a metallic clank. He looked down at some pots and pans, a pair of shoes, and a child's doll pressed into the mud, barely visible in the wet darkness.

Had the people here made it away? Had any of them been caught in the bombardment? He'd seen enough of the refugees who'd been clogging the roads for months, fleeing the German advance, to know that many of them had escaped. The expressions on their faces and his own common sense said that plenty had not, caught by the rapid pace of the armies.

He remembered Emily's terror during the barrage at the Red Cross camp, his own fear every time the shelling started. He tried not to think of what it would be like for a child, an elderly person. He looked away, lowered his head, and stepped around a twisted bicycle. His discomfort and rage at the rain and the long march coalesced into a quiet fury against the Germans—the people who had done this, the people who had brought him and his friends out here in the rain, at night.

We'll get the bastards soon.

He held on to that thought, and kept moving.

IT WAS MORE than an hour later before they finally reached their trenches. The French guides pointed each unit to the right place, the American officers struggling to keep their platoons together in the dark.

"Sergeant, set your men up here." Robinson pointed along the trench, trudging through the mud and down the line. "Have them see to their weapons. Not long until we're going over."

"Yes, sir."

Not long?

James eased his tired body into one of the shallow dugouts scraped in the side of the trench wall, grateful the mud hadn't made it into this one. How late was it? Would they even have time to sleep?

Not that sleeping would be easy. The rain might have stopped, but James was still soaked, and his nerves had drawn tighter during the night, fraying with the anticipation of the morning to come.

"Sarge." Caldwell dropped his pack, crouched down next to James. "What time is it?"

"About one in the morning." Daniels faced the men in James's squad, who had all tucked themselves into whatever comfortable spots were to be found in the soggy trench, the familiar, terrible odor of the frontline surrounding them.

"Shoals, Caldwell, I want you on the firestep. You've got first watch. The rest of you, clean your rifles and get some sleep. I'm going to see if I can get us more ammunition."

James shifted to the side to let Daniels step by.

Caldwell groaned, climbed up on the firestep. "More shit to carry."

"Better that than running out in front of the Hun." Shoals followed him.

James got to work on his rifle. He knew how to clean the weapon by feel. He pulled out the bolt, snorted in disgust. The action was gritty with mud.

William sat on his left. "That bad, huh?"

James glanced over, tried to find his friend's eyes in the dark. "That bad."

By the time James had cleaned and oiled the Springfield, Daniels was back, handing out spare cloth bandoliers of rifle clips. Robinson followed close behind him, making his rounds among the platoon to explain the objectives for the next day. Waddill and Glassco were on the parapet now, while Caldwell and Shoals cleaned their weapons.

James listened intently to Robinson, tried to imagine the lines on maps, the names of places he'd never heard of before. The Spaders were to cut the Paris-Soissons road, and their objective tomorrow was a place called Missy-aux-Bois. The Sixteenth Infantry would be on the left, and the Twenty-Eighth on their right. The French would be on either side of the First Division.

"This is part of a great counter-attack, straight down from Foch himself." Robinson met the gaze of each man, one at a time. "The Hun's been pushing us for months. This is our chance to push him back. I know you men are ready for that."

"Yes, sir!" A few of them spoke as one.

James nodded silently, holding on to the confidence in Robinson's voice. The lieutenant continued down the line, and James returned to his nest and shut his eyes, listening to the noise of the trench. Hushed conversations, a tense quiet settling over the men. The distant rumble of an engine, the thunder of far-off artillery.

He sighed, his skin itching with anticipation, and opened

his eyes. "I give up." He stood, picked up his rifle. "Shoals, are you tired?"

"Are you wearing khaki?"

"Let me up, then." James stood, picked up his rifle. He let Shoals step down, then took the man's place on the parapet, sticking his rifle through the loophole.

"Glassco, you too." William stepped up beside James as Glassco descended.

James glanced over at his friend. "Are you giving up sleep for my sake?"

William scoffed. "Of course not. I'm bored."

James smiled. "Right."

They stayed silently like that for hours, their rifles facing No Man's Land and the flashes of war on the horizon.

"Fɪx ʙᴀʏᴏɴᴇᴛs!"

Daniels's shout was one in a chorus down the line, other sergeants in other squads giving the same order.

James pulled the blade from its scabbard, fitted it over the muzzle of his rifle. His heart pounded in his temples, and he took a deep breath, trying to calm his nerves. He'd been through Cantigny. War wasn't an abstract idea anymore— he'd seen it, smelled it. He'd fought and killed.

Why should this bother him?

Because that was then and this is now.

He wasn't tired, felt energized, alert despite the lack of sleep. He stared through the loophole at the light that had begun to gather in the sky to the east, the coming dawn. He wondered for a moment if he would still be breathing by the time the sun climbed high overhead and set that night.

Focus!

The ground in front of them wasn't like the trenches

they'd seen near Verdun. Here, there were only a few shell craters, and a great, rippling field of wheat spread out before them.

Clearly, the line hadn't been here for long.

The sky roared, an awful sound, shells shrieking high overhead. James looked up, heard the sharp boom of the French guns a second later, firing from wherever they'd been placed behind the infantry.

The rolling barrage.

The artillerymen would adjust their guns so their shells would hit just ahead of the infantry moving with them, keeping a curtain of fire on the enemy until the US forces were almost on top of them.

A shrill whistle blasted somewhere down the line, the officers giving their men the signal.

"That's it!" Daniels shouted, cupping his hands over his mouth. "Up and over!"

Soldiers clambered out of the trench, moving into formation with their platoons before pressing on.

James hauled himself up the rough wooden ladders they'd placed along the firestep, stumbled, and was up in the open. The NCOs shouted to get men in formation, but James knew what to do, moving according to memory.

How many times had they practiced this now?

Two platoons up front, one half of each in the first line, each man spread apart from his neighbor to minimize artillery casualties. Next, a gap of twenty-five yards, then the other halves of the two front platoons in a second, dispersed line. Seventy-five yards behind them, the support platoons deployed in squad columns.

James rushed forward, keeping pace with the mass of soldiers to either side of him, the heavy grenades clunking off each other in the bag he'd slung over his shoulder. Far ahead, the ground exploded, shells falling on what must be the German line.

They moved through the wheat, which billowed about their waists in the light breeze. James shivered, his uniform still damp from the rain and his tumble into the shell hole.

"Look!"

He turned to his left, saw William pointing at—

"Frenchie tanks!" Caldwell voiced James's thought, waving at the strange mechanical beasts.

They were huge, an awkward shape, big boxes with tapered, pointed noses, their prows so much like the front of a boat, a small cannon jutting out from the right front quarter. The tanks moved at an angle across the field and toward them at a walking pace, taking their place among the Spaders, who shifted to make room. Then the machines turned to roll straight toward the German positions. One of the tanks, painted in splotches of brown, gray, and tan, was moving beside James's platoon now, hardly fifty feet away.

James tightened his grip on his rifle, felt the power of the machine rumbling through the ground, the growl of its engine joining the incredible boom and scream of the artillery passing overhead. This was the strength of the Allies on display, and James's fear ebbed, replaced by a giddy excitement. He kept low as he waded through the wheat, his bayonet pointing forward, intoxicated by the force around him.

The unmistakable pop of rifles firing carried over the field from the right. James strained to look, saw a few soldiers running a hundred yards down the line, firing at something.

"Keep moving forward! Don't stop!" Robinson was just ahead and off to the left, pistol in hand.

James looked back toward where the fighting was happening. One of the tanks down on that end of the line stopped, fired. The Spaders continued their advance, and the tank rumbled on.

They continued like that for what felt like an eternity—a few hours, at least—the sun fully above the horizon now and rising higher. They encountered the occasional German resistance, which they swept aside quickly and with very few losses. Even the German artillery mostly ignored the American force, only the occasional shell striking near the advancing regiment. A stray bullet caught Lobato, a man from another squad, and he stayed behind with a medic, bleeding from the arm. Some of the tanks sputtered to a halt as the infantry kept moving. James had heard the rumors that the machines always broke down before they were really needed. He glanced at the closest tank, its reassuring mass, and hoped the stories weren't true.

Shoals, just to the right, wiped sweat from his forehead. "I think the Boche just packed up and left."

Bird held his Chauchat down by his waist, shook his head. "If I lugged this damned thing here for nothing, I'm gonna be angry."

The ground sloped gently down now, moving toward what looked like a large, scrubby ravine, a long dark line that cut across the landscape, the scraggly shapes of brush and the odd clump of trees clinging to its sides. Wheat gave way to open grass, the occasional shell crater a telltale sign of the work the Allied artillery had done earlier.

"Move down and through the ravine." Robinson punched his pistol forward. "Keep advancing. Don't bunch up."

Almost as soon as Robinson had spoken, James heard it— the chatter of a Maxim gun. Then another weapon erupted into life, and another, the gulley ahead coming alive with dozens of muzzle flashes, pouring fire out toward the advancing Americans.

James's heart knocked against his ribs. He could see them

now, the little pillboxes and dugouts, the German fortifications tucked in and concealed along the gulch.

How had he missed them before?

"Damn it, Bird!" Caldwell's voice was barely audible over the gunfire. "You just had to curse it, didn't you?"

CHAPTER 19

"Move into the ravine, go!" Daniels broke into a run, and the others followed.

"Shit!" James sprinted forward, the air around him hissing, clods of dirt shooting up where bullets struck earth. Rounds thwacked against the hull of the tank, a loud, metallic drumming. He stumbled as a shell struck nearby, showering him with dirt, the blast ringing in his ears. He heard someone scream, saw men dropping as the spray of bullets from the machine guns caught them. He tried to keep track of his squad as he ran, of William, but the blur of running men, the flurry of motion, and the onslaught of noise pushed every thought from his head except the will to move forward, to get into cover.

"Get out of the open!" Robinson was just ahead, running down into the ravine. "Get to the other—"

Robinson's words were drowned out by the report of the French tank's cannon. One of the German pillboxes exploded, chunks of concrete and gray smoke racing skyward.

Get the bastards!

The ground was sloping away steeply now, and James had to slow his pace to keep from falling over his feet. He wound through the thick brush covering the sides of the ravine, which jerked and rustled as bullets sheared off branches and tore through leaves. The Spaders filtered through the bushes, some of them dropping down to a crawl while others ran forward, the bark and chatter of the machine guns a continuous roar. A shell detonated to James's right, and a man collapsed in front of him, a piece of jagged metal protruding from the side of his helmet. James dodged to the side, his uniform snagging against a bush. The tank fired again, shattering another of the German machine gun nests.

James was nearly to the bottom of the ravine now. He picked his way through rocks, water splashing around his boots. A shallow, slow creek ran through the gulley, boiling with bullet strikes and the footfalls of the doughboys who were stumbling across it. James glanced to his right, saw the muzzle flashes of machine guns shooting down the ravine, a bolt of panic constricting his chest.

The Huns were enfilading the ravine, shooting down it from both sides.

Men were falling all around, some of them jerking around as if struck, others seeming to suddenly go limp, as if they were dead and had only just then remembered the fact.

James's eyes fixed on Lieutenant Robinson, who was tucked into a small notch in the steep, opposite bank of the ravine and framed by some large boulders and thick bushes, a cluster of soldiers around him. A faint, sunken path ran up from the notch toward the top of the other side of the ravine. James drove himself forward, slipping on the rocks, the few yards left between him and Robinson an absurd distance.

A shell hit the creek near James and blasted water into the air, engulfing him. He gasped, his vision blurred by the dirty water. He stumbled, pitched forward, and hit dry ground hard. He blinked, crawled forward, keeping his grip on his rifle.

Someone grabbed hold of him and pulled him up.

"You hit?"

Disoriented, James shook his head, focusing on Caldwell's face in front of him. "I don't think so."

He was in the notch now, along with a few men from his squad and some others he didn't recognize. Daniels was there, too, as were Bird, Shoals, Caldwell—and William.

Thank God!

Almost weak with relief, James met the gaze of his friend, nodded.

The small group stood or crouched with their backs up against the earthen wall, the same confusion and fear that James felt written on their faces.

"Where the hell are the rest of the tanks? Why don't they come closer?" Daniels pointed.

James followed Daniels's arm with his eyes as he looked back up the ravine. Only one of the French tanks, the one that had moved alongside their platoon, was there, turning in place to point its gun toward a new target. Dirt was blasted into the air just beside it, a near miss from the German artillery. The opposite slope of the ravine was still swarming with activity as men dove into cover whenever the Maxims spat their way, then got up and ran in short bursts when the enemy paused to reload. More than a few of the Americans did not get up again, lying still where they had gone down.

"The tanks can't come down here." Robinson craned his neck to look around the notch toward the closest machine gun position. "They'll get stuck."

A tremendous blast tore the air, and James gaped at the tank, which had burst into flames, struck by a shell. His stomach turned as he watched the machine burn, imagining the men inside the inferno.

"Bird, get your damned weapon set up!" Robinson barked. "Shoals, help him!"

James tore his eyes from the tank, looked at Robinson.

"You two—" Robinson pointed to two men from another platoon. "Set up some rifle grenades. I want suppressing fire on that emplacement. Daniels, take charge of it. Once you fire, I'll lead the others up the path here and work around up top to get rid of these damned Maxims."

Daniels nodded as Bird and Shoals moved toward the edge of the notch.

Robinson pointed at James. "Garrison, Caldwell, Culver— come with me. I need your aim."

A small bubble of pride expanded in James's chest despite his fear. He and William had earned the reputation as good shots in training and at Cantigny. He held his rifle close, trying to ignore the screams of the wounded and dying men still out in the ravine.

Nothing felt better than the idea of using his skill now to get back at the murderers behind the machine guns.

Bird folded out the bipod on the front of his Chauchat and rested it on the pile of boulders at the edge of the notch. Shoals stood beside him, fresh magazine in hand, while the other two men fitted the odd metal rifle grenade cups onto their weapons and loaded them. Bird pivoted a magazine into the weapon, pulled the bolt back, and looked around at Robinson.

"Ready, sir."

Robinson nodded, and Bird poked the barrel of his weapon past the edge of the notch.

"Son of a bitch!" He recoiled back, a spray of rock fragments and the thwack of metal on stone announcing the strafing fire of one of the Maxims.

James tried to swallow, his mouth dry. The Huns had their sights on the notch. If Bird couldn't get that machine gunner to keep his head down, he and the others would be shot the moment they broke from cover.

"Wait for him to reload." Robinson stepped forward, put a hand on Bird's shoulder. The Maxim kept chattering away, then suddenly stopped. "Now."

Bird thrust the barrel forward, settled the weapon in his shoulder, and opened fire. The Chauchat shook in Bird's hands as it fired in a slow, staccato rhythm. A second later, the other two men stepped forward and to the side of Bird, set their rifles onto the ground, and angled them to shoot over and past the boulder. They fired their grenades, the charges leaving the cups on the ends of their rifles with a loud pop.

"Let's go." Robinson motioned for James, William, and Caldwell to follow, then dashed out of the other side of the notch from where Bird was firing, heading for the sunken path. James took a breath and plunged after him, his friends a step behind. Bullets tore up the dirt around them, sizzled through the air, but the Americans were only exposed for a second.

James threw himself onto the hard dirt of the path, grateful for the earthen banks protecting the spot. He looked up the slope, where Robinson had taken cover and was crawling upward. He felt someone tap his toe and looked down to see William and Caldwell lying prone just below him, peering up at him from under the brims of their helmets.

"Come on." William scooted up the path, his rifle held across his arms.

James nodded, then crawled after Robinson. Dirt sprayed across the trail, spattered his back as the German machine guns raked the lip of the bank protecting the path. He grimaced, keeping as flat as possible as he dragged himself up the packed dirt path. Robinson had stopped ahead at a tangle of barbed wire strung across the trail. James cursed to himself under his breath. It was just like the Germans to not leave a path like this without some kind of defense.

Clever bastards.

Beyond the wire, the trail ran another twenty feet or so before disappearing over the edge of the ravine, where a few sandbags had been piled, a clear sign that the Germans had also dug some kind of trench or foxhole up there.

"You boys keep me covered." Robinson holstered his pistol, pulled a pair of wire cutters from his belt.

James propped himself on his elbows, checked to make sure that the safety tab on the back of his rifle's bolt was set to FIRE, and sighted his weapon on the sandbags. He took a deep breath, tried to slow his breathing, listening to the dull snapping sound of the lieutenant clipping the barbed wire, the constant roar of the Maxim guns firing on the ravine below, the occasional sharp crack of a Springfield, the chatter of Bird's Chauchat—

A dark shape moved above the sandbags for a second, in silhouette.

A German helmet.

James fired, spraying sand into the air where his round struck the emplacement above. Unsure whether he'd hit his target, he cycled his bolt, sighted again on the sandbags. A jolt of fear shot through him when he saw it—a German grenade turning end over end as it sailed through the air.

"Hun grenade!" James shouted, trying to get the attention of the others. He watched the grenade as it tumbled and hit the ground with a thud a foot below where Caldwell and William were lying.

"Christ!" William kicked out and hit the grenade, sending it rolling down the steep path. Instinctively, James covered his head as the enemy weapon exploded, then looked down.

He breathed a sigh of relief. William and Caldwell looked shaken, but they were both uninjured.

"Here comes another!" Caldwell pointed, and James watched a second grenade sail over the path. This one fell farther down and rolled away on its own.

James glanced at Robinson, saw that the lieutenant was nearly through the wire. A sharp cry brought his gaze up toward the sandbags. He shouldered his rifle just as four Germans launched themselves over the lip of the ravine. James fired, knew before his target fell that the shot had been true. He cycled his bolt as the enemy soldier fell, heard the blasts of William and Caldwell's rifles. Two more Germans toppled to the ground, rolling down the path a few feet before stopping, tripping the last German. The man fell, his rifle clattering to the ground, his arms and legs flailing as he tried to catch himself. He skidded to a stop just in front of the wire, only a few feet away. James watched the man, saw his terrified expression as he tried to stand up. He hesitated, his finger on the trigger.

"Stop!" James pushed himself up higher, waving the tip of his rifle to get the man's attention. "Stop!"

But the German was on his feet, running to his rifle, his back toward them.

"Damn you!" James fired.

The German pitched forward. He writhed on the ground for long, agonizing seconds before lying still. James's hand shook as he worked the bolt and aimed the rifle at the sandbags, waiting for more Germans to appear.

Why hadn't the bastard just surrendered?

Robinson tucked his cutters away, pulled a grenade. "Garrison, grenade. Culver, Caldwell, keep us covered. We all move right after the blast."

James set down his Springfield, searching for one of his grenades. He pulled the pin, held the striker closed, and watched as Robinson did the same. The lieutenant nodded. James pointed his left arm, remembering the form he'd practiced with the French instructors, and threw the grenade high and far with his right. His and Robinson's charges tumbled through the air, disappearing over the edge. The grenades detonated, two blasts in quick succession, the roar split by a scream.

James grabbed his rifle and sprang to his feet, running after Robinson and slipping through the small gap the lieutenant had cut in the wire. He stepped over the sandbags at the top of the path and jumped into a shallow trench running parallel to the ravine. His stomach turned, a pair of dead Germans sprawled out on the trench floor, their uniforms torn from the concussion of the grenade, a bloody mess.

Caldwell and William jumped down next to him, breathing hard. They all trained their rifles down the trench, searching for targets.

Empty.

"This way." Robinson had drawn his pistol again and the four of them turned to the right, heading toward the machine gun nest at which Bird had fired. After fifty yards, they reached a bend in the trench, and James heard voices speaking in German.

Robinson made a silent throwing gesture at the enlisted men, and James took out another grenade. They threw the small bombs and waited for the double explosion, the surprised screams, then ran around the corner, bayonets ready.

The trench was clear. Three Germans lay in a mangled heap, a few boxes of machine gun ammunition torn open beside them.

Ammunition carriers.

They had to be close to the machine guns. James's pulse pounded in his temples as they walked farther down the trench, reached an intersection—other trench lines leading to other machine gun nests—and turned right.

The sound of a Maxim gun grew louder, deafening. They stopped at another bend in the trench and Robinson paused, putting his back against the side of the trench.

"Make ready," he hissed.

James opened the bolt of his rifle, slid a clip from his belt into the action, and stripped three rounds into his weapon. He tucked the partially emptied clip back in its belt pouch, then caught Robinson's eyes to show he was finished. Robinson waited a second longer while the others topped off their weapons.

He tapped William on the shoulder. "Grenade."

William nodded, took out a grenade, and pulled the pin.

James moved himself right next to Caldwell and Robinson, ready to dash around the corner. William stepped back, cocked his arm, and threw the grenade.

An explosion, a long scream, the chatter of the machine gun falling suddenly quiet.

James exhaled and lunged around the corner, running down a short length of trench before the dirt walls opened up into a small clearing, a gun pit by the looks of it. The machine gun was knocked over, the gunner and assistant gunner shredded. A German on the opposite end of the clearing was crawling on the ground, dazed, next to the opening of another trench line—where four more enemies were emerging into the gun pit, carrying boxes of ammunition.

James knew the moment the Germans saw him. He rushed to shoulder his rifle, fired—and missed.

"Son of a—" He worked the bolt—too late.

The Germans had dropped their ammunition and were rushing to unsling rifles and draw pistols.

Acting on instinct, James charged forward.

Two of the enemies screamed and fell before James could reach them, the bark of Robinson's pistol ringing in his ears. He lowered his bayonet and caught one of the Germans in the act of drawing a handgun. The blade punched through the man's chest, pinning him against the gun pit's earth wall. James tried to ignore the wet rasping sound that escaped his opponent's mouth, removed his blade, and smashed the butt of his rifle across the German's face.

He turned to his final opponent, saw the man swinging an entrenching shovel high into the air, but Caldwell was there, parrying the blow and sending the man stumbling back. The German tried to stand up, but Robinson shot him where he lay on the ground.

"James, move!"

He looked around, saw William pointing at him from the other side of the gun pit. He saw movement out of the corner of his eye, turned in time to see the last German—the dazed one—on his feet again and brandishing a Luger.

James ducked just as the man fired, ran the five paces to him, and tackled him. They hit the side of the trench and fell together. They struggled, the German trying to point the pistol at James. James leaned sideways, putting his elbow into the man's upper arm, pinning the pistol hand to the ground. A second later, a rifle butt came out of nowhere and smashed the man's face in, striking again and again. The German stopped fighting, and James looked over his shoulder to find William standing over him, a grim expression on his face.

"Thanks." James used his rifle to push himself to his feet.

But William stared down at the dead German, his face contorted. He stepped past James, and ran his bayonet through the enemy's still body. "Goddamned bastard!"

James gaped at his friend, surprised by this show of hatred, so unlike William's mild temper.

William withdrew his blade, met James's gaze, a look of loathing on his face.

"What's wrong?" The question sounded stupid.

You're on a battlefield, idiot.

William said nothing, only pointed.

James looked around, and understood. Robinson was kneeling next to Caldwell, who lay on his back, his rifle on the ground beside him, a surprised expression on his face—at least the part that had been spared by the ragged hole that parted and mangled his nose.

James stared at his dead friend, shook his head, his insides in a knot, his throat constricting.

"Nothing we can do. Come on." Robinson snapped Caldwell's dog tags from around the dead man's neck, stood, and pointed down the trench from where the Germans had come. "I bet there's another gun this way. Let's see if we can get more men up here and take it on."

James tore his eyes from Caldwell's body, met Robinson's determined expression. "Yes, sir."

The lieutenant led the way, and James walked numbly after him, William beside him, leaving Caldwell where he lay.

CHAPTER 20

July 21, 1918

James struck the dirt, stabbed it, worked it with his shovel, and tossed it out onto the ground in front of his foxhole. He focused on the work, his body numb with fatigue. All the better to keep his mind off the past four days —the empty, persistent hunger in his stomach, the stale smell of his filthy uniform and his own, unwashed body, the maddening itch of the lice, and the sore, exhausted muscles that resisted every thrust of his spade.

And he wouldn't have to think about Caldwell, his cracked face, or the bullet that James had dodged. Had he not ducked under the German's barrel at the last second, he'd be dead.

And Caldwell would be alive.

James stopped, took a deep breath, tried to think about something else. Emily, the kiss in the booth. He chuckled, the sweet memory so absurd, so distant from what was around him, from the other images overwhelming him. If he closed his eyes, he could almost see her, feel her lips—

"What's funny?" William's voice broke James's concentration.

"Nothing." He hacked at the earth with renewed vigor. He was too damned tired to hold it together, anyway.

It had taken the regiment almost two hours to clear the Missy ravine, where they'd left Caldwell and so many others. After the battle in the ravine, the regiment had advanced all afternoon through a wasp's nest of sunken roads and wheat fields toward Missy-aux-Bois. James had watched the sunset that night, thinking back to when he'd watched the dawn.

He was still breathing, but so many others weren't.

And the fight wasn't over.

The next day had been no different—hard, close-in fighting to push across the Paris-Soissons road, sweep the Germans out of a village called Ploissy, and fend off the inevitable enemy counter-attacks. Another long, taut night in foxholes, and then they had pushed on to take the railroad beside Berzy-le-Sec.

They'd made little ground at first, but this morning they'd tried again and succeeded, and Berzy was in the hands of the Twenty-Eighth Infantry, with the Spaders digging in beyond the rail lines. Of course, the Germans hadn't let them rest in this position, and the remainder of the day had passed in a blur as the Doughboys had beaten off several German counter-attacks. Now, it was quieter—sporadic, inaccurate German shellfire, the occasional burst from a machine gun somewhere out front—and the Spaders could finally see to their foxholes and settle in for the night.

He tried not to think of anything beyond the facts, dates, and places. The rest of it, the things James had seen, the men who'd been whittled away from the shrinking American force, the violence James had done with bullets, his bayonet, and his bare hands—it was all one ugly mess, uncoordinated and mixed up in his head. Except for Caldwell.

That was clear as crystal. Better to not think about it. Better to dig.

James paused for a moment, wiped sweat off his forehead, shifted his helmet, and attacked the dirt once more.

"You about have that thing back together?" William spoke up in the darkness, his voice barely a whisper. It had become an instinct to keep quiet at night after so many days spent so close to the enemy. James knew he was lying on the opposite side of the foxhole from him, keeping his rifle pointed toward the German positions.

"Getting bored?" Something metal clinked and rattled as Bird responded from where he was sitting beside William. He'd been cleaning the Chauchat for the past half hour, disassembling the French gun onto a tent section that they'd spread over the side of the foxhole. It was slow going in the dark.

William snorted. "The Hun probably is. If he comes over to play again, I doubt he'll bother to help you with that first."

"Cut it out, and pay attention." James tossed another spade full of dirt out of the foxhole, heard the sharp tone in his voice, and didn't care. It was true that having the Chauchat up and running in a hurry would be their best chance of survival if the Germans counter-attacked during the night—or worse, sent raiders—but Bird wasn't going to do it any faster with William pestering him.

William didn't reply, and James didn't bother to look around at him. He kept digging, trying to deepen the hole, widen it so the three of them could have enough room to fire from cover should they need to repulse another attack. The sweet, green smell of the moist dirt filled his nose, carrying with it the reek of burned explosives. The foxhole had started as a small shell crater they'd found, and it still smelled like one.

James stopped for a moment, listened to the long scream

of a shell somewhere, a muffled explosion a few hundred yards away. He relaxed, kept digging, heard a few shouts and muttered curses from other Doughboys in foxholes near their own, men he didn't know. The regiment had been totally scattered and confused during the fighting. What men remained were mixed together with troops from other platoons, other companies. William, Bird, and James had managed to stay close to Lieutenant Robinson—one of the only officers who seemed to be around anymore—but they hadn't seen many of the other men from their platoon since the first attack on Berzy.

James knew a lot of them were probably dead, but he was too tired at the moment to think about what that meant.

At least William had made it, and at least Bird and Robinson were there. He could hold on to those specifics. The ifs and maybes of who was still alive were too much.

He stopped digging, suddenly regretting the way he'd spoken to his friend. The hole was big enough now, anyway.

"Will." James planted the shovel in the ground and turned to look around at William, who was hunched over his rifle. "I'll take watch for a while."

William looked over his shoulder, nodded, then—the whites of his widened eyes gleamed through the inky night, and he put a finger to his lips.

James listened, heard the sound—the scrape and rustle of someone moving toward them.

"Where?" Bird hissed, drawing his sidearm.

William pointed over James's shoulder.

James's heartbeat increased, pounding in his throat. He reached beside him for his rifle, pulled it up into his hands, felt that the bayonet was mounted. He turned, lay belly-down on the side of the foxhole, and pointed the rifle out into the darkness.

If Germans were there, they must have found a way

behind the rest of the line. James had heard of the raiders, the fierce men with clubs and knives and the brutal ways they fought. He moved his hand to the safety tab on his Springfield, rotated it to the fire position. William was there now, taking position beside him.

The sound grew louder, closer, then stopped.

"This Bird's foxhole?" A voice hissed from the darkness, oddly familiar.

James and William looked at each other, then back at Bird, who shrugged.

"Yeah. Who's there?" James strained his eyes to see, focusing on a spray of bushes maybe five yards away.

"Robinson."

James relaxed and let out the breath he'd been holding, his pulse slowing. "Come out, uh, sir."

A dark shape moved from behind the bushes, running low. James waited until he recognized Robinson's shape to flip the safety tab back over. The Hun bastards weren't above tricks, after all.

James and William moved to make room for Robinson, who slid quietly into the foxhole, his pistol in one hand.

"You boys were hard to find." Robinson pointed his pistol toward the dissembled Chauchat. "You're lucky one of the guys to your right saw Bird's monstrosity. They knew where to send me."

James glanced at Bird's weapon, took a steadying breath.

Thank God for small miracles.

Robinson holstered his weapon, pulled a few bags off his shoulder, and held them out to Bird with both hands. "Here you are."

Bird put away his own pistol, his arms bowing from the weight of the bags as he took them in hand. "Full?"

"Yes. A load made it in."

James recognized the bags now—a batch of the Chauchat's half-moon magazines.

Bird took the pouch, pulled a magazine free. "Any chance some food came with them?"

Robinson smiled, a flash of white teeth in the dark. "Sure. Over there with the Hun, along with hot showers and fluffy pillows."

James sighed, holding back a moan. Save for some food carts that had made it forward yesterday, they'd been subsisting on their dwindling rations ever since jump off.

Robinson's grin faded, and he leaned forward, looking at them each in turn. "How are you guys holding up? Need anything?"

They responded with a chorus of low grunts. James wasn't about to tell his officer that he was tired to the point of agony, or that he wished he could go home, see his parents, pull Emily close and hold her there.

William shifted his rifle, resting against the side of the hole. "Do you know where Sergeant Daniels is, sir?"

"He may be with another group. I haven't seen him."

Or he could be dead.

After a moment, Robinson pointed off and over James's shoulder. "There's a sergeant in the foxhole about fifty yards to your left. I've let him know you're here. You report to him for the moment."

"Which sergeant?" James looked out into the blank darkness.

"Rico, from F Company."

William gave a low whistle. "We really are mixed up."

"We won't be for too much longer."

James glanced back at Robinson, trying to study his expression in the darkness. "Are we attacking again, sir?"

"No, private, the fighting's done. We're being relieved. The Scots are taking our place."

James gaped at him. "When?"

"Tomorrow, maybe the day after."

James looked at his friends, sensed the unspoken change in their moods. He held himself up with his rifle, suddenly so much more tired, the relief at getting out of that awful, bloody place opening the floodgates of his fatigue.

"Right," Robinson continued. "You boys keep low, stay out of trouble. And get that Chauchat up again. I doubt the Boche are happy we're here."

"Yes, sir." Bird started toward his weapon.

Robinson made to leave, but stopped suddenly and turned to William and James. "You two did well. At the ravine. I know Caldwell was your friend."

James's throat grew tight at the sound of his pal's name. "Yes."

Robinson took a deep breath and let it out, seemed to be searching for words. "It doesn't ever make sense, who gets hit and who doesn't, but you can't blame yourself for it."

Tears stung James's eyes. Surprised at his own reaction, he looked at the ground, grateful for the darkness.

"You gave the Hun back as good as he gave. Better, even. We've made them pay. That's got to mean something."

James couldn't speak, but nodded.

"Thank you, sir," William said.

Robinson cleared his throat. "I guess that's enough of that. You let Sergeant Rico know if you need anything. Stay alert. The Ladies from Hell will be here soon enough."

Bird chuckled at the old, silly nickname for the Scottish troops and their kilts. James couldn't bring himself to laugh, still fighting the sting in his eyes.

Pull it together!

The soft rustle of boots on dirt announced Robinson's departure. James looked up a second later and saw the lieutenant's dark shape moving back toward the rear, crouched low. He wordlessly slid past William and pulled himself over to the other side of the foxhole, past Bird, who was starting to put his machine gun together again.

James rested his rifle on the dirt, facing toward the German line now—wherever it was out there.

He stared into the murk, the occasional darting fireflies of machine gun tracers fired into the night, the flash of artillery off somewhere. Death and more death. At least it gave him something to watch, to keep from falling asleep.

"He's right, you know." William's voice almost made James jump. "There's nothing we could have done to save Caldwell… or any of the others."

The others.

A long list—no one could even know how long yet.

"Yeah." James tried to feel convinced, to sound it—and failed. "I suppose he is."

CHAPTER 21

September 20, 1919

"Y ou've got it on backward, Em."

"Oh?" Emily turned to the mirror, looked at her hat, and saw that it was, indeed, reversed. She reached for the pins fixing the hat to her hair and removed them. "Thanks, Marion."

"He really does have you in a flutter, doesn't he?" Alice giggled, dangling her feet off the edge of Emily's bed.

Emily righted the hat, studied her reflection for a second. "Can you blame me?"

Marion stood and walked up behind Emily. She reached up and re-positioned the hat slightly. "I think it's natural that he'd act strangely sometimes after everything he's seen. Walt's the same. There you are, my dear."

"Thank you." Emily turned from the mirror to face her friends, smoothing the white dress she'd just finished putting on.

They were all in light, airy dresses in shades of neutral white, ivory, and pastel colors. And if they didn't hurry up, they would all be late, as well. The boys were going to arrive with the motor cars at any moment. They'd spent much of the time they should have been using to get ready talking about James—or, rather, the troubling way he'd been acting.

Emily checked the blue ribbon tied around her waist and the bow at the back. "Do you really think it's nothing to worry about?"

Marion nodded. "He'll come around."

Alice stood. "I'm sure it's just nerves. You shouldn't expect a man to make sense."

"I hope you're right." Emily wasn't convinced.

She pretended to examine some other part of her outfit rather than continue the conversation. Talking about it wasn't helping, and her friends couldn't know more than she did—which was not much at all.

The past few weeks with James had been better than wonderful. They had seen each other several more times, always under her mother's watchful eye—a fact that hadn't prevented them from kissing again twice, each time finding some clever way to sneak around her mother's vigilance and share a moment of...

Passion? Could she call it that?

Oh, yes, she could, if her own heartbeat and the intensity of their embrace were any indication. But why, then, had James been withdrawn at times? Angry, even?

Sometimes he was his old self, and she could tell he was happy, but then he'd pull away, close up, or be short with her. It didn't make sense, and the War, Marion's simple scapegoat, couldn't account for it all. Emily had been to France, too, and she was certain he understood that. Their shared experience had been a point of common ground. She remembered that first, awful dinner with her parents, how he'd touched her arm when she'd been remembering the horror of the casualty clearing station. Why wouldn't he tell her what was wrong?

"James, what are you thinking about?" She had tried to broach the topic a few days ago, when they'd been on a walk together around the neighborhood, her mother a few steps behind.

"Nothing." He had stared straight ahead, his posture going rigid.

"You can't possibly be thinking nothing."

He hadn't responded, but had kept staring ahead of him, all the light gone from his eyes.

Shouldn't he confide in her, let her help him?

Perhaps you're not as close as you think you are.

She had tried to bury the thought, but it nagged at her again and again. What if all he wanted was to kiss her—or more? It wouldn't be the first time a man had wanted nothing more from a young woman than what her body could provide.

No, that couldn't be it. Or at least, she hoped it couldn't.

If his intentions had been dishonest, how could he be so thoughtful and kind? The way he showed interest in her life, in what she thought, how he encouraged her to keep up her fight with her parents about college, something so few people—and fewer men in particular—had ever done.

Was it all just a ploy?

No. She knew him well enough—and trusted her own feelings enough—to know that couldn't be the case. And she did know him, didn't she?

Of course, she knew him! She'd known him since they'd all been little children.

That was before the War.

Emily took a deep breath, her thoughts going in fruitless circles. She wasn't about to figure her troubles out now with everyone watching her. Rather than screaming in frustration, Emily looked for her parasol, found it leaning by the bedside. "Let's go down."

"Didn't I say she was in a flutter?" Alice winked at Marion, no doubt noticing the annoyed edge to Emily's voice.

Emily would have snapped at her friend had Marion not piped up.

"Let her be, Alice."

They filed out of her room and descended the stairs, hitching up their skirts as they walked. Emily's mother was perched on the edge of the settee with Brianna and Julius, the two large picnic baskets Mrs. Rawlins had put together sitting by the door.

"Go on, now." Her mother looked up at the approach of the three young women, and Emily could see at once that she'd been crying. "Outside with you two."

The children hopped to their feet, their expressions very serious —and were those tears on Brianna's cheeks?

Emily's concern for them broke through the quagmire of her own thoughts, and she reached for the little girl. "I'll see you both tonight, OK?"

Brianna returned her hug, sniffed. "Yes, Emmy."

"Julius?"

The boy nodded, his face grim. "Say hello to Mr. Garrison."

She gave his shoulder a squeeze. She deepened her voice, made it sound serious and official. "I will, Mr. Culver."

The kids walked toward the front door, and Emily turned to her mother. "What's the matter?"

Her mother waved a hand at the door. "Your gentlemen have been here for five minutes already."

"Oh dear." Marion laughed, put a hand to her cheek. "I knew we'd be late."

Alice grinned. "Better to make them wait."

Emily studied her mother's face. "Go ahead out front, girls. We'll join you in a minute."

She waited to speak until her friends had left, stopping to pick up the baskets as they went. She heard the door open and close, then took a step toward her mother. "What happened?"

It almost wasn't necessary to ask. These days, it wasn't hard to guess why her mother was upset. She rarely cried now, at least not that Emily knew, but the loss of William still hung behind every word, the unspoken grief they all wore.

"Oh, nothing." Her mother wiped her eyes, smiling faintly.

Emily took another step forward. "Tell me. Please."

Her mother sighed, seemed to be staring at a bookshelf, refusing to meet Emily's eyes. "Your sister wanted to know if the parade tomorrow is about William. She doesn't really understand the War. She thinks everything about it has to do with him, because that's where he went. She doesn't understand why he isn't home when so many other soldiers are."

Emily swallowed, her throat constricting, the usual, dull ache in her chest. She wanted to say something, but couldn't find the words.

"And how could she understand?" Her mother shrugged, her voice thick. "How could she comprehend that he is gone when he died so far away, and when no one knows *how* he died, or even where he is buried. Except..."

She trailed off, though Emily knew what she was thinking.

No one except for James.

Her mother looked at her suddenly, and when she spoke again, there was a pleading tone to her voice. "Emmy. You're close to James. I've seen you two together. I know he cares for you, and you for him."

Emily knew where this was going. She shook her head. "I can't."

But her mother closed the distance between them and

took Emily's hand in hers. "Couldn't you just try? If he'd tell anyone, surely he'd tell you. Oh please, couldn't you just—"

"No!" Emily pulled her hand back, anything to silence that desperate tone in her mother's voice. Her mother gaped at her, and Emily instantly regretted her actions.

But how could she possibly explain?

"Mother," Emily began again, trying to keep her voice even, soothing, the tears in her mother's eyes a torment to her. "I can't push him. Whatever happened hurt him terribly. You saw how he was when you and Dad asked him for details. With time, I'm sure he'll tell me. I don't want to force him."

They stared at each other, the only sound the persistent tick of the clock. Emily watched the play of emotions on her mother's face, half expecting her to shout.

"Right, then." Her mother dabbed her eyes and rounded the settee. "Let's not make a scene in front of your fellow. We can't lose face or upset him. God knows his problems are important. Come on."

She led the way toward the door, and Emily followed, her mood even darker than it had been before, her heart sinking.

Her mother was angry at her, upset. Worse, Emily couldn't blame her. She watched her mother's deliberate motions, heard the slight catch in her breathing, the suppressed tears. Emily had decided weeks ago to put her and her family's desire to know about her brother behind James's well-being, to respect his obvious torment and let the story come out when he was ready. Her parents couldn't possibly understand what the War had been like. Emily did, and she knew better than to push James somewhere he didn't want to go.

She stared at the back of her mother's head as she opened the front door and stepped outside. Was she wrong to choose James's good over that of her own family? How could she still make that choice? Guilt settled thick and cold in her stomach as she followed her mother outside and shut the door behind them.

And didn't she want to know, too? Didn't James owe her the truth? How could she and James ever enjoy a romance together if the question of William's death lay unanswered between them?

Emily's stomach turned, the back-and-forth of her own emotions making her dizzy.

Maybe she could ask him. Maybe she could at least try. Why not today?

Because a picnic with friends is the best place for that sort of discussion.

"There's our girl."

She looked up and saw James beaming at her from where he stood by his parents' car, the Gould's Model T parked just behind. Marion had already climbed in with Walter, whose face was concealed under his hood. Tommy Webb was sitting next to Walt, grinning like a schoolboy as he helped Alice inside.

Emily tried to return James's happy expression and inject some cheer into her voice, but failed. "Good morning."

His grin shrank, and she knew he must have noticed her and her mother's demeanors. "You look lovely."

The smallest balloon of happiness lifted her up, and she really did grin now, albeit faintly. "Thank you." He was looking good himself, dressed in a cool gray suit with a blue tie and a matching gray hat. He was so handsome, so happy to see her, the obvious concern that weighed down his smile a genuine sign of his affection.

"Mr. Garrison, I'm sure my daughter is mistaken and that your flirtatious language was intended for me." Her mother crossed her arms, her voice sharp.

"Of course, ma'am. Who else?" He winked at Emily,

though she could see that her mother's harsh tone had surprised him. He gestured toward the car. "Let's get going."

Emily watched as James first helped her mother into the back seat, then accepted James's hand as he guided her up into the vehicle. She felt him give a slight squeeze, looked over, and met his gaze.

"Is anything the matter?" He studied her face, his mouth drawn into a line of concern.

She tucked her parasol under her feet. "Nothing at all."

He didn't look convinced, but he released her hand and walked around the vehicle. After a few minutes of fiddling with the engine, James started the car, and they were off, rolling over dry dirt roads and up toward the mountains.

Emily breathed in the clean air that whipped around them, trying to let it carry away her darker emotions. She'd been looking forward to this picnic and knew her friends were excited, too. She looked over at James, his brow furrowed slightly with concentration as he drove.

She turned her head, saw her mother staring out the side of the car, a weary expression on her face. Emily's feelings warred with each other, twisting into a knot. She wouldn't hurt James, couldn't force him to relive whatever it was he'd seen. She'd experienced enough in France, observed enough in James's behavior to know how terrible that memory must be.

But how could she refuse her own mother, deny her family closure, and draw out their pain?

She leaned back into her seat and closed her eyes, listening to the motor, searching for some answer she couldn't see that would resolve the problem for everyone. She couldn't find one.

She would have to hurt James, or she would have to ignore her family's suffering.

How could she possibly make that choice?

"So, Alice tells me you two were in the World War, too." Tom Webb sat cross-legged across the picnic blanket from James, leaning back on his hands.

James held back a laugh. "That's right."

How else could Walter have acquired his wounds? A nasty fall down the stairs?

"Tommy is an *officer*." Alice pronounced the final word with awe, as if she were speaking about something miraculous and rare.

"Now we're in trouble." Walter winked at James with his good eye, a grin curving up the edge of his mouth as he gave Marion a nudge with his shoulder. "You had better get the car started."

It was good to be up here, away from other people, where Walter could have the foolish hood off. To Tom and Alice's credit, neither of them had seemed bothered by Walt's appearance.

"Oh, stop!" Webb waved a hand. "My commission ended with the War." Then his face took on a more serious expression, and he leaned forward. "You guys have my utmost respect. The guys who fought, I mean."

"And you didn't?" James looked at the man's open eyes, his warm sincerity, all of it speaking of wholeness, of a clean, untroubled spirit.

Clearly, he didn't.

"I didn't get the chance. I finished with OTC at the beginning of October. I had just arrived in France and was in one of those cramped forty-and-eight boxcars to the front with other replacements when the show ended." He held up his pointer finger, looked over at Alice. "But I did serve with the occupation force in Germany."

James and Walter looked at each other, and James saw the

same mix of amusement and annoyance in his friend's eyes that he felt.

OTC? James had seen enough of the men to come out of the Officer Training Camps, the so-called ninety-day wonders. Plenty of them had been good leaders, but many had been dangerously green, hadn't known the first thing about fighting, and hadn't been good for much of anything beyond getting themselves—or others—killed.

James had been lucky to have Robinson.

He sighed, the usual crush of pain at the thought of his leader's name.

"Did you guys see a lot of fighting? Which battles were you at?" He pointed at James's chest. "I read what you did. You're the town hero."

James shifted, trying to think of something to shut Webb up without hurting his feelings. He knew Webb didn't mean wrong, but the last thing James wanted to do was let the War spoil the picnic.

"I don't think we need to talk about that, do we?" Marion spoke up, looked across Walter and James toward Emily. "Do we, Em?"

"Mm," Emily agreed. She was running a blade of grass between her fingers, her brow knotted as she seemed to examine the plant, her delicate features weighed down by… what?

She'd been like this ever since James had picked her up, distracted, distant. James could tell something was bothering her, even though she'd insisted that she was fine.

He stared at her for a moment, taking in the brilliant white dress and blue ribbon she was wearing, her pursed lips, the stray strand of her hair escaping the chignon at the back of her neck and blowing in the breeze. She noticed he was watching her, lifted her chin, seemed to look right through him.

He grinned at her, hoping to make her smile. Her mouth curved up slightly, but it was only for a second, and then she was back to examining that blade of grass.

James peered down the hill to where Mrs. Culver was sitting with a book on a blanket, about twenty-five yards away. She hadn't been the same, either, had almost ignored the group of young people—hardly the behavior of a chaperone. Something must have happened between her and Emily, and James wasn't sure which emotion was stronger—his concern for Emily, or his irritation that she wouldn't talk to him about it.

Not that he had any right to be irritated. He'd been moody with Emily a few times over the past few weeks during the moments when the guilt had been the worst, when the sheer irony of his dating William's sister had been too much to stomach. He'd deflected or ignored her questions when they had risked forcing him to talk about William's death. He had seen the frustration, the hurt in her eyes whenever he had done that.

It was yet another sign he didn't deserve to be with her. After what he'd done, the least he could do was treat her well —and tell her the truth.

No matter how good his time with Emily had been— great beyond his expectations—he could not shake his guilt. How could he have thought this would work, courting Emily while withholding what he knew from her?

No use running through it all again.

Not here, not with the others around.

He looked down the grassy meadow slope, toward the auditorium, dining hall, and assortment of little cottages that made up the Colorado Chautauqua. It was a bright, perfect day—warm and sunny, but not too hot, the approaching autumn in the air, the hum of insects wafting over the tall grass. He watched the breeze ripple the golden-brown meadow.

The grass transformed into waist-high wheat, and the spray of trees at the edge of the Chautauqua became the dark line of a ravine, the flashes of machine guns sparkling at him.

That isn't now.

He blinked, watching a car driving by the dining hall below, the sun flashing off its glass.

"Then again, why not?" Emily spoke so suddenly that James jumped, his thoughts scattered by her voice.

"Why not what?"

"Why not talk about it?" She looked him in eye. Her expression was calm, flat even, but there was something in her voice, a note of vulnerability, of pleading. "I—I was in France. Walter, too. Tom was in the Army, and Marion's seen everything Walt's gone through. Alice heard you talk about the trenches before."

James's mouth went dry. He didn't want to do this, not here, not now.

She's not giving you a choice.

She leaned toward him and put a hand on his arm. "You can trust us. You know you can. It wouldn't be so terrible to talk to us about it, would it?"

James stared back at her, unsure what to say.

Was she asking what he thought she was asking?

He looked down at his hands, saw they were clenched tight. "I'm sorry, I can't."

"You can't? Or ..." She trailed off.

No one spoke for a moment, then—

"Let's get this cleaned up, shall we?" Marion's cheerful voice broke the silence, and they all went to pack the leftovers into the basket and clear away the dishes. James barely paid attention to what he was doing. He tried to meet Emily's gaze again, but she always seemed to be looking away.

Something was truly wrong, and it was on the tip of James's tongue to suggest he and Emily excuse themselves from the group for a moment to talk when Webb spoke again.

"I suppose you'll have to talk about it tomorrow, whether you like it or not." Webb chuckled. "I read that we can expect a speech from you."

Tomorrow. The damned parade was finally here. James had found out only a few days ago that the parade planners expected him, as the so-called town hero, to say a few words. He'd wanted to find whoever was to blame for the idiot idea and knock his teeth out.

"But think of the honor they're giving you!" His father had shaken a newspaper in James's face, clearly perplexed by his son's reluctance to take the podium. "My son, in front of the whole town!"

Yes, it was an honor—an honor James knew he didn't deserve and didn't want.

He kept his attention on the stack of plates he was handing to Marion, keeping his flaring temper under control. "I wouldn't be too excited about it. If I could get out of it, I would."

"But whatever for?"

James looked around at the faces turned his way— everyone except Emily, who was staring at her mother—and tried to find an explanation they would accept.

"The whole thing is a pack of lies." He gestured at Walt. "They say it's to welcome us home, but they support laws that keep you hidden away."

Walter sighed, put his hand over Marion's. "I'll be there watching."

"Watching?" Emily gaped at him. "You mean...?"

Walter shook his head. "Mom waited for an invitation.

She's still waiting. She doesn't think the town would leave a veteran out."

James's heart sank, his own problems forgotten for a moment. "Walt, I'm so sorry."

Walt shrugged, looking down at the grass. "You shouldn't let it ruin your chance to be part of that celebration."

"Sure." James couldn't help but laugh, a harsh sound. "My chance to see people wave flags and hear them talk about something they can never understand. They just want to have a good time and look at the men in uniform and feel like they did their part. They don't give a damn about the War."

It was the truth, as far as he was concerned—though not all of it.

"No one means any harm." Alice shifted her hat nervously. "And I don't think you're being very fair. We *did* do our part. You weren't here. A lot of people knitted for the soldiers, gave bonds, ate less, or collected scrap. We did meatless Mondays every week."

Bonds? Meatless Mondays?

How could any of that compare to a trench?

Marion tucked the last few items into the basket. "It's not as if we at home were untouched by what was going on. The influenza hit hard here, too. We worried all the time about our loved ones overseas."

James realized they were expecting him to acknowledge them. "I'm certain you did."

It sounded far more condescending than James had intended, and Alice and Marion looked at each other, hurt written on their faces.

Walt shook his head. "They give you a golden invitation, and you don't want to go. I want to go, but they won't let me march." He chuckled, but the brightness in his eyes betrayed the tears he was holding back. "You act as if they've insulted you. Hell, I'd be proud to see you up there, James, even if I can't be beside you. Why can't you accept the honor for what you did?"

This was getting out of hand. They were touching far too close to it. James shook his head. "Forget about it. You don't understand."

"*I* don't understand?" Walt's voice took on a hard edge, and he glared back at James. "Who the hell do you think you are?"

Webb cleared his throat. "I'm sorry I brought this up. Please, let's change—"

"You keep saying that we don't understand, but you never try to explain." Emily bolted to her feet. "No matter that some of us were there, that the War took from us, too. Do you think you're the only one who suffered?" Her voice trembled as she spoke, shook with ragged anger and some sharper emotion, though her eyes were dry.

James looked up at her, stunned to momentary silence by her sudden reaction. "I—"

"Here you've been given the chance to speak, a chance you could use to tell everyone how it was, and you won't take it. And you have the nerve to say that no one understands? How can anyone understand if you won't talk about it?"

James got to his feet, stuffing down the words he wished he could say, met the hard, blue steel of Emily's gaze, his own anger rising to match hers. "Because they don't want to hear!"

Because you mean everything to me. Because you'd hate me if I did.

"I do." Her voice trailed off and she looked down the hill again.

All at once, James understood, his anger melting away. This wasn't about the parade at all. He reached for her. "Emily, I—"

She stepped back, squared her shoulders, and picked up her parasol. For a split second, James thought she'd hit him with it. Instead, she raised her chin and fixed him with an icy expression. "There is an entire town full of people who want to honor you, and hear what you have to say. And what do you do? You whine about it and throw their gesture away. I would think you'd be more grateful. Not everyone got that chance."

James took a step back, feeling as if he'd been struck. Before he could respond, she turned and marched down the hill toward her mother, her dress fluttering in the breeze.

"But…" He searched for words. "How will you get home?"

"I'll walk."

"No, we'll drive you." Walter got to his feet, Marion at his arm, and the two of them started after Emily, leaving James alone with Alice and Webb.

He stood for a moment, torn between shouting and running after them. He sat down instead, noticed the others were staring at him.

"Sorry about that." It was a stupid, inadequate thing to say, even to his own ears. "I didn't mean to be… unpleasant."

"Quite alright." Webb smiled, or tried to.

Alice pursed her lips, gave James a disapproving look. "We didn't even eat the butter cake."

CHAPTER 22

"Doesn't he look handsome in that uniform, Miss Marion?" Walt's mother walked into the parlor, Marion a couple steps behind.

Walt looked down, pretending to examine the olive-drab tunic he wore. It was better than rolling his eyes at his mother's comment. How typical of her to say something cheerful like that, even if it couldn't possibly be true. Handsome was not a word to which Walt could lay any claim, not anymore. Not now that half his face looked like clay that some lazy sculptor had twisted and smeared.

Marion laughed. "I think you know I'm biased, ma'am."

Walt looked up, met Marion's warm smile, his chest swelling in the same idiot way it always did when he was around her. She looked bright and beautiful, her dark hair done up under a wide hat with red, white, and blue ribbons pinned onto it, a similarly patriotic sash across her white blouse.

How could she ever see anything in him, a man with half a face?

A freak.

"You darling girl." His mother motioned for a chair. "Let me get you something to drink."

"Thank you." Marion sat, smoothed her skirts. "But don't forget we need to be moving on soon."

Walter's pulse tripped. Only a few more minutes before they would leave, before he'd be out in public, watching the parade with the rest of the town, in his uniform—and the damned hood.

"Of course. Anything for you, Walter?"

"No thanks, Mother."

She nodded and strode toward the kitchen, shouting up the stairs as she went. "Hurry up, dear! Don't make your son late!"

As soon as Walt's mother was out of the room, a mischievous grin spread across Marion's face, and she quietly slid off her chair and onto the settee beside Walt. She scooted over until they were side by side, leaned against him, and planted a kiss on his cheek.

"You *do* look handsome," she whispered in his ear.

He looked at her, found her lips waiting for him. They kissed—this was not their first time doing this, sneaking kisses when they were out together, or when his parents weren't in the room. Their covert affections excited him— and made no sense at all.

How can this possibly be?

Her hand slid across his chest and up to his face, cupping the numb, warped skin on his right cheek. A bolt of alarm shot through him, and he pulled away.

"Stop."

Her brow knotted in concern. "Did I hurt you?"

"No. I..." He looked at the floor, felt an insane desire to grab his hood off the coffee table and slip it on. "Forget about it."

The room was silent for a long moment, then Marion

sighed. "Walter, you know it doesn't bother me."

He didn't know what to say. She was so kind, so good. How could she stand to look at him and call him handsome when he couldn't stand to look at himself?

"Don't you believe me?"

The note of vulnerability in her voice brought his eyes back up to hers.

"Of course I do, and that's what bothers me."

She tilted her head to one side. "I don't understand."

"Marion...." He searched for the words, hated the uncertainty in his voice, the emotion that tightened his throat. "Don't you think this ought to end eventually, for your sake?"

Her eyes widened, and her head jerked back as if he'd hit her. "What are you saying? Aren't we happy together?"

"Yes, more than I could have imagined."

It wasn't a lie. He remembered the first time he'd seen his new face, how it had made him sick to his stomach, made him yearn for a glorious, honorable death. He remembered the long days in recovery before being sent back to the States, when Marion's letters had stopped and he'd known she'd abandoned him.

During those endless, miserable days of painful surgeries and aching, head-splitting pain, he'd never imagined that she would come back—or that he would ever be so happy again. So many times, he had been on the point of ending it. It was hard to believe he *had* tried to end it so recently, but the past weeks had seen so much progress in rebuilding his life, each success breathing life into him. His job at High Valley had gone well. He could work again, be useful again. Above all, he and Marion were together, closer than ever.

"Then how could you say something like that?"

He swallowed, tried to explain. "You are so beautiful, Marion, and you deserve someone in one piece."

She pursed her lips, annoyance flashing across her face. "There is more to this world than looks, Walter Gould."

"Of course, but..." He fought to keep his voice even. "I want you to have the best. You deserve a man who can be outside with you, who you don't have to worry about or look after. It wouldn't be right for a girl like you to settle on me, don't you see? It just wouldn't be right."

"But why?"

Because I love you.

He couldn't bring himself to say it, didn't want to frighten her with the intensity of his feeling. He searched for another reason. "Because you could have so much more. I want you to have that. I want you to live a beautiful, fine life. Don't waste it on me."

His voice cracked on those last words, and he closed his eyes, ashamed to be so emotional in front of her.

Her hand took hold of his, and he opened his eyes to see her watching him, tears on her cheeks.

She smiled, a ray of light. "The only waste would be to ignore the way I feel for you. Why ever would you want to throw this away?"

He gripped her hand tighter, tilting the mutilated half of his face toward her. "And I should let you live the rest of your life with this?"

"That isn't your choice."

"Marion." He cupped her face with his hand, wiped away her tear with his thumb. If he was ever going to tell her, this was the moment.

"For goodness' sakes, Robert! Come down!"

They had just enough time to pull apart and make themselves look casual before Walt's mother walked into the room, a cup in each hand.

"Here you are, my dear." She handed one cup to Marion, sat down beside her, and raised the other one to her lips, her face folded in concentration, her gaze directed toward the front window. "Do you suppose your friend will even come?"

Relieved that his mother hadn't noticed Marion's change in sitting location, it took Walter a moment to realize that she was talking about James. He and Marion had told her about the disastrous picnic yesterday after leaving Emily, tight-lipped and withdrawn, at her home.

Marion sipped her tea. "Your guess is as good as ours. I don't know what got into him."

Neither did Walter, and that was the problem.

"Think about the other guys who didn't get the chance you have now, to build something with what you've got. You owe it to those guys to do the things they couldn't."

Walter saw James standing in front of him the day when Walter had tried to hang himself, a determined look on his face. Somehow, he wasn't the same man Walter had seen yesterday—erratic, so quick to anger, and so unwilling to explain himself. When they'd left James standing in the meadow, Walter had been furious at his friend, his dismissal of everything they'd been through, his insistence that none of them could understand.

Now Walter's anger had become worry. Something was wrong with James, something they had all missed. Whatever it was, Walt wouldn't let him deal with it alone, not after the way his friend had encouraged and helped him before.

"Will Emily be there?" Walter would find time to talk to her, ask her to explain her side of things. She and James had been so close during the past weeks, and if anyone knew, she would.

Marion shrugged. "I think so. I haven't talked to her since yesterday."

"Hmmm." Walter massaged his good temple, thinking. If Emily weren't there, certainly Mr. and Mrs. Jones would be present to see their nephew. They'd been so helpful and understanding, so generous to take him on at the ranch. Surely, they'd help Walter figure out what was wrong with James.

A clatter of footsteps on the stairs announced Mr. Gould's entry into the room. A second later, he rounded the corner, still buttoning his brown jacket shut, all in a fluster. "What are you all sitting around for? Let's start walking!"

Walter hauled himself to his feet, grateful that his muscles were less stiff than they'd been before, the benefit of so much movement and exercise at the ranch. He smoothed his rough woolen tunic, felt strange to be wearing his uniform again. He half-expected his sergeant to burst into the room bellowing orders.

He reached for his hood, hesitated, his nerves tightening.

His mother set her cup down, stood. "Son, you know we're proud of you, even if you aren't marching today."

"I know." Walter slipped the hood over his head, tucked the bottom into his tunic collar.

"You're twice the man any of them are." His father crossed his arms. "I'm glad you're still going. The way they've treated you, no one would blame you if you stayed away. Damned hypocritical affair—"

"Language, Robert!" His mother put her hands on her hips, though she was smiling.

His father waved her off, kept speaking. "I'm proud you're not letting them keep you down, that you're taking this chance to stand for what you did over there."

Walter looked down beside him, where Marion was still seated, watching him. He offered her his hand. "I'd be crazy to let an opportunity like that go by."

She smiled, accepted his hand, and stood. "My thinking exactly."

He threaded his arm through hers, and they started for the door.

~

"WE OUGHT to have a good view from there." Emily's father pointed to a spot a few yards down the path from the stage. "Brianna, Julius, you stand up front."

Emily trailed behind her family, her insides numb, the autumn sunlight more than hot enough to make her boil in the black skirt and blouse she was wearing. They'd all come in black today, and they weren't alone, the occasional solemn stand of people scattered amid the mostly happy crowd that was beginning to gather all along Pearl Street.

Silence hung in the air, each member of the family wearing a grave, closed expression—except for Brianna, who was scuffing her shoe against the ground, playing with a pebble.

Her father stopped next to a fat spruce tree, herding the children to stand in front of him. "Shouldn't be too long until it starts."

Her mother nodded, her mouth in a hard line. "No, I expect not."

Not able to bear the veiled grief on her parents' faces any longer, Emily turned her attention to the wooden stage erected just in front of the stairs of the red brick courthouse. Patriotic ribbons and banners festooned the structure, a small podium in its center. A large banner with the words, "Welcome Home Saint Vrain Fighting Men" hung over the podium, fluttering in the light breeze.

She saw motion out of the corner of her eye and looked across the stage at the people on the other side of the path up to the courthouse. It was James's Uncle Chester and Aunt Maggie, waving at her. She waved back and glanced around her at the gathering crowd on the grass in front of the court-house and along Pearl Street, to her back. The newspaper had said the parade would come down from the campus, turn onto Pearl Street, and then end here for a speech by the mayor and the town's most decorated soldier.

James.

She hadn't spoken to him since yesterday. She had slept fitfully, lost in her own battle between her anger at James for not confiding in her, and regret for how she'd spoken to him. She had already felt raw from her conversation with her mother, and James's attitude at the picnic had ignited an explosive anger within her.

She had meant every word she'd said to James, knew that what she'd said had been correct. It made no sense that he should resist being in the parade so forcefully, or that he wouldn't explain himself to his friends, even to her. He had no business treating her and Walter like ignorant parlor soldiers, the kind of person who talked about the War without having ever seen it.

Yes, she'd meant every word. He wasn't the only one who'd lost something from the War, and he was a fool if he thought he was.

But was it right to have confronted him then, in that way? Every time she closed her eyes, she could see the shock on his face when she'd shouted at him.

She'd hurt him, and she regretted that. More than that, she'd done it in front of everyone. And hadn't she just told her mother that she couldn't, wouldn't push him? That she wouldn't put him through reliving the horror he must have seen in the War and when William died?

First, she had refused her mother's wishes, putting James's needs ahead of her mother's grief. Then, she'd turned around and lost her temper with that same man. In short, she'd managed to disappoint as a daughter and as a lover in the course of one short afternoon.

Emily fanned herself, squinted up at the sun, and wished it would move behind the spruce tree and cast her in shade.

"Emily!"

She turned and saw Marion walking toward her, her spirits lifting at the sight of her friend.

"Hello." She looked behind Marion, searching for the Goulds. "Where are the others?"

Marion squeezed past a pair of men in work overalls and stopped in front of Emily. "They're a bit farther up the street. I just wanted to find you before it started."

The concerned look on Marion's face told Emily exactly why this was.

"I'm fine." Emily tried to smile. "Really."

Marion fixed her with a knowing look from under the brim of her hat.

Emily's composure broke under her friends' gaze.

"I feel..." She trailed off, searching for the words to describe the feeling that inundated her every time she heard the words she'd spoken to James in her head, every time she glanced up at the words *Welcome Home* above the stage.

"I feel sick." Emily's voice was barely a whisper. Her eyes stung, but stayed dry. Tears were worthless, and they wouldn't change anything.

"I don't expect this is easy for any of you." Marion gestured toward Emily's family, who had yet to notice her. She leaned in closer, her expression becoming more serious. "Yesterday couldn't have helped. We're worried about James, Em."

"You're what?"

"We're not defending how he acted. You had every reason to be angry, but..." She shifted uncomfortably. "Well, Walter wants to talk to you when you can."

Emily took a deep breath, the weight of a new worry settling in her stomach. If Walter and Marion were concerned about James, perhaps it meant he was more troubled than she had imagined.

I bet it helped to yell at him, didn't it?

"I'll come over when I can." She looked down at her feet. "I should have been softer on him."

Marion touched her arm. "I wish I'd never shut Walter out when he first got home. I let myself get scared off and, well... You apologize and you do the best you can to move forward. It's not easy when you hurt the one you love."

What was that word she'd used?

Emily stared at her friend. "Marion, I don't... That is to say, I don't think we..."

"Love each other?" Marion raised an eyebrow.

Emily opened her mouth, but no sound came out. She cared for James, yes. She had cared for him for a long time, maybe always, as her brother's best friend. But love? She searched for a response to Marion's questioning look. The answer terrified her.

Before Emily had a chance to collect herself, her mother nudged her way through the crowd, interrupting the conversation. "Hello there, Marion. How do you do, young lady?"

"Fine, ma'am." Marion inclined her head politely. "It's quite the show today."

"Yes." Emily's mother peered out into the crowd. "Yes, I suppose it is."

Marion cleared her throat, took a step backward. "I ought to go join Walt. I'll see you all afterward?"

Emily nodded, still unable to speak.

With that, Marion turned and vanished into the growing crowd.

Emily looked around for a chair, suddenly light-headed.

How could she have not seen it? Had it not been obvious so many times before?

Yes, she did love him. There was no other explanation for the happiness she'd felt when she'd been with him—or for the pain she felt knowing her words had wounded him. She peered over her shoulder toward Pearl Street, suddenly desperate to find him, desperate to talk to him, to apologize.

Her head buzzed with questions. Did he feel the same? And after their argument yesterday, would he still want to be with her? How could they ever resolve the question of William's death lying between them?

She almost felt like laughing at the absurdity of it. She'd always imagined love would make her feel blissfully happy, and here she was, afraid and miserable. All of the problems she'd wondered at yesterday were still there, and all of them still needed to be resolved, but now, the stakes were higher.

JAMES EXAMINED his own reflection in his bedroom mirror, the man in uniform. It wasn't at all right like this, with just his tunic, trousers, puttees, and boots. Compared to his memory of how the other men had looked, he seemed small, bare. No cartridge belt, no entrenching tool, bayonet, trench spike, or grenades. No gas mask pouch hung over his chest. No bandoliers of extra rifle clips across his chest, no helmet, no haversack, no rifle slung over his shoulder. No mud, no bloodstains on his boots and cuffs, no choking odor, no itch of lice.

He didn't have any medals, either, much to the consternation of his parents, whose letters to the War Department had received a clipped reply. The medals weren't ready yet, and wouldn't be sent for some time. James didn't mind. He was unworthy to wear a medal, and he felt plenty ornate without the extra decoration.

The two French *fourragères*—short red-and-green braided ropes with brass ends—for the regiment's two *Croix de Guerre* citations were there, wrapped carefully around one shoulder and tucked through his tunic's epaulettes. On his left sleeve were his four service chevrons, his single wound chevron on his right. His expert marksmanship pin was attached over his left breast pocket, glinting faintly in the light that streamed through his open window.

He straightened his tunic and checked that his notecards were still in his pocket—an awful, empty speech he'd managed to put together after staring at a piece of paper for four hours. He looked around for his campaign hat, the wide-brimmed affair they'd stopped using almost as soon as they had arrived in France because it had been too bulky to pack around and not useful in a cloudy, European climate.

He imagined all the people who would be watching today, all the people who would say to themselves, "This was the War, and these were our soldiers." They would see nothing of the truth in how he or the others were dressed today, clean, well-fed men in perfect safety.

"James!" His mother's voice carried from downstairs. "You'll be late."

"I'll be right down." He found the hat, hidden by a turned-up corner of his bed sheets.

He looked at himself again, met his own gaze. "It's only for an hour or two."

He drew a breath, trying to calm his nerves.

There is an entire town full of people who want to honor you, and hear what you have to say.

Yes, people had been streaming down the street and toward the courthouse for a half hour already, eager to honor their veterans and celebrate something after years of war and influenza and uncertainty. James had seen the notice in the paper about the parade, knew what everyone was expecting.

He would play the role of a hero for an afternoon, a role he didn't deserve.

That wouldn't be too hard, would it? To be someone else for an hour?

"You whine about it and throw their gesture away as if it were nothing. I would think you'd be more grateful. Not everyone got that chance."

James remembered Emily standing in front of him, remembered the anger in her voice. Would she be there? After yesterday, he wouldn't be surprised if she never talked to him again. He'd ruined his picnic with her, had spoken too harshly and hurt her and Walter. Her response had knocked him flat.

Worse, she'd been right. There were so many people who deserved to be in parades like this, giving speeches, and here he was wishing he could avoid it.

It should be William.

And what if William had been the one to survive? If their positions had been reversed, what would William do?

James's reflection stared back at him. No, he didn't deserve what he was getting, and if the others knew, they'd surely agree. But was it too much to put up with it, to do it for those who didn't get the choice? Wouldn't doing his part, making his appearance, honor them, too?

"James!" His father's voice broke through his thoughts. "They're going to start without you. Come on, now!"

"I'm coming." His mind made up, James set the hat on his head and turned on his heel, making for the door.

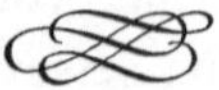

CHAPTER 23

"We'll be watching for you at the courthouse." James's father gave his hand a firm shake, clapped him on the shoulder.

"Don't be nervous." His mother smiled, and James suddenly felt as if he were some small child being left at school.

"I'll be fine."

"Of course you will." His father locked arms with his mother and started to tug her away. "Come along. It'll be slow going getting down there."

"Good luck!" His mother waved as she and his father walked away across the grass toward the parked car.

James watched them go, took a steadying breath. Just about everyone was ready, no more than a hundred men in uniform on the quadrangle in front of Old Main. James took a few steps and stopped again, unsure where to go.

There was a small marching band in front, a color guard next, followed by a small line of officers, along with some gray-haired captain, and then the enlisted men behind. James started toward the ranks of the enlisted men, but a pair of hands came out of nowhere and steered him toward the officers.

James looked about, saw the owner of the hands was an official-looking man in a sand-colored suit, straw hat, and a red, white, and blue sash. "What do you think you're doing?"

"We want you here." The man pointed to a spot next to the captain.

Not sure how the man had even recognized him, James resisted, pushing against the hand on his back. "But shouldn't I be over—"

"How can we get you to the stage if you're behind everyone?" The man fixed him with the kind of look one reserves for idiots and small children, then bustled off to do something else without any word.

James felt the eyes of others on him, looked around to see the officers staring at him, clearly trying to figure out who this enlisted dope was. Tom Webb was there, just behind James and to the left.

He held out his hand. "I hope you don't have any more butterflies, Garrison."

A couple of the officers chuckled.

James took Webb's hand, grateful for the man's humor. "I don't suppose I have the option, now… sir."

"Garrison?" The captain's eyebrows rose. "You're the one to blame for this whole thing?"

"Yes, sir."

The older man chuckled, offered his hand. "Well done, then. Captain James Merritt. I run the university's new reserve officer training program."

"James Garrison." He accepted the handshake, self-conscious to be rubbing elbows with officers like this. "I'm here because they told me to be."

"And I suppose they couldn't just put you in charge, could they?"

James shrugged his shoulders. "It wasn't my idea."

"I don't doubt it, son." The old man winked.

James couldn't help but smile.

The band coughed, banged, and spluttered to life, some old marching tune.

Merritt squared his shoulders. "Don't look now, but I think we're starting."

A moment later, Merritt shouted the order to march, and the column flowed forward, the men falling naturally into step with each other, the benefit of countless drill practices.

They marched across the quadrangle and over to Broadway, then turned right, heading downhill. People lined both sides of the street, some waving, most just watching the men go by. The band finished its song, started another one— "Over There."

An odd calm settled over James, the effect of doing something he'd been so used to doing, the comfort of being in an ordered line, part of a disciplined whole. How many times had he fallen into formation, walked like this?

Hell, how many times had they sung this very song?

He searched his mind for the answer, couldn't find one. Before he knew it, the houses of Saint Vrain vanished and he was walking in his own memory, back in the sparse, straggling line they'd made coming off the line at Soissons a year ago, marching to the assembly area at Bois-de-Retz. Some of the soldiers had started humming "Over There" under their breath, anything to distract themselves from the blisters on their feet, their soggy boots, their chafed necks and aching shoulders, their dry mouths and throats, their mind-breaking exhaustion.

"Louder, men!" Lieutenant Robinson had shouted. "Sing like Spaders! For the colonel!"

The word had come that morning that Colonel Hamilton Smith, the man who'd given them the blue arrowhead insignia, the man who had made them Spaders, had been killed. They started murmuring the words together, their voices a crescendo. James had sung as loud as he could manage, singing for all the men they were leaving, his voice raspy with thirst.

"Tommy!"

Alice's shout jogged James's brain back to the present. He looked to his right, saw Alice's folks standing with people who looked like they must be Webb's family. They all waved, and James heard one of the other officers snickering.

"Is that your girl, Webb?"

"Not bad," another added. "Not bad at all. I wouldn't mind rolling—"

"Leave her alone, will you?" Webb cut the other man off, sounding more than a little embarrassed.

Luckily for him, they were past Alice and her folks now, almost at the bottom of the hill, the crowds alongside the road getting thicker as they neared the intersection with Pearl Street.

The band was playing "It's A Long, Long Way to Tipperary" now, and they were just about at Pearl Street when James spied a couple people leaning out slightly into the street up ahead, waving at the marching veterans. It took a moment for him to realize they were waving at *him*, and just a second longer to recognize them.

Walter and Marion. Marion wore bright, patriotic ribbons, and Walt was in his uniform—and the hood.

A gentle relief washed through him at the sight of his friends, their display of affection for him. After what had happened, he had worried he'd alienated them forever, right along with Emily. He raised his hand to wave back.

"Who is that?" One of the voices that had teased Webb before spoke up.

"A friend of Alice's," Webb replied. "Got hit in the face."

"And he couldn't march with us?" Merritt spoke now, his tone incredulous.

"You know the law, sir." Webb sighed.

The first voice whistled. "Damned shame."

"Yeah, it is." James said, more to himself than anyone. He was almost even with his friends now, and could see Marion's happy expression, but could only guess at Walt's.

This wasn't right.

James clenched his fists, found himself breaking from line, walking over to his friend.

"Hey, Garrison!" Webb shouted after him. "What are you doing?"

James ignored the curious faces looking toward him in the crowd, the men in uniform staring as they passed him.

He stopped in front of Walter and crossed his arms, taking in the inquisitive stares of Mr. and Mrs. Gould, who stood right behind their son.

Marion gaped at him. "James! They're leaving you behind."

He ignored her, staring into the pool of darkness cast over Walter's face by the heavy black hood. "Fall in."

"You don't outrank me." Walt's voice was unreadable, and for a second, James doubted his decision. He'd put his friend on the spot, made a scene.

What if Walter didn't want to march after all? What if he preferred to hide from view?

But then he stepped forward, slowly at first. "I'll catch up with you later, Marion."

She wiped her eyes. "Go."

"You hold your head up high, son!" Mrs. Gould shouted after them, her voice choked with emotion.

Walter waved back, murmuring under his breath. "I think you've let that medal get to your head, giving orders like that."

James grinned. "You told me I should accept the opportunity. There, I've accepted it."

They quickened their pace to reach the front of the line, James glancing at his friend, noticing his slight limp. It was so much less than it had been, and he noticed with a start that Walt hadn't brought his cane.

They stepped into formation alongside Captain Merritt, the other officers gawking at them with incredulous expressions.

Merritt gave them a sideways glance, nodded, and pointed toward the hood. "You're out of uniform, private."

"I...." Walter trailed off, and James could sense his friend's hesitation.

"He *does* outrank you, pal." James gave Walt's shoulder a squeeze.

Walt reached up and pulled the hood over his head, revealing his broken face. James distinctly heard a gasp from somewhere in the crowd, but Walter raised his chin, kept his eyes forward.

James stared into the crowd, satisfied at the occasional shocked face he saw there.

Let them look. Let them see the War. Let them see what it did.

How could they ever really know?

The parade turned onto Pearl Street, the band music reverberating off the store fronts, the paved sidewalk on both sides of the narrow street packed with people. In a few blocks, the street opened up on the left, the small park surrounding the courthouse. James wiped his forehead, a small trill of fear in his throat.

There were so many people, more than he'd thought there would be.

The flash of cameras caught him off guard, made him blink as the parade column came even with the path that led from the street to a stage that had been erected in front of the courthouse's front steps. The band turned left toward the stage, and the color guard followed.

"Left face, private." Merritt gestured for James to turn with him toward the stage as they neared the path.

James looked at Walter.

"You said you'd accepted it." He smiled. "Go."

"My big mouth…."

James followed Merritt as he turned sharply onto the path, leaving the body of the parade. He glanced over his shoulder, saw that the rest of the column was continuing down Pearl, filling the length of the street in front of the Courthouse.

James swallowed, turned his attention forward, glad to at least have Merritt beside him. The crowd was so close here, an arm's reach away, smiling, curious gazes turned his way, pressing in on him, the long, narrow walk somehow unsettling. He blinked hard, putting away the image that sprung to his mind, of men filing down a trench, tilting shoulders to pass each other.

Don't lose your composure now, not here.

He raised his chin, willed himself to focus on the present. The color guard had come to stand on stage, while the band was below it and off to the left.

"Halt!"

A voice called out from behind, and James looked behind him, saw the column come to a stop out on the street.

"Left… face!"

Only a few more yards left to the stage, and James caught the eyes of Uncle Chester and Aunt Maggie, who were just in front of the stage on the left side. They waved, and he could see his parents on tiptoe behind, waving, too.

James attempted to smile at them, but knew that he'd only managed a grimace, his nerves winding tighter with each step. Then he saw Emily.

She was standing with her family, looking up at the stage, her face unreadable, her brow furrowed.

His heart sank. She still looked upset.

How could she not be?

She turned, and he knew the moment she saw him. She met his gaze, held it. For the briefest moment, James didn't hear the music, didn't feel the weight of the crowd around him. Everything fell silent, his step slowed. Then she nodded, and the smallest smile curved her lips upward, a light moving through her expression, softening the intense blue of her eyes.

He really did smile now, the chaotic mix of band music and chattering voices returning to him in a rush, his nerves quiet, a strange calm stealing over him.

The moment passed, and he followed Merritt up the narrow wooden steps to the top of the stage, where a man in a dark coat and tall hat was standing, undoubtedly the mayor.

"Welcome, Captain. Thank you for coming." He beamed at Merritt, and the two men shook hands.

"Mr. Mayor."

The man turned toward James and thrust out a hand. "A pleasure to meet you, Private Garrison. You've done your town proud."

He took the mayor's hand, hid his grimace at the man's vice-like grip. "Thank you, sir."

"Over here, gentlemen." Another man, short, round, and wearing a brown suit, pointed to a spot beside the podium.

James nodded and moved to the correct place, Merritt beside him. He looked out at the sea of heads, hats, and parasols in front of him, the broad khaki band of veterans at attention among the lighter colors of the happy crowd. Reporters stepped out onto the path below, hauling their cameras with them. They stuck their heads under their light hoods, dazzling the stage with the pop and sparkle of their flash lamps. A quick movement caught James's eye, and he looked down at his parents, who were still waving. Not sure what else to do, he waved back.

With a final flourish of brass and drums, the band stopped playing.

The crowd hushed.

The mayor stepped forward, waved his arms. "Ladies and gentlemen!"

James's nerves began tightening again. He looked down at Emily, saw she was still watching him. He concentrated only on her, only half-listening to the mayor's speech. The man talked about love of country, the great, proud heroism of Saint Vrain men, their joyful return home.

"Not as conquerors, but as liberators and heroes, wearing the laurels of glorious victory!"

The people cheered and clapped.

Emily's eyes flicked to the mayor and back to James, and she shook her head gently.

James nodded.

Only a politician could describe a war like that.

"Let me present Captain James Merritt, commander of the University of Colorado Reserve Officer Training Corps."

Merritt walked over to the podium, accepted another handshake from the mayor.

The old captain cleared his throat. "Ladies and gentlemen, today I have the distinct honor of presenting to you a young man of remarkable courage."

James kept his attention on Emily, trying to ignore the awkward feeling of having a stranger talk about him as if they were old friends, as if Merritt had been there with him throughout the past three years.

As if James deserved any of the glowing praise the captain was heaping on his name.

"Enlisted in 1916 for peace," he was saying, "but sent to the battlefields of the Great War."

Merritt summarized the engagements James's regiment had been in, spoke of the citations the unit had received, a procession of facts from his service dossier, and his expert marksman qualification.

"I'd say I rubbed off on him."

Uncle Chester's familiar voice brought James's attention away from Emily, and he saw his uncle tapping Aunt Maggie's shoulder. "Hey, didn't you hear me?"

"Oh, stop it, you," Maggie said, smiling.

"And now, I am proud to present Private James Garrison, recipient of the Distinguished Service Cross and French Croix de Guerre, a hero of the World War."

The people erupted into cheers and applause, a roar of sound. Someone nudged James's arm, and he turned to see Merritt looking at him. It took James a second to realize what the man was expecting.

He saluted, waited for Merritt to return the gesture, and then stepped toward the podium.

Merritt leaned toward him, barely audible over the crowd. "They're clay in your hands. You'll do fine, son. Relax."

James nodded, his mouth full of cotton. He slipped a shaking hand into his pocket, pulled out the few notecards he had prepared.

Beside him, the mayor raised a hand, quieting the uproar.

"Um...." James's voice came out a whisper. He took a steadying breath, trying to read what he'd written. "Ladies and gentlemen. I am glad to be in front of you today, to represent for you the just and noble cause we fought for, and to show the gratitude we all feel for the nation that stood behind..."

He trailed off, the words sounding hollow, forced. He

caught Emily's gaze again, saw her encouraging smile. Seconds ticked by, a cough from somewhere below. He looked beside Emily, saw little Brianna and Julius, the boy who looked so much like his brother.

He knew what he had to do. He looked out over the people, cleared his throat again. "Ladies and gentlemen, I know many of you had hoped I'd talk about how I got my medal, but I'm afraid I will disappoint you today. I'd like to talk instead about the men I knew in the Army. I had a lot of friends in the service. After a day in the trenches, I can tell you we didn't wonder too much about causes or glory or what it was for. We were too tired and too scared to think much about any of that. What we did in France, we had to do, and I'd like to believe we were right to do it. Sometimes, I don't know."

James heard the growing confidence in his voice, ignored the perplexed look on the mayor's face. He pressed on. "But I do know that all of the fellows I served with were good men, much better than I am. A lot of them couldn't be here today. *Those* men are heroes."

He heard a sniffle, saw Mrs. Culver holding a handkerchief to her mouth, her face crumpled.

James looked toward the column of men at attention, searching for Walter. "Other guys suffered worse than I ever did and came home in pieces only to be made to hide away, as if they'd done something wrong, or shameful. Those men are heroes, too."

James saw some heads nodding in the crowd. He found Walter among the soldiers, standing at attention, his head held high.

If only William were with them.

James's throat tightened, and he fought to keep his voice even. "I was asked to stand here so you can see a hero. Look around you, at the families in mourning. Remember their sons, fathers, and brothers in our cemeteries, and the ones who lie in French soil. Those are your heroes. I am not half what those men were."

Worse, you're a damned fraud.

It was too close to the truth, and James knew he had to finish this, had to get off this stage, away from the mass of people who were watching him, totally silent now.

"I am honored by the warmth and affection you have shown me today. Truly, I am. There are many who should have got the chance to be here, and for them I am glad to accept your kindness." He meant it, hoped Emily could hear that he meant it. "But please don't save all of your praise for me. There are others who deserve it more. Thank you."

He stepped back and made way for the mayor, who rushed to the podium.

"Thank you, Mr. Garrison, and let us all express our thanks for your selfless service and distinguished gallantry!"

The crowd applauded, and the mayor continued his speech, the same rhetoric as before, the same grand gestures.

Captain Merritt grinned. "I don't think he was expecting that."

The mayor finished his speech, the people clapped again and began to disperse, a few final flashes from the cameras. The band started up, and the round man in brown reappeared, pointing for James and the captain to vacate the stage.

Thank goodness.

James let Merritt pass in front of him, followed him back down the stairs. He reached the ground and had only made it a few steps away from the stage before Emily was there in front of him. He swallowed, searching for the words he'd wanted to say since he'd last seen her.

"I'm sorry, Emily. You were ri—"

She interrupted him, flung her arms around his neck, and

pulled him against her. "Let's forget about all that. Just for a minute."

He took off his hat, ducked his head under the brim of hers, and wrapped his arms around her, holding her fast. He breathed in the clean scent of her hair, her face warm against his, and he closed his eyes, savoring the feel of her against him.

God, she was everything. How could he let anything threaten what was between them?

How could he ever hope to keep her?

"Ahem."

James knew without looking that Emily's parents were there now, too. He opened his eyes and pulled himself away from her. Mr. and Mrs. Culver were standing there with the children.

"Good afternoon, sir." He turned toward Mrs. Culver. "Ma'am."

Mr. Culver seemed to study him for a moment, and James was sure the man was about to scold him. Instead, he took hold of James's hand, shook it. "I must confess that yours was an unusual speech, but I appreciate that you turned the focus to the dead. I think that was…appropriate."

"Thank you, sir."

"Unlike that display just now." He pointed at Emily. "Remember you're in public."

She sighed, and Mrs. Culver dragged the children forward with her, wiping at her red eyes. "We're very happy for your award, James. I imagine William would be, too."

Her words cut him, and he couldn't help but wince.

"Thank you, ma'am."

"There he is!" James's father pushed through the thinning crowd, his mother, Uncle Chester, and Aunt Maggie behind, all of them talking at once.

"Didn't I say you could do it?" His father rubbed his hands together. "You didn't look nervous at all up there, did you?"

"I think that's hard to believe—"

"We're so proud of you for finally doing it." His mother pulled him into a hug. "I know you had your doubts, but I think you said the right things."

"I hope—"

"I don't think the mayor appreciated that part of it." Chester shook James's hand, clapped him on the shoulder. "All for the good, my boy."

Maggie scoffed in exaggerated disgust. "You're impossible." She looked at James, smiled. "I heard some of the newsmen talking about what you did with Walter. Well done."

James held up his arms to cut the stream of conversation. "Thank you. Truly, thank you. Now, can we go home?"

He wound an arm through Emily's and pointed toward the path. They turned and strode slowly back toward Pearl Street—before the reporters stepped in front of them, blocking their way.

"A photo for the paper, Private Garrison?"

"Say, is that your girl? A photo with you and your lady?"

James waved the men away. "That isn't necessary, thanks."

"I don't see why not!" His father nudged him on the back. "Go ahead!"

James opened his mouth, but the men with the cameras were already puttering about, working their devices.

"Right, now hold still!"

"James Garrison?"

He blinked, the burst of light from the cameras' flash lamps in his eyes.

Had someone been calling his name?

"James Garrison?"

He looked around, saw a young woman wading against

the stream of people heading back toward Pearl Street. Everyone around him had noticed her, too, had turned to look at her approach.

"A new fan of yours?" One of the photographers winked at James.

The other man turned to Emily. "You may have competition, miss."

The young woman slid between the cameras and came to stand in front of them. "James Garrison?" She was breathless, urgency in her voice and her green eyes.

"Y-yes." James looked at the woman, tried to remember if he'd seen her before. "Do we know each other, miss?"

She looked to be about his age, wore a dark skirt and ivory blouse, her light brown hair in a bun beneath a wide hat, a black band around her arm.

"I'm Susan, Susan Mabee."

James shared a glance with Emily, saw she was just as confused as he was. "I'm sorry, Miss Mabee, but I don't think we've met."

"We haven't. He may not have mentioned me to you. Maybe it wouldn't have been proper protocol..." Susan's voice trailed off.

James shook his head, confused. What was this about?

"Who wouldn't have mentioned you?"

She raised her chin. "I'm Dwight Robinson's fiancée."

CHAPTER 24

August 6, 1918
Near Pont-à-Mousson

"Keep low, dammit!" James reached up, slapped the helmet of the kid in front of him.

Cole was his name, Virgil Cole. One of the new guys.

Cole flinched, crouched down, his step faltering as they all wound down the narrow zigzag of the communication trench.

"Sorry!" Fear pinched Cole's voice, made James's already thin nerves fray even more. There was no room for that kind of fear, that warm, soft inexperience.

That sort of thing got people killed.

"Don't be sorry." Sergeant Daniels, in front of Cole, turned his head to speak over his shoulder. "Just pay the hell attention." He tapped the shoulder of the man in front of him, Mullins. "Both of you."

"Yes, Sarge." They both spoke at once.

Collins, tromping behind James, laughed. "We're breaking you kids in the US Army way."

Cole and Mullins weren't the only ones who needed breaking in. Just about half the men in the regiment were replacements for the guys they'd lost at Soissons, fellows fresh off the trains from St. Nazaire, where shiploads of raw, untested American troops were arriving every day. In some ways, it was good to see the regiment back up to strength. When they'd formed ranks at Orry-la-Ville after the long march back from their foxholes near Berzy-le-Sec, James had stared at the assembled regiment with a kind of numb shock —the most emotion he'd been capable of mustering in his exhaustion. Some companies had been reduced to the size of platoons, and even those that had fared well in the fighting had lost a huge number of their effectives.

In James's own squad, they'd lost almost half their number. Glassco, Waddill, and Caldwell, gone. Ripa and Miller wounded. Since he and William had been separated from the squad during the fighting, James had feared it would be worse. Thankfully, Daniels and Corporal Rodriguez had survived, along with Collins, Killeen, Dobson, McLean, Pippert, and, of course, William and himself. Bird and Shoals had made it, but their squad, the platoon's automatic rifle squad, had lost seven men. The regiment had returned from Soissons as a shell of its former self, the survivors tattered and worn out. That, combined with the deaths of Colonel Smith and Lt. Colonel Elliott, had left not a few of the men wondering what would become of the regiment and if they would ever be in good fighting order again.

But then they'd taken the train to Pont-à-Mousson, and the replacements had started streaming in by the hundreds. Their green enthusiasm had given the regiment new life— and annoyed the hell of out James. It was as if the men *wanted* to have their heads shot off, talking about adventure and glory, and not paying attention. They made James nervous, on edge—and he wasn't the only one.

"Sergeant, your squad has the listening post today." Lieutenant Robinson, newly promoted to command of the company, had stopped by in the morning to issue orders and inspect the platoon's progress with the new men. "Make sure to take a mix of experienced men and replacements with you. I want these soldiers fit for service."

"Yes, sir." Daniels had nodded grimly, picked up the shotgun he'd taken to carrying in lieu of a Springfield as he'd turned to the squad. "Cole, Mullins, you're with me. Garrison, Collins, you too."

James had just started his letter from Emily, had read she and some of the other Red Cross girls would be in Paris soon on leave. The mail service had finally caught up with the regiment early that morning, bringing him and William two letters each from Emily. Seeing her handwriting and hearing her voice in his head as he read the letters was a small taste of something beautiful and clean amid the filth of the front lines.

It was something to which James had looked forward ever since he'd seen the two envelopes with his name on them. It was also a pleasant way to pass the time, something to get his mind off Caldwell, that split moment in the German machine gun nest. He saw the German in front of him again, raising his pistol. He ducked, pushed forward, gripping his rifle, heard the blast of the man's weapon —

James blinked, took a deep breath.

Not here. Not now. Focus on the present.

James wouldn't be any better than Cole if he couldn't concentrate. He focused on his own footsteps, picking his way over the soggy wooden duckboards along the bottom of the trench, tilting the muzzle of his rifle higher to fit its long form through the narrow sections. The post shouldn't be too far away now, just a few dozen more yards. The air overhead, getting brighter each minute in the growing morning light, was eerily quiet, a faint whistle of breeze through barbed wire.

James gripped his rifle tighter.

They were alone out here.

The listening post was well forward of the frontline trench, a small island in the middle of No-Man's-Land. It was the ideal spot to monitor the enemy and warn of attacks —or simply a very convenient place to get killed in a German raid.

"I was the fourth man to go in with that whore," Daniels was saying, his gaze fixed on the top of the parapet, weapon ready, betraying his casual tone. "And I didn't want to be working in some other man's seed, so I had her give me a French job. She must have had a big mouth, because she took my whole cock in it."

Cole and Mullins looked at each other, clearly not used to this kind of language.

Daniels chuckled, shaking his head as he walked. "Women. I ended up here because of some farm girl in the nineties. She said I got her in trouble. I had to leave. No work anywhere, so I joined the Army."

Mullins adjusted his helmet on his head. "Well, did you get her in trouble, Sarge?"

"She got herself in trouble." He rubbed his stubble, grinned. "But I suppose I helped."

Mullins chuckled, though it was obvious the bawdy story hadn't taken his fear away.

James crouched lower, the trench shallower as they moved forward, its walls in a worse state of repair, crumbling inward. Typical. The day listening posts were abandoned every night and didn't benefit from the constant frenzy of repair work and activity the regular trenches received.

Daniels held up his hand.

James stopped, his heartbeat kicking up.

"Huns," Daniels hissed under his breath.

James shouldered his rifle, prepared to shoot at the first sign of motion on the parapet. He heard it then—voices in the harsh, strange rhythm of German. They all stayed like that, crouched in the trench, weapons ready, as seconds ticked by with agonizing slowness. None of them spoke, their breathing unbelievably loud. The voices faded away, replaced again by the sighing breeze.

Daniels relaxed. "That's just the wind changing, blowing their voices over from their trench." He turned and fixed Cole with a serious expression. "We're not far from their front line."

Cole nodded, sweat trickling down his temple.

Give it some time, and you'll be in *their front line, kid.*

The men started moving again, and after another minute of walking, the trench opened up on both sides into a small clearing, not unlike a shell crater, save for the old, gray wooden revetting holding up the sides and the trench periscope mounted on the front, pointing toward the German lines. James scanned around, looking for any signs of danger. It wasn't unusual for the Hun to sneak into their posts at night and leave delayed explosives or other booby traps to kill the Allied troops who came to man the spot in the morning.

Some enterprising individual had taken hundreds of empty ration cans and pressed them into the ground to make a strange sort of tiled floor that clicked under the hobnails of their boots. Someone had nailed a few hooks into wooden boards for hanging gear, and an empty shell case hung on fraying twine from a board jutting out from under some of the parapet sandbags, a makeshift gas alarm.

A shrill whistle, an explosion.

They all flinched—but the new men crumpled, dropped

to a squat, their eyes squinted shut. James slung his rifle on his shoulder, couldn't decide whether he wanted to laugh or smack the men upside the head. If they acted like this from a single mortar, how would they react under a bombardment?

"Son of a bitch!" Mullins opened his eyes, looked around at them. "Are they shelling us?"

"Nah, they don't want to ruin a quiet sector." Daniels sniffed, kicked at the ration tin floor. "They just want to keep their mortars from rusting and impress their officers. Say, they did a nice job with the floor."

Collins snickered, and James watched Mullins and Cole stand up, the embarrassment on their faces obvious.

They were so damned young.

And they aren't the only ones.

An image flashed into James's mind. The first time he'd been in a trench, the callous humor in the eyes of the French soldiers at his reaction to the artillery, the corpse in the trench well, vomiting in the muddy water. Guilt tugged at him, and he searched for something to say, some wisdom to impart to make the men feel more at ease.

"If you hear the whistle, that means you're alright."

Cole and Mullins looked at him, confused.

James tried again. "If you can hear the whistle of the shell, it's not going to hit you. You can't hear the ones that hit close to you."

"Okay." Cole swallowed, but didn't look reassured at all.

"Right, let's get to work." Daniels pointed at the periscope. "Mullins, you go ahead and man the periscope. Collins, you can take the parapet next to him. We three are going to do some work shoring up the revetting a few yards down. Drop your packs and get out your tools. Take your weapons, too."

James suppressed a groan. He'd been hoping to spend some time opening his letters from Emily while waiting for his shift at the parapet. He hadn't had time to write since before Soissons, and he wanted to let her know he was alive before she became too worried.

James leaned his rifle against the side of the post near the entrance to the trench, made room for Collins to walk past him. He unhooked his haversack from his cartridge belt, and eased it to the ground. He freed his bayonet and T-handle entrenching shovel from straps securing them to the haversack. He worked the bayonet scabbard's hooks into the eyelets on his belt and took the shovel in his hand. He stood, picked his rifle back up, and slung it over his shoulder, adjusting the gas mask bag hanging in front of his chest.

Cole was fumbling with his haversack on the ground, his hands shaking nervously. Collins was already at the parapet, and Mullins was beside him, awkwardly traversing the periscope around.

Daniels stepped toward Cole.

"Do you need help with that, son?"

Cole shook his head, grinned. "No, Sarge. Just nervous."

Daniels sighed. "Take a moment."

Cole took a deep breath, stood with haversack in hand, and looked behind him. There was something that looked like a small bench there, a box fashioned out of fresh wood—colored blonde rather than the old, sodden gray of the revetting supports—with a neatly folded pile of empty sandbags on top of it.

James stared at it, such a new, comfortable-looking thing, oddly out of place in the dirty, worn post. He noticed the small sprinkling of sawdust on the ground around it, a metallic glint between gaps in the bench's wooden boards. Fear skittered up his spine. "Cole, wait a second."

"What?" Cole was making to sit down, didn't seem to understand.

Daniels had noticed, too, was reaching for Cole. "Stop! Don't sit—"

James toppled backward, knocked over by the sharp blast. He hit the revetting, rolled off it and onto the ground, dazed, his helmet clattering over the ration can floor. He shook his head, blinked, tried to stop the Earth from spinning around him.

Someone was screaming, moaning, something warm and wet trickling down his face. He heard a groan, realized it was coming from his own mouth. He brought a hand up to his face, wiped at the moisture. His eyes finally focused on his own fingers. His hands were covered in blood, his nose choked with the smell of it. He rolled onto his back, looked down his body, and his stomach turned. He was spattered with blood from head to toe, covered with it. But—

He patted himself, found no injuries, no torn cloth.

The blood wasn't his own.

Someone was still groaning, and James pushed himself slowly to a sitting position, took in the devastated post. The spot where Cole had been was blasted to bits, the revetting torn and blackened, splattered with blood. Collins and Mullins were on the ground below the parapet, getting to their feet, also covered in blood. Daniels was writhing on the ground, moaning.

Where was Cole? James looked around, his mind in a fog, working slowly. He realized with a hard knock in his chest.

The explosion had blasted the kid to pieces.

He heard shouts, distant calls in English and German. Both sides would have heard the explosion, seen the puff of smoke and fire—which meant the Huns could be coming to press their advantage and knock out the post.

James shook his head again, looked for his rifle, found it lying a few feet from him. He took hold of it, dragging it behind him as he worked his way over toward Daniels.

"Collins." His voice was a raspy whisper in his throat. He swallowed, tried again. "Collins!"

"I'm alright." Collins was standing now, helping Mullins to his feet.

"Get on your rifle, Collins. If they're coming—"

"Right." Collins turned shakily toward the parapet, trained his rifle out. Mullins just stood there, staring at Daniels.

James had reached the sergeant now, was searching for the man's bandage pouch on his belt—impossible to do when he wouldn't hold still. "Take it easy, Sarge. I've got you."

"Oh God." Mullins's voice held an edge of panic.

They didn't have time for this.

"Mullins, run and get reinforcements and first aid." James found the bandage, removed it from the pouch, and opened its packaging. He looked at Daniels's bloodied uniform, couldn't tell which of the gore came from Cole and which came from Daniels himself. A few wooden shrapnel shards were sticking out of the sergeant's body here and there. James stared at the one bandage he had, fought the insane desire to laugh. He found a tear across the Sergeant's chest, saw blood oozing up out of it. He pressed the bandage in, holding it against Daniels's wound. "It's alright, Sarge. We're getting help."

James looked up, saw Mullins still standing there, gaping at him. "Mullins, go! Now!"

Mullins jumped as if waking from sleep and bolted back down the trench.

"GO ON, KEEP READING." William tapped at the paper in James's hands, smiled. "Emily would be terribly disappointed if she knew you were so unenthusiastic about her letters."

James let out a breath, forced himself to focus on the

writing, fighting the incredible fatigue that had crept over him, filling every corner of his body.

Why the hell was William making him do this, anyway? He'd returned from the listening post about a half hour ago, met the shocked faces of the rest of the squad, and told them what had happened. The company medic had come to check him out, told him that he was fine, said he'd come back with a fresh uniform and something to wash up with.

Then William had sat him down in the little dugout—just a scoop out of the side of the trench, really—and asked him to read Emily's letters to him.

"Don't you have your own?" James had pulled them out of the breast pocket of his tunic, his stomach turning when he'd seen the stains on them where Cole's blood had soaked through.

"I want to know if she's keeping anything from me." William had winked, nudged James with his elbow. "Come on, pal, read."

But why was it so damned hard to focus? He could barely read a couple sentences before he found himself losing his place on the page, his attention drifting off. And the shaking —it didn't help either. He hadn't shaken when he'd been with Daniels, hadn't shaken when the reinforcements had come, or when the medic had taken the sergeant out on a stretcher —but now he couldn't stop, his emotions ragged.

It was damned embarrassing. He was a soldier. He hadn't been hurt. Collins and Mullins had both received minor wounds, had followed Daniels to the aid post. James had escaped without a scratch. He should be glad. Why the hell should he be so rattled? Was he some sort of coward?

Control yourself, Garrison!

"I don't see the point. I already read this part." James felt something on his face, a fly. He reached for it, touched something wet instead, a tear. Had he been crying this whole time? He wiped at his face, hoping William didn't see.

"Humor me." William drummed his fingers on his legs.

James sighed, took a deep breath, and read. "Mrs. Wolfe has been her usual self. Her temper keeps us all in good form and on time. We're very busy here, and many units pass through every day. Most of the troops feel confident they'll see action soon, and many are new arrivals to France. Seeing them makes me think of you and William all the time. I…" He trailed off, skipping past the part in which Emily talked about their kiss, how she kept thinking about it, how much she missed him and wanted to see him again.

He found an unoffending line further down, restarted. "I have some exciting news to share. I will be in Paris next month, ten through fourteen August. Mrs. Wolfe says the Red Cross is giving us a brief leave for all our hard work. I don't think she approves. It's just a few days, but we are so excited to…to…."

He couldn't read any more. His vision blurred, and he wiped the tears from his eyes, smelling the dried blood on his hands. He tried to find the line where he'd stopped reading, his concentration wandering.

A pair of boots and puttees appeared in front of the dugout and a familiar voice spoke. "Is Garrison in there?"

"Yeah," someone responded in a hushed, dark tone.

William scooted out of the dugout, stood. James stared at the letter in front of him, still trying to find where he'd left off.

"How is he?"

William cleared his throat. "He's a bit dazed still … I think he needs to be cleaned off."

"Why didn't you get him clean earlier?" The first voice was sharp now, angry.

Another voice spoke up, the medic. "We didn't have anything with us to do it. We had to get Daniels back—"

"Right. Private? Garrison? Can I see you for a minute?"

James fumbled with the letter, tucked it back in his pocket, and slowly pulled himself from the dugout, every motion slow, so damned difficult.

He stood up next to William and found himself looking into the eyes of Lieutenant Robinson, whose grim expression melted into a smile when he saw him. "I hear you did quite the good job today."

James could tell Robinson's smile was real, that the man was trying to cheer him up. James looked over Robinson's shoulder and saw the medic and Lieutenant Lanning, the new platoon officer, staring back at him with obvious concern.

"Uh, thank you, sir." James wasn't sure how anything he'd done could qualify as a good job.

"You got everyone moving quickly. You may have saved the post, had the Germans attacked."

"Daniels…" James sniffed and hoped he wasn't still crying. He hated the slight tremble in his voice. "H—How's Daniels?"

"He was doing alright when I left him." The medic took a step forward. "I think he may make it, but I don't know when you'll see him back here."

James nodded. At least that was something. Maybe Daniels would get a ticket back home. "Good."

Robinson pursed his lips, seemed to be measuring something in his mind. He reached into a pocket and pulled out a couple slips of clean white paper. "I've been thinking, Garrison. I've been invited to a gathering the French are throwing in the capital on the eleventh. They saved some places for the AEF, and the brass thought they'd give a few days of liberty to some of the officers from units that fought well at Soissons. I need… an orderly to come along with me, but I don't have one. Would you like the extra pass?"

James looked at William, saw his friend's surprised expression. "You mean I'd go to Paris with you?"

Robinson wagged the passes at him. "You'd have work to do, and you'd have to accompany me to the ball. But I don't think it would hurt much to let you out in the city a bit. What do you say?"

A small bubble of happiness expanded in his chest. The eleventh was during Emily's stay in Paris. Surely, he'd be able to arrange seeing her. But... He glanced back at William, shook his head. "I can't."

Robinson frowned. "Why not?"

"You should take William here. His sister's going to be in Paris. He ought to go."

"Are you crazy?" William clapped him on the shoulder.

"Don't you want to see her?" James knew they were close, knew William missed her.

His friend hesitated for a moment, and James could see the play of emotion in his eyes. "No," he said with a wink. "I saw her every day for eighteen years. Besides, I know you're sweet on her."

"She's your girl, eh?" Robinson tucked away the passes. "It's settled, then. Report to the company C.P. on the morning of the tenth at seven o'clock."

"Yes, sir."

"And in the meantime—" Robinson turned to Lanning and the medic. "—get him back to the rear for a while. I want him cleaned up and in a fresh uniform." He looked back at James and William. "Take Culver, too."

"Yes, sir." Lanning and the medic spoke at the same time.

"Well." Robinson rubbed his hands together. "You two will be spending a little time in the rear line, near Jezainville. Just a night. I hear the engineers dammed a creek and made a swimming pool. There's a nice wine shop in town, too. Friendly family there."

James couldn't help but smile, imagining the odd sight of soldiers swimming in a pond with the front line so close by.

"Carry on then." Robinson stepped out of the way as Lanning and the medic gestured for James to follow. James nodded slowly, picked up his rifle and his gear from where it sat next to the dugout, then plodded after them, William right behind him.

He felt tears on his face again, wiped at them, his steps heavy, his legs wooden beneath him. He was getting off the line for a real rest. He was going to Paris.

He turned, wanting to say something to Robinson, something to thank him for his kindness—but Robinson was gone, already walking farther down the trench, talking to the rest of the squad as he passed.

CHAPTER 25

August 11, 1918
Paris

Emily tapped her foot as she stared at the imposing, soot-stained stone façade of the Gare de l'Est, the great half-rose window, the French flag drifting lazily in a light breeze, the long, ornate awning running the length the building. The station hummed and buzzed with activity. Trucks, taxis, and cars idled on the street, taking in and disgorging hurried passengers. The occasional couple, too old for military service, strolled past arm in arm, walking in and out of the building with the air of going nowhere very quickly. The great throngs of soldiers, almost all the young men in sight, milled and moved about, the sky blue of the French troops mixing with the drab brown of the British and American soldiers in a whirl of movement.

"Do you think something's wrong? He said he'd be here by ten." She turned to Gertrude and Clara, her anxiety turning instantly to annoyance when she saw their amused expressions.

"Which was all of ten minutes ago." Gertrude pointed at the clock on the front of the building.

Clara nodded. "Don't work yourself up about it, dear."

Emily glanced back at the rest of the women, who were gathered in a little group a few feet behind them.

Easier said than done.

She'd received the latest letters from William and James just before she and the other girls were to leave for Paris. Flooded with relief to hear from them after the recent fighting, she'd torn them open at once, only to discover something so wonderful that it seemed impossible. James had, for some vague reason, been given a special leave to the capital along with his company commander, and would arrive at the Gare de l'Est at ten on the eleventh.

She'd fought to conceal her delight, worried Mrs. Wolfe would keep her from going to Paris for fear of an immoral liaison with a man. She had, of course, completely failed to hide her joy from the other women, who had by now guessed that she was sweet on James. Worse, with a bit of insistent prodding from Gertrude, Emily had yielded the secret of their kiss, a secret she had otherwise guarded closely to prevent Mrs. Wolfe from finding out.

"How could you have kept that from us for all these months?" Gertrude had put her hands on her hips, a scathing look on her face.

"He saved you from the shells." Clara had sighed, looked up into the sky. "It's so romantic."

"I don't think he saved anything." Emily had explained, embarrassed and annoyed at her friends' growing obsession with her romance. "We were lucky. If we'd been hit directly—"

Rose had cut her off with a wave of her hand. "Don't spoil it for the rest of us."

Emily supposed she couldn't blame them. Under Mrs.

Wolfe's strict guidance, there had been precious little in the way of romance or gossip. Nor was there likely to be any in Paris.

"During the day, I will be visiting my son, who is on leave," Mrs. Wolfe had explained, giving them her sternest expression. "I expect you ladies to stay together in groups of three at all times, and to be at the hotel and in your rooms by the curfew." She'd pointed at them each, one at a time. "Any one of you who breaks these rules will find herself on a boat to New York."

The women's disappointment had been tremendous, but Emily had to concede that it was probably better that way. They were in France to do a job, not to find husbands or get themselves in trouble. Still, Emily could understand their boredom.

What she couldn't understand was why every single one of them had insisted they wanted to meet James with her at the station. A group of nine was hardly necessary to follow Mrs. Wolfe's guidelines.

They just wanted a look at James, and none of Emily's efforts to convince them of how silly that was had been effective. On the contrary, her friends had only become more determined.

Emily fidgeted with her light blue dress, one of the only ones she'd brought to France besides her blue-and-white uniform. It was nice to wear normal clothes again, to be out of the hooded hat. If it weren't for all the soldiers around the station, she could almost pretend that the War didn't exist, that William and James and all the boys she knew from back home were safe and wouldn't be in danger any more.

"Is that him?"

Gertrude's voice brought Emily out of her reverie, and she looked up, her heart jolting in her chest.

"Where?" Emily searched the milling people around the

front gate, caught sight of him. He was facing another man, talking. "Yes, that's him."

Gertrude pointed. "Ooh, and he has a friend with him."

"An officer!" Helen clapped her hands together.

Grace nudged Emily. "You didn't tell us he'd have a friend."

There was something familiar about the other soldier, and Emily tried to figure out where she'd seen him before. Too late—James saluted, and the other man—definitely an officer, the company commander—returned the gesture and started off in his own direction.

A ripple of disappointed sighs passed through the group of women.

Emily rolled her eyes.

Clara saw her expression, shrugged. "Can't blame a girl for hoping."

Emily ignored her, stepped forward, trying to put a little distance between her and the others. She waved, trying to catch James's attention as he turned and searched the crowd. She knew the moment his gaze stopped on her, a grin spreading across his face as he walked toward her. She felt herself smiling, too, and didn't care anymore that the others were watching. She hurried toward him, walking as fast she could manage in her dress, suddenly impatient.

And then he was there in front of her, pulling her into a hug, smelling of soap and fresh woolen cloth. She slid her arms around him, held him fast. He was here, he was safe, he was whole. The knot she carried with her always, the one she'd become so used to that she hardly noticed anymore, the knot of worry about him, about William, eased ever so slightly.

"God, I've missed you." His voice was tight, and she could tell he was fighting to control himself. He pulled her back into his arms, held her tightly against him.

She slid her hands around his neck, drunk with happiness, with relief, wanting to feel all of him in her arms, finding it impossible to hold him close enough.

"I'm here," she whispered. "I've got you."

Neither of them spoke for a moment as they stood there, swaying slightly, wrapped tightly together. Through the haze of her emotions, Emily heard a note of alarm in the back of her mind, shock at the intensity of his—and her own—reaction. They'd only kissed once before, had only exchanged letters since then. Since when had things become this fierce? What had come over them? Shouldn't they be acting more moderately?

Not when you may never see him again.

They pulled apart, and she smiled up at him and saw he was grinning, too, though somehow it didn't reach his eyes. There were shadows there she hadn't seen the last time they'd met.

"I hope you weren't waiting long. How has Paris been so far? God, you look wonderful."

"It's been—"

"Ahem."

Oh no.

James looked past her, and his expression changed to one of curiosity. Emily stepped back, turned, and saw the other women standing a few feet behind her, all of them wearing identical, knowing smirks.

Emily took a deep breath. "James, these are my friends, the other girls from the canteen."

James's eyes widened, and color crept up into his cheeks. "Oh."

Gertrude giggled, held out her hand. "How do you do?"

James took it, gave it a light shake. "Um, fine thanks. I remember you, miss...?"

"Gertrude. You can call me Gertie."

Emily huffed, crossed her arms. They were going to make this moment as embarrassing as they possibly could, and there was nothing she could do to stop them. One by one, her friends introduced themselves, suppressing giggles and exchanging looks with each other as they shook his hand.

"Right." Emily put her hands on her hips. "Where would we like to go?"

The sooner they got distracted with sightseeing and left James alone, the better.

"Well, *we* are going to see the Pantheon." Gertrude wagged her finger at Emily. "I'm not sure what you two are going to do."

"What?" Were they leaving her behind with James? The idea held a certain appeal—no more giggling, for one—but offered more than its share of risk. "What if Mrs. Wolfe—"

"Don't be dismal. Just be back on time. We'll catch up later tonight, okay?" The women started to step away, some of them still watching James with smiles that sent a prickle of irritation up the back of Emily's neck.

"But Mrs. Wolfe said—"

"Don't worry about her. We'll cover for you." Gertrude waved. "Bye-bye now!"

"Have fun!" Clara winked.

Emily watched her friends walk away, disappearing into the constant motion of the busy street. She wasn't sure whether to be relieved or irritated. First, they'd been all over James. Now, they were leaving her alone with him. What were they playing at? When they weren't embarrassing her, they were trying to get her into trouble.

"What was that about?"

She turned and saw James's expression, somewhere between amusement and confusion. "Your guess is as good as mine."

James shook his head, offered his arm. "Well, we have a

few hours before the lieutenant wants me at the officer's ball. What shall we do?"

Only a few hours?

Might as well make the most of them.

She tucked her arm through his, smiled, her happiness at being with him burying her lingering annoyance with her friends. She pointed down a random street. "Doesn't matter. That way looks perfect."

"Very well, ma'am." He saluted her, and they walked off together arm in arm into the crowd.

"SHALL WE SIT DOWN FOR A WHILE?" Emily pointed to a dozen small, black iron tables and chairs clumped together in the shade of a huge oak tree. "There's a free table there."

It wouldn't be open for long, given the rate at which people were streaming out of the park and up to the small café stand a few yards away.

James nodded, but didn't say anything. Fine, white gravel crunched beneath their feet as they walked to the table, slid out the chairs, and sat down.

Thank goodness.

She couldn't remember the last time she had done so much walking, and judging by how they felt, neither could her feet or legs. They had passed the morning and afternoon standing on the crowded metro trains they'd taken between the city's monuments, walking along the picturesque boule-vards, wondering at the long rows of stately ivory buildings with blue-gray roofs, strolling through the leafy, shaded parks. All of this tourism had amounted to a lot of time on their feet—more, even, than a typical, long day at the canteen.

It was more than worth the effort.

Emily had been through Paris on her way to join the Red Cross canteen for the first time a few months earlier. She'd only glimpsed the city then, and it had been under the damp gray of the early French spring. Still, she'd wondered how any place could be so beautiful. Now that she was able to see the city in its entirety beneath the August sun, she was overwhelmed by it. Even the occasional reminders of the War— air defense emplacements set in parks and open places, small groups of soldiers manning skyward-pointing cannons in sandbagged gun nests—were not enough to dim the city's loveliness.

Whether James found it as wonderful, Emily couldn't tell. His initial happiness at seeing her had faded as the day went on, and he'd become quieter and quieter. She had tried to engage him with questions, about life at the front, about how William and the other men in the regiment were doing, but his responses were always short, vague, trailing off into dark silence, a frown clouding his features.

"I want to hear about you." He'd interrupted her in the middle of another question. "Tell me about the canteen."

Emily had understood his unspoken request. He didn't want to talk about the front, not here in the Paris sunshine. "What do you want to know?"

There were few things he *hadn't* wanted to know. He'd asked about the work she did, where she slept, what she ate. He had also asked her to fully explain the things she'd only mentioned in passing in letters, and she'd answered, walking beside him, her hand in his. Sometimes, neither of them spoke, and they stood together in silence, taking in the great city. But every time the silence had lasted for too long, James's expression had slipped toward barren numbness, and Emily had revived the conversation, trying to snap his attention back to the present. The weather, random observations about the French and their customs—any topic was acceptable if it kept James away from whatever darkness plagued him.

"Monsieur, Madame, je vous écoute."

A waiter appeared beside them, slicking his short, salt-and-pepper hair back with one hand while he dug a notepad out of his white apron with the other.

"Do you want anything?" James looked at her, his voice flat.

Emily considered for a moment. "Coffee, please."

While James ordered in French, Emily looked out at the park and the people in it. A small band setting up their instruments in an open space beside the café. A few children playing. A group of soldiers sitting around a fountain in the auburn, late-afternoon sunshine. Couples strolling together, the men almost always in uniform, the women wearing defiant smiles. It all seemed so peaceful, so neat and pretty, a stark contrast to the mud of the canteen and violence of the front. That these places were only a train ride away from each other was unreal, a cruel irony. She felt an absurd impulse then to go home and leave the War behind. She almost laughed at the thought of trading the beauty of Paris for the ugly browns of the sun-parched Colorado summer in shabby little Saint Vrain.

The waiter returned with two miniscule cups of dark, strong coffee set on little saucers with paper-wrapped cubes of sugar. James handed the waiter a few coins.

"I sure need this." Emily put on a cheerful tone, smiled at him. "I'm all worn out!"

"Hmm." James frowned, reached for his cup.

She searched her mind for a topic to get James's attention, found one. "I'm glad you boys are getting a nice rest after the last battle."

She unwrapped a cube of sugar, dropped it into the coffee.

"We're still on the front. It's not really a rest."

"Oh." She ignored the sharp edge of his tone, stirred the sugar into her drink, her spoon clinking off the cup's sides. "But it *is* a bit safer than where you were before, yes?"

"Yes, I suppose so."

More silence, though now the band was rasping out a light waltz.

Emily raised her coffee to her lips, sipped, her knot of worry tightening. She looked across the table at James, comparing the brooding man staring out into the park with the cocky, gregarious boy she'd known back home, or even to the confident soldier she'd seen—and kissed—back in May.

What was it in the trenches that had changed James like this? What had it done to William? How much worse would it get before the fighting finally stopped? She wasn't naïve. She'd seen enough men go through the canteen in states of exhaustion and fear to know the front was beyond terrible. But to see someone she knew so well changed so profoundly was…. Disturbing? Outraging? Terrifying?

Yes, to all three.

Damn this stupid war!

James met her gaze, seemed to study her for a second, then sighed. "I'm sorry."

"For what?"

"You would probably have had a better afternoon if you'd stuck with your friends. I'm…" He looked for the words. "I'm not very good company."

Emily waved a hand at him. "Nonsense. We've had a great time, haven't we?"

"You were frowning just now."

"Oh." She hadn't known her worries were showing. "That's something else."

He shook his head. "I've ruined your afternoon."

She reached across the table, rested her hand on his. "I don't think that's possible in Paris."

She didn't really believe that, but she didn't want him to feel bad, even if the day hadn't quite been what she'd wanted.

James stared down at her hand, his expression unreadable.

The band finished playing, and the people seated around them gave a light patter of applause. They started again, and a few people gathered in the open space next to them and started to dance.

"I don't deserve to be here." James spoke so suddenly that Emily jumped in her seat.

"Of course you do. Otherwise your lieutenant wouldn't have—"

"No, I mean I don't deserve to be here, alive with you, drinking coffee. How can I just sit here when the other guys are still in the trenches?"

"I think they'd be glad you're here. I'm certain William is."

She knew without a doubt that her brother would be glad James was safe, that they were passing their time together.

"No, I...." He trailed off. "I shouldn't bother you with it."

She squeezed his hand tighter. "James, what happened?"

He spoke quietly, his voice flat, emotionless, as if he were recounting the facts of someone else's life. Emily listened as he talked about the ravine, the brutal fighting to take it, the machine guns that shot men down in hundreds. She listened as he talked about a friend, Caldwell, and about a new soldier, Cole. She felt almost weak with grief as she saw the horrors he had witnessed in her own mind, the anguish of lives cut short, blasted to oblivion.

"I got lucky twice. I moved one way while they moved another." He met her gaze. "Why wasn't it me? Or William? And when is it going to be?"

Emily's throat tightened, the question striking close to

her own constant fears. "You don't know that it will be."

He snorted. "Half of us didn't come back from Soissons. *Half.* That was one battle, and I don't think the Huns are finished yet. When I sit here, and I look at you…"

"What?"

"I wonder what the point of it is." His voice was barely more than a whisper now. "I don't think I'll ever see you again."

Emily struggled to find something to say, overwhelmed by the bleakness of what he'd said and the crushing pain that wrapped itself around her chest. "James…"

The band finished, and people clapped. A second later, the musicians began again, another waltz. The dancing couples floated over the gravel, their movements graceful, light.

"Dance with me." Emily didn't realize she'd spoken the words aloud until she noticed the surprise on James's face.

"What?"

"Dance with me."

"I don't know if I remember how."

Emily hadn't danced the waltz in years, not since cotillion school. It didn't matter. She stood, still holding his hand. "Dance with me."

JAMES GOT TO HIS FEET, and they walked together to where the other people were dancing. He slid his right hand over the soft fabric of her dress to rest between her shoulder blades and held out his left for her. She took it, rested her left arm over his right. He straightened up, making a rigid frame with his body. He breathed in the light floral scent of her perfume, met the intense gaze in her eyes, felt the electricity between them.

He waited for a gap in the twirling couples, then led her out into the line of dance.

One, two, three. One, two, three.

James looked down at his feet, counting the steps in his head as they turned, determined not to step on Emily's feet.

One, two, three. One, two, three.

"Look out!"

Emily's voice brought James's gaze up in time to avoid running into another couple.

His cheeks flushed. "Sorry."

"I don't think your feet will run away if you look up."

He thought back to when he'd learned the waltz, remembering the teacher's shouted instructions to look over his partner's right shoulder.

"You can't steer if you can't see where you're going!"

They traveled around the clearing, their steps becoming smoother and more coordinated as they went.

One, two, three. One, two, three.

James caught the curious stares of a few other people, did his best to ignore them.

He cleared his throat, uneasy. "It's funny."

"What is?" Emily glanced sideways at him, her head turned to look over his right shoulder.

"I think we must seem very awkward. People are looking at us."

"I think it's because you're counting."

James gaped at her. "What?"

"You're counting." She deepened her voice, imitating his. "One, two, three! One, two, three!"

He stared at her, unable to keep his embarrassment off his face. And then they both laughed, her smile chasing away some of the shadows in his mind.

She was so beautiful, so alive and perfect and free of the filth and misery of the trenches, and he'd spent most of the day in his head instead of relishing his time with her. Rather than seeing the monuments and architecture of Paris, he'd relived that moment when Cole had sat down on the German trap, heard again the gunshot that had passed over him and into Caldwell—over and over and over again. Lieutenant Robinson had brought him to Paris, he'd had a chance to see Emily, and he'd wasted it all.

You may not get another chance.

He pulled her closer, and she didn't resist. He felt her head come to rest on his shoulder, savored the feel of her in front of him. He fought the urge to wrap her up in his arms and bury his face in her hair. He didn't want to end the moment by crashing into another couple. James lost count of the songs they danced that way, swaying and turning together in the dappled afternoon light.

Too soon, the band stopped playing and began to pack away their instruments, accepting the coins and bills that the people tossed into their instrument cases with a cheerful "merci." James still held Emily in a ballroom frame as they both stood unmoving, reluctant to let go of her. Her hand slid up his shoulder to the nape of his neck, drawing him gently toward her. He knew what she was doing, and he tilted his face down, met her lips with his own.

Laughter, excited chatter in French.

James remembered they were in public, in front of many other people, and he pulled away from the kiss. The people sitting at the café were looking at them. An older couple standing near the musicians frowned.

He looked back at Emily, the expression on her face making it more than clear she still wanted to be kissing him.

She stood on tiptoe and whispered in his ear. "Come on."

Without another word, they walked away from the park together.

CHAPTER 26

This was a bad idea, insane.

Emily didn't care.

She waited just long enough for James to lock the door to his hotel room and turn toward her, then wrapped her arms around his neck and stepped up on her toes to kiss him. She could sense the same intensity in him that she felt, and she didn't know if it excited or terrified her more.

Their emotions were dangerously out of control.

Was this going too far?

She wasn't entirely sure what that even meant. She'd heard stories, of course, warnings about girls who'd surrendered their virtue and invited ruin. If kissing a man alone in his hotel room wasn't going too far, she wasn't sure what else could be.

But none of that seemed important now. What mattered was that he was here.

"I don't think I'll ever see you again."

She wanted to keep him with her, to find the hurts in him and soothe them. She wanted to feel him, warm and alive. She slid her hands over the rough woolen fabric of his uniform and down to his chest, fumbling with one of his buttons.

His kiss faltered for a second, but his hands moved to help her, and in a moment, he was wriggling off his tunic, letting it drop to the floor. Emily's heart knocked in her chest as she ran her hands over the smooth skin of his arms. He pulled her closer, his hands moving around to her back, and her pulse pounded in her neck.

He was trying to undo her dress.

Without thinking, she broke the kiss and turned around. She felt his hands on the eyelets of her dress, his movements awkward and unsure.

"Sorry." He laughed. "I've never taken one of these off before."

She was about to laugh, too, but the sound caught in her throat, turned into a gasp as the last eyelet came free and his hands moved to peel off her dress. She worked her arms out of the sleeves and felt the garment fall around her ankles.

She stood there, a shiver running through her despite the room's stuffy warmth. She could hear James's fast breathing, his intake of breath as she took a step forward and out of the dress. She'd never been exposed to any man like this, and she reached up to cross her arms over the front of her corset. She wanted to turn around again, to keep kissing him, but her cheeks were hot with embarrassment, and she couldn't make herself do it.

She didn't need to.

James's arm closed around her waist, pulling her back against him.

"Em." His lips brushed over her exposed shoulder, the straps of her chemise slip, the base of her neck. She tilted her head to one side, leaned back against him as he kissed her there.

Stop, Emily. You need to stop this.

Didn't she want to stop? Wouldn't any young lady?

She ignored the voice in her head, entwined one hand with the hand James had splayed across her belly, then reached up with the other and threaded her fingers into his hair.

This is wrong, Emily. Stop this.

Of course, she wanted to stop. This wasn't what respectable young women did. She *had* to stop him. But how could she do that when it felt so good?

She heard someone whimper, realized the sound had come from her, the feeling of James's lips on her nape silencing her worries entirely.

Those lips. She wanted them again.

She turned around now, completely forgetting her shyness, and he met her, kissing her again, harder and more insistent than before. She felt herself moving backward, realized he was backing her toward the small bed in the corner. The edge of it bumped into the back of her knees, and she fell, pulling him with her. He was on top of her now, his lips brushing over her cheek, her ear, and back to her neck.

Realization hit her, a bolt of fear immediately behind it.

She didn't want to stop at all.

JAMES WAS INTOXICATED, caught in some kind of feverish trance. He slipped a hand into Emily's hair, not caring that he was messing it up. She was everything, in every sense, his entire world, her skin soft against his lips, her scent in his head like some kind of drug. She pulled his face downward and he flinched, the soft wetness of her lips on his neck taking him by surprise.

She wants to try that, too.

Not sure what to do, he held still, tilting his head to the

side to give her access. He thought back to the bawdy stories he'd heard in the trenches—about wives, girlfriends, prostitutes—and tried to remember any tips and advice that might be useful.

He saw Daniels again, heard his voice.

"I was the fourth man to go in with that whore, and I didn't want to be working in some other man's seed, so I had her give me a French job. She must have had a big mouth, because she took my whole cock in it."

What could possibly be useful about that? It seemed an insult to take any of those crude words and apply them to Emily.

Emily, who he couldn't remember not knowing. Emily, who had annoyed and pestered him and William in their childhood. Emily, who had become a woman, the preoccupation of his free thoughts. Emily, who lay there, soft and warm and beautiful.

Surely, he couldn't do that to her.

And what you're doing now isn't bad enough?

It would be if they kept going. He kept waiting for her to tell him to stop, kept pushing forward when she did not.

What the hell were they doing?

James wasn't sure, but he wanted to find out.

Something hard pinched against his calf. "Ouch!"

"Oh." She looked up at him, ran a hand over his cheek. "My shoes."

James fought the impulse to laugh. They'd made it to the bed, and they both still had their shoes on.

You're not the only one who doesn't know what to do.

The thought calmed his nerves, and an idea came to him. He pushed himself up, planting a trail of kisses across the cloth covering her bosom. She gasped, pressed her hands harder into his back. He kept going, kissing his way across her belly, his lips brushing against the thick fabric of her corset. He propped himself up on all fours and pushed himself back to stand in front of her. He took in the sight of her lying there, her tousled blonde hair, her clean white corset and slip showing the curves of her body, the swell of her chest, her black stockings against her white petticoat, and, of course, her shoes.

He reached for them, unlaced them, and slipped them off. He looked back at her face, knew enough to recognize the hunger in it. Emboldened, he slid his hands up her legs, first one and then the other, and unhooked her garter clasp—damn this fumbling! —peeling back her stockings and letting them drop to the floor. He'd never seen any woman so bare, and he ran his hands over her ankles, up her legs, following his touch with little kisses.

He couldn't get enough of her, wanted to touch her everywhere, see her everywhere, feel every inch of her soft, clean skin.

She whimpered, reached down, and took hold of him by the nape of his neck. He understood, allowed himself to be pulled upward until they were kissing again, her lips meeting his with an urgency that thrilled him.

He slipped one hand down, felt the bottom of her slip, slid his hand beneath it, and began moving it up her leg.

"I ended up here because of some farm girl in the nineties. She said I got her in trouble. I had to leave. No work anywhere, so I joined the Army."

"Well, did you get her in trouble, Sarge?"

"She got herself in trouble. But I suppose I helped."

James met the soft cloth of her knickerbockers, retreated, then slipped under them, sliding higher up her thigh. She whimpered again, arched her back, pressing harder into the kiss.

"I don't think I'll ever see you again."

James remembered his own words, froze. He pulled back,

looked down at Emily's closed eyes, her perfect face brushed by a soft beam of light streaming in from the window. When this was over, he would go back to the War, probably to his death.

This was his only chance to be with her, to take a pretty memory with him to the trenches, and leave her with a memory of him when he was gone.

Yes, he'd be gone, and she'd still be here to face the consequences.

Could he do that to Emily?

She opened her eyes, her brow furrowed, and for a split second he could see the girl in the young woman. William's sister, the person he'd always known.

No, he couldn't, no matter how much he wanted to.

He pulled his hand out from her drawers and shook his head, still breathing hard.

"I won't do it. I-I can't."

"What's the matter?" She reached up, stroked his hair. "I want to."

Did she even know what that meant? Did he?

"I can't. I won't get you in trouble." He kissed her gently on her forehead, resting his face against hers. For a long time, neither of them spoke, their breathing gradually slowing. She wrapped her arms around him, and something wet touched his cheek.

"Don't take any risks, nothing more than what they ask of you." Her voice was thick with tears, and James knew she was crying. "I… I need you to come home."

What the hell could he say to that? He had no more control over bullets and shells than the next man. He couldn't very well make some foolish promise to her, but he couldn't tell her off, either.

He pulled away to look at her, saw the anguish on her

face, and brushed away the tears running out of the corner of her eye. "I would never want to hurt you."

It was a weak response, stupid, and he knew it. But what else could he say?

She nodded, sniffed. "Kiss me."

He caressed her cheek and pressed his lips to hers. They kissed gently, slowly—until James heard a soft chiming sound and looked at the clock sitting on the rickety wooden nightstand by the bed.

"Dammit."

EMILY CREPT up the stairs and peered around the corner before stepping out into the hall. The doors were all shut, though there was light shining through the crack beneath the first door on the right.

The one in which she and Gertie were staying.

Was one of the other girls in there, waiting up for her to tell Mrs. Wolfe when she returned? And where were the rest of them? It was still too early for them to be asleep.

She tiptoed up to the door, pushed it slowly open.

Empty.

Perplexed, she stared at her own bed and trunk, wondering what was going on.

Footsteps. Someone was coming up the stairs.

Emily bolted inside, shut the door behind her. She sat down on the bed and started untying one shoe.

Too late. The steps were too close.

Not knowing what else to do, Emily threw back the blankets, lay down on the bed, and covered herself up again. There was a soft knock at the door, but she ignored it. She closed her eyes, ready to pretend to be asleep, only...the light! She opened her eyes, looked for the button, and found it beside the door—just as the knob started to turn.

Hoping against hope, she turned her back to the door and shut her eyes again.

Whoever it was stepped into the room, took a couple steps forward. Emily's pulse pounded in her ears.

Please be Gertie. Please be Gertie.

"Miss Culver?"

No!

It was Mrs. Wolfe.

"Miss Culver, are you awake?"

Emily played along, moving herself as if she was stirring from sleep. She rolled over to face Mrs. Wolfe, who was standing a few feet from the bed, a concerned look on her face.

Mrs. Wolfe held out a hand, put it to her forehead. "How are you feeling?"

"Awful." Emily thought of symptoms that would be hard for someone to see. "My stomach."

Mrs. Wolfe pursed her lips. "You're all flushed." She stepped back, put a hand on her hips.

Seconds passed in agonizing silence as Emily looked back at her.

"You should have listened to Miss Dibbs and avoided the confections." She clucked her tongue. "Given the number of them you ate, I'm not surprised you're feeling ill."

Relief flooded through her.

Thank you, Gertie!

"I almost feel the same way, to be honest. Trevor made me eat more of this rich French food than I can stand."

"Trevor?"

"My son." Mrs. Wolfe smiled, and Emily had to keep herself from gaping. She'd never seen the woman so relaxed and cheerful.

Mrs. Wolfe turned to leave. "I'll have Miss Dibbs bring you up some soup when she's finished eating. We're downstairs in the dining area if you need us."

"Thank you, ma'am."

Mrs. Wolfe walked out of the room and closed the door behind her, the muffled tap of her shoes on the hotel's wooden floors fading into silence.

Emily let out a long breath. She owed Gertie for that story. She must have just missed everyone heading down to dinner.

She pushed back the covers and slid out of bed. Listening for footsteps, she went about the business of preparing for sleep. She reached around and undid the eyelets on her dress, her mind filling with the memory of James's hands on her, undressing her. By the time she was in her nightgown, her close call with Mrs. Wolfe was totally out of her mind, her thoughts instead on what had happened in James's hotel room.

She didn't know whether she was delighted, horrified, embarrassed, ashamed, disappointed—or all of those things at once. She'd allowed the kiss to go too far, had *wanted* it to go further. Had James not stopped himself, would she have asked him to?

Emily climbed back in bed, left the covers rolled down, her body burning with strange, new sensations, singing its satisfaction with the way James had kissed her, touched her, her emotions raw and confused.

Did James feel this way, too? Did he think less of her because of what they'd done?

She remembered the look on his face when he said he'd never want to hurt her, the tenderness of the kiss that had followed. Surely, he still cared for her.

And maybe much more than that.

If only Emily hadn't had to run back to this hotel. If only

they'd been able to talk about what their experience meant, what they could be for each other in the future.

If they even had a future.

Emily rolled onto her back, stared up at the ceiling.

James would be going back to the front with William. She had no idea when—or if—she'd see either of them again.

She closed her eyes, felt fresh tears coming.

Mrs. Wolfe might not have caught her, but one thing was certain: Emily was definitely in trouble.

CHAPTER 27

September 12, 1918
Near Vigneulles, France

"Stop!" The hoarse whisper passed down the line, repeated man to man. "Halt!"

James stopped in his tracks, knelt next to a large bush, and trained his rifle forward into the crushing, inky black of the woods ahead. Nighttime was one thing, but nighttime in this thick forest was another. Not so much as a glimpse of the sky, no stars or moonlight to illuminate their path. Only the Army would expect someone to fight a war when they couldn't see.

"Christ!" Sergeant Rodriguez cursed under his breath somewhere to James's right. "Again?"

"Maybe they've found Second Platoon?" The hopeful note in Mullins's voice made the new soldier sound even younger than he was, a boy.

"Maybe." William crouched down on the opposite side of the tree from James. "But I think Lanning's more worried about finding ourselves than the others."

"Don't move, any of you." There was a rustle as Rodriguez stood and passed behind them, bent low as he half-ran off to the right, into the darkness.

James sighed, leaned against the tree, and rested the butt of his Springfield on the ground, the tip of his bayonet pointing up at the black roof of tree branches. The platoon had been moving like this for what seemed like hours. They'd entered the woods in the afternoon, pushing on toward Hattonville and Vigneulles after a morning of incredible successes. Following a fierce barrage, they'd moved forward at oh-five-hundred, secured their first objective within an hour, pushed through the main line of enemy resistance at the woods near the Quart de Reserve by ten, and taken their primary objective, the Lamarche-Nonsard Road, by noon. A sharp contrast to the slaughter at Soissons, their attack had progressed perfectly, and with few casualties. In James's squad, only one man, Pippert, had been wounded.

Everyone had been in high spirits, elated with their easy victory. If this momentum continued, they'd pinch out the St. Mihiel salient, their ultimate objective, in a matter of days. The replacements began to wonder openly if they'd get through the whole battle without losing anyone. Then the regiment had entered these damned woods.

At first, it had been a relief to escape the open, marshy ground they'd been crossing for most of the attack. No longer were they under the German guns on Montsec, the glowering hill that dominated the horizon to their left. The Hun had harassed them with sporadic shell fire from that hill all day, and strong, persistent winds had blown away the smoke screen the US artillery had tried to create.

Trees would not blow away, and the regiment's concealment from Montsec had been complete.

Trees were also good for getting people lost, and with night had come confusion. They'd gradually lost contact with the other platoons, creeping forward at an excruciating snail's pace. It seemed that every time they got started again, Lieutenant Lanning called everyone to a stop to look at his compass once more.

"Anyone got a smoke?" Bird's voice, coming from a spray of bushes off to the right, almost made James jump.

William clucked his tongue. "No open flames. Unless you want a bullet with that cigarette."

"Hey, I'll give him a smoke!" The voice belonged to Collins, just a little forward and to the left.

"I'll contribute!" Killeen laughed.

Bird huffed. "Thanks, guys."

"Shhh!" James pressed a finger to his mouth, the pointless chatter of his fellow soldiers grating on his nerves. They were vulnerable to enemy attack—spread out, confused—and they didn't need to advertise their position to the Germans with silly conversation. Why the enemy hadn't exploited this fact was something James couldn't figure out.

Maybe they really are broken. Maybe this will be over soon.

James held on to the glimmer of hope for just a second and threw it away.

I'll believe it when I see it.

He didn't need false hopes to distract him. He was distracted enough already. He'd spent more time than he should have this past month reliving his visit with Emily. He'd found himself imagining her in her slip, kissing him, her body beneath his, her skin soft, bare. What if they'd gone just a bit further? What would it have been like to see her naked? To make love with her? He almost regretted not accepting what she had tacitly offered him, and he couldn't help but feel excited at what might happen when he saw her again.

If you see her again.

And even if he did, how would she act toward him now?

Her letters had been as affectionate as ever, but she'd stopped well short of declaring love or suggesting improper activities, as had James. It was as if nothing had happened between them.

He knew the reason.

She didn't want to be involved with a dead man any more than he wanted to get her in trouble and leave her heartbroken. She was doing the right thing, protecting herself.

You're probably overthinking this.

He shifted uncomfortably, adjusting his helmet on his head. Maybe he had offended her and ruined whatever romantic sentiment she had felt for him by insulting her honor. Hell, he'd had a hard time looking William in the eye when he'd returned from Paris and had been vague with his summary of his time with Emily—something his friend had noticed.

"You mean you spent the entire time sightseeing?" William had raised his eyebrow so high that it had vanished under the brim of his helmet. "That's it?"

"The time I didn't spend helping Lieutenant Robinson, yes."

"Huh." William had crossed his arms. "Then I suppose you got to know Paris very, very well."

The less William knew, the better. James couldn't imagine any brother approving of a man who'd kissed his sister so intimately, not to mention in a state of undress. But did Emily approve? She'd initiated the kiss, but had James done too much?

She's not the one who stopped you.

James took a deep breath, blew the little worries away. It didn't matter, any of it. Not now, anyway.

He brushed his hands over his damp puttees and trousers, flaking off some of the mud crusted there. The march to their jump-off positions had been even worse than at Soissons, rain and deep mud every step of the way, the road choked by the flow of men and equipment. At least this forest was on dry ground, and he wasn't sinking up to his knees in mud every time he took a step—when the platoon was actually moving, that is.

James drummed his fingers on the stock of his rifle, impatience sharpening within him. He listened to the sigh of the wind moving through the trees and the breathing of the other men of his squad around him, waiting for the rustle of Sergeant Rodriguez coming back to them.

James jerked his head up, heard himself gasp. Had he been nodding off? He shook his head, trying to focus on something out in the confused mass of shadows in front of him. How long had they been there now?

"Hey." Someone nudged James on the shoulder, and he looked around to see William's dark outline leaning around the tree. "Are you alright?"

"Tired."

Bird snorted. "I wonder why that is."

William ignored him, nudged James again. "Here."

James looked down, saw his friend's open hand. He reached for it, and William tilted his palm, dropping something light and rough into his hand. James held the thing up to his face.

"Hard tack?"

"I swiped some extra at lunch." William's teeth were a patch of white in the darkness as he smiled.

"You didn't happen to get some of the bully beef, did you?" James gnawed on one end, suddenly energized—and very hungry.

"Just the biscuits. Eat up, I've got a couple more."

Bird groaned. "Oh, for God's sake, don't talk about food!"

"Shut up over there!" The voice belonged to Rodriguez.

James straightened up, slipping the hunk of bread into his

pocket. A moment later, the dark shape of Rodriguez came into view as he dashed over to the bush next to Bird and took a knee.

"Right. We're changing direction." Rodriguez pointed his arm forward and a little to the left. "That way. Get moving, and stick together. Remain in sight of each other at all times."

They all got to their feet, appearing out from behind trees and bushes, and started forward. James winced as he stood, his tired muscles stiff from the brief rest. He double-checked the safety tab on his rifle and trudged after the others, careful to keep William on his left and Rodriguez on his right.

The ground was sloping gently down now, the forest stretched out before them, an expanse of silent, black-and-gray shapes. James stumbled on a root, cursed under his breath, and kept going. He walked on, suppressing a yawn. He wondered how late it was, glanced up to see—was that a patch of sky? The woods were thinning out, soft silver light spilling through the leaves and onto the ground. Ahead, the forest was brighter, a small glade lit by the stars. James strained his eyes, made out the hard, regular lines of a building, a little house.

"Lieutenant says hold up!" The words echoed down the line, and Rodriguez halted, held up a hand.

James huffed, annoyed to be stopping again so soon.

William knelt down. "Maybe I should give one of these biscuits to Lieutenant Lanning."

James couldn't help but grin. "If anyone needs one, he does."

The bright starburst of a muzzle flash erupted from the building, and James dove to the ground. Bright red tracer rounds spat out in a regular, rapid rhythm, filling the air with sizzling lead.

A machine gun.

James crawled a few feet on his elbows, raised his rifle to

his eyes. He tried to aim for the muzzle flash, fired. The machine gun kept shooting—and swung the arc of bullets toward him.

"Son of a—" He flattened himself against the dirt and dead, damp leaves, cool earth spraying him where the bullets struck the ground. The other doughboys were firing back, the sporadic pops from their Springfields drowned out by the steady roar of the machine gun.

"Auto rifles, set up here!"

James looked over to see Rodriguez in cover behind some rocks and a thick stump, directing Bird and the other men from the Chauchat squad into position.

"Garrison!" Rodriguez met his gaze. "Take a few others around the left."

James swallowed hard. He'd never been given a responsibility like this. Maybe Rodriguez's promotion had got to his head. "Yes, sergeant!"

James looked around, saw William, Mullins, Collins, Killeen, and Dobson in cover to his left, their faces half lit by the flicker of gunfire. "Come with me!"

He waited for a break in the machine gun's fire, then pushed himself to his feet. Bent low, he sprinted forward and to the left, the other soldiers standing up and following him, crashing through the brush.

"Down!" William's shout was barely audible over the gunfire.

James dove, gasping as something punched the wind out of his lungs. Through the haze of pain, he was aware of the hiss of bullets cutting the air overhead, the spray of dirt and sharp splinters as the deadly rounds struck nearby. Had he been hit? James reached down, felt his torso for the bloody wound he feared would be there—and felt the rock on which he'd landed. Relieved, he held still, waiting for the slow thumping fire from the Chauchats to begin.

A second later, it came, and the German machine gun fire stopped, the gunners no doubt keeping their heads down to avoid the wall of American lead.

"Move!" James pushed himself back to his feet with his rifle, still gasping for air. He spied a long, black line slicing through the forest floor a few yards ahead—a ditch! He turned toward it, yelled over the back-and-forth argument between the German Maxim and the American Chauchats. "Take cover in there!"

James glanced to his right, saw he was almost at ninety degrees to the house now, well out of the German gunner's arc. This position would be perfect. They could follow the ditch toward the back of the house and—

The ground in front of James exploded into a dozen puffs of dirt as bullets raked the forest floor.

He saw William dive to the right, did the same himself. He crashed through a bush, rolled down a slight embankment, and came to rest against a tree stump, his cheek and hands stinging where the shrub had cut him.

His rifle! Panic seized him, and he reached around for it in the dark, found it next to his left hand.

Thank God.

"James? James!" William crawled up next to him. "Are you hit?"

"I'm fine." James looked around. "Where'd the others go?"

"No idea. Was that fire from the house? Did we go the wrong way?"

"I don't think so." James crawled forward and slowly raised his head to look up the embankment.

A new machine gun ahead of them was firing sporadically into the forest to the left, the noise of its report mixing with the din of the other Maxim and the Chauchats behind them. James lowered himself back into cover. Did Lanning or Rodriguez know they were pinned down here? What the hell were they supposed to do? If they didn't stay close to this embankment, they'd be in the open and exposed to the German gun ahead. If they stayed here, the Germans in the house would eventually notice their neighbors were firing at someone and send troops over to pick them off.

They could already be on their way.

James swallowed, his mind racing. "I-I think we should follow this embankment and get around the gun ahead of us, circle back, and get the first gun after." He met William's gaze, but couldn't read his friend's expression in the dark.

"After you."

They crawled forward, sticking tight to the embankment, stopping to hug the ground every time the machine gun fire swept close to them.

They'd gone perhaps twenty-five yards when the bursts of fire from the Maxim quickened, a sudden crescendo of rifle shots. A second later there were two explosions, then a long, agonized scream.

What the hell was happening out there?

The machine gun in front of them had gone silent, and the only gunfire now came from the house and Rodriguez's position.

"What should we do?" William leaned closer to make his whisper heard.

"I don't know. Maybe go ba—"

James cut his sentence short, rolled onto his back as a dark shape jumped over him. He swiveled his rifle around and saw the man turning toward him, pointing a pistol, his face catching a small patch of moonlight.

"Lieutenant Robinson?" James gaped up at the officer, cold sweat on his forehead.

"Garrison?" Robinson knelt down, then waved to someone on the other side of the embankment. "Get over here!"

A dozen or so doughboys slid over the embankment and squatted around James and William. James looked at their faces, recognized Mullins, Collins, Killeen, and Dobson.

"We've been advancing about a hundred yards that way, and I found the rest of your squad in cover a few dozen yards from here." Robinson clicked on his pistol's safety. "What's going on?"

"Our platoon's back there." William pointed back the way they'd come. "German Maxim in that house."

"Right." No one spoke for a minute as Robinson seemed to think things through. "Come on. Let's get that MG and see about linking up your platoon with the rest of the company."

"Do you know the direction we're supposed to be going, sir?" James pulled himself up to a sitting position. "We've been lost all night."

"I'm not sure." Robinson chuckled, the smile in his voice a sharp contrast to the muffled gunfire. "But we're better off lost together."

"Yes, sir."

"Come on, soldiers."

The other troops helped James and William to their feet, and they started through the thick forest back toward the house and the clearing. The German machine gunners seemed completely unaware of what was going on, still distracted by the slow thump of the Chauchat gunners.

They reached a low stone wall, hopped over it and into the flat, grassy area around the house. James scanned the darkness, searching for movement, checking the shadows. They were almost to the house now, its stone walls a dull, dark gray. They kept low, the air thick with bullets from the American position. There was a wagon loaded with what looked like gasoline canisters parked next to the house. James couldn't see a door, figured it must be on the other side, but just below the roofline, toward the top of the wall, was a huge, jagged hole in the structure's masonry, no doubt the work of a light artillery shell.

They reached a small outbuilding, and Robinson stopped. He pointed at Dobson and Collins, made a fist, then pretended to pull a pin away from it before pointing at the hole.

Dobson and Collins nodded, dug into their equipment bags for grenades.

James wrinkled his nose, the smell of human waste filling his senses. They had to be near an outhouse. He readied himself to move, knew what his and the others' jobs would be. As soon as those grenades went off, they'd have to rush in and deal with whoever was left alive. His hand went instinctively to the grip of his bayonet, locked in tight.

He watched as Dobson and Collins crawled across the space between the outhouse and the house, their slung rifles bobbing on their backs. They got to their feet, kept their backs flat against the wall. They pulled the pins from their grenades, turned around, and tossed the grenades up and into the hole. They dove for the ground, and seconds ticked by. Then—

Two muffled explosions, a scream. The machine gun fell silent.

"Go!" Robinson stood, swinging his pistol through the air.

James was already on his feet, bayonet forward, charging toward the house. He'd only taken a few strides when another, larger explosion rocked the ground under him. A cloud of fire belched out of the hole in the roof, the building suddenly ablaze.

James's step faltered, and then he heard the screams. Three balls of flame came running around the house, shrieking, stumbling, their helmets distinctly German, the light from their burning bodies illuminating the clearing.

James stared in disbelief, unable to move. "Good God."

Smaller, sharper explosions tore the air as the men's cartridge belts went off like firecrackers. Still they ran, fell to the ground, rolled.

"Shoot them!" Robinson's voice was distant, drowned out by the screams and explosions. "For God's sake!"

James raised his rifle, thought of Caldwell lying there, his face split open, of Cole splattered across the listening post.

Let the bastards burn.

"Shoot them!" Robinson fired his pistol, and the noise jarred James out of his trance.

He flipped over the safety tab of his rifle and moved his finger to the trigger, but it was too late. A chorus of shots assaulted his ears as the other men around him fired. The Germans jerked, stopped screaming, and lay still, the occasional cartridge still detonating in their belts.

Robinson was still shouting. "Move away from them! They'll be visible for miles!"

Hardly a moment later, the clearing exploded again. James dropped and covered his head with his hands as the ground shook a half-dozen times. Dirt showered over him, fell down the back of his tunic, bounced off his helmet like hailstones. The explosions moved now, striking the woods to the right, creeping farther away. The noise stopped, and James peeked out from under his hands. The house was still burning, but had been broken apart even more, a few small craters dotting the yard around it. Men were getting to their feet, helping their buddies up. James looked around for William, spotted him a few yards to his left, giving another man a hand. Robinson was a few feet from him, holstering his sidearm.

"First aid! First aid!" The cry came from somewhere behind him, but James didn't have time to see who it was as Lanning came charging into the clearing around the house with the rest of the platoon in tow, gaping at the burning

German corpses on the ground. James wrinkled his nose, coughed as the unmistakable smell of scorched flesh filled his head.

"We thought for sure you guys were goners when we saw the shells hit." Lanning walked past James, blocking the grisly view, and stood in front of Robinson. "Is the rest of the company nearby?"

Robinson waved off toward the direction he'd come from. "A couple hundred yards that way."

The relief on Lanning's face was obvious, even in the flickering firelight. "We figured we were just about lost. It's good to—"

"We can worry about that later. Get your platoon on the move. I'm sure whoever threw those mortars can still see the flames."

"Right." Lanning turned around. "Let's move on, everyone. Sergeants, get your squads back together."

Lanning glanced at the Germans one more time, straightened his helmet, and walked away from the clearing, moving in the direction Robinson had indicated. The rest of the platoon followed, squads shifting and regrouping.

James looked around for Rodriguez, saw him crouched ten yards behind him, next to the medics.

Who was on the ground?

"Whew!" Bird walked up next to James, clapped him on the back. "You guys are lucky. It's good the Hun truck didn't get hit. This whole clearing would be torched."

James ignored him, walked toward the small huddle of men.

Rodriguez stood. "Take his tags. I don't know how easy it will be to find this place again."

Rodriguez saw James, met his gaze, and held it for a moment. "Come on."

He shouldered his rifle and moved after Lanning.

But James couldn't listen, found himself walking right up to the medics, looking down.

It was Dobson, another one of the replacements, his face and body dark with blood.

James hardly knew him, didn't remember any of the information he'd shared when he'd joined the squad—details like his hometown, whether he was married, what he'd done before the War. Now, none of it mattered.

James slung his rifle over his shoulder, and one of the medics looked up at him.

"Shrapnel. He didn't get down fast enough."

"Yeah." James knew he should feel something, some sadness at the death of this new squad mate, but he felt nothing, his chest empty, numb.

"We're going to fall behind." William appeared beside him with Bird. He looked down, shook his head. "And here it is I thought we might make it without losing anyone."

Bird shifted the heavy Chauchat in his arms. "Bad luck."

"Bird, your squad's already moving." Robinson's voice made them all look around. He was standing a few feet behind them, his arms at his side. "Culver, Garrison, you, too. Just keep moving."

James nodded, turned, and started after Rodriguez, William and Bird in tow. The clean darkness of the woods was welcome, a relief from the smoke and sickly, dying light of the now smoldering Germans.

After a few minutes, William cleared his throat. "Poor bastards. They must have brought some of the fuel inside the house."

"Yeah. Poor bastards." James didn't mean it, didn't want to think about any of it. He stuck his hand in his pocket, searching for the hard tack William had given him.

It was broken into pieces.

CHAPTER 28

September 21, 1919

James trailed off, and silence filled the parlor. Emily stared at him, seeing it all in her head. The deadly fire-fight in the dark woods, the blaze of the burning Germans, the squad mate cut down so randomly. She shuddered, felt something wet against her hand. She looked down and saw the coffee she'd forgotten, the small splash across her skin where her movement had caused the drink to spill. She set the cup down and reached for a napkin.

James had been speaking for a couple hours now, ever since they'd come back to the Culver house after the parade. He'd talked on about the War, while everyone sat and listened—her parents, Mr. and Mrs. Garrison, James's Uncle Chester and Aunt Maggie, and Susan Mabee, the young woman they'd met at the parade, the one who said she was Lieutenant Robinson's fiancée.

Or at least she had been, before Robinson had died.

Emily was grateful they'd sent the children to the front lawn to play. She didn't want them to hear about this. She picked her cup back up and took a sip, found it had gone cold. She drank anyway, imagining William there, in the forest, confronted with such horrors.

What did he feel? Was he afraid? Did something similar happen to him?

"Thank you for talking to me about this." Susan dabbed her eyes, her voice breaking the silence. "I know it isn't easy. Everyone thinks they are doing me a favor by refusing to tell me how it really was. It's much better to know."

Crying won't change anything.

"It is." Emily reached across the coffee table and put a hand on Susan's arm. How she wished that she *could* know about William, too. She looked at James, a swirl of emotions filling her. She wanted him to keep talking, to share every detail until he'd reached the one she was desperate to know. She wanted him to never talk about the War again, to end the obvious pain it brought him to share what he'd seen.

James sat back in his seat, his voice heavy. "It's the least I can do. Robinson always took care of us. He was always there when we needed him."

James paused, and Emily could tell he was fighting to keep his composure. "He was the best of us. It shouldn't have been him."

"Thank you." Susan smiled through her tears. "If it makes you feel better, he'd have been glad you made it. He spoke about you a few times when he was your platoon leader." She glanced over at Emily's parents. "And about William Culver, too."

"Is that how you knew to come find us?" Mr. Garrison handed his empty coffee cup to Mrs. Rawlins, who moved through her duties slowly, her attention focused on the conversation.

Susan nodded. "A friend of mine lives with her husband in Saint Vrain. She wrote to me last month that the town was going to honor its soldiers and a decorated hero from the War."

James frowned, but didn't say anything.

Susan looked over at James. "She mentioned your name. I recognized it from somewhere, and I read through Dwight's old letters. Liza, my friend, sent me a copy of the newspaper with the description of what you did. I saw you earned your medal on the same day that Dwight died. I figured if anyone would know about him, you would."

Emily leaned forward, her pulse pounding in her ears. If Robinson had died the same day James had attacked the machine gun, that meant he'd died the same day as William. Had the two men died together, killed by the same shell, the same burst of machine gun fire?

"You mean the War Department never told you the facts?" Emily's father crossed his arms, shared a glance with her mother.

"N-no." Susan sniffed. "Just that he died in the line of duty."

Emily squeezed Susan's arm. She understood that pain, the pain of not knowing, of inventing and imagining horrors to fill the void of information.

Susan turned to James. "That's why I wanted to come. I was hoping you could tell me how it happened."

James's face drained of color, and all the air seemed to leave the room. Everyone was staring at him for a long moment as he shifted in his seat. "I…"

"You did see it happen, didn't you? You saw Dwight die?"

James met Susan's gaze. "Yes."

Tingles marched up the back of Emily's neck. This was it. She was finally going to hear about the day William died, would maybe hear how it happened.

Susan leaned over, put a hand on the armrest of James's

chair. "You've told me so much already about his life, the battles he was in. Please."

For a long time, he said nothing.

Emily's father cleared his throat. "I think it's about time to get dressed for dinner. You're all welcome to stay and continue this conversation afterward."

Susan glanced at her watch. "Oh! Liza is going to wonder where I've been. I'm supposed to meet her at the train station in ten minutes. I have to go." She looked back at James. "Will you promise to tell me?"

James closed his eyes and nodded his head. "Call at my house tomorrow."

Emily shook her head in disbelief. He was going to tell Susan? Susan, but not her? After all the times she'd tried to get him to talk about William's death, all Susan had to do was ask politely? Anger blazed to life inside her, and her hands shook as she set down her cup.

"We'll take you to the station." Chester stood, holding out his hand to help his wife to her feet.

"That's very kind of you. Thank you all for your hospitality." Susan reached across the coffee table and took hold of Emily's mother's hand. "I'm so sorry for your loss."

Emily's mother squeezed Susan's hand tightly. "And we for yours."

"I suppose we'll get started home, too." Mr. Garrison nudged James's arm. "Come on, soldier."

They all stood up, but Emily couldn't move, every ounce of her self-control tied up in containing her explosive anger. James was still sitting, too, his eyes closed, his hand massaging his temple.

Everyone said their goodbyes and thank-yous, and Chester and Maggie walked out the front door with Susan in tow.

"Come along, Emmy. Go bring Brianna and Julius inside,

and get dressed for dinner." Her parents climbed the stairs, heading for their room.

"Oh! I think someone ought to give that girl our address." Mrs. Garrison walked to the door, too.

"I'll get the car started." Mr. Garrison went outside after her, leaving James and Emily in the room alone.

Emily's hands shook. She looked down, saw she'd balled them into fists. James was still sitting there silently.

"How could you do it?" Emily spoke quietly, fighting to keep her voice even.

He opened his eyes, met her gaze. "What?"

"You're willing to tell *her*, but you won't tell me?" Emily shook her head, unable to believe it. "How could you do this to me? To my parents? To William?"

James shot to his feet, straightened his uniform tunic. "It's different."

Emily stood, too. "How? Can you at least explain that?"

He stared back at her, seemed to be weighing his words. "You don't want to know. Trust me."

"But you heard Susan. It's better to know."

Why couldn't he understand that?

"Is it?" He crossed his arms. "Would you like to live with those memories?"

"It can't be worse than all the things I've imagined."

"I wouldn't be so sure of that." He started around the settee, heading for the door.

She wouldn't let him leave without telling her, not this time. She stepped in front of him, blocking his way. "You are going to tell me."

JAMES LOOKED DOWN AT EMILY, at the hard lines of determination on her face. His heart hurt to see her so angry, so tattered and raw.

He took a deep breath. "Emily, I'm trying to protect you."

How could he make her understand?

"From what? Susan's strong enough to take it. Do you think I'm not?"

"That's not what I meant." He searched for some way to explain himself. "I don't want you to remember him that way."

Better that Emily invent some heroic death in her head, anything but the truth. Couldn't she see it was better this way?

For her, or for you?

She took his hand. "James, can't you see what this is doing to my parents? To me?" Her voice was barely more than a whisper now. "I thought… I thought you loved me."

The words hit him like a fist, and he wanted to reach for her, pull her against him and kiss away the pain in her eyes.

Yes, he loved her. For God's sake, he loved her more than anything. The realization terrified him, made his head spin.

"Emily… I don't want to hurt you."

"This is killing me."

He shut his eyes, knew there was no way out now. He couldn't make her suffer like this anymore. And if it meant losing her?

If it took the pain out of her eyes, it would be worthwhile, wouldn't it?

"He died because of me." The words tumbled out of his mouth before he could stop them.

Emily's eyes widened. "What?"

There was nothing for it now.

"We were attacking an enemy position. We were going to make one more try before getting pulled off the line. They were dug in well along a ridge." He swallowed, his heart pulsing in his throat. "I ignored the order to hold position."

He closed his eyes, could feel again the searing anger that drove him forward, the spray of machine gun fire that had ripped the air around him as he'd plunged toward the enemy. "I assaulted the German positions, and William came after me."

"James! What the hell are you doing? Come back!"

"But..." Emily took a step back. "That means... William was in that machine gun nest, too, wasn't he? He took it with you?"

James hesitated. He'd never thought she'd draw such a conclusion.

Good. It was better that way.

"William came after me," he repeated. "He got hit, and I got wounded just afterward. I fell unconscious. I disobeyed orders, got my friend killed, and they gave me a medal."

Emily shook her head silently, took a step back, her voice trembling. "But you were supposed to take that nest, weren't you? You were just taking initiative. You were a hero."

"No!" He hadn't intended to shout, but his anger at himself was boiling over. It was time she finally saw him for what he was. "I didn't. We were supposed to hold position. The attack stalled, and we were supposed to wait for reinforcements."

His voice cracked, but he kept talking. "I went forward against orders because I wanted to kill those Hun bastards, every goddamned one! William tried to stop me, and he died."

Emily took another step back, her brow knotted as if working through some impossible problem. "He took that nest with you, and you never said anything? You let them... let *us* think he was missing? How could you....?"

Something snapped in her, and color flooded into her

face. She pointed at his face. "Stop crying. What good is it now?"

James hadn't felt the tears gathering in his eyes, felt them now. He didn't know how to respond.

"Answer me!" Emily yelled, her voice reverberating in the enclosed space of the house. "Do you think that helps anything? Does it bring him back? You got him killed, and you think you have a right to…How dare you!"

James wanted to say something, but held himself back.

Let her hate you. This is how it should be.

She took a step backward, catching herself against the back of the settee, breathing in hard gasps. "You killed him! And all this time I've been… I let you… Oh God!"

James resisted the urge to help her, to pull her into his arms.

Ragged, crushing pain twisted through him. He'd lost her now, forever. There would be no going back.

"Emily?" Mr. Culver appeared at the top of the stairs, came running down. "Emily, what's the—"

"Get out!" She straightened up, took a step toward James, her hands balled at her side.

Mr. Culver was there now, putting an arm around her. "But Emily, what's gotten into you?"

"Get out!" Her voice was the bellow of a wounded animal. She pointed an accusing finger at him, her body shaking with the ferocity of her grief. "He killed William!"

Mr. Culver looked at him, perplexed. "James, what is this about?"

But James couldn't stay there another second. For her sake, it was time to go. "Goodbye, Emily."

He turned on his heel, and walked out the door.

CHAPTER 29

September 30, 1918
Near Neuvilly-en-Argonne, France

"What the hell is this?" William pointed toward the edge of the road to his right.

"What the hell is what?" James followed his friend's gesture and saw a tall lieutenant, one of the officers from battalion headquarters, standing by the road, shouting at them as they all marched by.

"Have any of you seen the sign for Vauquois? Anyone at all?"

"No, sir."

"Sorry, sir."

The column kept marching, and James shuddered, some of the damp creeping under his duster. "I hope someone has seen it."

The village of Vauquois was the next landmark on the way to Cheppy, where the Blue Spaders and the rest of the First Division were to relieve the bloodied 35th Division, the end of their long march.

"What do you fellows suppose you'll do after all this?" Private Corbett interrupted James's thoughts, looking back over his shoulder at James as he marched, the brim of his helmet bonking the muzzle of his rifle with a dull metallic clang.

James shifted the weight of his full marching kit on his shoulders. "Eat. Sleep, if they'll let me."

William chuckled next to him. "Don't be too ambitious there, soldier. I haven't seen the supply train in days."

For that matter, none of them had seen it. After the end of offensive operations at St. Mihiel four days earlier, the regiment's logistical apparatus had struggled to keep up with the troops' constant motion.

"Where do you think they're hiding?" The voice of Bird, marching in the row in front of Mullins and Corbett, was unmistakable.

"Not here, that's for sure." William shook his head. "There's nowhere to hide."

That's the damned truth.

James looked out at the broken terrain around them. There wasn't a tree or building as far as the eye could see, only overlapping craters and churned up, pulverized earth, the occasional scrap of a uniform or a twisted, broken helmet, the grim trace of the fighting that had seesawed across these rolling hills for four years.

Corbett clucked his tongue, as if chiding a kid. "No, you noodles. I mean after the War. What do you think you'll do?"

"I... Well, I..." James searched for an answer, taken aback by the question. "I don't know. I've never thought about it. There isn't much point."

He didn't need to explain, not to the older men, the ones who'd been at Soissons. They knew just as well as he did there was no use planning when they probably wouldn't survive the fighting. The constant, distant rumbling ahead, the sounds of Marshal Foch's great Allied offensive that the officers were always talking about, was more than enough to maintain this conviction.

Of course, Corbett was not one of the older men, but a replacement who'd joined them for the light fighting at St. Mihiel.

Light fighting.

James's mind flashed back to the clearing in the wood, the burning Germans, Dobson lying on the ground, his body mutilated by shrapnel wounds. And yet the regiment had lost only a handful of men at St. Mihiel, the half-hearted German resistance crumbling before the American advance. More than one man had begun to voice the same enthusiasm Corbett clearly felt, that the Huns were on their last legs and the War would be over soon.

"I want to go to California." Corbett sighed, the longing in his voice evident. "I have a cousin out there, in Los Angeles. Works for an oil company. Says he can get me in." He nudged Mullins, who was marching beside him. "He says the girls there are keen, too."

"I'd like to go to school." Collins's voice carried over from the next row back. "I'd like to work on airplanes."

Mullins snorted. "You don't need schooling for that— Jesus, another one!"

James followed Mullins's gaze. Another of the huge craters, more than a hundred feet across. They were everywhere in this zone, the work of the great railroad guns.

After a moment, Collins spoke again. "I mean I want to design them. I'd like to be an engineer."

James pushed back his helmet brim and looked behind him at Collins. "You never said you wanted to be an engineer."

Collins shrugged, his mud-spattered khaki duster fluttering about his puttees in the breeze. His gaze followed a truck passing in the other direction, dragging a cannon behind it. "Dad worked in a garage. I guess machines always interested me. He'd love to see what we've got out here."

James stumbled, brought his gaze forward again. How long had he known Collins? The man was one of the originals, had been in his squad since before Cantigny. They weren't particularly close, but James had never known Collins liked machines, or that his dad had worked on cars. What else didn't he know about his squad mates?

"I want to be a journalist." William spoke so suddenly that James flinched.

"A journalist?" He gaped at his friend. "Since when?"

Bird laughed. "Since he saw that Frenchie article about how we have pool tables and fencing mats at the front line. He can't resist getting in on the fun."

The men all chuckled, the same dark laughter. Many of them had given up on reading anything but the Army's own newspapers, the flagrant misinformation of the civilian publications more than they could stomach.

"No, that's the kind of thing that makes me want to do it." William's voice rose, a hard determination driving his words. "Someone ought to know what really happened out here, what's still happening. When the War's over, they'll need people like that to help create a better world."

"Hey guys!" Bird shouted. "Woodrow Wilson himself is with us."

"Cut it out." James could just see Bird's helmet from between Mullins's and Corbett's shoulders. "It's a good idea."

"It's what we're fighting for," William continued, the steel still in his voice. "Truth. A world safe for democracy."

"You still believe in any of that?" Bird's voice had changed, all humor gone from it, replaced by some sharper emotion. "Where the hell have you been?"

"Hey, lay off him!" Corbett nudged Bird in the back.

"What's eating you up?"

"Forget it." Bird kept marching, but said no more.

William met James's gaze, shrugged. "Why else would we be doing all this?"

James didn't have a response, so he kept marching in silence. A minute later, the tall lieutenant reappeared, sitting in a truck that rumbled past the men.

Corbett shook his head. "The officers never march."

"Robinson always marches," Mullins replied.

James cupped a hand around his mouth and shouted over the noise of the motor. "Sir, did you find Vauquois?"

The lieutenant pointed at a small spur in the road a hundred yards ahead and to the right. "You're looking at it."

James stared at the lieutenant, perplexed, as the truck sped on. "What did he mean by that?" He swept his arm over the vast, empty wasteland around them. "There's nothing here."

William pointed. "Look."

They were abreast of the spur now, and James looked down the road that seemed to go nowhere. Jumbles of rocks dotted funny little mounds, and just by the road was half of a white metal sign with a red border around it, the letters "VAUQ" written on it in black.

Not rocks. Bricks.

James stared at the ruined village for a moment, trying to imagine what it had looked like when each mound had been a house, a church, a shop. He heard low whistles from some of the men.

"Someone's got to talk about this," William muttered.

"Who would believe you?" James tore his gaze from the spectacle of destruction, and when William didn't answer, he shifted his pack again and kept marching.

~

October 1, 1918
Near Éclisfontaine, France
First Day in the Line

JAMES HACKED at the dirt with his entrenching tool, tossing the dark, moist earth on the growing pile in front of him. He couldn't dig fast enough.

"Shit!" He flattened himself against the ground and grit his teeth as more shells exploded nearby, the noise constant, filling the air around him. He looked at William, who was crouched in the shallow pit beside him. "You alright?"

"Dandy. Whose fucking idea was this?"

"Dig."

They got back to their hands and knees and started working again, deepening their foxhole, expanding it out to the sides, sweating despite the cold, damp air. Explosions vibrated through the ground beneath them, rang inside James's skull, shaking his bones.

How could anyone possibly expect them to hold position here, under those German guns?

The same fools who left our own big guns behind, that's who.

Sergeant Rodriguez had broken the news to them when they'd arrived, crouching beside them as they'd started work on their foxhole. "We're holding here until the artillery can catch up and get into position."

"How long will that be?"

"Two days. Maybe three."

The shelling had started just afterward, merciless, precise, pounding the American positions with a relentless rain of steel.

James glanced to either side, at the long, serried line of foxholes the doughboys were digging into the slope of the shallow ravine where the battalion had positioned itself. Nothing moved above ground, but little clods of dirt flew out of the foxholes here and there as the men dug, their helmets bobbing and ducking at the rumble of the German artillery.

He felt an absurd impulse to laugh. Now the regiment's nickname made sense. The Blue Spaders. The men who dig.

"I think that's deep enough!" William shouted over the barrage.

James nodded, and started whacking the dirt pile they'd made in the front of the hole, packing it down while William threw a few more shovelfuls onto it for good measure.

James stuck his shovel into the dirt, reached above ground, and dragged his pack and rifle into the hole. Then he saw to his Springfield, brushed away the loose dirt that had fallen on its action. He rested the rifle against the side of the hole and reached around his belt for his water canteen. He unscrewed it, took only enough to wet his mouth.

The same idiots who'd left the artillery behind had neglected the water as well.

"Dammit!" William hugged his rifle close, blinking as dirt showered over them.

The rate of explosions crescendoed, merged together into an ear-splitting roar, driving all thoughts from James's brain. He clenched his canteen in his hands, moving his head side to side, anything to shake off the unbelievable noise and power of the enemy guns.

He wasn't sure how much later, but the shells suddenly stopped and moved off somewhere else, a distant rumble.

"First aid!" A voice James didn't recognize, filled with panic, screamed from somewhere along the line. "First aid!"

How many of the men had been hit? James raised his head ever so slightly over the lip of foxhole, but couldn't see anyone above ground, everyone no doubt as low as they could get. A few craters had broken in among the line, smoking gently, the acrid smell of explosives burning his dry throat.

He raised his head higher, looking out over the lip of the ravine toward the German positions. The bastards were out there somewhere, among the rolling high ridges and hills, their slopes dense with woods, the valleys and ravines between them clouded by heavy, damp mist.

James swallowed hard, staring up the gentle slope in front of him. He could just make out the dark outline of where the ground dropped away into the Rau de Mayache and Exermont Ravine, two broad, steep-sided gullies running across the regiment's front. It would be one of their first objectives —whenever they got around to attacking.

James gripped his rifle tighter, tried not to think about the ravine at Soissons, the murderous fire the Germans had poured into it.

Tried, and failed.

Not this. Not again.

"Stay in your holes!" The voice belonged to Rodriguez, somewhere to the right. "They'll start again soon."

James groaned, ducked back into the hole. He sagged against the dirt, brushed clods of it off his duster and the gas mask bag across his chest. "Why did he have to say that?"

"I don't believe it."

"What?" James looked out William's side of the foxhole and saw a marvelous sight.

Lieutenant Robinson was running beside a line of men with thick wooden yokes over their shoulders, large steel pots dangling from them. Lieutenant Lanning cantered behind Robinson, his eyes squinted, crouching low, as if under a rain storm.

Hot rations. Real food.

"God bless the Army." William shook his head. "Crazy bastards, running in the open like that."

"They can do what they want, so long as that food is hot."

The first of the mess contingent had already passed their

foxhole and were running down the line, eliciting throaty cheers from the men belowground. One of the men, a short guy with freckles and a pointy nose, stepped down into their hole.

"Move over guys. Make way!"

James and William both scooted to make room.

"You all have what you need? Ammunition? Bandages?" Robinson and Lanning were there now, too, squatting beside their hole.

James held up his canteen. "We could use water, sir."

Robinson looked at Lanning.

"Water, right," Lanning said, breathing hard. "Anything else?"

James and William shook their heads.

Robinson stood. "Let's keep moving."

The officers ran off down the line, while the other soldier eased his load off his back and began unscrewing the lid of one of his containers. "You guys holding up?"

James opened up his pack and pulled out his ration tin and utensils. "It's not raining."

"Yet." The soldier smiled and held out a hand. "I'm Rhoades, Arthur Rhoades."

James and William shook the man's hand in turn.

"Your name could be Jesus Christ as far as I'm concerned." William wiped his nose. "We haven't had hot food in a week."

Rhoades finished unscrewing the canister, pulled a ladle out from a sack at his side. "I'm not surprised. We've been trying to catch up to you guys since St. Mihiel. The Hun has been shelling the rear, too. They hit an entire train of pack horses, and we had to spend a couple hours cleaning up the mess and getting replacements." He leaned over the canister, took in a deep smell. "I think it's still hot."

"Not if you keep jawing!" James held out his tin, his

mouth watering as the smell of stewed meat and vegetables hit him.

Rhoades dipped his ladle into the canister, slopped a spoonful onto James's tin, then turned to William and served him, scooping the thick, steaming stew onto his pail. "I can't give you more than two ladles for now. Got to make sure it lasts."

James didn't respond, but immediately dug in, gulping the food down as fast as he could move it from the tin to his mouth.

Rhoades wiped the ladle on a cloth and screwed the cap back on the canister. "I'll come back along if I've got extra."

"Will we be getting regular rations now before we assault Exermont Ravine?" William pointed a thumb over his shoulder toward the front.

"Excrement, you mean?" Rhoades smiled. "I wish I knew. Enjoy it while you've got it!"

"Thanks," James managed to say between bites.

Rhoades had just gotten to his feet when the air ripped apart around them. He flattened back on the ground next to James. "Holy hell!"

"Can't they wait?" William covered his mess tin, trying to protect it from the dirt the German shells had thrown into the air.

A shell struck nearby, the thud of its impact followed by a faint pop. James frowned, his heart jumping into his throat.

Oh God, no!

A hissing sound, another pop. He poked his head up over the edge of the foxhole, and saw a small, dark metal canister a few dozen yards ahead of them, a jet of greenish-yellow vapor shooting out of one side. At that moment, the unearthly wail of the klaxon started.

"Gas!" James's voice cracked as he tore his helmet off and reached for the sack at his chest.

The call was repeated up and down the line, frantic voices shouting the same, hated word.

James's hands shook as he pulled the mask over his face, tightened the straps around the back of his head. He forced his nose into the clips, winced as his nostrils were pinched shut, and opened his mouth to take in the mouthpiece. He drew a breath, saliva pooling in his mouth as it always did when the mouthpiece was shoved in it. He looked around through the thick, yellowish lenses of the mask at William and Rhoades putting on their own masks, the long, elephantine tubes leading from their masks to their filter cans, still stuffed in their sacks.

The air around them thickened, filled with the heavy vapor that billowed over them, settling down into the bottom of their foxhole. James felt for his helmet, put it back on his head, then found his rifle. It would make sense for the Germans to send a counter-attack now while they were disoriented. He knew the others were thinking the same thing because William reached for his Springfield and Rhoades had drawn a trench spike and a revolver from his belt.

James crawled up to the dirt pile in front of their foxhole and aimed his rifle into the thick pall of gas filling the air, trying to find the sights through the narrow, fuzzy field of vision offered by his mask. The sound of his own breathing filled his ears, one breath after another, his lungs straining with the effort to pull the air through his mask's filter. Then

—

Christ!

He flattened himself against the dirt, his heart pounding against the dirt beneath him as the German artillery picked up its dreadful pace again, explosions rippling around them in a constant, mind-breaking chain.

James squeezed his eyes shut, felt the ground lurch, his

ears ringing from a hot blast to their left. He opened his eyes, saw a jagged piece of shrapnel embedded in the ground beside him.

That one was close...

Something bumped his foot, and he looked around. His heart stopped.

Rhoades was writhing on the ground, his weapons cast aside, his hands clenched around his mask. William was trying to hold him still.

"Where is it? Where'd they get you?" William's voice was almost incomprehensible through his mouthpiece, but the frantic edge to it was clear, betrayed his terror.

Rhoades didn't respond, choking, spluttering as he rolled and bucked in William's grip. James stared, not sure what to do, and then he saw it between Rhoades's hands—a jagged tear a couple inches long across the mask's long tube.

The shrapnel.

William looked over at James, the expression in his eyes pleading for help.

James reached over and took hold of Rhoades's other arm, his helmet toppling off with the man's frantic motions.

"Hold still, dammit! Let me help!" He tried to place a hand over the tear in Rhoades's mask, anything to seal out the poisonous fumes, but the man was jerking around too much for James to get a grip.

Rhoades's hands ripped at his mask, tore it off, his uncovered face tinted yellow in the thick, toxic air. Frothy liquid trickling from the side of his mouth, his eyes wide, so wide they seemed ready to pop from their sockets.

Dammit, what do we do?

James wanted to yell.

William shook his head, his expression hidden by his mask.

James found Rhoades's hand, felt him grab hold, his

clammy grip a vice. James bit his lip, squeezed back, and held tight through the agonizing minutes. He wanted it to end, the awful sounds of Rhoades's frothy, hacking coughs, the man's agonized squirming.

How long could it possibly take for a man to die?

Rhoades choked, his entire body shaking with the effort to cough. His movements grew weaker, his head lolling side to side. He turned and stared at James, and, finally, let go of his hand.

James looked away from the dead man's unblinking stare, collapsed against the side of the foxhole, breathing hard, his throat dry, his mouth filled with watery spit. Neither of them spoke as they sat there, both of them looking anywhere but at Rhoades. The blast of the artillery had lessened, was tapering off.

William turned around, picked up his rifle, and went up to lie at the parapet. James saw his helmet, next to Rhoades's revolver and trench spike. He picked up the trench spike, stuck it in his belt. He reached for the revolver and put his helmet back on. Wordlessly, he set the revolver next to William, who remained still. As James turned to his own rifle, he saw his tin of food, abandoned and filled with clods of dirt, the stew thickened and coagulated, tinged green.

It would be no good now that the gas was in it.

Anger surged in him, and he picked the tin up and threw it across the hole. It banged against the ration canisters, splattering stew across its dented metal sides. The food inside would still be good if the seal held, if it kept the gas out. It might even be hot.

James's eyes darted from the canister and over to Rhoades, the man who had run through the open to bring them chow. His stomach turned, and he looked away, bent low over his rifle, the sound of his own breathing filling his head.

CHAPTER 30

October 4, 1918
Fourth Day in the Line

"Make ready! Fix bayonets!" The call drifted along the American foxholes, repeated by each man over the boom of the artillery.

Finally.

James massaged his stiff muscles, his joints swollen from the cold and inactivity. He shifted his position in the foxhole, checked his weapon one last time. He reached around for his bayonet, drew it from its sheath, and slid it into place.

"You check your grenades?" William scooted next to James, his own bayonet pointing skyward, Rhoades's holster and revolver swinging on his belt.

"Am I an idiot?" It came out more harshly than James had intended, the days of cold and fear fraying his nerves.

"That remains to be seen."

James turned to meet William's gaze, saw the same exhaustion and tension written there that he felt. "You check them?"

William nodded. "Always."

James turned to face the terrain in front of the foxhole again, eager to jump up and out, anything to get away from the funk of the last few days, the piles of their own waste and filth.

Excrement Ravine, indeed.

At least the artillery wasn't only on them now. James looked out toward the Rau de Mayache, through the fog, toward where the American shells were blasting the enemy lines, the flashes and distant booms a testament to the ferocity of the barrage.

William trained his rifle out over the lip of the foxhole. "I hope they like their own medicine."

James looked over at him and couldn't help but smile.

Serves the bastards right.

After four days of being under constant German bombardment, it felt good to hit back. James looked over his shoulder to where Rhoades's torn gas mask was still lying in the dirt.

Yes, it felt very good.

The rushing bellow of the artillery shells passing high overhead faltered for a minute, then resumed, the noise different somehow.

James's insides tensed. The American cannons had switched their targets, beginning the creeping barrage. It was time for the infantry to attack.

"Let's hope that did the trick." William adjusted his helmet.

James didn't say anything, but moved to get his feet under him, ready to spring up and out of the foxhole. Seconds ticked by, and James focused on keeping his breathing even and steady.

The shrill call of a whistle broke through the low bark of exploding shells, and James launched himself to his feet.

"Dammit!" He groaned, his stiff, cramped muscles protesting the motion. He limped forward, his feet numb.

On either side, soldiers were rising out of their foxholes and clambering up the last few feet of the ravine's slope onto open ground. William strode forward to James's right, his rifle held at high ready, his face hard with determination. Beyond William and farther to the right, a pair of tanks—the new, small ones with the round turrets on top—crept forward ahead of the infantry, their motors growling.

James stared into the fog, peering forward toward the Rau de Mayache and the Exermont Ravine. It was impossible that the two ravines would be undefended, but maybe the doughboys could just make it across the open and get down lower before the enemy artillery found them.

Had the Germans left the approaches to the ravine clear?

The air hissed to his left. A second later, a soldier on that side grunted and pitched to the side.

So much for that idea.

"Move!" Lieutenant Lanning, fifty yards to James's left, waved with his pistol. "Double time it! Spread out for—"

Lanning vanished in an explosion of dirt and fire, the men around him to either side thrown by the blast.

"First aid!" Someone was shouting. "First aid!"

James fought down his panic. What the hell were they going to do without an officer?

"Keep moving!" Rodriguez ran to the front, cupping one hand over his mouth to shout. "To the ravine! Go!"

James broke into a jog, gritting his teeth.

Soissons all over again.

The earth vibrated and pitched beneath James's feet, the world around him crashing down as the German guns found their range, tearing the ground to pieces around him, raining dirt and shards of sharp steel in every direction. Bullets whispered and sizzled around his head. Men screamed and fell along the advancing line, their comrades stepping over them as they charged forward.

James bent low, pointed his bayonet forward. The pace of the German guns quickened until the explosions blended together, thundering and staggering around him. James heard a sound like the howl of an animal, realized it was his own voice screaming, defying the cacophony.

A putrid smell stung James's nose and he nearly tripped. He glanced down, seeing for the first time the rotting, scattered bodies of men from the 35th Division who had attempted this attack before them—black, their dried blood caked in the dirt and grass.

"Goddamn it!"

James looked around and caught sight of William staring far off to the right, beyond the advancing lines of doughboys. Muzzle flashes lit up the fog, sparkling from woods and ridge tops.

"Our flank is in the air!" William pointed, shouting. "Why the hell isn't the Ninety-First Division advancing?"

James couldn't respond, his breath stolen by the blast of the German shells around them, awestruck by the long, unbroken crescent of flashes from enemy guns in front of them and to the side. The Germans had them from multiple directions, and there was nowhere to go but forward.

"Come on! Keep moving!" Rodriguez's voice was like a beacon in the turbulence and fire. "We're nearly there!"

James held his rifle close, focused on the broad ravine opening up in front of him. It was only a hundred yards ahead now. He didn't care what could be in it, wanted only to get down and out of the open.

A shell burst up ahead, sending shrapnel whistling past him. Something stung his right arm, and a man ahead and to his right fell over, grabbing a stump where his leg had been. James kept moving, didn't bother to look at his own wound.

The roar of the tank's engines grew louder as they reached the lip of the ravine. A flash erupted from the turret of the closer tank as it fired toward the other side of the gulley.

James cheered, and he heard other soldiers join him.

Make the Huns pay!

The machines started down into the ravine, but hadn't gone more than a few yards before one of them stopped cold, fire blasting out the top of its turret. The other tank pressed forward, then lurched as a German shell hit it. It spun completely around and lifted a few feet off the ground as the ammunition inside it detonated.

"Christ!" James instinctively put an arm over his face and felt something wet, his own blood smearing on his cheeks.

Rodriguez had reached the edge of the Rau de Mayache, and he turned around and waved before disappearing over the lip. "Assault into the ravine!"

A few seconds later, James reached the edge of the ravine, William right beside him. James had only enough time to register the thickly wooded slope in front of him before the gulley exploded with gunfire, the air even thicker with bullets than it had been in the open.

There was nothing for it. With a shout, James pointed his rifle into the maelstrom of fire and plunged after Rodriguez.

~

October 6, 1918
Near Vavincourt, France

EMILY STEPPED inside the wooden booth, carrying a crate of pea-green sweaters in her arms, cartons of cigarettes stacked up to her chin. She squeezed past Clara, who was leaning against the counter, her head in her hands.

"Where is Mrs. Wolfe?" Emily set the crate on the counter with a huff, a few of the cigarette cartons toppling off the sides. She straightened the gas mask bag across her chest, a chilling reminder of their proximity to the fighting. "Clara?"

Emily turned to look at her friend, but found her staring off across the courtyard toward the road into the village. Army trucks bearing the red cross of the medical services were streaming into the square and over to the little church on the other side, the growl of their engines reverberating off the little houses and cobblestones.

"They've been like that for hours now." Clara's voice was distant, flat. "More and more all the time."

Ever since the Army had established an aid station in Vavincourt a few days ago, the medical traffic from the front had been increasing. The aid station had filled almost to bursting overnight, forcing the canteen to move across the square, even though they'd only just finished setting up after their move from the St. Mihiel area. It was the first time the canteen had been set up next to an aid post, and the nonstop traffic of men through the area had kept them busy.

For days, everyone had been talking about a big offensive elsewhere, north of Verdun and near the Argonne Forest. Emily watched as a few orderlies helped men out of the back of the truck, the blood on white bandages obvious even from across the square. If this many wounded were coming back every day, the fighting there must be severe.

Please, please let William and James be safe!

Emily didn't want to think about it. She couldn't afford to worry about who could be in those trucks, wounded and in pain, not when she had so much work to do. She had to keep functioning. There was a lull right now while most of the men were eating luncheon, so they needed to take the opportunity to restock for the evening.

She snapped her fingers in front of Clara's face. "Where's Mrs. Wolfe?"

Clara recoiled back, frowned. "I don't know. I haven't seen her in a half hour. What's the matter with you?"

Emily tapped her foot on the floor, thinking. It wasn't like Mrs. Wolfe to step back from managing the canteen like this.

What was going on?

"Never mind." Emily reached for the cigarette cartons and started putting them in the shelves below the counter. "Just help me with these things."

Clara nodded, and they got to work organizing their wares and putting them away. They kept a few cigarette cartons out on the counter, along with a few of the folded sweaters. Emily rested her hand on the rough, pea-green wool. They were knitted and donated by people back home, the hopes of a nation for their young men in peril.

How many of those people were losing their sons right now?

A few of the stretcher-bearers filed over to the booth from across the canteen, their faces hard.

Emily put on a smile as the men approached. "Would you like some hot chocolate, soldier?"

They nodded, but didn't say anything. None of the normal flirting, the shy banter. Just polite nods and the faintest of smiles as they held out their mess tins for the hot, sweet liquid and paid for their cigarettes.

"Can I?" One of the men pointed at a sweater, his eyes two points of brown and white in his dirty face.

Emily couldn't remember if Mrs. Wolfe had said they were supposed to charge. She didn't care, either. "Of course."

"Thanks, miss." The soldier took the sweater and put it over his shoulder, his fingers leaving dark smudges on the cloth.

Without another word, they walked away.

"Poor dears." Clara set down the hot chocolate kettle with a soft clunk. "It must really be something this time."

"Yes." Emily drummed her fingers on the counter, anxiety building inside of her. More trucks were entering the courtyard and parking now, filling it. A low, plaintive noise reached Emily's ears.

The moans of the wounded.

"Oh." Clara put her hand to her mouth. "How awful."

Emily tried to focus on something else, set about folding and refolding the sweaters. But the trucks continued to arrive, parking closer and closer to the canteen, the moans and cries of the men being pulled off the trucks getting louder with each vehicle that arrived.

"Help me! Someone, please!

"Mother, help me!"

Emily couldn't stand it anymore. "I'm going to find Mrs. Wolfe."

She stepped around Clara, opened the door of the booth, and almost ran into a tall, thin man with a bald head and mustache.

"Oh," Emily said, noticing the blood stains on the man's white coat. "Pardon m—"

The man held up his hand, cutting her off. "I'm sorry, but are any of you trained as nurses?"

Emily looked back at Clara, who shrugged her shoulders, her expression blank.

"Nurses?" Emily shook her head. "No, we just offer refreshments. We're—"

"Today, you're nurses." The man pointed across the courtyard. "I need as many hands as you can spare. Find me over at the church in ten minutes."

"But sir, I..." Emily started to object, but the man had already turned around and was striding back across the courtyard between the trucks.

She heard the thud of footsteps as Clara came to stand behind her. "What do we do?"

There was a quaver in Clara's voice, and Emily didn't blame her. They didn't know much at all about medicine, not to mention treating wounded men. How could they possibly help? Emily stood there, listening to the terrible sound of the wounded.

She couldn't do it. She would just get in the way.

Is that the real reason you're afraid?

Emily raised her chin, reached up to straighten her hat. She would not be a coward, not now. "I'm going to find Mrs. Wolfe. You stay here."

She set off into the canteen. Unsure where to go, she let her feet carry her to the galley tent. She poked her head in, saw Ruth, Florence, and Gertie working on another batch of doughnuts while Rose and Helen poured more hot chocolate into a kettle.

Emily looked between the faces of the other women. "Have you seen Mrs. Wolfe?"

"I think she was in the mess tent." Gertie wiped the flour off her hands and onto her apron, the pale powder smudging her face. "She passed by a while ago."

"Three of you go talk to Clara at the booth. We…" Emily hesitated, not sure what to say. "We have a bigger job to do. She can explain. I'll be there in a few minutes, too."

Emily didn't wait to respond to the women's questions, but ducked back outside. She angled toward the mess tent, shivering in the cold. She stepped inside, slipping past two soldiers headed the other way. Her gaze swept the rows of tables, where men sat bent over letters, eating their rations, or sipping cups of coffee and hot chocolate, their heads resting in their hands. Lilly and Grace walked between the rows, stopping to help men with their spelling.

"Where's Mrs. Wolfe?" Emily put her hands on her hips, annoyed.

After all the harsh discipline, the woman had chosen this critical moment when they needed her guidance to run off.

Lilly looked up from a soldier's letter, a grave expression on her face. "She just left a few minutes ago."

"Left? Where?"

"I don't know." Lilly turned back to the soldier she was helping.

Why does she look so glum?

Emily walked toward the entrance on the opposite side of the tent, passing between the rows of tables, the scents of dirty men, paper, and tobacco in the air. She stopped at the entrance, cold air washing over her. She looked out ahead of her at a supply dump and a few houses beyond.

Where is she?

Movement to the side caught Emily's eye, and she looked to see—

"Mrs. Wolfe?"

She was sitting on a stack of crates, her back to Emily, a woolen blanket pulled over her shoulders, a piece of paper in her hand.

Emily walked toward her. "Ma'am, a medical officer says he needs us over at the aid station and—"

She stopped, sensing something was wrong. "What are you doing here?"

Mrs. Wolfe looked around. Her eyes were red and swollen, her cheeks wet, her pointy nose red. She turned back around and pulled her blanket tighter, staring into the distance.

"Mrs. Wolfe." Emily stood directly behind her now. "What's wrong?"

She'd never seen the gruff woman like this before. Through every moment in France, Mrs. Wolfe had been a rock, the person who always knew how to keep the women organized and on task. Seeing her in this state... Emily suddenly felt disoriented, lost.

After long seconds of agonized silence, Mrs. Wolfe looked down at the letter. "Trevor's gone."

"Trevor? Who's—" Emily stopped herself.

Trevor. Mrs. Wolfe's son.

Oh, God.

"Mrs. Wolfe, I'm...I..." Emily didn't know what to do, the weight of the woman's grief pressing in on her. She reached out, put a hand on her shoulder. "Ma'am, I'm so sorry."

Mrs. Wolfe didn't respond, but reached up and took Emily's hand. They stood there in silence.

"Emily!" Helen appeared around the corner of the mess tent, fastening a fresh apron around her waist. "They need you right now. More trucks are arriving."

Emily looked back at Mrs. Wolfe, gave the woman's hand a squeeze. "I'm coming."

"It's very simple." Captain Buchanan, one of the Army surgeons, led the way between the trucks and toward the church. "You'll do basic tasks for us. Triage, taking the rags and bandages out to be burned, anything to free up skilled members of my staff for other work."

"Triage? Will that require any medical knowledge?" Emily almost had to run to keep up with him, the other women from the canteen in a group around her.

Buchanan shook his head. "No. The stretcher-bearers can help you."

They rounded the back end of another truck and emerged in front of the church, the sounds of the injured men all around them now, the reek of blood, filth, and vehicle exhaust choking the air. Buchanan turned left and walked down a narrow street between the church and a brick wall before turning right again. He stopped in front of an open gate so suddenly that Emily almost ran into him.

He pointed down the street. "We want the walking wounded brought around this way and over to that building there."

"Walking wounded?" Emily's gaze followed his arm to look at a dilapidated *bains-douches* a few doors down. Nurses and orderlies were helping a few men limp inside while others rushed in and out, carrying armfuls of bandages and boxes filled with little glass bottles.

"Yes, that's men with more minor wounds." Buchanan gestured back the way they came. "Take cases that need immediate attention into the church."

"It seems straightforward enough." Clara nodded, her tone cheerful, though the clenched hands at her waist betrayed the same tension Emily felt.

What if they chose incorrectly, sorted a man into the wrong group, and cost him any chance of survival?

Buchanan turned again and pointed through the stone gate in front of them. "Anyone too far gone to treat goes here."

Emily leaned out to look inside the gate. Beyond was a wide courtyard, part of the church's cloister. A covered walkway ran around the periphery, closed in by elaborate gothic stonework. In the center of the courtyard was a small fountain, surrounded by a closely cropped green lawn, a stocky apple tree in one corner. A few rays of afternoon sunshine cut through the clouds and past the church spire to fall in golden patches on the green grass. Emily's gaze rested on two mud-colored bundles lying near the tree. She swallowed hard, her mouth going dry when she realized what they were.

Those bundles were soldiers, their drab uniforms blood-stained and torn, their forms still.

"We were putting them in an alley behind the church, but it filled up." Buchanan started back the way they had come.

Emily held out a hand, stopping the surgeon in his tracks. "We're just leaving men there to die?"

Buchanan met her gaze, his eyes distant. "They were dead before they got here."

Emily opened her mouth to say something else, but he held up a hand, stopping her. "We can't waste staff on men who are beyond our ability to help. I'm sorry."

Emily glared at him. How could he say that? How would these men's families react if they knew their sons and fathers were abandoned and alone at the end? Through what torment did it put the men to lie there, hopeless and alone? What if some nurse somewhere were dragging William to a place like that and leaving him in a heap?

None of that mattered now. There was no other choice.

Emily nodded. "I understand."

Buchanan pointed at Helen and Rose. "You two, head inside the church and report to Nurse Carselli. She'll explain your jobs in there."

The two women turned and walked away without a word.

Buchanan turned to Gertie, Clara, and Emily. "The rest of you work on triage with the stretcher-bearers. They'll help you make any hard choices."

"You can count on us, sir." Gertie crossed her arms, determination on her face.

Buchanan tilted his head in acknowledgement. "I'll check on your progress in a few hours and see about rotating you with the others."

He walked off and left the three of them standing there.

Emily looked down at her shoes on the gray stone, suddenly wishing she could be anywhere else.

You baby.

As long as James or William didn't have that choice, Emily didn't, either.

She cleared her throat. "Let's get to work, ladies."

They walked back to the front of the church, and Emily saw Buchanan disappear inside just as two new trucks pulled up.

A pair of men—the same ones who'd come to the canteen earlier—ran up to the vehicles.

"Nurses!" One of them shouted, looking around him. "We've got more wounded!"

Emily followed Clara and Gertie toward the trucks, hoping that her nerves didn't show.

Gertie waved as they reached the two men. "I'm Miss Dibbs, and this is Miss Robbins and Miss Culver." She gestured at Clara and Emily. "We're here to assist you."

The one wearing the pea-green sweater pointed at his chest. "I'm Moore, that's Devitt. God bless you."

CHAPTER 31

Emily was not tired. She was not hungry. She was not thirsty. She was not upset.

She was busy, and there was not a moment for anything else.

She lost track of time, gave up on trying to keep the blood off her dress, focused instead on the routine. As each new truck stopped in the square, she, Clara, and Gertie would help the wounded men inside clamber down, then Devitt and Moore would hop into the trucks to evaluate the men who couldn't get out on their own.

"You girls focus on getting the walking wounded to the bathhouse. We'll worry about the men headed to the church and the others."

The others. The ones they carried to the courtyard to die.

"Can you walk? Can you walk this way?" Emily moved between the crowd of men behind the truck, asking each one of them in turn, trying to judge the severity of their wounds. Bandages around heads, around limbs, wet with blood and caked with mud and dirt. The soldiers turned to look at her, exhaustion and bewilderment on their faces.

"I can try, ma'am."

"Which way, miss?"

"Get these men moving along!" Devitt poked his head out the back of the truck. "We need them out of the way to load the stretchers."

"Come on!" Emily waved to get the attention of the soldiers milling around behind the truck. "This way."

They led the soldiers down the narrow street toward the *bains-douches,* the men groaning and cursing as they walked, and passed them off to the nurses waiting at the doorstep.

Emily looked behind her, saw one man had fallen behind, limping. She ran back to him, threw his arm over her shoulder, and walked with him, struggling under his weight.

"You're going to be alright." She didn't know what else to say, tried to make her voice sound pleasant. "We're taking care of you."

He nodded his head, gritting his teeth.

Gertie appeared on his other side and took some of the weight off Emily. "Aren't you lucky, soldier? How many of your pals have two girls on their arms?"

The soldier laughed faintly. "I don't reckon my pals can put their arms on anyone anymore, ma'am."

Emily met Gertie's gaze, saw the same anxiety there that she felt.

What was going on in this battle to the west? Could it be that the Allies were losing after all? Was the Army collapsing?

They reached the steps of the bathhouse and a pair of nurses walked over to them. "We've got him."

Emily and Gertie transferred the soldier to the nurses' care, turned, and made their way back. No time to worry what became of him, or even know his name, the same process repeating itself without end.

"Oh, hell." Emily wiped her forehead, sweating despite the autumn chill. In the time it had taken them to get the last bunch to the bathhouse, two more trucks had arrived. Clara was already moving between the men, trying to determine who could walk while Devitt and Moore hauled themselves into the vehicle's bed, their bloodstained stretcher held between them.

"Can you walk?" Clara's voice was almost lost among the groans of the soldiers and the growl of automobiles. "Can you walk, soldier?"

"We're taking too long." Gertie sighed and started forward.

Emily nodded, following a step behind. If only there were a way to evaluate them more quickly…

She stopped in her tracks and grabbed Gertie by the sleeve. "Let me try something." She cupped her hands over her mouth and shouted. "If you can walk, come toward me!"

All of the soldiers turned to look at her, then limped and shuffled in her direction, their eyes staring out of filthy, blackened faces. Emily and Gertie met them, arms threaded around shoulders, and they walked together to the bath-house, Clara supporting a man in the back of the group.

The soldier Emily was helping smiled at her, his green eyes bright. "You're the most beautiful thing I've ever seen."

She looked down at her dirty gray dress, spattered here and there with blood, and fought the insane urge to laugh. "You're going to be alright, soldier. I've got you."

The seconds and minutes and hours blurred together, stained red and khaki. More trucks, more soldiers, the sun sinking lower into the sky, Emily's voice hoarse from shouting.

"If you can walk, come this way!"

Emily handed off a man she was helping to one of the bathhouse nurses. She pulled her hat off, squeezed her eyes shut, and leaned against the cool stone by the gate.

I am not tired. I am not *tired.*

She opened her eyes just as Gertie passed behind her, running.

"Come on!" Gertie hiked her skirt up with her hands as she moved. "Another batch!"

Emily pushed her hat back on and followed. In the square, Devitt and Moore were unloading a man on their stretcher while the other wounded men stood around, dazed.

"If you can walk, come toward me!"

Clara and Gertie took a limping man between them and led the way while Emily followed behind, watching for stragglers.

"Don't put me in there! Please!" The hoarse whisper was barely audible over the din of the idling motors, but the note of panic made Emily turn to look.

The soldier on Devitt and Moore's stretcher was writhing around, his head lolling back and forth, a look of terror on his pale face.

"No!" He choked, his voice hardly more than a whisper. "Don't leave me back there!"

Moore and Devitt didn't respond, a pinched expression on their faces. They walked over to the cloister gate and disappeared from view.

Emily swallowed, a sickly feeling wrapping itself around the pit of her stomach. Somehow the man's terrified murmurs were still audible from inside the cloister when Moore and Devitt emerged a moment later, their stretcher empty.

You can't help him.

Emily forced herself to turn away and ran to catch up with the group.

"What's going on back there?" Clara looked over her shoulder at Emily as she helped the soldier she and Gertie had been assisting into the hands of the nurses.

Emily shook her head. She couldn't speak, the man's voice carrying up the noisy street despite how quiet it was.

Or was she imagining it?

"Someone... Please... I don't want to die!"

Clara's eyes widened, and they both stood there a moment, unable to move, rooted to the spot.

"Nurses!" Devitt's shout broke over the soldier's cries. "Come on!"

Emily wiped her cheeks, tears she didn't even know were there. She locked arms with Clara, and they walked together to the square.

WHEN THEY PASSED the cloister gate again with a fresh group of soldiers, the whispers of the dying soldier had become fainter, less frequent. The men stared, horrified, into the cloister as they passed, or looked down at their boots, their expressions blank.

When the bathhouse filled and they began taking the men to a covered market farther down the street, he was barely audible, no more than a whimper.

"Mother... Mother..."

Emily gritted her teeth, trying to shut out the awful sound.

Please. Just make it stop. Let him die. Let it be over.

Fewer ambulance trucks were arriving now, the pace slowing to a trickle, the evening air making Emily shiver and wish she'd remembered her cloak. She looked across the square at the canteen and saw Florence wave from the booth. She didn't have the energy to wave back. It seemed a long time ago that she'd been there, handing out hot chocolate and sweaters. Was Mrs. Wolfe faring well? She'd almost forgotten about the woman and her son in the chaos.

A single truck was waiting, the wounded men hopping out of the back, wincing and groaning as their feet struck the cobblestones.

Gertie came to a stop at Emily's elbow, cupped a hand around her mouth. "If you can walk, head over this way!"

This group was smaller, and none of the men needed help getting to the market. Emily walked at the edge of the group, repeating the same encouraging phrases she'd said a hundred times. They were almost at the cloister gate, and Emily girded herself for the gasps of the dying man—but they never came.

She breathed a sigh, her relief at not having to endure the awful noise anymore at war with her sorrow for the man.

What a hideous way to die.

"Make way. Coming through."

The group of soldiers parted and Emily stepped to the side as a pair of stretcher-bearers walked out of the bathhouse and squeezed past, carrying a soldier between them. She caught sight of the man's green eyes staring blankly into space and recognized him instantly. The one who'd called her beautiful.

Emily stopped in her tracks. "But… He wasn't that badly hurt!" The words tumbled out of her. "Why?"

One of the stretcher-bearers looked over his shoulder. "Beats me."

Emily stared after them. She balled her hands into fists, squeezed shut her burning eyes.

I am not upset. I am not upset!

"Please. Please, help me."

I am not upset.

"Sister? Can you hear me?"

Emily opened her eyes. Someone was talking to her. The group of soldiers she'd been walking with were ahead now,

Clara and Gertie's white hats bobbing among the olive drab uniforms.

"Over here. Please…"

Emily looked to the side through the open cloister gate. It was the dying man, lying by the fountain between the still forms of two other soldiers.

How could he still be alive? And if he was alive, could he be moved to the church and treated? Emily hesitated, Buchanan's words coming back to her.

We can't waste staff on men who are beyond our ability to help.

"Please," the man whimpered. "Help me."

Before she knew what she was doing, Emily was walking forward, stepping between the still, blue-lipped bodies of the men laid out in the cloister, their limbs jutting out in odd, stiff angles. Her eyes rested on the face of one of the dead men, the lower jaw and half of one side torn away, the one good eye staring up at her. She stopped.

"Please don't leave me here."

Emily fought her instinct to run away and leave the ghastly cloister behind her. She bit her lip, picking her way among the dead until she stood over the wounded man.

He peered up at her, his brown hair matted and tousled, his skin almost white, his lips tinged blue, an odd green hue to the foam at the corners of his mouth. He drew shallow, rattling breaths, his hands folded across a mangled torso stained red with blood. His mouth moved, but Emily couldn't understand what he said.

"What did you say?" She knelt beside him, resisting the urge to wrinkle her nose at the strange chemical odor that mixed with the smells of blood and soggy, rotting wool.

He licked his lips. "Please help me." His voice was so quiet that Emily had to bend forward over him.

"I…" Emily looked for words, found the same, threadbare

ones she'd used all morning. "I'm here, soldier. You're going to be alright."

He coughed, shook his head. "Please help me. I'm freezing to death."

Emily felt something cold against her skin, looked down, and saw his hand nudging hers. She took it, shocked at how icy the man's fingers were.

"I'll find you something warm. What's your name?"

"Brian."

"Let me see here, Brian." Emily twisted about, careful to keep her grip on the man's hand. There was a blanket wadded up at the feet of the man laid out behind her. She reached over, pulled it from the dead man's feet, and spread it over Brian's legs, her one-handed motions clumsy. "There you are."

Brian coughed, more of the green foam gathering at the corners of his mouth. "Please."

"Is that better?" Emily tucked the blanket around him. "Do…Do you need something else?"

He stared at her. "Please."

"Please what?" Emily instantly regretted the exasperated tone in her voice.

What was she supposed to do? Moore and Devitt had made a mistake. If Brian was still alive after all this time, he should be in the church, where the surgeons could help him.

Maybe they still could.

She had to let them know. "I'll be right back."

Emily tried to release Brian's hand, but he held on tight, his eyes flying wide. "No! Don't leave!"

"I'll just be gone a minute." She untangled her fingers from his. "I'm going to get help for you."

Brian shook his head, his voice husky with tears, desperate. "No! Don't leave me here! Don't leave me alone!"

Emily stood, her throat tight. "I'll be right back."

She turned and stepped as fast as she could through the obstacle course of dead soldiers, Brian's feeble cries following her as she went. She reached the cloister gate, turned, and sprinted toward the square.

"Emily?" Gertie was walking past carrying a crate of bandages. "Where are you going?"

Emily didn't answer, but ran past her friend. She emerged into the square, and spied Moore and Devitt by the church door, folding up their stretcher. The square was oddly empty now, the ambulance trucks gone, an unfamiliar hush hanging in the air.

Emily ran up to the two men, pointed back down the street. "The man you brought back there, Brian, the one who protested. He's still alive!"

Moore and Devitt looked at each other, but didn't move.

Emily stepped toward them. "Well, aren't you going to do something?"

Moore scratched his temple. "Miss, there's nothing we can do for any of the—"

Emily waved her hands, cutting him off. "Yes, I know. This one is different. He's been crying out since you left him there." Emily's voice cracked. She balled her fists, refusing to let the men's impassive stares deter her. "I think he might make it if he gets treatment."

They didn't move.

Emily took another step forward, stomping her foot. "Well?"

They stared at her for a moment before Devitt hauled up the stretcher. "Come on."

Emily led them back down the street and through the cloister gate. "He's right over here."

She stepped between the bodies, averting her gaze from the one with the mangled face, and stopped next to Brian. "Let's get him up and inside."

Moore and Devitt put the ends of the stretcher poles on the ground and leaned against them.

Emily bent down. "Well hurry up! He's cold." She turned to face the man on the ground. "Brian? I'm here."

Brian didn't say anything back, his gaze fixed on something over her shoulder.

She took his ice-cold hand, squeezed. "Brian? Brian, I've brought people to help you."

His hand remained limp, his eyes unfocused, a puddle of green foam accumulating in the grass beneath his mouth, which lolled open.

Emily fought to breathe, a crushing pain in her chest, tears stinging her eyes. "Brian?"

Devitt cleared his throat. "Like I told you, miss. There wasn't any hope for him."

She shook her head. "You just left him here. You didn't even try. He begged me to stay, and I..." She held Brian's hand with both of hers, pulled it against her chest. She shuddered, fought not to cry.

I am not upset. I am not upset.

Something touched her shoulder. She looked around and saw Moore standing over her, his face in hard lines. "Miss, can I get you anything? A coat? It's freezing here."

She shook her head. "He was cold, too."

Moore nodded, turned on his heels, and walked away with Devitt, leaving Emily alone with the dead.

She fought to rein in her emotions. Fought, and failed. The tears she'd been holding in all afternoon burst out of her, and she rocked back and forth sobbing, her emotions jagged, confused, out of control. She cried for Brian, for the dead men lying around her like bundles of junk, for her fears, for every terrible thing she'd ever imagined could happen to William and James, for all the new ones she now knew were possible.

"Emily!" Clara's voice cut through her grief. "Captain Buchanan says it's time to rotate. Nurse Carselli needs us inside!"

Emily looked over her shoulder, saw her friend standing at the gate. "I'm… I'm coming!"

Clara nodded and walked away.

Emily looked back down at Brian's staring eyes.

I am not upset.

She let go of his hand, wiped her cheeks dry. What good were tears now? They wouldn't make one bit of difference, wouldn't help anyone. She stood, forcing her emotions down, regaining her composure.

Tears were useless. They served no purpose. She wouldn't let them overcome her again, not while others depended on her.

She took one more look at Brian, then turned on her heel and walked between the empty bodies. There was nothing more she could do for him, but there were wounded men she could still help, and she wouldn't let some damned pointless crying stop her.

Emily lifted her chin and stepped out of the cloister, leaving it to the dead. By the time she passed out of the gate, her eyes were dry again.

~

September 21, 1919

JAMES EASED his bedroom door shut, closed his eyes, and leaned back against it.

It was done. Emily knew.

"Are you sure you don't want anything for dinner?" His mother's voice carried up the stairs, muffled through the door.

James barely heard her, his mind racing. Emily would never want to see him again. They were through. Any idiot could see that. But at least she wouldn't wonder about William anymore. She now knew what she needed to know.

"James?" His mother's voice was closer now, just outside his door.

"No." When his mother didn't reply, he added, more softly, "Thank you."

He listened for her footsteps, heard only silence.

After a moment, she let out a sigh. "We'll save you a plate if you change your mind."

Her feet scraped on the floor as she turned, her soft footsteps fading away down the hallway.

James opened his eyes, walked to his bed, and sat down.

Yes, Emily and her family wouldn't have to suffer uncertainty anymore. Wasn't that what James had wanted for months? Hadn't he struggled and debated how to do what now was done? Emily would be better now. She could begin to heal. Hell, she'd filled in the story better than he could have imagined.

He saw again her expression as she'd put the pieces together, realization hitting her.

"He took that nest with you."

She would spend the rest of her life seeing William in the machine gun emplacement, dying face-to-face with the enemy, a hero. This was the best possible outcome. And if it meant Emily hated him?

He'd been a fool to think it could end any other way.

"You killed him!"

Yes, he had, as surely as if he'd pulled the trigger. That, at least, was a fact, and he more than deserved her anger.

That didn't make the pain of losing her any more bearable. He massaged his chest, trying to get at the ragged ache there.

Failing, he stood up, unbuttoning his uniform tunic, eager to be out of the thick wool. Maybe word of this would spread, and all the people who'd cheered for him at the parade today would come to revile him.

He probably deserved that, too.

"You never said anything? You let them... let us *think he was missing?"*

James folded his tunic and set it on the bed. He walked over to the window and looked outside, over at Walt's house.

What would he have to say? He probably wouldn't want to see James again, either. And what about Uncle Chester and Aunt Maggie? How would they react to it all?

No Emily. No Walt. Not a single friend in Saint Vrain, except his parents, maybe. It would not be easy to live like that, but that's how it would be.

James continued undressing, put on a pair of dark twill trousers and a white shirt. He hung up his uniform and walked to the middle of the room, unsure what to do next.

His stomach growled. He actually *was* hungry. He could wait for a while and go down to eat once his parents had retired for the evening. He didn't want to face their questions about what had happened at the Culver house, not now.

He paced back and forth, and his gaze landed on a picture on the wall. He walked to it, picked it carefully off its hook.

It was his cousin Henri, his Aunt Ethyl, and his Uncle Cyrille together in France. The picture was a few years old, from sometime before the War.

James ran a finger over the glass, an idea coalescing in his mind.

Henri knew already, and he'd accepted James without judgment.

Better than you deserve.

James set the picture back and strode over to his desk.

Finding a piece of paper and pencil, he started writing. He could draft the message now and send a telegram tomorrow.

He chuckled in spite of himself. Months ago, he'd been eager to leave that wrecked country and return to a place removed from the War. Now, he wanted to run away to France. The absurdity of the situation almost made up for how awful it was.

Running away.

That's exactly what it was.

James looked down at his note, tempted for a second to crumple it up and throw it in the wastebasket. He took the note in his hand, moved to crush it into a ball. Things would get better here. Nothing was impossible, was it?

He saw again the perfect rage in Emily's face as she'd walked toward him, her fists clenched at her sides.

Some things *were* impossible.

He'd never been the kind to run, not before the War, and certainly not during it.

There's always a time to start.

And what had he been doing all these months besides running? Putting off the inevitable?

He smoothed the note on the desk and folded it in half. There was nothing else to do.

Nothing to do but leave.

~

October 9, 1918
Hill 263, France
Ninth Day in the Line

JAMES GASPED, fought to breathe, his heart pounding in his ears as he pushed himself up the steep, wooded slope. Bullets sliced through the forest from somewhere up ahead, blasting splinters off tree trunks and shearing off autumn leaves to flutter to the ground like an odd kind of yellow-brown snow.

James leaned forward, used the butt of his rifle as a cane, put all of his might into moving up the hill, his legs and chest burning. He paused and leaned against a tree—and panic seized him.

Where the fuck is William?

For that matter, where the fuck was anyone? He'd been by his squad mates a minute ago, to the right of William and Collins. Had he not even seen them go down? Was he completely alone now?

Damn this forest!

It kept scattering the doughboys, turning them around, dispersing platoons and companies until everyone was lost and confused, as if the landscape itself were trying to aid the Germans and break up the American attack.

He turned around on the spot, peering through the trees and brush, trying to find someone else, listening for voices between the boom of gunfire and the occasional scream.

"Don't stop! Keep moving!"

James looked to his left, where the call had come from. Was that Captain Robinson's voice?

"Help that gunner up!"

Yes, that sounded like Robinson. James caught sight of some khaki shapes in that direction, angled himself to intercept their path higher up the hill, and started off again.

Sweat dripped down his temples and forehead despite the heavy chill in the air. The slope was getting steeper with every step, and he was falling behind.

Come on, dammit. Move!

He broke into a slow canter, his breath coming in painful gasps. The distance between him and the other Americans closed, and in a minute, he was pulling in behind them. He recognized Corbett, Mullins, Peterson, and Wadleigh, and there was Bird with Shoals and some of the other Chauchat gunners. He saw an officer with a pistol farther to the left, helping one of the gunners to his feet.

Definitely Robinson.

Relief took away the sharpest edge of James's panic, giving him new energy. But where the hell were William and Collins? And where was Sergeant Rodriguez?

No time to stop and figure it out.

They pushed up the hill, everyone bent low. The bullets were flying thicker now, the spray of splinters and fluttering leaves in the air a constant, stinging blizzard.

James cursed under his breath, his left cheek searing where a bit of wood had scratched it. Something warm trickled down his face, but he kept moving.

"Son of a bitch!" He tried to raise his leg and couldn't bring it up high enough, the slope so steep now that it was almost a wall. He stopped, breathless. How could they possibly attack through this?

Ahead, the men were crawling, scrambling, clawing their way up the slope, cursing and stumbling as they went.

Bullets smacked into a tree to the right of him. Staying still was certainly not an option. There was nothing for it. He'd have to climb.

James reached up, grabbed hold of a sapling, and pulled himself up, pushing off the ground with his rifle, the tip of his bayonet bobbing dangerously next to his ear. His arm throbbed, the shrapnel cut from days ago aching through its bandage. He gritted his teeth, planted his left foot on the ground, and lifted himself up the slope.

He came up, then fell forward onto his knees, steadied himself, reached up for the next trunk, then a root, then a bunch of branches. He hauled and dragged himself upward, dirt spattering his face as the boots of the men above him kicked and fought with the earth, bullets spitting up dust where they hit.

A strangled cry brought James's gaze upward just as one of the men above fell from the slope, clutching his abdomen, a ragged hole in his back. He toppled over backward, caught in a set of low branches. The man thrashed and screamed, trying to free himself. More holes burst out of his back, and he jerked and lay still, strung up in the branches.

James pulled himself to the side, avoiding the man's rifle as it bounced and slid back down the hill, clattering as it went. He grabbed hold of the next tree and kept climbing. When he came even with the man, he couldn't help but glance at his face.

Mullins, his face frozen in an expression of terror, blood trailing out of his mouth and spattered across his face.

James swallowed, his mouth dry.

Don't stop. Keep moving.

He pushed and clawed, the branches grabbing at him as he went. Something caught on his sleeve. He pulled, heard a tearing sound, and scrambled up.

The slope was leveling off now, the steps becoming easier. James grabbed his rifle with both hands, finally able to move without pulling on anything, the thwack of bullets gone. That was good on both counts, because the trees were thinning out. Were they at the summit?

He ran to catch up with the men ahead, just as they reached the edge of the trees. There was a small glade ahead of them, then more forest. The broad shoulder of the hill was to their left, its summit beyond. The American troops stopped, panting.

"Set up here!" Robinson motioned to the Chauchat gunners. "Get ready to cover us moving across that opening."

James knelt near a tree trunk, dread filling him as he watched Bird get down on his stomach and train his gun across the glade. Where was the machine gun that had been shooting at them? Was its line of sight blocked now by the shoulder of the hill?

Do the bastards have another one?

Robinson turned to a group of about ten men to his left that James didn't recognize. "You men come with me."

"Yes sir!" they shouted together.

Then Robinson looked over at Corbett, Wadleigh, Peterson, and the four other infantrymen clustered near James. "Be ready to flank around whoever opens fire."

James nodded, held his rifle tighter.

"Let's go!" Robinson launched himself into the glade at a sprint, the soldiers he'd chosen to follow him a couple steps behind.

James shouldered his rifle, counted the agonizing seconds by the beat of his heart, his gaze fixed on Robinson.

One beat. Two. Three.

A machine gun tore the air, and two men fell instantly.

"Dammit!" James searched for a target in the woods on the opposite side. Two more men fell, and another, gripping his side. The man crawled forward—and jerked as the Maxim finished him off.

"To the right!" Robinson yelled over his shoulder as he ran. "They're to the right. Two hundred yards!"

James rotated, aimed his Springfield into the woods… and saw nothing. The woods were too thick from this angle, and there was no way the doughboys could last out in the clearing.

Shit.

"Fucking dirty Huns!" Bird pivoted, pointing his Chauchat to the right. He opened fire, and James could see the rounds blasting out bits of trees ahead. The German gun faltered, then kept shooting.

Ahead, Robinson and the surviving soldiers with him

dove into the woods on the other side of the glade. A second later, their rifles barked, a slow reply to the chatter of the Maxim.

James wasn't about to let Robinson die out there. He reached down for a fresh clip, stripped it into his Springfield. "Let's go."

He stood, readying himself to head down the hill and to the right. He looked down the slope. "Christ."

They'd done this a hundred times in the past week, the same routine repeated with each new bunker, pillbox, and machine gun nest. A damned hill shouldn't change anything.

Corbett and three others turned to follow him —and froze.

A second later, James heard it, too.

A long scream, an unearthly wail, getting louder and louder until—

"Incoming!"

CHAPTER 32

James hit the ground as a tremendous explosion shook the earth beneath him. Dirt and debris showered over him as another long wail filled his ears.

Mortars.

The big kind.

He covered his head, squeezing his eyes shut against the awful screech, breathing in the musty smell of dirt and soggy leaves mixed with the acrid chemical odor of explosives.

The ground pitched and rolled, and then was still. James raised his head, could see a couple gaps blasted in the trees below, trunks split and torn, huge pale shards of wood scattered everywhere.

He pushed himself to his feet as the Chauchat gunners got back to work. He looked across the clearing, but he couldn't see Robinson or the others. They were firing their rifles, though, so at least some of them were still alive.

James turned to the other riflemen. "Come on! Before they fire again!" He picked a line through the trees, angling off down and to the left to take him behind the machine gun, and started at a run.

The snap of branches and panting of the other men told him they were following. The slope down became steeper, and soon James couldn't run, but had to step down sideways, holding on to the trees.

"Fucking again?" Corbett's terrified shout was almost inaudible as the terrible whistle of the mortars returned.

James turned and let himself fall into the slope, covering his face and head.

The hill shuddered, the air ripped apart by the terrific explosion somewhere behind them. He pushed himself up, kept going. A different noise now—the thwack and snap of bullets coming from the other machine gun, the one shooting from behind the hill's shoulder.

Another mortar announced its arrival with a long shriek, and James hit the ground. He started to roll down the slope, his own yell lost against the explosion. He hit a tree and lay against it, winded.

"You hit?" Wadleigh stood over him, held out a hand.

James took it, got to his feet. "Keep moving!"

They crashed and stumbled down the hill, hugging the dirt with every blast of the German mortars. The entire forest seemed ablaze with explosions and gunfire, the pace of the barrage accelerating.

James stopped in his tracks. There was a squad of Americans below, pushing up the hill and to the left.

"Hey!" James held his rifle in the air. "Over here!"

They could use all the help they could get flanking the machine gun.

One of the men, a sergeant, judging by the chevrons on his sleeve, saw James and pointed. The troops started in his direction.

A wail, a deafening crash, screams. James threw himself at the ground. Bits of wood and dirt covered him, falling down the collar of his tunic, bouncing off his helmet with a metallic clank.

He pushed himself to his feet, looking for the sergeant and his troops, and saw mangled, toppled trees instead, bits of scarlet-stained khaki cloth scattered here and there.

"The whole squad?" Corbett was next to James, breathing hard.

James didn't answer, but continued down the hill. After a few dozen yards, he angled more to the left, following the hill's contour. They'd gone down far enough now and needed to traverse over. Robinson had said two hundred yards, but how far over had they come when they'd descended?

Fifty, maybe? Seventy-five? It was damned impossible to know in these thick woods.

He looked around him as he ran, and saw it, a narrow little path a few yards below them, barely visible between the trees. It was angling up the hill, toward them and over to the left.

If I had to haul a Maxim up this hill, I'd take a path like that.

James turned to head toward the trail, pointed at it, wincing as a bullet struck the tree next to his head. "Make for the path!"

A wet thud. An agonized groan.

James looked in time to see Wadleigh clutch his arm, blood seeping between his fingers.

The man stumbled, lost his footing, and fell. James reached for him, his fingers closing around air. Wadleigh pitched forward, hit the ground, and rolled, knocking into trees as he went down screaming, his rifle and helmet following him as he careened toward the path. A second later, he crashed through a stand of bushes at the edge of the path and vanished.

James picked his way down the hill toward where Wadleigh had disappeared, Corbett and Peterson on either side of him, the others behind. They reached a gap in the bushes, and James peered through them at a short, steep embankment and the path below. He started to climb carefully down, the shriek of the mortar somewhere behind them. The trees and bushes around him crackled as a spray of machine gun fire hit them.

James cursed and jumped, the bush tearing and scratching at him as he fell. He landed on his feet, his tired legs buckling, the embankment shielding him from the machine gun. He sank to his knees as the others landed next to him. He straightened his helmet, made to stand up, and froze.

Not five yards in front of them were five Germans. They were standing over Wadleigh, one of them withdrawing a bayonet from his body.

The Germans looked over, saw them.

A shout.

A gunshot.

James threw himself forward, a step behind the others as he finished getting to his feet.

Peterson lunged with his bayonet, but one of the Germans slashed down with a shovel, catching him between the shoulder and the neck. James didn't look to see if Peterson was still alive, didn't wait for the Hun to withdraw his shovel, but punched his blade forward, catching his enemy in the ribs.

The German screamed and grabbed hold of James's rifle. James yelled and tried to withdraw his bayonet, but the German held it fast, shrieking. Something moved in the corner of James's vision, and he ducked, the wooden stock of a Mauser missing his head and striking his rifle. James let go of his weapon, lowered his shoulder, and threw himself in the direction of his assailant.

The German grunted, and they fell together, the odor of the man's sweat filling James's nose. A hand closed around James's throat, choking him.

James found the man's face with his hands, scratched at it, digging his fingers into his enemy's eyes, trying to gouge them out. The German screamed, loosened his grip on James's throat, and punched at his head.

The trench spike!

James reached for his belt, found the weapon he'd taken from Rhoades, and drew it out. He slashed the blade across the German's throat, the man's choking, gurgling scream hissing from between James's fingers. He didn't stop, but stabbed at the base of his enemy's neck until the German stopped struggling.

James spat out the vomit that surged into his mouth and jumped to his feet, knife out, ready to fight again. Corbett was there, smashing the butt of his rifle across the face of a German, knocking the man off the path and down the hill. Two of the other Americans were bayonetting a German again and again, while the third was reloading his rifle, a headless enemy leaning against the embankment in front of him, gore splattered over the dirt. Peterson lay still, the shovel embedded halfway down his torso, and another doughboy, one of the men James didn't know, lay still next to Wadleigh.

James wiped his knife on his pants and tried to sheath it, his shaking hands making the task difficult. "Come on, damn you!"

He finally succeeded and walked over to where his rifle and bayonet were still embedded in a writhing enemy soldier. James picked up his rifle, put a foot on his enemy's arm and pulled back hard. The man shrieked and moaned. James looked away and fired, silencing the man's cries.

Without a word, the Spaders regrouped, leaving their

own dead beside the Germans. They stepped just downhill of the path, keeping to the trees as they walked, rifles up, ready to fire. James tried to concentrate on his sights, the woods around him. He gripped the stock of his weapon, chasing away the feeling of his fingers digging into the German's face.

The path curved around, climbed back up the hill. A machine gun was firing, but the sound was different.

They were behind it.

"There!" James pointed his rifle at a dark shape, just a few yards off the path to the left. The entrance to a concrete machine gun emplacement. There were no other Germans around, the men they'd just killed probably part of the gun's infantry protection.

A rifle fired, then the slow thump of a Chauchat. A long shriek, followed by a huge explosion. After a pause, the Chauchat stuttered back to life.

James crouched down as bullets dug into a tree nearby. Was there another machine gun?

He waited, looking between the wide-eyed expressions of the other soldiers.

The Chauchat fired again. More bullets, more bits of bark and wood.

These were shots from their own side. They'd need to finish with this emplacement quickly. James hadn't made it this far to be shot by his own unit. He looked at Corbett, made a fist shape. Corbett nodded, dug out a grenade.

They all crawled to within a few yards of the bunker, then Corbett got to his knees, looking over his shoulder. James nodded, stood to a low crouch, bayonet ready while the other three trained their rifles around them, ready to repel any defenders.

Corbett pulled the pin, tossed the grenade in. They all ducked low.

The machine gun stopped, and James heard a panicked yell, followed by the sharp *boom* of the grenade's explosion.

James charged forward and into the bunker. He choked on the acrid smoke, his cough echoing off the narrow concrete corridor. He blinked, darkness closing in around him. He raised his rifle, aimed it forward at the slumped forms of the Germans, in silhouette from the light of the gun port, a small cloud of steam rising from the punctured water jacket of the toppled machine gun. The Germans looked dead, but James wasn't taking any chances. He shot one, worked his bolt, and shot the other, his ears ringing.

"Hold your fire!" Corbett was shouting outside the bunker. "We're Americans!"

James watched through the gun port as doughboys emerged from the trees. He turned and walked back toward the entrance, relief filling him when he saw Captain Robinson standing next to Corbett, Bird and Shoals a few feet behind them.

But no William, or any of the others from his squad.

He swallowed, sick to his stomach. At this point, how could they be anything but dead?

"We left Peterson, Wadleigh, and Dines down there, sir," Corbett was saying.

Robinson took out a notebook, wrote something down, and stuck it back in his pocket. He turned to face the others. "Good work. Let's keep moving up and to the left, see if we can't take out that other Maxim over the shoulder of the hill there. It's got the whole approach in its beaten zone. I'd like to get out of here before those mortars open up again."

James almost wanted to laugh at Robinson's understatement.

He stepped out of the bunker, slinging his rifle over his shoulder. The unit was moving off now, resuming the climb up the hill through the trees, angling to the left, past the glade and toward the distant chatter of a Maxim gun. James followed behind Corbett and Robinson, suddenly exhausted.

"Shit, James." Bird hefted his Chauchat, fell in step with James. "What the hell happened to you?"

"What do you…?" For the first time, he looked down at himself. His duster was completely spattered with blood, his hands and rifle coated with it.

"It's… it's not mine." James didn't know what else to say.

Bird nodded, and without another word, they followed the others up the hill.

~

October 12, 1918
Near Arietal Farm, France
Twelfth Day in the Line

"I COMPANY? Has anyone seen I Company?" A soldier stood at a bend in the path the men were taking across the draw, a dark shape beside the ragged column of soldiers trudging away from the front line.

James shook his head as he passed, though he doubted the man could see him in the dim, flickering light of the distant artillery explosions. "Sorry, no."

"Dammit." The soldier put his hands on his hips, turned to face back along the line. "Has anyone seen I Company?"

James kept walking, shifting his rifle on his shoulder, turning to focus on the inky shape of Corbett a few steps ahead of him.

Somewhere behind him, Bird snorted in disgust. "How much you want to bet that guy was shirking back here while his company got shot up?"

A few of the men muttered in agreement. More than a few soldiers from the regiment had turned up miraculously as they'd started the march back from their final positions at the Bois de Romagne, suddenly figuring out which way was north.

"Everyone's mixed up, Bird." Corbett turned his head to speak over his shoulder. "Or he could have been wounded or sent off as a stretcher bearer."

Bird ignored Corbett, the anger and fatigue in his voice obvious. "He looked fine to me. Stupid bastards. We should just send them over to the Germans."

"They're on our side, you fucker."

"Just shut up, the both of you." James didn't want to hear any of this bullshit, not now. He was too tired and too cold, his nerves frayed and raw.

Bird mumbled something inaudible, and Corbett faced forward again. The column marched in silence, their footfalls and breathing mingling with the rumble of the artillery behind them, back at the battle lines and that awful, keening sound.

Wounded men calling for help somewhere out there in the darkness, moaning in agony, pleading for someone to find them.

James tried to shut out their cries, the sound almost more than he could bear in his exhausted state.

The stretcher-bearers will find them. They'll help them.

Maybe.

Right now, James just had to get to the rear, get away from the battle, and, for God's sake, find something to eat.

He rested a hand across his abdomen, willing the painful, gnawing ache to subside. He stuck a hand in the musette bag at his side, but knew he wouldn't find anything in there this time, like the past half-dozen times.

You can always hope.

How long had it even been since any food had made it up to the front lines? James tried to count the days, gave up, his mind fuzzy and dim with weariness. Hopefully, there'd be plenty of slumgullion to go around in the rear.

The rear.

Behind the lines. Food. Rest.

It didn't seem real. The orders had come a few hours ago, just after 22:00.

The runner from Regimental HQ had found them at the front, digging foxholes, and told them the good news while catching his breath. "Colonel Erickson… says… get ready…to pull… back toward Cheppy… The Forty-Second Division… is relieving us."

"Do you hear that, boys?" Robinson had turned to the men in the dark, a smile in his voice. "We're moving out. Get yourselves ready, and stay sharp."

After a few more excruciating hours of waiting, the men from the 42nd had arrived, filing up through the woods and filtering into the foxholes the Blue Spaders had just finished digging.

"We saw the ground coming up this way," one man had said, his face hidden in the night. "You boys had one hell of a fight."

That was the truth.

"Watch your step." The phrase repeated down the line, and James lifted his leg high to step over a jumble of broken rubble. A smashed supply wagon, maybe? He looked out over the draw, at dark, irregular shapes scattered here and there. A particularly large flash erupted from somewhere behind them, and for a second it was bright enough to identify what all the shapes were.

Bodies. Bent, twisted, and contorted in the strange ways that men fell in combat. But the moment of brightness faded, and the draw returned to darkness, the low boom of the great explosion washing over them in the wind.

William could be out there, probably *was* out there.

James took a deep breath, let it out slowly, trying to focus on the dull ache in his feet rather than the pain in his chest.

What the hell was he going to tell Emily?

James pictured her face, imagined her shock, her tears at the awful news. It was almost too much for James to consider. Thankfully, the image faded away, his exhaustion too great to allow for much emotion beyond the heavy weight that settled behind his breastbone.

As soon as he had leave, he'd have to find her. Hopefully, he could get to her before the Army did. It would be better hearing from him.

They filed past the dark shape of broad, rolling hills, each one a monument to suffering. Hill 272. Hill 212. The ground sloped down and the column descended into Exermont Ravine. The stink of explosives and gas was still in the air, the ground torn and uneven from shellfire.

James gasped and pulled his head up. Had he nodded off walking?

"Move." Beggs, the man behind him, gave him a little push.

James spotted Corbett a few feet ahead and numbly plodded after him. He reached up, smacked himself on the cheek a couple times. He wasn't about to be the reason the unit got lost.

They climbed back up the wooded slopes of the ravine, a soft blue glow on the horizon announcing the arrival of the new day. It was easier to see now, the branches and roots cast in soft, dim light. As he stepped over the lip of the ravine and onto flat ground, James looked off to the left and saw the distant, dark shapes of the tanks he'd seen destroyed in the first attack, maybe two hundred yards away. How peaceful they looked now, like big boulders.

Were the bodies of the men inside still there? Was there even anything left of them?

James saw again the image of them burning, spinning from the force of their own explosions. At least William hadn't died in a tank, unless he'd done something stupid and tried to drive one somewhere at the end.

That's the fatigue talking, idiot.

By the time the column marched past the sign announcing the village of Cheppy—a shelled-out mess of wrecked houses and toppled bricks—it was nearly dawn.

"Halt!"

Corbett stopped in his tracks, and James did the same, peering around his squad mate to see what was happening. A dozen yards up the line, Captain Robinson was stepping over to an officer who stood at the corner of a hollowed-out church, a notebook in hand.

"Is this your company, Robinson?"

"No, Captain Thomas." Robinson pointed back at the men. "This is all First Battalion."

Thomas looked up from his book and stared at Robinson. "*That's* a battalion?"

They shared a look in silence that James couldn't quite see.

After a moment, Robinson cleared his throat. "Major Legge should be along soon with more details."

Thomas whistled. "Good God."

James shifted, the ache in his feet worse now that he wasn't walking.

Come on, already.

Thomas wrote something down in his notebook. "Keep heading south about two kilometers. You'll see some supply trucks there with your gear. You'll all bivouac there tonight."

"Yes, Captain." Robinson stepped back into line. "Forward!"

They started off again, passing through the village and back into countryside. The march couldn't have taken more than a half hour, but it felt like an eternity, every step agony.

"Thank God." James spied a few trucks ahead next to a little stand of woods by the road. A few men were there, unloading equipment and setting it in a big pile beside them. That would be their marching packs and shelter halves. There would be many spares.

When they came abreast of the trucks, the officers in the column gave the orders to halt and fall out. Some of the men dragged themselves over to the pile of equipment, but James didn't bother. He found a patch of ground beside a tree, looked around it for rocks. His head snapped up. He'd nodded off standing again.

James slipped his rifle off his shoulder and lay it on the ground next to him. He pulled off his helmet, dropped it with a clatter, and sank to his knees. Resting his head on the crook of his arm, he was asleep without another thought.

Music. Slowly at first. Only a few instruments. A drum, now a trumpet.

James groaned, opened his eyes to stare up at the branches of the tree above him. The sun was high in the sky now, its light filtering through a thin veil of clouds and the canopy of the forest.

"For the love of Christ!" Someone nearby cursed.

That was putting it mildly.

James sat up, gritting his teeth in pain, every muscle of his body aching. He looked around for the source of the noise and spotted it. Out by the road, past the sagging pup tents and bundles of men who were stirring on the ground, was a regimental band and—

He bolted to his feet, all of his pain forgotten. He stumbled forward on stiff limbs, and as he stepped out from the cover of the trees, the smell hit him.

Food.

There was a field kitchen set up on top of a cart, big soup canisters glinting silver in the weak sunlight.

James reached in his musette bag, dug out his mess tin, and had to keep himself from running. He was one of the first in line, his stomach growling and churning in expectation, the cheerful song of the band an afterthought. He held out his tin and accepted the thick, meaty stew from the soldier with a white apron over his uniform.

Slumgullion.

It was the most beautiful stew he'd ever seen.

"Thanks." James turned and trudged toward the trees, shoveling the food into his mouth while he walked. When he was back with his rifle and helmet, he sat down, his back against the trunk, and ate. It was delicious, better than good, better than anything he'd ever tasted. Only the band was playing now, everyone too focused on eating to speak, the clatter of spoons on mess tins a happy accompaniment to the music.

All too soon, James was licking his empty tin. He reached for his canteen on his belt, slipped it out of its cover, and shook it.

Empty.

"Damn."

He heard the stuttering growl of a motor and saw another truck pulling up, a large tank on its bed.

Just in time.

James stood again and started out for the road, tin in hand. With so many casualties, maybe there'd be extra grub.

A khaki wave was sweeping toward the water truck as soldiers emerged from their bivvies to refill their canteens.

James stopped mid-stride.

Sergeant Rodriguez. He'd seen a glimpse of him through the crowd for just a second.

James pushed past the other men, ignoring their curses and shouts.

It *was* Rodriguez, looking the other way toward the water truck.

James punched him on the shoulder.

"Ouch!" Rodriguez turned and elbowed the two men standing next to him, surprised recognition on his face. "Well I'll be damned. Hey, look at this, you guys!"

The two men turned to look.

James's heart jumped into his throat, did a summersault.

It was William and Collins, their mess tins and canteens out, looking at James in complete surprise.

In a second they were all talking at once, shaking hands, slapping each other on the shoulder.

"I thought you were dead!"

"We thought *you* dead."

"Did you get hit?"

"Only little scratches."

"How could they miss that big, fat head of yours?"

They laughed, smiled, the flow of men breaking around them.

James felt something wet on his cheek, wiped it away quickly. "Where the hell were you guys?"

"We drifted coming up Hill 263." William's expression darkened. "We ended up fighting along with Second Battalion for the past few days."

"Any of the others from the squad make it?" Collins pointed toward the water truck, and they all started moving for it, merging back into the traffic of thirsty soldiers.

"Corbett, Beggs, and Killeen were with me." James unscrewed his canteen's lid.

Rodriguez nodded. "McLean is with us, too."

James did the math in his head. Seven of twelve. Almost half of the squad gone.

No one spoke as they filled their canteens from the spouts on the side of the tank, gulping the water down as they stepped away. What was there to say?

"Let's get some more of this." James pointed at his mess tin. "And I bet Bird will want to see you, too."

"Bird made it?" William grinned, raising his canteen. "Now *that's* worth a drink."

James clanked his own canteen against William's, and they walked with their squad mates toward the mess cart.

CHAPTER 33

September 22, 1919

"Can I get you some coffee, dear?" Mrs. Gould put her hand on Emily's shoulder. "Or maybe something stronger?"

Emily made herself smile. "Coffee would be wonderful, thank you."

Mrs. Gould nodded and made for the kitchen. "I think I may take the stronger. Better to drink it than pour it down the drain come January."

Emily laughed, glad for Mrs. Gould's levity. It was a reminder that the world would keep on spinning, even if it didn't feel that way.

She rubbed her eyes, her lids heavy. She'd hardly slept at all last night, running over and over what James had told her. She'd punched the bed, rocked back and forth with her arms wrapped around her knees, grief and anger alternating in sharp waves. She'd almost wished she *could* cry, something to let out the awful, crushing emotion inside her.

All this time, she'd been courting the man whose negligence had killed her brother. Not just courted. She'd managed to fall in love with him. How could she have allowed things to go so far? Why hadn't she insisted on knowing sooner?

She'd chosen her love for him, her desire to not hurt him, over her own welfare and that of her family. This was the price.

And James had let her make that mistake. He'd tricked her, misled her. He'd *kissed* her with that knowledge inside him.

"Emily, I'm trying to protect you."

Protect himself, more like.

Emily wrestled down her flaring temper and looked over at Walt, who'd been standing silently at the window looking across the street at the Garrison house ever since she had finished telling him what she'd learned from James.

Walt scratched the good side of his face. "I wish I understood why he didn't tell us sooner."

Emily fidgeted with her hands, her swirl of emotions making her impatient. "Isn't it obvious? He knew how we'd all feel knowing he got William killed."

"Maybe. But I don't think it would have caused quite this much pain if he'd said something earlier. It just makes me wonder…"

"What?"

Walt turned to look at her. "What happened to him to make him act that way? It doesn't make sense."

Was Walter really going to show James sympathy? Now, in front of her?

She scoffed, her temper rising in her voice. "It makes sense to everyone else. He lied because he didn't want to accept the consequences of his actions."

Walt's good eyebrow raised. "*Everyone* else? Or just you? I don't think anyone else understands, either."

Emily raised a hand, ignoring his question. "I don't see why you're defending him. Who cares when he told us or why he did what he did. He still killed William."

Walt stared at her, and she realized she'd nearly shouted the last part.

After a moment, Walt started for his chair, his cane tapping on the floor. "I'm sorry, Emily. I'm so sorry for you."

She smoothed her dark blue morning skirt, regretting her harsh tone. She knew Walter didn't mean to upset her. He was James's friend, too. She couldn't blame him for wanting to make sense of things.

Walt eased himself into the armchair with a little groan. He settled himself and pivoted to face her. "I know this is especially hard since you two have been... so close lately."

"It's..." Emily searched for the words, managed only a whisper. "It's awful."

Mrs. Gould entered the room and handed Emily a cup.

"Thank you." Emily took the steaming drink, grateful for something to distract her attention. She sniffed the coffee and took a sip of the hot, bitter liquid. She wrinkled her nose. Wasn't that the taste of....?

She looked at Mrs. Gould, who settled herself onto the settee. The woman winked at her, a conspiratorial smile on her face.

Maybe a little whiskey wouldn't hurt after all.

Walter drummed his fingers on his thighs, looking toward the window again. "Men do strange things in combat."

"Like kill their friends?" Emily took another sip.

Walter snapped around to meet her gaze. "He didn't pull the trigger."

"It's his fault nonetheless." Emily's hands began to shake, and she set the cup down on the end table, afraid she might spill it.

Why was he defending James again?

"Yes, perhaps." Walt looked back at the window. "It doesn't add up, though."

"Add up?" Emily held her hands out to her sides, exasperated. "What is there to add? He confessed all the details himself."

Walt tilted his head to the side. "He said he went forward against orders. William followed him. And he said William was in the trench with him when he stormed the machine gun emplacement."

"Yes, and that's when William got… got hit." Emily picked her coffee back up. She needed more of it—and that little bit extra—to go through this again. She took a sip, remembering James's words. "Well, he didn't say that exactly, but William would have to have been there."

"And that's what I don't understand." Walt held up a finger. "Why didn't the Army recover William's body? If he went forward with James, why didn't he get a posthumous citation?"

"Because James lied, Walt." Emily's voice rose again, but she didn't care, another wave of anger overtaking her. "He wanted the glory for himself, and he didn't want anyone to know he was culpable."

Emily stopped herself, holding onto her coffee cup so hard she thought it might break, the pain in her chest making it almost impossible to breathe.

Walter shook his head but didn't say anything.

Emily looked at Mrs. Gould's sad, shocked expression. She cleared her throat and sipped her coffee, hiding her emotions behind the cup. "I'm not very good company today. I'm sorry, Mrs. Gould."

"You're alright, dear." Mrs. Gould reached over and put a hand on her arm.

"He wanted the glory…" Walt repeated Emily's words,

trailed off. "He seemed eager to avoid it before the parade, though. He didn't want to be the center of attention at all."

Emily shrugged. "Feigned modesty, perhaps?"

Walt shook his head. "Not James."

"James before the War, you mean."

"Not James," Walt repeated. "Even if he did lie, why was William marked missing? Wouldn't they have found a body eventually?"

Emily fought back images of the torn and mangled men she'd seen at the field hospital in Vavincourt, shuddering to think of her brother like that. "You know how the War was. Anything could have happened."

"Maybe." Walt took a deep breath and let it out. "It's all very strange."

She stared back at Walt, and her anger cooled, replaced by another emotion.

Doubt.

It *was* strange, and it didn't seem to fit the James she'd thought she'd known. And he hadn't exactly said that William had been in the trench with him. Emily had figured that part out herself.

Figured out, or assumed?

"Perhaps this is a topic we should leave behind us." Mrs. Gould set her cup down, stood, and walked to the window. "I don't think it does our Miss Emily much good to dwell on it now. It's a beautiful day out."

"Yes, it is." Emily set her cup down and walked to stand beside her. "What shall we do with it?"

"I expect Walter has to get to the ranch before long, but we ladies can find plenty to do."

Mrs. Gould began to rattle off a list of activities, but Emily wasn't listening. She watched as a motorcar turned onto the street and parked in front of James's house. A second later, the young woman from yesterday, Susan

Mabee, stepped out, and the car drove away. Susan turned and walked up the front steps of the Garrison house. She paused, then knocked.

"And I expect Marion would love to join us, too," Mrs. Gould was saying. "How about I telephone her?"

"Hmm." Emily pursed her lips, thinking. Something was missing, some detail James hadn't shared. Had he lied to her again? And if she confronted him once more, would he tell her the whole truth?

The door opened, and Susan stepped inside.

~

November 7, 1918
South of St. Aignan, France

"FIRST AID! FIRST AID!" James dove to the ground, dirt exploding upward as the German machine gun swept the rise in front of them. He rolled over and reached out for Bird, who was writhing and cursing where he lay.

"Son of a bitch!" Bird moaned, cradling his hand.

James grabbed hold of Bird's arm, took in the injury. The Hun bullet had struck him in the hand, shearing off two fingers and mangling the top of his palm.

James shouted over the gunfire, tried to sound cheerful. "That's your ticket out of here!"

Bird gritted his teeth, sweat trickling down his forehead from under his forehead. "Just don't fucking ask me to play the piano. Christ!"

James looked back down the wooded slope. "First aid! Where are those guys?"

"Keep your head down, idiot." William, on James's other side, put a hand on James's helmet and pushed him down.

"Lieutenant!" Robinson's voice sounded from farther down the line to the right.

James looked around, saw Robinson twenty yards away, waving at Lieutenant Merriam, who was behind James, a few feet past Bird to the left.

"Merriam, auto rifles and rifle grenades, now!"

"Right, right," Merriam mumbled under his breath, fear and confusion written on his young face. He cupped a hand around his mouth. "Pour it on them, boys! Chauchats up front."

Bird yelped as he turned over, grabbing his Chauchat with his bloodied hand. "Shoot, James!"

James didn't need to be told twice. He seated his rifle in his shoulder, searching for the enemy gun port with his sights. There was a fair amount of brush in front of the German position. The bastards had concealed it well, and James couldn't find the muzzle flash. He spied the cool gray color of concrete, a regular, hard shape amid the tangle of trees and brush. It was perhaps two hundred yards away, on the other side of a small embrasure that cut through the hillside.

James fired, worked his bolt, and fired again, rattling off shots as fast as he could, the report of his rifle subsumed by the thump-thump of the Chauchat. Several dull pops announced that someone had fired off rifle grenades, and a second later, a couple small explosions appeared just this side of the ravine. Useless, but hopefully it would keep the Hun's head down.

James's rifle bolt refused to go forward, and he realized he'd emptied his magazine. He rolled onto his side, reaching for a clip from his cartridge belt.

Officers were shouting down the line, and off to the right, the men rose from cover, moving to attack under the curtain of fire from the rest of the company. James's gaze came to rest on Captain Robinson.

Time seemed to slow down as Robinson stood, pointing his pistol in the direction of the enemy. He took a step forward, then jerked. He crumpled to his knees, tried to stand, and jerked again, his helmet knocked askew, a red mist spraying back from his head. He swayed, fell sideways, and lay still.

James opened his mouth to yell, but nothing came out, the air punched out of his lungs, grief hitting him in the sternum. His head spun, his eyes stinging, his throat tight, too tight for him to even breathe.

No! God, no!

The soldiers around Robinson fell back into cover, some of them knocked down as the deadly machine gun fire thinned their ranks. A second later, the panicked shout broke over the cacophony. "The Captain's hit! Robinson is hit!"

Some of the doughboys tried to stand and move again, but the German machine guns forced them down once more.

Then James heard it—between the bursts of the machine gun fire and the American rifle shots, faint, but unmistakable. The Germans were cheering.

James's brain buzzed, rage searing his temples, making him shake, filling his chest.

"Collins, Culver!" Lt. Merriam pointed behind him, back down the hill the way they'd come. "Start back that way and get some Stokes mortars and a one-pounder this way. See if the French can spot us some artillery."

James squeezed his rifle, fighting to rein in his emotions. They'd hold position now, wait for the heavier weapons to come up and help them break through. He looked over at where Robinson lay, face down in the dirt.

There it was again, the cheering.

To hell with waiting.

James's lungs burned, sucking down ragged gasps of air, his emotions jagged, his face hot. He looked over at Bird, who had set the Chauchat back down to cradle his hand, a look of despair on his face. James slung his rifle over his shoulder, pulled the Chauchat from the ground, and ran forward.

William's alarmed shout followed him. "James! What the hell are you doing?"

~

"AND THEN, I..." James trailed off, noticing Susan wasn't watching him anymore, but had put her face in her hands as she cried softly, shaking her head back and forth. "Well, I suppose the rest isn't important."

"There there, dear." James's mother, seated next to Susan, reached over and took the younger woman's hand, her face drawn into a concerned frown. "I think that's enough for today."

Susan shook her head harder, meeting James's eyes. "No... No, it's not that. I've spent months imagining this. But to hear it now... Did he suffer? Was it terribly painful?"

"Well... I..." James weighed his words. He could soften the truth and give her a fantasy, but Susan had insisted from the beginning that he not spare her any detail. He would honor her wishes. The very least he could do for Robinson now was to send his loved one off with the truth—and resolution.

"He was hit several times, so I think he must have felt a great deal of pain after the first shot, but not for long. He died very quickly." James swallowed, fending away the image of Robinson swaying there, his body wrenched by the impact of the German bullets. "It was a quick death—quicker than many I saw in the War."

Susan's face crumpled again, and she sobbed, rocking back and forth.

James opened his mouth to say something else, but no words came out.

Had he said too much after all?

"Miss Mabee, forgive me. I didn't mean to—"

She held up a hand, interrupting him. "No. No, you see, I'm relieved. I've heard so many stories, about the gas and about men burning alive or… or lingering for days in pain, begging for help. It's a mercy Dwight didn't have to endure that."

"It sounds like he was the kind of man who deserved a decent end." James's father, sitting in the chair across from his wife, leaned forward. "Like the men truly loved him."

"Yes." James looked down at his hands. He wasn't sure there was such a thing as a decent end in war. "Any one of us would have traded ourselves for him."

He silently cursed the emotion that had crept into his voice. Susan had come here to have her own grief addressed, not to see an unbecoming display from him.

No one said anything for a moment, then Susan broke the silence. "Thank you."

James looked up, found her gaze fixed on him, her eyes red and swollen from crying. Not knowing what to say, he tilted his head in acknowledgement.

"Truly," she continued. "You've done me a great kindness. I've talked to enough men who served in the War to know that was not easy for you."

"It's… not a problem." James leaned back in his chair, suddenly very tired. He'd been up late packing for France. He had no idea when he'd return to Saint Vrain, if ever, and the task of choosing what to leave behind had proved more difficult than he'd imagined.

His mother stood. "I think luncheon is just about ready. Will you be staying for the meal, Miss Mabee?"

Susan folded her handkerchief. "Not if it's an imposition."

"Hardly." James's mother smiled, though it didn't quite reach her eyes.

James watched her walk out of the room, frowning. She hadn't taken the news about his returning to France well, and had spent the past few days quiet and subdued. Even his father's normally cheerful demeanor had changed.

"Whatever it is you and Emily argued about, I'm sure you can mend it." His mother had wrung her hands, tears in her eyes.

His father had put his hands on James's shoulders, his voice gentle, imploring. "What is so terrible here that you have to run that far?"

James hadn't answered them but had left to go buy his train tickets to New York.

He listened to the ticking of the grandfather clock, wishing he could just go upstairs and take a nap. He realized with a start that Susan was still watching him. He shifted, uncomfortable. She was studying him intently, as if she could answer a question by looking at him.

"You said you ran forward from the line," she said at last. "Why?"

"I…" James blinked, taken aback by the question, unsure what to say. "I wanted to kill them."

His father raised an eyebrow. "Isn't this when you earned your medal?"

Susan didn't say anything but kept staring at him.

After a few seconds under her gaze, James shook his head. "What other reason are you looking for?"

"You could have waited. You said they were bringing up the big weapons. Why didn't you wait?"

It was on the tip of James's tongue to ask her why this mattered, but instead he looked away, out the window at the trees that lined the street, their green leaves fading to gold and brown. He felt again the insane rage searing him, could hear the chatter of the machine gun, and behind it, in the distance—

He looked back at Susan. "I couldn't stand their cheering. They—"

"They'd just killed Dwight," she said, interrupting him. "And then they were happy about it."

"Yes." James spoke so quietly he could barely hear his own voice, and he wondered if she had heard him. "They were happy to stop us there, even if only for a few minutes. It was almost the end for them."

"But they didn't stop *you*." His father pointed a finger at the ceiling, his body swelling with pride beneath his brown jacket. "You destroyed those machine guns."

James suppressed a groan. Couldn't he just let it go?

Instead, his father turned to Susan. "That's how he earned his Distinguished Service Cross from the Army. The army of his home. America. Your *home*, James."

Please, not now!

James closed his eyes and massaged the bridge of his nose, holding back the harsher words that came to him. "She heard the speech, Dad."

"It was a very brave thing you did," Susan said.

James opened his eyes and looked at her, shaking his head. "I just told you what it was about. Bravery had nothing to do with it."

Susan narrowed her eyes. "You talk as if you're ashamed you did it. You should be proud. You loved Dwight. You did it for him. I think that's noble."

How could he make them understand? "Yes, but—"

His father interrupted him. "Listen to this girl, James." He turned to Susan. "He's been whining about this medal since he learned he got it. He has these insane ideas about running away to France. Did you know that?"

"Not now, Dad. Please."

"France?" Susan shook her head, clearly taken aback by his father's intensity.

"Maybe you can talk some sense into him." His father gestured wildly. "It all started with this medal. You'd expect him to be proud, like a man should be, but—"

James stood, his anger spiking out of nowhere. "It was a goddamned mistake! Why don't you understand?"

His father stood then, too. "No, I don't. And rather than running to your room like a child or telling us we can't know because we weren't there, why don't you try explaining it?"

He took a step toward James, his voice softer now. "What would you keep from your own father?"

James gaped at him, his anger draining away, leaving behind a worse emotion.

Guilt.

What had the past months been like for his parents? How had they felt to be kept in the dark? Had he ever even tried to explain to them?

No, because they'd insisted on fussing over this damned medal.

Wouldn't any *parent do that?*

James shifted under his father's gaze. It was clear his parents had no idea about the War, and never would.

Did you ever give them the chance?

His mother reentered the room, her eyes wide. "What on earth are you men shouting about?"

Susan looked between James and his father, a perplexed look on her face.

What have you got to lose?

He was already going to France. Emily was gone from his

life forever. The least he could do was leave his parents with the truth.

All of it.

"Mother, please sit down." James eased himself back into his chair, his knee protesting the sudden movement, and turned to face his father. "Don't interrupt me and tell me about heroism or medals or any of that nonsense. Just listen. Can you do that?"

His father flinched at James's tone, but he nodded and sat down. "You're our son."

James took a deep breath. "Miss Mabee, where did I leave off?"

CHAPTER 34

October 18, 1918
Near Vavincourt, France

E mily walked to the steel barrel and tossed the armful of bloody cloths and bandages inside it. The fire smoldering within the barrel flared to life, sputtering and hissing. She wrinkled her nose, the familiar odor of burning cloth and scorched blood filling her nostrils.

She stepped back from the barrel and walked through the garden gate and around the corner of the church, adjusting her sleeve protectors as she went. On the other side of the building, Devitt, Moore, and a few of the other men were sitting on the steps of the *bains-douches*, resting, their stretchers set out beside them. Emily avoided looking toward the entrance of the cloister and glanced instead across the square. It was just about empty. The flood of trucks that had come in for many days had slowed to a trickle—though the rumble of the guns in the distance had continued without pause.

"They're diverting the casualties to a different facility,"

Buchanan had explained. "They're letting us catch up before they send more."

Rather than spending entire days on hospital duty, she and the canteen women only had to work short shifts now, assisting the medical staff for a few hours before rotating back to help distribute refreshments to the stream of men heading to and from the front. There were a few soldiers clustered around the canteen booth now. Mrs. Wolfe was there, handing out more of the pea-green sweaters—they disappeared just as soon as more arrived—and Gertie was with her, holding the hot chocolate kettle.

Mrs. Wolfe saw Emily looking, and nodded her head in acknowledgement. She had been a rock for them the past few days, concealing her own grief to keep the women under her command healthy and in good spirits despite the terrible long hours among the dead and dying.

"I can't eat, Mrs. Wolfe," Emily had said when she'd come to relieve her during one long hospital shift, pointing at the many patients disembarking from the trucks in the square.

Mrs. Wolfe had simply pointed across the square at the canteen. "Eat, or retire to your cot for the evening."

"I am not tired."

"Tired has nothing to do with it, Miss Culver." Mrs. Wolfe had put a hand on her arm, giving her a gentle squeeze. "We've left some of the hot chocolate by your plate. Go, before it gets cold."

How Mrs. Wolfe could take care of them all after hearing the news about Trevor, Emily couldn't possibly understand. But she was grateful.

She returned Mrs. Wolfe's nod and found a new, small pile of used bandages waiting for her in the trough they'd set up by the church steps. She adjusted her gas mask bag where it hung at her side—it got less bloody there than when she hung it across her chest—and took the rags in hand. When she got to the bottom of the pile, she noticed the shallow pool of blood in the bottom of the trough.

Filling up again.

She bunched the rags under one arm and tilted the trough over, spilling out the blood on the rain-dampened cobblestones. When the trough had drained, she righted it, transferred her bundle into both arms, and made her way back to the burn barrel, her boots tapping on the cobblestones. She tossed in the new load and put a hand on her lower back, massaging her sore muscles.

I am not tired. I am not tired.

She straightened up, turned around, and almost ran into Devitt, Moore a few steps behind him.

"Oh!" She made to move past him. "Pardon me."

"We'll take a few loads, Miss Culver."

"That's quite alright, Corporal. I am not a feeble schoolgirl."

"We've been sitting for a while now, and Moore here is getting bored."

He leaned out from behind Devitt. "I fall asleep if I sit too long, miss."

"Yes." Devitt nodded. "Fast asleep."

Emily looked between the two men, not sure whether she felt charmed by their kindness or irritated.

She put her hands on her hips. "I'm… I'm not tired."

Do you really believe that?

"Oh." Devitt stared blankly back at her.

Emily took a deep breath, every muscle and joint aching. She smiled. "But my feet certainly hurt."

"You boys decide yet what you're going to do with those things?" Clarence, the driver, pointed at the piece of paper in James's hands, shouting over the roar of the truck's engine.

"You mean this?" James raised the paper to his lips, kissed it.

"As much as we possibly can!" William, seated in the middle, held up his own pass.

James laughed, his heart light. Two weeks of leave. Two full weeks away from the front, starting today. After that, training and rest while replacements arrived to fill out the regiment.

"The final tally says we lost more than half our number," Sergeant Rodriguez had said when he'd handed them the passes. "I expect we'll be out of action for several months at least."

Hell, given the rumors about German resistance crumbling away, it was possible—

"There might not be a war to return to by the time you boys come back." Clarence finished the sentence in James's head.

"A fellow can hope." James tucked his pass into the breast pocket of his stiff, new tunic. He stared out the window at the French countryside rolling past his window under gray, cloudy skies. Instinctively, his eyes sought out every point where the enemy could hide a machine gun—that church steeple in the distance, that little clump of trees on the hill there, that farmhouse across the field.

Relax.

James took a deep breath, listened to the soft cooing of Clarence's passengers, barely audible over the motor. It hadn't been all that long since he'd been behind the front. And yet, the civilian world seemed even stranger than it had when he'd gone to Paris to see Emily.

Emily.

James bit back his excitement. They were going to see her today. Or at least they were going to try.

Her letters from a couple weeks back had said she was in a village near Vavincourt—of course the Army censors would not allow anything more specific than that—which is where the regiment happened to find its new billet.

She hadn't sent anything since then, so there was no guarantee she'd still be in the area.

"Could she be sick?" James had looked up from Emily's last letter when he'd noticed the date.

There was some awful new influenza moving around the military camps, and working in a canteen must surely expose her to many people.

William's brow had furrowed with the same concern James felt. "Maybe she's just busy, or maybe her group is moving to a new area."

Or maybe the post had been lost or delivered to the wrong unit. They'd invented a few dozen theories to lessen their worries, but they agreed it was worth investigating if Emily was still around Vavincourt. Some boxes of cigarettes and a bar of chocolate William had saved were enough to gain the assistance of Clarence, his truck, and his many passengers.

There were several canteens located in the area, and Clarence had taken them to each in turn without success. There were only two left to search now, and James was beginning to wonder if Emily had indeed left the area.

The truck lurched and bumped on the uneven road, bringing James's attention back to the present.

"Watch out, birdies!" Clarence laughed, bent over the wheel. "That was a good one."

"Better drive carefully, or your passengers won't know which way to go anymore." William stuck his thumb over his shoulder.

"Nah." Clarence shook his head. "These guys never get lost."

James stuck his head out the window, looking around at the large, square structure on the truck's bed, towering over the cabin. It looked like a little house, except for the camouflage paint and the chicken wire covering the small windows along its top. James caught a glimpse of one of Clarence's passengers moving around behind the window, its head bobbing as it walked.

Carrier pigeons.

James couldn't help but grin. In this war, little pigeons kept company with tanks, machine guns, and modern, breech-loading artillery. It seemed funny somehow.

"You know, we have a friend who'd love riding with your passengers," William nudged James in the ribs. "An auto rifle gunner."

"Oh, yes." James worked a tone of exaggerated sincerity into his voice. "He's very good with pigeons. Speaks their language, you could say."

Clarence looked over at them, perplexed. "Oh yeah? What's his name?"

"Bird," James and William said together.

Clarence stared at them for a second, then started laughing. James couldn't help but join him, laughing until his belly ached and his eyes watered. It wasn't really that funny—it was just so good to be out and free, with no enemy and no orders.

"Here's the next stop, you shell-shock cases," Clarence chuckled, driving the vehicle down what looked like the central street of a small village. He cranked the wheel, and they turned into a large cobblestone square. On one side was a church, on the other a set of tents and wooden booth, each marked with a bright red cross.

That had to be the canteen. It looked familiar, more or

less like all of the canteens James had seen in France. There was a short line of soldiers at the booth, all of them the perfect image of exhaustion.

The pigeon loft truck stopped with a lurch in the center of the square. A few soldiers gathered around the church steps looked up at the truck, curious expressions on their faces.

"Give us a few minutes." James opened the door and hopped out, wincing at the blisters he'd worked up in his new pair of boots. He straightened his overseas cap, looking around him while William jumped to the ground. "Let's ask at the booth."

They walked over toward the canteen, a chill creeping up James's spine at the odd hush of this village. He stopped in his tracks.

The girl at the canteen. He recognized her, and his heart soared.

"I think this is it."

"How can you know?"

James didn't answer William's question, but broke into a run.

Yes. He absolutely recognized her. Gertrude was her name. Gertie.

He pushed past the line of soldiers, ignoring their curses. "Where is Emily Culver?"

Gertie looked up in the middle of pouring hot chocolate. Her eyebrows shot up as she recognized him. She pointed across the square.

"And just who are you?" An older woman next to Gertie set down a stack of sweaters and put her hands on her hips.

"Thanks." James didn't bother to answer the question but turned around, almost ran into William. "She's over by the church."

William's face split into a smile, and before James could say another word, he was already running across the square.

James followed him, giving Clarence a thumbs-up as he passed. "Thanks, driver!"

Clarence honked his horn in acknowledgement and began to turn his truck around.

They reached the church and stopped, breathless. The soldiers on the steps were staring at them, incredulous.

A tingle ran up James's spine. What was that noise?

A low moan. Someone calling out something unintelligible.

Just then, someone in a red-stained white surgeon's apron stepped out of the church.

There was a field hospital here, as well as a canteen. For the first time, James noticed the stretchers leaning against the church next to the men seated there.

Stretcher-bearers.

Was Emily in the hospital? James couldn't recall her ever doing medical work. Had she been wounded?

William pointed to the left, to an open gate. "Over there, maybe?"

They walked together toward the doorway, and James realized it must be part of the church itself. A cloister, perhaps?

"Good God."

Inside were men laid on stretchers, most of them motionless, some still squirming and moaning. Bodies had been piled several rows deep, along the back wall, next to a small tree.

James backed away, reaching to pull his rifle off his shoulder—only to realize it wasn't with him.

He closed his eyes, tried to calm his racing pulse.

This isn't a battlefield. You're not there anymore.

"What are you men doing here?"

James opened his eyes and saw a captain standing next to them, his arms crossed.

They both saluted.

The captain returned the salute, frowning. "Well?"

"We're on leave, sir." James held out his pass.

The captain took it, eyeing him suspiciously. "And you thought visiting a field hospital would be fun?"

William raised his chin. "We're looking for my sister on our way to the rear, sir."

The man stared at William, his expression blank. "Your sister?"

"Emily Culver, sir. She works at the canteen."

The captain nodded, handed back James's pass. "That's different, then. She's on duty right now. She'll be ending her shift soon."

On duty? Shift? When had Emily started working for a hospital?

James shook his head, confused. "But we were just at the canteen and didn't see—"

"Pardon me, Captain Buchanan." Another man had appeared at the captain's elbow.

"Yes, Mr. Devitt?"

"She's over in back, sir. We gave her a break to rest her feet."

"Sir, may we see her?" The hope in William's voice was almost too much to bear.

Buchanan looked at them both for a long second, before sighing. "Very well. But stop running. You're making people nervous, and we've had too much strain here for that."

"Yes, sir." They both saluted again.

Once Buchanan had saluted back, Devitt gestured for them to come along. "I'll show you."

They followed Devitt across the front of the church and through a gate into what looked like a large walled garden attached to the church. He pointed, and James followed the man's finger past a smoking metal barrel toward a double row of trees, their branches bare except for a last few, stubborn leaves.

"Thank you."

Devitt nodded, and they left him by the barrel to make their way toward the trees. James scanned among the trunks, looking, but couldn't see her. He was about to suggest turning around and asking Devitt if she could have moved somewhere else when he spotted a little bit of white sticking out from behind a tree trunk.

"There." He pointed so William could see.

"Oh, to hell with that captain." William broke into a run.

Hard to argue with that.

James sprinted after his friend, rounding the end of the row of trees until they were on the other side. Emily was fully in view now, no longer hidden by the trunk.

William stopped in his tracks.

James halted to avoid running into his friend. "What's….?" He trailed off as his gaze fell upon her.

She sat on a small wooden crate, her back against the trunk, her hat set next to her on the grass, her blonde hair disheveled. Dark circles shadowed her eyes, her gaze fixed on a blade of grass in her hands. She pulled, splitting the blade in two. That's when he noticed the bloodstains. On her apron, her skirts, her hands, the puffy cloth sleeve protectors covering her arms, and smudged on her face.

James stared at her, taking in the complete exhaustion written in her features. What had happened to her in the weeks since she'd written?

"Emily?" William took a step forward.

"I'll be right there." She threw the bits of grass aside as she stood, wincing when she put her weight on her feet, and saw them.

Her eyes flew wide.

In a heartbeat, she was in William's arms, laughing, swaying on the spot, kissing him on the cheek, knocking his hat askew, both of them talking at once.

"What the hell happened to you?"

"How on earth did you find me here?"

James realized he was grinning, the joy of the two people in front of him chasing away the shadows in the corners of his mind, the memories of the battle.

Emily withdrew from William, turned to face James, and then there was nothing but her, her scent, the soft warmth of her cheek against his, the press of her arms around the back of his neck, her beautiful, familiar voice in his ear.

"I can't believe it." She stepped back and took hold of their hands. "I must have imagined you both dead a hundred times."

James squeezed her hand, unable to stop smiling. "Only a hundred?"

CHAPTER 35

E mily held her cup of hot chocolate with both hands, giddy with happiness, staring at James and William, feasting on the sight of them.

It was like some kind of dream. They were alive. They were sitting right there, across from her.

Safe.

She'd noticed their injuries right away—little scrapes and bruises here and there, including one long cut on James's cheek. They were both thinner than she remembered, their motions quicker and different somehow, as if they were nervous, distracted, always watching the movements of the other soldiers milling around the mess tent. But they were there, with her, and after everything she'd seen in the past days, they seemed unbelievably, miraculously whole.

No, the real miracle was Mrs. Wolfe. The woman had found them talking and laughing in the orchard. Emily had prepared to face the woman's reprimand for shirking her duties and fraternizing with two men, had been ready to explain that this was her brother, for goodness' sakes, but

Mrs. Wolfe had merely held her hand out for James and William.

"We're so glad you two men were able to find our Miss Culver."

They'd taken her hand and given it a gentle shake, one after the other.

"Thank you, ma'am."

"We appreciate it."

Emily had realized her mouth was hanging open. "But… how did you…?"

"Captain Buchanan told me everything." Mrs. Wolfe had smiled, pointed toward the canteen. "Take these soldiers over to the mess tent and get them some proper refreshments. And please do put on a clean uniform, Miss Culver."

"Yes, Mrs. Wolfe."

"I didn't realize you'd taken up nursing." William's voice brought Emily's attention back to the present. He was studying her, a concerned expression on his face.

"I didn't. I…" She looked for the words, something to describe the awful blur of the past twelve days. "They drafted me."

James frowned. "I didn't know they could do that."

Emily shrugged. "We're here to serve. There were just so many wounded all the time. I… I thought the Army was collapsing and the Germans would come marching along any day."

She forced a smile onto her face. "I suppose that sounds silly."

William put his hand over hers. "No, it doesn't."

James leaned back in his chair, staring off into space. "We lost half the regiment at Soissons, and half again just now. I don't even know why we're here. Why us?" His voice was calm and even, but there was a hardness in there as well, a bitterness.

William and James's expressions had fallen, and Emily could tell that they were slipping away, their thoughts returning to the battle.

She heard again what Mrs. Wolfe had said when Emily had first started with the canteen, what felt like ages ago.

The first days after combat are always the most depressing for the men. You girls are here to help them through those times.

What could she possibly do?

"You're here to drink this." She nudged their cups. "And right now, you're letting it get cold."

They both looked down at their hot chocolate.

James took a sip. "Sorry we're not very good company."

Emily held his gaze. "You're here."

"Cheers to that." William raised his own cup and drank.

Emily pointed to the leave passes lying on the table between them. "Where will you go next?"

William set down his empty cup, licking his lips. "Paris, probably. Some other guys talked about going to Nice. I don't know if we can make it that far."

"I wish you could come." A spark flickered in James's eyes, and she knew he meant more than he was saying.

Memories of kissing him—of doing more than just kissing him—filled her with a warmth that collected in her cheeks, making them burn.

Not in front of William!

She pretended to look toward the tent opening, collecting herself. "Someone's got to keep this war in order while you're away."

"With any luck, there won't be a war for much longer."

"What?" Emily whipped around to look at her brother. "What do you mean?"

He grinned. "It may be nothing, but rumor is the Germans are on the run. And we've got months before we'll be back in action."

Emily leaned back in her chair, dumbstruck.

The Germans on the run? How was that possible when so many Americans were dying?

She realized they were both waiting for her to say something. "I'll believe it when it happens."

James huffed. "I don't suppose it matters much, does it?"

Emily shook her head. "What you are fighting for here matters to millions of people. It's the most important thing anyone on earth is doing."

She saw again the bodies in the cloister, the desperate pleas of the men they'd left there to die. Was anything worth that?

As if he was reading her thoughts, James raised an eyebrow. "You still believe that?"

She raised her chin. "Yes."

The alternative was too painful to contemplate.

"Same old Em." William smiled at her. "At least you've still got your idealism."

She poked him in the arm. "And I'll keep yours warm for whenever you come to your senses and want it back."

"Ouch!" William batted her arm away, laughing.

"Isn't it strange that we should be here?" James spoke suddenly, his expression distant, his eyes unfocused.

William winked at Emily "Well, you see, James, there was this guy named Kaiser Bill."

James smacked him on the arm. "No, I mean the three of us, in France, together, in all this."

He spread his arm wide, encompassing the tent with his gesture. "It's... strange. Who would have ever thought?"

William rubbed his arm. "Since when is everyone hitting me?"

Emily couldn't help but smile. "Maybe they put something extra in the hot chocolate."

James took a deep breath, looked across the table at her. "Let's come back some day."

"To France?" William laughed again.

"Yes. See it properly."

Emily tried to imagine it. What would it be like to tour the countryside in a motorcar? Or see the cities and monuments without the cannons and sandbags and soldiers all around them?

She sighed. "It's something to look forward to."

"I think I can look forward to this." William tapped his cup. "Where can we get more?"

"I'll get some." Emily stood and turned toward the door.

She had only taken a couple steps when Mrs. Wolfe stepped inside, followed by two soldiers, the large, white letters MP emblazoned on their dark blue brassards, pistols holstered at their hips. The hum of conversation around the mess tent died, all eyes turning toward the newcomers.

Military policemen.

Mrs. Wolfe pointed toward William and James, and the soldiers started in their direction.

Emily whirled around. "Are you two not supposed to be here?"

James stood. "Maybe they didn't want us wandering around the military zone."

"Or commandeering pigeons," William added, winking at Emily as he got to his feet.

"Pigeons?" She gaped at them. Had they gone insane?

The two soldiers came to a stop at the end of the table. "You men have to come with us."

James picked his pass up off the table, held it out for the men to see. "We're on leave. We were just on our way to the rear."

One of the soldiers, a tall man with a flat nose and dark

stubble on his chin, shook his head. "Not anymore, you're not. All passes for the First Division have been rescinded."

"What?" William held his hands to his sides. "That can't be true."

The other soldier, thin and wiry with green eyes, nodded. "The orders just came through. They want the division to start working up for the front again. They need the help of all experienced soldiers to train the replacements."

The tall man put his hands on his hips. "You're both to report back to your unit. We're sorry to do this, fellows, but you have to come along."

Emily's head spun, her ears ringing. Working up for the front? Would they be going back to the battle already?

"But you can't possibly…" She looked for anything she could say to keep them from going. "They only just arrived. At least give them some time."

The tall man pressed his lips together. "We have our orders, miss."

Mrs. Wolfe cleared her throat. "Why don't you soldiers come have some doughnuts while these two men say their goodbyes? I can vouch they won't do anything foolish."

A smile tugged at the corners of the green-eyed MP's mouth. "Doughnuts?"

Mrs. Wolfe gestured at the tent opening. "Fresh and hot."

The tall MP nodded. "Very well." He turned to James and William. "But I expect you men will be right outside."

The MPs turned and followed Mrs. Wolfe out of the tent.

Emily met William's gaze, and for a moment, they just stared at each other.

She sighed. "Well…"

William rounded the table in two steps and put his arms around her, hugging her close.

Emily closed her eyes, not wanting the moment to end, wanting to stretch it out as long as she could.

All too soon, William pulled away. "We'll get that hot chocolate next time."

"We'll have plenty." She turned to face James, who pulled her into his embrace. Then she felt his face against hers, his warm lips planting a soft kiss on her forehead.

"Write when you can," he whispered.

"Do I need to get those MPs back in here?"

William.

He probably had no idea about her and James's feelings for each other.

She pulled back from James to look at her brother, his arms crossed over his chest.

Was he angry?

"I was going to tell you eventually," Emily began.

"And you can be assured we'll do everything properly once the War is over," James added.

William shook his head slowly back and forth—and then his look of disapproval dissolved into a smile. He wagged his finger at James. "No time like the present, soldier. And if you think you've been subtle over the past few months, you're mistaken."

"Miss Culver?" Mrs. Wolfe's head poked through the tent opening. "They're waiting."

They walked together out of the mess tent, then followed Mrs. Wolfe back out to the square, where the MPs stood next to a large Army truck. About a half-dozen soldiers were sitting in the truck bed, glum expressions on their faces. One of them waved at James and William.

"You too, huh?"

James waved back. "Weren't you supposed to be in Lyon by now, Collins?"

The tall MP gestured at the vehicle with his half-eaten doughnut. "In the truck with you."

Emily found James's hand, gave it a squeeze. He squeezed

back, held her hand for a moment, then turned and walked to the truck.

William gave her an exaggerated salute, then followed James. James clambered up first, Collins helping him over the edge. William put a foot up, then stopped. He turned, ran back to Emily, and they hugged again. She buried her face in his shoulder.

"This war is nearly over." His voice vibrated in his chest against Emily's cheek.

She nodded, unable to speak for fear of betraying the emotion that was tightening her throat.

"Come on, now." The tall MP was next to them now, though his voice was softer.

William stepped back, turned on his heel, and climbed into the truck, James and Collins hauling him up.

The MPs stepped up into the cabin, and the truck's motor roared to life a second later. The vehicle turned, then crossed the square, headed for the street that led out of town. Emily waved, working to keep a smile on her face despite the crushing pain in her chest. Her eyes burned, but she would not cry.

Tears don't help anything.

James and William stood up, waving back to her. Then they passed behind some houses and were gone.

IT WAS A MERCIFULLY short ride on the bumpy, muddy roads back to the Army camp near Vavincourt. The soldiers were quiet the whole way, staring down at their boots or off into the distance. James looked past William, sitting on the other side of the truck bed, into the open countryside, his thoughts on Emily.

He hated that she was doing medical work now, that she'd

have to see every bit of the War's horror. Hell, based on the exhaustion he'd seen on her blood-smudged face, the shadows in her eyes, she probably already had.

Before, he'd taken comfort thinking of her in relative peace, handing out cigarettes and treats, sheltered from the worst. There seemed to be nothing this war couldn't touch and injure, even if it might end soon.

No more war. A boat back to America. A train ride home.

It was too much to hope for. If the Germans were running, why did the Army need the First Division back in action? And how quickly could the regiment rebuild itself?

With any luck, it would take a good, long while. Long enough for these rumors to prove true.

Wish in one hand...

The green fields and little woods gradually gave way to the stone houses of the village of Vavincourt, then to farm fields again, and finally to rows of wooden barracks and khaki tents, the familiar camp.

They passed groups of soldiers, all of them heading in the same direction, toward the parade ground. Some of them cursed, splashed with mud by the truck's tires.

William pointed ahead. "What the hell do you figure this is all about?"

"Beats me." James leaned over the side of the bed, looking past the front of the truck. A large group of men were gathered in the parade ground around a single man who stood up on a crate in the middle of the group. James squinted, trying to recognize him. It had to be an officer, judging by his Sam Browne belt and tall leather boots.

The truck lurched and came to a stop.

"This is it, boys." The tall MP stepped out from behind the steering wheel and waved them down.

One by one, the soldiers climbed out the back of the

truck, their boots splashing in puddles when they hit the ground.

"And I was just getting used to being clean." Collins looked down at the mud spattered across his boots and puttees.

"You've got to break them in sometime." William clapped him on the back.

"Come on." James waved for William and Collins to follow him, and they walked alongside the road the last few yards to the parade ground.

The man in the center was speaking, shouting over the helmets and caps of the assembled doughboys. James stopped at the back of the crowd.

"Who is that?" He nudged a soldier next to him.

The soldier glanced at him but said nothing.

James nudged him again. "Well?"

"General Summerall."

"The corps commander?"

This must really be something important.

"Shh!" Another soldier pushed James from behind.

James craned his neck to see over the men in front of him, cupped a hand behind one ear to hear better, but the noise of hooves and the squeak of a wagon made him look over his shoulder. A mule-drawn water cart had pulled behind the group, and a few men were filling their canteens while the driver peered over toward Summerall.

Irritated at the noise, James directed his attention back at Summerall, barely able to hear his voice.

"Men," he was saying, "You belong to a fighting division. You have pushed the enemy back on three fronts. You have gone far. You will go farther. You have suffered much. You will suffer more."

"Oh, perfect," William snorted.

"Shh!" Collins glared at him.

Summerall held his hands out to his sides, the pride in his voice unmistakable. "You have gone long without food. You will go longer. You have faced death. You will face it again. Your record will go down in history as a splendid example of courage and fortitude. Your name and fame will be immortal."

No one spoke, silence falling over the crowd as long seconds ticked by. And then—

"Who in hell is that guy, anyway?"

James looked for the source of the noise and found the mule driver, who shrank in his seat under the gaze of so many people.

"Well?" The driver shrugged.

A low ripple of laughter moved through the crowd.

Even Summerall chuckled. He put his hands on his hips, then continued speaking. "The German is on his last legs, and the First Division will help give him the final wallop."

Summerall kept talking for a few more minutes, but James hardly heard his words.

He caught William's gaze, imagined he saw the same emotions there that he felt. Pride at the general's praise. Resignation. Fatigue. Dread.

They were heading back to battle, back to the front. Were they going to lose half the regiment again? How could any of them possibly survive another fight like the one they'd just left?

Applause rippled through the audience as Summerall stepped down and the crowd broke up, each man heading to his own barracks or to whatever task he'd been doing before the general had arrived.

"I'll see you, fellas." Collins started off toward the barracks. "I've got some letters to write."

"Wait up." William followed Collins, and James trailed a few feet behind them.

They passed the mule driver, angled across the road and toward the barracks where they'd left their kits before quitting the camp for leave.

As they neared the barracks, William spoke up. "If the Huns are really teetering, maybe it'll be easy this time, like St. Mihiel."

Images filled James's mind, of the machine gun in the woods at night, the burning Germans, Dobson lying mangled on the ground, his lifeblood oozing out of him through shrapnel wounds.

"Yeah." James massaged his temple, willing the memories away. "Easy like St. Mihiel."

CHAPTER 36

September 23, 1919

"I'll get it." Emily stood up, smoothing her skirt, and set aside the book she'd been reading before someone had rung the doorbell. She couldn't concentrate, anyway, and Julius and Brianna would be home from school any minute. She rounded the settee and walked to the door, opening it to find—

"Miss Mabee?"

Susan stood on the porch, her hands folded in front of her, her subdued dress and black armband a perfect companion to the rainy fall weather.

Emily stared at her. Why was she here?

"May I come in?"

"Yes." Emily stepped aside, embarrassed at her lapse in manners. "Yes, of course."

"Thank you." Susan walked past Emily and leaned her umbrella by the door.

"Sit wherever you like." Emily led the way into the parlor. "Can I get you anything?"

"I've only got a little while." Susan crossed in front of the settee to sit in the armchair, fidgeting with the black lace gloves she wore.

Emily sat back down next to her book. "Very well."

The patter of rain on the roof filled the silence in the room, and Emily found herself drumming her fingers on the cushion beside her while Susan kept fidgeting with her gloves, clearly uncomfortable.

Finally, Emily cleared her throat. "Miss Mabee, I hate to be rude, but what exactly has brought you here?"

Susan took a deep breath. "I debated whether this was the right thing to do. It's a violation of trust. I debated it, prayed about it, and I can't allow you both to make a mistake. Someone has to do something."

Emily held up her hands. "What on earth are you talking about?"

Susan cocked her head to the side, her lips pressed into a thin line. "Did you know James is leaving for France?"

Emily fell back against the backrest of the settee as if someone had slapped her across the face. "France? No... I... What do you mean?"

"He's leaving the United States for France, and he says it's a permanent move."

"I didn't know…" Emily pressed her hands together in her lap, shock coalescing into anger.

He was running away, leaving the destruction he'd caused behind him without so much as an apology. And to think…

To think you loved him.

Worse, she'd once imagined he loved her, too.

She was almost too angry to speak, a terrible ache in her chest. "Good riddance, I suppose."

"Good riddance?" Now Susan looked as if someone had struck her.

Emily raised her chin. "Yes. You may not be aware, Miss

Mabee, but my family and I have legitimate reasons to wish never to see Mr. Garrison again."

Mr. Garrison.

It hurt to talk about James that way, but how else could she make Susan understand?

Susan waved a hand in the air. "I know all about that."

Emily gaped at her, her anger tightening and coiling in her chest "You do? I suppose that makes sense. James waited months to tell me everything he was willing to tell you in only an afternoon."

Susan raised an eyebrow. "He did not tell you everything."

Emily pointed at her, her manners forgotten in her anger. "Walter was right! You see, James lies to me and tells a stranger the truth. Why should I care if he—"

"Because he loves you!" Susan shouted, cutting her off.

"He told you that, did he?" Emily scoffed. "He has a peculiar way of showing it."

"I saw the way you embraced at the parade. Don't you understand?" Susan shook her head "He's trying to protect you with a fantasy rather than have you face the truth. What explains that kind of stupidity besides love?"

"The truth? How he got William killed?" Emily wouldn't hear anyone else defend James's actions, especially not this newcomer to whom he'd told everything while leaving Emily in the dark.

"It's not exactly—"

Emily didn't let her finish. "And who is he to protect me? Didn't you say knowing the truth was better?"

Susan stared at her but said nothing.

"Emily?" Her mother's voice carried down the stairs. "Who's shouting down there?"

Emily sighed. She didn't need to drag her mother through this, not again. "It's nothing, Mother. I'm...practicing a song."

Good work, Em. Very convincing.

She looked back at Susan as she stood and started toward the door "I think you had better go."

Susan didn't budge. "Did you know my Dwight got killed right before William?"

Emily stopped in her tracks. "No, I didn't."

The floodgates opened then, Susan talking so quickly that Emily almost couldn't follow her. She told Emily about the machine guns in the woods, her fiancé's agonized final moments, about the cold cheers from the German lines that drifted over the pinned-down Americans, and James charging forward, blind with rage.

Emily sank back onto the settee as she listened, chilled by the scene Susan described. It had been clear from James's story the other day how much he and the other soldiers had loved Robinson. She closed her eyes, her anger cooling as she imagined the insane grief that must have overcome James in that moment.

"William went to stop him, and James told me he died shortly thereafter."

"He never made it to the machine gun nest?" Emily opened her eyes, gripping the settee cushions to keep the room from spinning. "James really did go in there alone?"

"Yes." Susan folded her hands in her lap, almost breathless from her monologue. "Glory was the last thing on his mind."

Emily bit the inside of her lip, new questions swirling around the old ones in her head. This explained why James alone had received the Distinguished Service Cross, but not why the Army had marked William missing. And why had no one found his body? James hadn't lied to keep the medal to himself, but—

"Why didn't he say all this before?" Emily finished the sentence in her head.

"I told you already."

Emily resisted the urge to roll her eyes. "Yes, but how does the story he told before protect me?"

Susan shrugged. "Isn't it better to think your brother died heroically, taking an enemy position, than to think he just… died?"

"He's still dead."

"Yes, well…" Susan looked down at her hands.

Neither of them spoke for a minute, and Emily ran through Susan's account again, looking for anything to explain James's deception. She had seen and heard enough of the War to know that plenty of men died in No Man's Land, without ever reaching their enemy. Why would William's fate be so different?

Unless…

Emily leaned forward, put her hand on the coffee table to catch Susan's attention. "Did James say how William died? I mean the instrumentality of it? Was it gas? Was it shrapnel?"

She shivered, imagining a thousand horrifying possibilities.

Susan shook her head. "He didn't say anything about that. With the machine gun there, I'd assume the Germans shot him, like they did Dwight."

Susan put a hand to her lips, narrowed her eyes. "Come to think of it, he brushed over that part of the story. He just said William got hit."

"That could mean many things."

Susan put her lace gloves back on. "None of them are pretty to imagine, and your opportunity to know what it was for certain is leaving today."

Emily's stomach plummeted, her pulse suddenly painful in her neck.

Today?

"Do you know when?"

"I wish I did, but he didn't tell me." Susan glanced at the

clock, got to her feet. "It's late. My friend's husband will be here in a moment to pick me up."

Emily stood. "I… appreciate you coming. And I apologize for my harsh words."

Susan closed the distance between them and put a hand on Emily's shoulder, the smile on her face not quite reaching the grief in her eyes. "If our situations were reversed…"

Emily nodded, understanding. "Yes, I suppose."

They walked to the door, and Emily opened it. A car was waiting outside, a man climbing out of it. He stopped and waved when he saw them.

Susan took a step, then stopped. "You do love James, don't you?"

"I…" Emily stuttered, taken aback. "Yes, I do… Or I did."

She wasn't sure what she felt right now, and she certainly wasn't going to figure it out talking to a relative stranger on her doorstep.

"I loved my Dwight." Susan's brow furrowed, as if she was deep in thought. "He didn't wait to be drafted. He volunteered."

Emily shifted, unsure of what to say. "Oh?"

"I was so angry he was rushing off to danger before he needed to that I didn't talk to him for a week." She met Emily's gaze, held it. "Don't you think I'd do anything to have that week back now?"

With that, Susan stepped outside and down the front porch steps.

Emily took a step back and eased the door shut, thinking.

This would never be over, she would never have peace, unless…

She turned around and strode across the room and down the hall to the telephone. She lifted the receiver and turned the crank. "Hello? Operator? Saint Vrain four-thirteen, please."

"One moment, please."

Would James even talk to her? What if he was already gone?

"I'm sorry, ma'am, but no one is answering."

Emily cursed in her head, formulating a plan. "Try Saint Vrain four-oh-eight."

The speaker crackled with static. "Very well. One moment."

Emily tapped the phone's wooden case, waiting.

"Hello?" The familiar voice sounded on the other end of the line.

"Mrs. Gould? This is Emily. Is Walter there?"

JAMES LIFTED his trunk into the back seat of the Hupmobile, his sore leg protesting the motion.

"Is that the only one?" His father pointed at the suitcase.

"That's it."

The rest could stay here in boxes. He wouldn't need—or want—many reminders of home when he got to France. A clean break would make everything easier.

"And what will you do if your mother and I sell all of it?" His father crossed his arms, the tone of his voice barely concealing his anger.

James wouldn't be baited. "You can wire me a percentage, if you'd like. Or keep it."

His father huffed and walked around the car, inspecting the tires for the third time. James watched him, not sure what else to say to him.

He'd explained to them and Susan about William, told them just about everything—he'd spared them the gory details—and they still didn't understand why he had to leave. They had laid into him as soon as Susan left.

"Time will heal things with Emily, James, especially if you come clean and tell her what you've told us." His mother had pleaded with him, tears rolling down her cheeks. "I don't understand why you have to run away from this. Why won't you let us help you?"

He'd managed to keep calm. He hadn't wanted to argue with his parents on his last night at home. "I've tried putting my life together here. It isn't working."

His father had crossed his arms, his face red. "I haven't seen all that much trying. Have you got a job or gone back to school? You've hardly been home at all."

They'd continued arguing for hours, always talking in a circle until something in his mother had snapped.

She'd wiped her tears and stood, her voice hard. "If you want to leave, go. I won't gratify you by waving a handkerchief."

At that, she'd walked out of the room, and James hadn't seen her since.

James leaned against the car and looked back at the house, half hoping he'd see his mother looking out a window.

Nothing but curtains.

He swallowed, fighting down his emotions. "Dad, we need to get going."

This was harder than he'd thought it would be.

His father mumbled something to himself and climbed inside. "Fuel switch."

James opened the hood, found the switch, and turned it on. They went about the business of starting the car in silence—James pulling out the choke and cranking the engine while his father turned the key to magneto. He was about to start the car, his hand on the crank, when—

"James, what on God's green earth do you think you're doing?"

He looked over to see Walter walking toward him, cane in hand, his face concealed by his hood.

James straightened up, bracing himself. The last thing he needed now was another argument. "I'm leaving, Walter."

His friend stopped in front of him and pointed at the car with his free hand. "Leaving is a nice word for running away. Do you mind telling me why?"

James put a hand over his eyes, massaging his temples. "I'm not going through this again."

"Emily telephoned, James. She wants to talk to you. I'm sure you know why."

James opened his eyes, not believing what he'd heard. Why would she want to talk to him again? Had she figured out his omission?

Your lie, you mean.

She was too damned smart for her own good.

"Damn," James murmured.

Walt put his hand on his hip, his voice expressing the irritation his hood concealed. "Damn's right. Because I think you owe her the truth. You owe *William's sister* the truth."

"Walt, I…" James looked for words to defend his position, couldn't find any.

Because maybe it's a bad idea, idiot.

Walt threw up his hand, a slight waver in his voice. "No, I've heard it before. We can't understand, and so on. If all of us and everything you have here doesn't matter, go. But you damned well better give her the courtesy of the truth before you do."

"Hear, hear!" James's father called.

James and Walt both turned to look at him, then back at each other.

James started to talk, but Walt held up his hand.

"You told me to live because of the ones who died over there, who didn't have the chance we do to make something of ourselves. You said we owe it to them to do the things they couldn't. I don't know how I can take any of that seriously now."

"I'm sorry I've let you down, Walt." James didn't know what else to say.

"Fix bayonets, James." Walt turned and started across the street to his house. "Or run like a coward. Whichever suits you."

James stared after his friend, his chest aching. He didn't want to leave him like this, didn't want to cause so much hurt to everyone.

And how exactly did you think this would go?

James returned to the car crank, grabbed hold of it, and started the sputtering engine.

~

November 7, 1918
South of Omicourt, France

"HEY! Where do you think you're going?" James hissed, trying to catch the attention of the soldier who stumbled out of line, walking into the mud alongside the road in the blue, predawn light.

The man ignored him, his footsteps uneven, drunk. He stopped in his tracks, his head lolling back, his rifle slipping off his shoulder and dropping to the ground with a wet thud. He fell forward onto his knees and collapsed face-first into the mud.

A few medics rushed out of the line, and James made to help the man, but Lieutenant Merriam's voice stopped him.

"Stay in formation men, keep marching."

William spat on the ground, speaking so quietly that only James heard. "Until we're all dead?"

James shook his head, too tired and in too much pain to respond. They'd marched in cold rain for days to the area around Mouzon and attacked the enemy yesterday morning. Thankfully, the fighting had been light, and they'd had few losses. Even the new replacements, with no better training than what the experienced Spaders had given them at Vavincourt and Parois, had fared well. They'd been digging foxholes for the night when Captain Robinson had arrived to talk with the new lieutenant, Merriam, a ninety-day OTC graduate barely out of high school.

"The First Division has been given the… honor of spearheading the liberation of Sedan." The irritation in Robinson's voice when he'd said the word *honor* was unmistakable, except to Merriam.

"That is an honor indeed, sir." Merriam had beamed, his freckled face hidden in the dim light.

Robinson had ignored his enthusiasm. "We're marching overnight for Chémery-sur-Bar to begin the advance on Sedan. It's more than sixteen miles, and we need to be there by morning."

Shortly thereafter, they'd dropped their packs, taking only the most essential equipment, and begun the march. They'd moved in columns of two on either side of the road through a landscape choked with the wreckage of battle, ready to fight Germans who never showed up. Rumor was the enemy was simply retreating in front of them.

The Spaders had drawn more than a few ugly words from the doughboys they'd encountered as they'd cut across the supply trains of the other American divisions in the area.

"First Division making a grab for glory," one corporal had said, scowling at them.

"Dead or alive doesn't matter." Bird's voice brought James's attention back to the present. "Some fucking general somewhere will get to say he was the liberator of Sedan. That's what matters."

A grumble of agreement passed through the ranks.

"I don't like this." Collins, marching behind James, spoke up.

"Yeah?" Bird snorted. "Tell me who does."

"No, *this!*"

James looked behind him and saw Collins pointing off to the side, at the wooded slope rising up to their left. The road was running along the bottom of the valley, between two steep, forested ridges. If the Germans were in there, if they ambushed the column here…

"Shut your mouths and keep your eyes open." Sergeant Rodriguez's voice carried back over the line from somewhere, ending any discussion.

James shifted his rifle on his shoulder, his entire body protesting each step, hunger burning his stomach. They'd left the field kitchens behind long ago, passing through Chémery and continuing up the road to Omicourt.

They marched on in silence, their breathing and the squish of their boots in mud the only sounds. The sky was changing color now, turning gold and orange behind the ridge to their left.

"Good morning, Huns," Corbett said, somewhere up ahead.

James looked around, wondering why everyone just kept marching if Germans were there. Then he saw them, three men slumped over a Maxim gun, their uniforms soaked red.

The advance guard was clearly doing their job.

James put a hand on his rifle sling, ready to slide it off at any moment. He wasn't sure how much longer they marched, the sky brightening overhead, but suddenly the column passed back the command to halt.

Merriam walked back along the line. "Third Battalion is securing the town."

James watched the man pass, looking at his freckles, his youthful, untroubled eyes. He turned to William. "Does it worry you that the new guys seem young to me now?"

William grinned beneath the brim of his helmet. "Shut up, old man."

There were a few rifle shots ahead, the loud thump of grenades. Soon afterward—

"Forward!"

The line started moving again, and before long they passed a white metal sign with a red border, the word *Omicourt* written on it. Men up and down the line pulled their rifles off their shoulders, and James did the same, peering up at the stone houses lining the town's main street.

It would be just like the Huns to leave a sniper behind.

A cellar door burst open, and James raised his rifle to his shoulder and took aim. He blinked, realizing it was an old woman in front of his sights.

"Hold your fire!" He lowered his rifle. "Civilian!"

The woman gaped at him, her gray hair in a bun behind her head, stray wisps blowing in the breeze. She wrung her hands in her gray skirt, shaking her head side to side. "Les Allemands? Sont-ils partis?" *Are the Germans gone?*

James put what he hoped was a reassuring smile on his face. "Oui, ils sont partis."

"Et vous? Vous êtes Britanniques?"

"What's she saying?" Bird leaned on his Chauchat.

"She wants to know if we're British." James shook his head. "Non, nous sommes Américains."

"Américains?" The woman put a hand to her mouth, a smile spreading across her face. She teetered on the spot, and James realized with a lurch she was about to faint.

He ran forward and caught her, supporting her against his chest. "Help me with her!"

He bent his knees, getting low to drop his rifle on the ground, holding on to the woman with both hands.

Collins and William slung their weapons and helped James carry her back down into the cellar. The scent of straw and musty wood filled James's nostrils, and he strained to see in the dark. Setting her down gently with her back against a crate, they turned and walked back up the stairs, their boots clattering on the wooden boards.

"I didn't know seeing an American was such a big deal." Collins dusted off his hands.

William pulled his rifle back off his shoulder. "She hasn't seen a soldier who isn't a German in four years."

They emerged into daylight and found Sergeant Rodriguez there, waving them on. "Let's keep moving."

They hadn't gone more than a few steps before a loud rushing noise filled the air.

"Shit!" James hit the ground, the cobblestones punching the air out of him.

An explosion somewhere, the sound of bricks and rubble raining down on the street below and then—nothing.

"That's it?" James got back to his feet. "A single shell?"

"Don't tempt them." William pushed himself up with his rifle butt.

If that was all the Germans could muster, they really must be broken. The American column continued through the village, ducking into cover at the occasional, sporadic shell that crashed in the village. The German gunners were unfocused, half-hearted, their rounds landing haphazardly and far off target.

As they passed into the northern outskirts of the town, the houses became more widely dispersed, large walled gardens between them. Ahead, beyond the town, the road continued up into a large wood that sloped up to a broad, rolling hill.

"Halt!"

Merriam came walking down the line again. "We're holding position here. Take cover in the gardens."

James followed Rodriguez into one of the gardens with the rest of his squad—William, Collins, Corbett, Beggs, Killeen, and the replacements, Padis, Dawson, Craver, Rico, and Frew. They huddled close against the rough, blonde-colored stone, their rifles pointed skyward.

"Don't mind if I do."

James looked around to see Beggs picking some leaves off what looked like a lettuce plant.

So much for American goodwill.

"Careful, Beggs." Rodriguez peered outside the garden gate. "There are still froggies here."

Curious, James scooted over next to Rodriguez and leaned his head around the corner of the garden door. The road was practically empty, only the occasional rifle barrel sticking out from one of the gardens or side streets. A group of officers and a few NCOs stood next to a large building, sheltered from view of the woods. Robinson was there, and Major Legge. Two other majors were with them, standing next to Merriam and some other lieutenants. Among the sea of olive brown uniforms were a few men in the sky blue of the French army. The officers saluted each other and dispersed. One of them walked into the middle of the road and cupped his hands around his mouth.

"Company K, move up!"

Soldiers appeared out of wherever they'd tucked themselves and moved out of town, heading for the wooded slope.

"What's happening, sir?" Rodriguez moved to let Lieutenant Merriam enter the garden.

Merriam adjusted his helmet, breathless. "A coordinated

assault. Company K is attacking toward St. Aignan, over that hill. The French will support us on our right."

William raised an eyebrow. "And what will we do?"

"We're in reserve."

As Merriam walked out of the garden to pass the order to the rest of the platoon, James sat down, relieved to be off his aching feet. He set his rifle down, listened to the distant sound of gunfire, another shell exploding uselessly somewhere. His head bobbed onto his shoulders, and before he could stop himself, he was asleep.

CHAPTER 37

September 23, 1919

"Excuse me. Pardon me." Emily pushed through the crowd of people inside Union Depot, searching for James. Families, businessmen traveling to Denver alone, a few miners in blue denim headed in the other direction, up the canyon to Tungsten and Nederland. She made her way to the wide, arched door leading onto the platform. "Excuse me! Coming through. Pardon me."

He had to be out there, waiting for the train. She'd spotted Mr. Garrison pulling away from the station, alone in his car, when she'd arrived, breathless from her near run from her house to get here on time.

She was not going to let James leave, not before he gave her the truth—all of it.

Emily emerged onto the platform, scanning the people who stood in clumps alongside the yellow Union Pacific train that waited, steaming and huffing in the cool morning air.

She walked along the platform, searching. Where could

500

he be? Was he already on board? She turned around on the spot, looking for a conductor, someone who could let her on the train to look.

A whistle blew, and people crowded toward the doors of the train cars, waving to the loved ones they left behind on the platform, smiling and chattering. Emily started the other way on the platform, craning to look in each window as she walked.

"All aboard for Denver Union Station!"

The doors closed up and down the train, scraping and banging. Windows lowered and people poked their heads out, waving. The train lurched, started moving. Helpless to stop it, Emily watched it go, puffing clouds of coal smoke from its stack as it moved east along Water Street, gaining speed.

That was it, then. After everything, he hadn't even said goodbye.

She put a hand to her chest, the awful ache there taking the breath from her lungs. She pressed her eyes shut, grateful she couldn't cry. Tears wouldn't bring the train back, or make James get off it. She stood there, unable to move, overwhelmed by the bleak emptiness inside her.

James was gone, and she'd probably never see him again.

She opened her eyes and took a deep breath, steadying herself.

I am not upset. I am not upset.

The dozen or so well-wishers on the platform were filtering away now, leaving her alone.

She shivered, the autumn air cooling her perspiration. She couldn't stand here forever. She would have to move on from this, move on and keep living.

One moment and one step at a time.

She turned around, a gasp catching in her throat when she saw—

"James?"

He was sitting on a bench by the door, his suitcase tucked between his legs, his gaze fixed on her.

"How did I miss…?" She trailed off, almost not believing her eyes.

"You walked right past me when you charged out onto the platform." His voice was flat, tired.

"Oh." She didn't know what she wanted to do more—hug him or hit him.

Both, in whatever order feels best.

"We weren't even supposed to be there."

"What?" She took a step toward him.

He leaned back against the bench. "The day William died. We weren't supposed to be there. Another company was supposed to lead the attack, but there was a problem."

Chills ran up and down Emily's back. This was it. He was going to tell her all of it. She took another step. "Go on."

"We were waiting in reserve, and they called us to the front."

～

"Come on, James!"

He gasped, suddenly awake, fighting against the strong hands that shook him. His eyes focused on William's face.

"Wake up!" William shook him again.

"Alright, alright." James got to his feet, groggy and disoriented, every muscle stiff. He looked around him, remembering. The long march. The walled garden in Omicourt. The chatter of gunfire from the woods to the north of town had increased in tempo while he'd been asleep. So had the German artillery, judging by the occasional boom in the distance.

"Company C!" The voice was Robinson's, sounding from somewhere outside the garden. "Form up!"

"What's going on?" James found his rifle leaning against the stone wall, rubbed his eyes.

Rodriguez, standing next to the door, unslung his weapon from his shoulder, scowling. "The attack has stalled, and First Battalion is taking over. K Company is holding position up the hill. M Company... is taking its time moving forward."

James looked to William for an explanation.

His friend shook his head. "Rumor is their lieutenant says the War is ending. He doesn't want to take any risks with the end so close."

"Not a bad idea," Collins murmured.

"Enough of that shit." Rodriguez stepped out of the garden and onto the street. "Hurry up!"

They filed out of the garden and moved in column up the street, joining the stream of other soldiers from the two companies. They hadn't walked far before stone houses and gardens yielded to an open patchwork of green and brown fields, the stubble of crops poking up from rows of tilled dirt, the road cutting through it. The officers led them toward a sunken road, hiding them from view of the woods.

Robinson stood out front. "Company, attack formation!"

"First platoon, up front!" Lieutenant Merriam, to Robinson's right, drew his pistol, waving to get their attention.

The NCOs repeated the orders, urging the men forward, pushing them into formation, finding the straggling replacements and showing them where to stand.

And doesn't it figure we'd be the very front line?

James watched as Robinson looked between the platoon commanders, received a nod from each. "Fix bayonets!"

James drew his blade, fitted it over the end of the muzzle. The sleep was completely gone from his eyes now, his pulse kicking up, fear wrapping around his stomach.

A loud whistle, an explosion. James dropped down, waited for the shower of dirt and shrapnel to subside, then got back to his feet, crouching low, the men beside him doing the same.

He gritted his teeth. "Hurry it up, dammit."

They gave the order to hold weapons at the high carry, then—

"Double time…. March!"

The line of men surged forward, scrambling up over the embankment and into the open. James braced himself, ready for the storm of bullets from the hill. A bullet did sizzle overhead somewhere, and another, a shell bursting way out in front of them, blasting the tilled earth into the air—but there was no storm.

It wasn't very far to the woods, and within a few minutes they filtered between the trees, the sound of gunfire ahead growing louder. James bent low, picking a path between the gray trunks, careful to keep William on his left and Collins on his right. Dirt and bits of wood rained down on them, the ground churned by a deafening explosion.

"Watch your fire!" Lieutenant Merriam shouted over the noise. "Americans ahead!"

James strained his eyes, found the khaki shapes of K Company in front of him, hiding behind tree trunks, the root balls of toppled logs, and rocks, firing their rifles up the hill. He stepped on something soft and stumbled, knew without looking it was a body.

The crackle of bullets splitting the air increased in volume, surrounding him.

A scream behind him.

A wet thud and a groan to his right.

James picked up his pace, pumping his legs to push him up the hill.

Just ahead, an officer cupped his hands over his mouth. "K Company, hold your fire!"

The Americans charging up the hill passed around and between their comrades, who cheered them on as they moved out in front.

"Get the filthy Huns!"

"Come on, kill the bastards!"

I have to see one first.

James peered among the trees, trying to find the cool gray of the German uniforms, or a muzzle flash, or—

There!

He dropped to his knee behind a tree, sighted on the smooth, mushroom shape of a German helmet poking out above a log, and fired. His first shot went wide, and the helmet bobbed down for a second as the man beneath it crouched low.

"Come on, damn you." James worked his bolt, aimed again, his ears ringing.

This time, when he pulled the trigger, the helmet jerked back and vanished.

The rifle fire from the American line intensified as the men found their targets. To James's left, the auto rifles added their slow, thumping fire to the roar, Bird propping his Chauchat on a massive, downed trunk.

James looked for another target, saw the flash of a muzzle, and fired at it. A few seconds later, the Germans scattered out of cover, a flurry of movement as they broke from where they'd been hiding and ran up the hill.

"After them!" Robinson was standing already and charging up the slope. "Move in short rushes."

James launched himself from behind the trunk, a primitive, giddy excitement coursing through him at the sight of his enemy running.

The bastards are beat.

The running firefight sputtered on, the American tide sweeping up the hill in fits and starts, dislodging the enemy from each new place they tried to stand and fight, driving them up the hill with their rifles, leaving dead Germans behind them like a trail of crumbs.

They weren't alone. Doughboys stumbled and fell, grasping bullet wounds, screaming, lying still. Artillery ripped among the American ranks, striking closer now, blasting trees apart, tossing men aside and into the branches, their bodies torn.

James aligned his sights on the edge of the trunk, waited. Out popped the German, his rifle pointed down the hill. James fired, and the man's face crumpled in pain as he fell out from behind the tree.

Again, the Germans scattered, moving up and over what looked like a bare shoulder of the hill, a break in the trees.

The Huns had to be close to breaking, would run at any moment. James untucked himself from the cover of a boulder, caught sight of Lieutenant Merriam, William, and Bird to his left front, Collins to his right.

"We've got them running!" Robinson was far off to the right, too, pulling a replacement to his feet and pushing him on. "Drive them to Sedan!"

The American line broke through the trees and into the open, cresting the shoulder of the hill. James had just enough time to register the scene in front of him—a small, steep-sided embrasure cutting the hillside, the tangle of woods and brush beyond it—before the forest ahead exploded with the telltale rattle of Maxim guns.

James dove to the ground, an agonized scream right beside him almost drowned out by the gunfire. He looked around for the source of the scream, fear jolting through him.

Bird?

William?

It was Bird, cradling his arm, moaning.

James's heart thudded against his ribcage. "First aid! First aid!"

~

"You were pinned down." Emily sat down beside James, her skirts rustling.

James nodded, staring straight ahead of him at the empty train tracks, the echoes of the battle in his head, making him shiver. "They had their guns in a checkerboard pattern in the woods ahead of us. As soon as we came into view…"

He looked down at his hands in his lap, hating the tremble in his voice.

"And that's when Dwight Robinson died."

James looked up, found her blue eyes studying him, her brow furrowed. "How did you know?"

The corners of her mouth curved upward, the slightest smile. "Susan."

He held her gaze, almost afraid of the softness of her expression, the soothing tone of her voice.

After everything he'd put her through, was that compassion he saw? Compassion for him?

His throat tightened, choking off his words before he could say them. He nodded. He saw it all again in his mind—Robinson standing, trying to lead the men forward, falling, jerking again and again as the German lead tore through him.

Don't fall apart. Not now.

There was nothing for it now. He had to finish it.

James swallowed, found his voice. "The bastards cheered. They cheered when they saw him die."

"And you grabbed your friend's machine gun and ran at them."

James wiped his cheeks. "Yes."

~

"GARRISON, STOP! STOP!"

James hardly heard Lieutenant Merriam's shout as he stood, the heavy Chauchat in his hands, the sling of his own rifle cutting into his shoulder. He sprinted forward, his eyes fixed on the woods beyond the embrasure, his breathing ragged, his face burning hot.

"James!" William's panicked shout followed him. "What the hell are you doing?"

He ignored his friend, yelled as he ran, an awful, raw sound even to his own ears.

For a moment, everyone stopped firing, the occasional rifle shot breaking the sudden silence on the hillside. James caught sight of a doughboy in cover off to his left, staring at him, his mouth open.

It was only a dozen more yards to the edge of the embrasure. If he could only make it before…

"James! Goddamn you!"

He glanced over his shoulder, saw William standing up, his eyes wide, his face white with fear.

The entire world crashed in around him as everyone opened fire at once. The German machine guns spat their deadly fire at him, blasting up clods of dirt and leaves all around him. Rifle shots, the thud of a rifle grenade touching off, an explosion in front of him. The air vibrated and snapped around him as he ran, the ground pitching beneath him as the dirt to his left exploded into the air. He stumbled, the shell's blast knocking him off balance for a moment, his footsteps faltering.

He was so close now, so close to the safety of the gulley. He summoned all his energy and threw himself forward. He hit the ground just below the lip of the embrasure, his legs buckled and he rolled, coming to a stop when he slammed into a stump, the wind knocked out of him, black spots floating in front of his eyes. He heard the metal clatter of the Chauchat falling somewhere below him but couldn't move to stop it.

He lay there, gasping for breath, his mind finally catching up with him and taking in his surroundings. The embrasure was wider and deeper than it had looked, more of a small ravine, brush and tree stumps choking its slopes. On the far side was an opening to a shallow trench line.

The Germans would be there any minute. They had to have seen him go down here.

Cold sweat trickled down the back of his neck, fear replacing the heat of anger.

What the hell had he just done and where was—?

Oh, God.

"William!" James choked, fighting to breathe.

Had he got back to cover in time? He'd been standing to follow James, exposed to the enemy.

James reached above him, fisted his hand in the dirt, and pulled, dragging himself back up the slope. He saw his rifle lying above him and took it in hand. He crawled on his belly, his head low, the sigh of bullets flying overhead. Instinctively, he put a hand up to push his helmet down—only to find it was missing. He kept crawling, reached the lip of the ravine, and peered carefully over.

And there was William, alone.

Running, stumbling, sprinting toward the embrasure, twenty yards to the right from where James lay. He vanished as the ground in front of him erupted into the air from a shell blast. He burst through the smoke a second later, still running, his bayonet forward.

James stared, transfixed, rooted to the spot. He spun around and looked for a target to shoot, but the slope was higher on the other side, blocking his view, and he couldn't find the German machine gunners.

"Dammit!" He turned back around, helpless, panic seizing him. "Come on!"

William was just about to the edge of the ravine now, was lifting his foot to step down when a red mist puffed out of his side, near the hip.

No!

William crumpled forward, screaming, and fell headfirst into the ravine, sliding down the soft dirt to rest a few yards below the lip. He clutched his side, writhing in pain, a low, agonized groan escaping his mouth.

The sound tore into James, ripping his tattered nerves to pieces. "I'm coming, William!"

He slid a few feet lower down the slope, then stood and started running toward his friend. "Don't move!"

William raised his head, met James's eyes, the seconds slowing as a long, horrible shriek filled the air.

The slope where William lay vanished, engulfed by fire, ripped apart and thrown into the air. Something slammed James in the leg, the force of the blast knocking him backward, spinning the world around him.

His vision swam, the noise of battle suddenly distant, his ears ringing. He tried to stand, but his body wouldn't cooperate, his leg heavy. He sat up, then sagged back down against the slope, dizzy. He looked toward the spot where William had been, hoping against hope to still see him there.

Nothing but a crater torn in the earth.

James shook his head, refusing to believe, desperation electrifying every nerve.

"Come on." He tried to stand again, but his dizzy head forced him down.

He rolled onto his belly and started dragging himself across the ground. "Come on, damn you!"

He pulled himself through the brush and grass until his hands sank in the soft earth of the blasted area. The stink of explosives filled his nose as he crawled, searching the churned earth for some sign of his friend. He looked down the slope, toward the spray of bushes there, anywhere William could have hidden. He reached the edge of the crater and looked in, the chemical smell of the shell overpowering, gagging him.

Nothing.

His fingers closed on something soft. He looked down and saw them—just a few bits of khaki cloth, stained red with blood.

William's blood.

James's arms collapsed out from under him and he sagged against the ground, shaking, unable to control the sobs that burst from his mouth as he squeezed the patch of cloth in his hand, his scream lost in the din of the battle around him.

CHAPTER 38

Emily fisted her hand in the front of her blouse, her heart pounding. She swallowed, sick to her stomach, her chest splitting with the force of her grief. "That's why they couldn't find a body. The shell hit him directly."

James shook his head, his gaze fixed in front of him. "Don't you understand? There *was* no body. The blast vaporized him, blew him completely apart. He was there one second, and then…"

"Gone." Emily finished his sentence. Her vision wobbled in front of her, and she closed her eyes, tried to slow down her breathing. She felt like she was falling, tumbling, breaking apart.

Something warm covered her hand, resting next to her on the bench. She opened her eyes and looked. It was James's hand. Without thinking, she took it, held on for dear life.

"I'm so sorry, Emily. I'm sorry I didn't tell you sooner. I didn't want you to think of him ending that way." His voice wavered, but there was a steel in it to which she clung, a buoy in the chaos of her emotions.

"I suppose it was painless."

James nodded. "But to suddenly cease to exist… It's as if he never was there, like he was nothing."

Emily shuddered, her throat tight. "And the other soldiers didn't see?"

"He was too far down the slope. I'm sure they saw the explosion, but they couldn't have known for sure. I'm sure the Maxims occupied their attention."

She looked over at him, her own voice distant to her ears, as if it came from someone else. "Then how did they see you earn your medal?"

James laughed, a harsh, mirthless sound. "They didn't. I'm sure they just found the results and put it together afterward. I suppose I might as well tell you that part. My heroism."

He spat the last word, his disgust for it evident.

Emily opened her mouth to tell him he didn't need to relive any more of the battle, but he had already started talking, the words spilling out of him, and all she could do was listen.

THERE IT WAS. Between the gunshots, sure as anything.

James raised his head, looked along the ravine in front of him. A handful of Germans, grouped in front of the opening into the shallow trench. Some were carrying sandbags, their rifles slung on their backs. Others were setting up one of the lighter Maxim guns, carrying ammunition. They were preparing to enfilade the ravine, no doubt. Mow down the American attackers as soon as they moved into it—and they seemed completely oblivious to his presence.

He watched them move, his hatred for their gray uniforms, the very shape of their helmets, the sound of their damned language, smoldering to life beneath his grief.

He was already in a perfect position, prone and slightly

uphill. Trembling, he slid his rifle forward in the dirt, raised it up to his shoulder, and took aim.

His sights danced across his target, the man stooping to sit behind the Maxim gun, his front covered in smooth armor plates.

What the hell is wrong with you?

James tried to steady his sights, failed. He exhaled, squeezed the trigger.

The rifle kicked his shoulder, but when he cycled his bolt and looked over the end of the barrel to see his handiwork, the German at whom he'd fired had stood upright, looking at him, unhurt.

The other Germans shouted, unslung their rifles.

James took aim, fired again. This time, one of the Germans fell sideways, gripping his shoulder.

Not a killing shot.

The other enemy soldiers fired back, and dirt sprayed James in the face, bullets whistling overhead.

James worked his bolt, wishing he had—

A machine gun.

Where had the Chauchat fallen? He looked around, searching the ravine near where he'd entered it, twenty yards behind him. He spotted it, snagged on a bush just a few yards above the embrasure's bottom.

James turned his attention back to his rifle, fired again at his enemy, and didn't wait to see if he'd hit or not. He pushed himself up to his feet, the sudden pain in his leg wrenching a cry from his throat. He hobbled down the side of the ravine, cutting a diagonal path for the Chauchat. The brush tore at him as he went, snagging his uniform.

More gunshots. Shouts in German.

He didn't look around, gritting his teeth as he broke into a full sprint. Panting, he slid feet first to the ground next to the Chauchat. Leaving his rifle in the dirt beside him, he flattened himself against the ground and hauled the Chauchat out of the bush. He turned it sideways, smacked it hard to throw out any dirt.

He shouldered it, resting its bipod on the earth in front of him, and took aim. The Germans were loading the Maxim gun, only a few seconds left before they'd be ready.

James pulled the trigger.

An ominous clunk, then nothing.

"Christ!" His hands flew over the weapon, felt the round lodged at an odd angle.

The German worked the handle on his Maxim.

James racked the bolt, raised the gun back to his shoulder.

The German swiveled the Maxim to point his way.

James pulled the trigger, and the Chauchat chattered to life, smacking him in the shoulder. Little jets of dirt erupted around the Germans, who tried to scatter. James cut them down, ripping them up while they were still grouped together.

Click.

The Chauchat stopped firing, and James didn't wait. He grabbed his rifle and sprang forward, groaning as soon as his weight came onto his injured leg. And what was the odd clicking sensation in that knee?

He ignored it, pointing his rifle ahead of him, and reached for a grenade.

Dammit!

They'd fallen off somewhere. He didn't stop to look for them but kept running. One of the Germans was still alive, trying to move his dead comrade and get to the machine gun. James reached him first.

He swung the butt of his rifle up, catching the man under the chin. The German grunted and fell backward, into the trench. James stayed with him, ending him with two thrusts of his bayonet, drawing a long, gurgling rasp from the man's mouth.

James withdrew his blade, turned to the Maxim gun. He topped off his rifle, shoving the partial clip into his pocket, and slung the weapon over his shoulder. Stooping down, he hauled up the Maxim, the pain in his leg causing him to moan. He looked over the weapon, its unfamiliar controls, the funny magazine sticking out one side, the belt of cartridges feeding from it and into the gun.

Above him, the German machine gunners were still firing.

The bastards who killed Robinson, shot William.

He stumbled forward, pointing the Maxim in front of him, his hands sweaty, slipping on its handles. The trench turned, sloping upward, zigzagging as it climbed the ravine. He turned a corner, found three Germans gaping at him.

He fired and they fell, jerking as the rounds tore through them.

A sickly, intoxicating pleasure filled him at the sight of his enemies' deaths.

Make the bastards pay.

He stumbled on again, stepping over their bodies. He stopped, sagged for a moment against the wooden revetting on the side of the trench, his heart racing. Unable to catch his breath, he pushed on, limping.

Another few zigzags and the trench leveled out. James peered down its length, stopping again to rest. There were two concrete bunkers built into the trench ahead, facing out toward the ravine. He couldn't see their gun ports, but he could hear the work of the enemy machine guns, spraying short bursts out over the embrasure.

How many more men in James's battalion had they already killed?

No more. Not one more.

He rested a hand on his pounding heart, trying and failing to steady himself. He stumbled forward, advancing on the first bunker. He gasped, the lip of the trench exploding in a spray of dirt.

Shots from the American side.

He crouched lower, dragging his injured leg as he closed on the bunker. A German emerged, carrying an ammo can. He spotted James, and his eyes widened.

James pulled the trigger, hosing his enemy down with bullets. A few more Germans appeared, rifles up, and James mowed those down, too, the Maxim killing them with perfect efficiency. He kept moving toward the emplacement and pivoted as he reached it, pointing the monstrous weapon inside. The German machine gunners looked around, but James cut them to pieces before they could turn.

"Nein!"

He spun, saw another German running from the first bunker to the next. James fired, held down the trigger. The man jerked, dropped, and the Maxim went dry. James heaved the machine gun aside and reached for his rifle.

The momentum of the heavy weapon threw him off balance, and he fell forward. He caught himself against the trench wall, his head suddenly spinning. For the first time, he looked down at his leg. His breeches and puttees were soaked in blood from just above the knee down to his boot. The woolen fabric was torn open around the knee, and James could see his own mangled flesh through the hole.

A shout in German drew his attention from his wound, another enemy at the other end of the trench, moving toward him, brandishing an entrenching tool and a pistol. James fired from the hip, missed. The man screamed at him, broke into a sprint. James raised the rifle to his shoulder, leaning against the trench wall for support, and fired again, dropping his opponent.

James wanted to run, to charge the other emplacement, but his feet were so heavy, the effort of walking more difficult with each step. Cold sweat poured over his face, trickling down the back of his tunic. He gasped, panted with exertion. He reached the entrance to the bunker, leaned against it, then half-jumped, half-fell inside.

There were five Germans, grouped around the gun, turning to face him.

There was no aiming, the distance so short. He fired, worked his bolt, and fired again, the blast of his weapon contained and magnified in the concrete box, ringing his ears. The gunner and his assistant screamed and fell over. The others reached for pistols and a rifle leaned in the corner. James knocked one German down with his next shot, but when he moved the bolt forward it stuck, the rifle's magazine empty.

Shit.

No time to reach for a clip.

He lunged forward, catching the closest enemy in the gut with his bayonet. James fell forward, his own momentum carrying him over, pushing his skewered opponent in front of him. He caught his fall with his bayonet, felt something snap. He withdrew his blade, saw the tip was broken.

James turned on the last German, who was babbling, trying to run out of the bunker.

The man tripped over one of his dead comrades and started to crawl away. James put his foot on the man's back, pushed him to the ground, and thrust his bayonet between his shoulders. The man screamed, the blunt, ragged edge of the broken blade taking much longer to break through skin and bone.

James couldn't hold himself up anymore. He fell onto his rifle, his body weight driving his weapon down, the odd twitching of his enemy's body telling him he'd finished the job.

He wavered, his head spinning, black gathering at the edges of his vision. He couldn't hold onto the rifle any longer, slipped off it and onto the body of the man he'd just killed. He crawled toward the bunker's exit, his last coherent thought on getting out, getting away from the stink of blood that filled his head. The black fog in his eyes thickened, closing in on the center of his vision. Sunshine warmed his face as he emerged from the bunker and breathed in the dirt of the trench floor.

He heard someone yelling his name, a crescendo of gunfire.

Then he sagged to the ground and knew no more.

"THEN WHAT HAPPENED?" Emily squeezed James's hand tight, the warmth of his skin, the pulse of his heart a miracle.

How in God's name had he survived?

He stared straight ahead, though his grip on her hand tightened. His voice was distant, his tone matter-of-fact, as if he were talking about someone else. "Once those two bunkers were gone, the battalion advanced through the gap. They must have found me and brought me to the rear. I don't remember much. It was a day or two afterward before I was coherent again, a pathetic invalid in a bed somewhere."

Emily looked for words that might comfort him. "You saved American lives that day. I don't think that's pathetic."

James pursed his lips, his face pinched. "Do you know what the regiment did next?"

She shook her head.

"Collins and Rodriguez told me a few weeks later, when they came to visit." He took a deep breath. "They advanced to the woods just south of St. Aignan and stopped to send out patrols. They were ready to attack the village when the French ordered them out. Our guys were crossing into their line of advance, and it turned out the French wanted to liberate Sedan more than we did. All that marching for nothing."

Emily could understand that. "I suppose it was their city."

James looked at her, his expression desolate. "Just a few hours after my little stunt, the regiment withdrew and didn't fight again before the armistice. A few hours, Emily. Had I kept my head, had I not run forward, William might have made it. He missed the end by a hair."

She studied his face, the anguish written in his eyes. Only hours ago, she'd been so angry with him, hated him for the reckless stab for glory that had killed her brother.

Now she knew it was different. She could see it all—James stumbling along the trench, bleeding to death, driven on by grief and vengeance. She imagined the other soldiers, lying on the edge of the ravine, pinned down by the enemy guns, waiting for the heavy weapons to arrive. What must they have thought when the German guns went silent, one after the other? What must they have felt?

She had to make him understand. "James, what would have happened if you hadn't gone forward?"

He wiped his cheeks. "We'd have stayed pinned down until the one-pounders and the mortars arrived. We might have tried to flank them again, like we usually did. For all I know, they did exactly that. I couldn't see what our side was doing."

"And this flanking, is it dangerous?"

His eyes widened and he laughed. "Is that a serious question? You've heard me talk about it."

"So, you spared others that danger." She spoke slowly, kept her voice as calm and soothing as she could. "You got rid of those machine guns faster than anyone else could have."

He let go of her hand. "It was stupid luck. The Germans thought the same shell that killed William got me, too. They overlooked me, and I slipped through. Nothing more."

She raised her chin, holding his gaze. "Luck or not, you saved men's lives that day."

"Saved them?" He raised an eyebrow. "Didn't you hear me? I killed all those Huns."

"You just said the regiment would have flanked them or blown them up with bigger guns. Someone else would have killed them."

"At least it wouldn't have been me." He looked at his hands, his voice barely a whisper. "I suppose they almost made it to the end, too."

Emily opened her mouth to respond, closed it. She'd never heard him express regrets for the Germans before. And why wouldn't he? Were there people in a train station in Germany right now, having some version of this conversation? Wondering about the Frenchman, the American, the British Tommy they'd killed at the end? What would it be like to live with that blood on his hands?

Emily thought of the man Devitt and Moore had left in the cloister, the one who had died alone, begging her not to leave. How long had she felt responsible for the fact that his last, awful moments passed without comfort? Had she ever stopped?

She had no idea what to say, to him or to herself. "James…"

He waved his hand. "No, I know. It was war. I guess anyone would have done it."

She reached to reclaim his hand. "It's not every man who would have kept going with that injury."

James huffed, ignoring her gesture. "It's not every man who gets his friend killed, either. Don't you see?"

People were gathering on the platform for the next train, and some of them stopped to stare, but he seemed not to notice them.

He stood up, turned to face her, his voice rising. "We weren't even supposed to be there. The French—"

"Didn't order your regiment back for hours. You all would have faced those machine guns regardless." She paused, her throat tightening. "William might have been killed doing your flanking maneuvers, or in the advance afterward."

He closed his eyes as he stood there, shaking his head silently. "You don't know that. He might have lived had I not killed him. It was all for nothing."

"Nothing?" Emily's temper flared now, and she stood. She put her hands on either side of his face, the rasp of his stubble beneath her palms. "He was trying to rescue you. Isn't that something?"

James opened his eyes and met her gaze, shaking his head.

"No." She held him still. "Now it's your turn to listen. I know what you meant to him. He saw you run out there alone, and he couldn't bear watching the Germans gun you down. William tried to save his friend, and he died for it. For you."

Her voice cracked, emotion making it waver. "As far as I'm concerned, that's pretty damned noble. Don't you dare steal that from him now."

"And you don't hate me for that? You should hate me, Emily." His expression was stern, his words hard, but the note of vulnerability in his voice was unmistakable.

She studied his face, the tears in the corners of his gray eyes, gauging her own emotions. She was angry, yes. Angry that he hadn't told her for so long, angry that he'd lied. But could she hate him, knowing what she now knew?

"Hate you?" She craned her neck and kissed him, just the lightest touch on the lips. She pulled away, stroking his cheek with her thumb. "You're the person my brother loved more than his own life. How could I do anything but love you, too?"

He pulled her into his arms, and they stood there together, not speaking, rocking gently as the crowd flowed around them, coming from and going to their journeys, washed in the steam from the waiting engine.

Emily could not cry, and she reckoned she never would again. What good would it do any of them now? But when she felt James's tears on her cheek, she was not angry with him. Instead, she held him closer, his tears washing them both clean.

CHAPTER 39

Near Vavincourt, France
November 11, 1918

"Hurry up with your things, girls." Mrs. Wolfe bustled around behind the women as they lugged their trunks over to the Red Cross truck. "We're behind schedule already."

Emily hefted her trunk up and into the bed, then moved out of the way for Gertie to do the same. She started across the square toward where the canteen had stood for more than a month, now a jumble of partially collapsed tents and stacks of supply boxes, the booth disassembled and laid out in pieces. They were moving northeast, following the advance of the US Army. The battle must be going well—and judging by the lack of letters from James or William during the past ten days or so, it must still be hard fighting.

She ignored the tension that had settled in her stomach and walked over to help Ruth and Clara pick up the pieces of the booth and move them to the truck. She was just bending

524

over when a shout from the direction of the church drew her attention.

Were more wounded men arriving?

There were no trucks, only Devitt and Moore running across the cobblestones toward them, a stream of doctors, nurses, and limping soldiers flowing out of the church, cheering, hugging each other.

"What's going on?" Clara wiped her forehead, holding a wooden board under her arm,

Before Emily could respond, the two stretcher-bearers had made it over to them. They stopped, breathing hard.

"Just… heard…" Devitt put his hands on his knees, half laughing, half panting. "It's… over."

"What?" Emily shook her head, not understanding.

He couldn't possibly mean…

Ruth gasped. "Oh, my goodness."

Moore's face split in a smile. "The War… it's over at eleven o'clock."

Emily's knees shook, the news hitting her with the force of a punch. "Are you sure?"

"Positive." Devitt stood upright. "We heard it from a major in the next village. Everyone's talking about it."

"What's going on over here?" Mrs. Wolfe walked over, the other women in tow, her hands on her hips. Her serious expression became one of shock as Devitt and Moore repeated the news.

Emily looked around at the other women, the disbelief on their faces a mirror to her own emotions. "What time is it?"

Mrs. Wolfe glanced at her wristwatch. "A quarter to nine."

Only a couple hours.

Emily turned to face the northeast, listening to the distant rumble of the guns. Could it possibly be true?

~

JAMES OPENED HIS EYES, his vision unfocused. He reached up to hold his spinning head still, trying to determine his surroundings.

Where the hell was he?

"We thought you'd never wake up, soldier."

A shadow fell across James's eyes. He blinked, his gaze focusing on the face of a young woman bent over him, a red cross cap on her head.

"Emily?"

The woman shook her head, smiling. "Edith. I'm your nurse. Is Emily your sweetheart?"

A nurse? Had he been wounded?

Oh, God.

It all flooded back to him. Robinson. William. The Germans in the ravine, the trench, the bunkers.

He tried to sit up, panic making his heart pound.

Please, let it be a dream.

"Easy." Edith held him down, her brow knit with concern. "We don't want you putting any weight on that knee."

James sagged back against the bed, wincing at the pain that lanced up and down his leg. "My knee?"

She pulled a blanket up to his chin. "You took a lot of shrapnel. It's a miracle we were able to save the leg."

He gripped the blanket, unable to control the hot tears that filled his eyes.

It wasn't a dream.

William was dead, and Robinson, and how many others?

Did Emily know?

James sniffed, trying to pull himself together. "How long have I been here?"

"Oh, a couple days." Edith took hold of his hand. "There, now. It's alright. We're taking good care of you. You woke up just in time."

"In time?"

"Mm hmm. The War is about to be over."

He stared at her. "What did you say?"

She nodded, her hat bobbing on her head. "In just a minute or two. It's all over at eleven. You almost missed it."

"But how?" James looked to his side, trying to get a view of the room.

He was in a long building of some kind, filled with rows of beds, most of them holding bandaged men. Some were asleep, or unconscious, while others huddled together, expectant looks on their faces. Nurses and doctors filtered between the rows, talking in excited whispers, smiles on their faces.

"The Germans have signed an armistice."

An armistice?

This *had* to be a dream. James looked back at the other soldiers. "What are they doing?"

"They're listening to the guns." Edith put her free hand to an ear, closed her eyes. "They've slowed down."

James strained his ears, trying to hear the artillery, the unending rumble that had permeated every moment at the front during the past year. It *was* slowing down, the constant noise diminished to a slow trickle of muffled booms.

There was one. And another. And then…

Silence.

Everyone who had been moving stopped in their tracks. The nurses held perfectly still, their eyes wide. The doctors beamed at each other. The soldiers bowed their heads in prayer, or stared toward the windows, listening.

Still, there was silence.

The room erupted into cheers. Men who could stand got to their feet, danced, hugged each other. The doctors shook each other's hands, laughing while the nurses joined in with the soldiers. *The Star-Spangled Banner* rose above the din, sung by a hundred voices.

Edith bent forward and kissed James on the forehead. "You see? It's really over."

He shook his head, his vision dissolving in tears. "I killed him."

"Whatever is the matter?" She held his hand tighter. "This is a happy day."

James shook his head, his body trembling, the joyful noise of the others surrounding him as he repeated himself over and over again. "I killed him. I killed him. I killed him."

EMILY HEARD the last shell fall just after 11:20, though by then it was hard to hear anything but the revelry around her. Soldiers and nurses danced together in the square along with the women from the canteen. French villagers emerged from their houses, passing out wine bottles, kissing their American guests. Somewhere, someone was letting off flares, drawing excited cheers and applause from the crowd.

"We did it!" Gertie pulled Emily into her embrace, laughing. "It's over!"

Emily hugged her friend, unable to stop smiling. "It really is over."

She had to keep repeating it to believe it.

Gertie pulled away and accepted a bottle from a passing Frenchman, who was singing *La Marseillaise* and weeping as he danced through the throng. She took a swig and shoved it into Emily's hands.

Emily laughed and drank, the liquid warming her, almost chasing away the shadows that still clung to her heart despite the festivities.

Were William and James safe? Were they still training replacements, like their last letters had said? Had they made it back to the front before the fighting ended?

Gertie took the bottle back from Emily. "I'm surprised Mrs. Wolfe isn't putting a stop to all this."

"Where is she, anyhow?" Emily looked around her. Come to think of it, she hadn't seen the woman in a little while, not since everyone had started celebrating at eleven.

Gertie took another swig. "I don't know."

"I'll go look." Emily pushed and slid through the crowd, making her way back toward the disassembled canteen. She put her hands to her mouth. "Mrs. Wolfe?"

No use, not with all this shouting and singing.

Emily walked to the middle of the collapsed tents, put her hands on her hips. Maybe Mrs. Wolfe was somewhere in the crowd and she just hadn't seen her. Emily turned to retrace her steps, but stopped in her tracks.

There was Mrs. Wolfe, leaning against the Red Cross truck, hidden from view of the square, crying.

Emily had moved right past her without seeing. "Mrs. Wolfe?"

The older woman looked at her with red, puffy eyes. "A month."

"Pardon me?"

"My boy Trevor missed it by a month."

Emily shifted on the spot, uncomfortable with the woman's tears. Hadn't she learned yet, as Emily had learned, that they served no purpose? She walked over to Mrs. Wolfe and put her hand around her shoulder. "He'd be proud the War is over."

"Over?" Mrs. Wolfe shook her head. "Not for Trevor, I think. And for me? Go and enjoy yourself, Miss Culver."

Emily hesitated. She couldn't just leave her like this. "Ma'am?"

"You've earned it."

Emily gave her shoulder a squeeze, then started for the square. She stopped herself and turned. "It'll all be alright in the end. You'll see. The world will be a better place now. With time…"

What else was she supposed to say?

Another flare sailed into the air, and applause and cheers echoed off the stone houses around the square.

Mrs. Wolfe met her gaze, smiled faintly. "It's a nice thought."

An ache in her heart, Emily left the grieving woman behind and returned to the celebration, the flare burning red against the gray sky.

Beyond, the church bell started to ring.

September 27, 1919

"The truth is easier—you'll see."

Emily sat down on the settee and gave James what she hoped was a reassuring smile.

He took his place next to her, the sweat on his forehead betraying his nerves.

Him and me both.

How would her parents tolerate what they were about to hear?

James crossed his hands in his lap, took a breath. "I'd like to tell you everything now, everything you want to know, and then I never want to speak of the War again."

Emily's parents nodded wordlessly, apprehension written on their faces. Her father had a notebook and pencil in hand, ready to record whatever James told him. Mrs. Rawlins stood behind them, a feather duster in hand, her tasks forgotten.

"I...." James cleared his throat, his hesitation plain to see.

Emily placed her hand over his, gave it a light squeeze.

You can do this.

He met her gaze, his face pale. He nodded ever so slightly, then looked back at her parents. "I think William joined the Army because it was the opposite of what everyone expected of him. He was always the smart one. The star student, the great athlete."

"Everyone? You mean what *we* expected." Emily's father frowned, but his voice was calm, no accusation in it.

James held her father's gaze. "Yes, what you expected."

Then he spoke without interruption for what felt like hours, telling them all about William's time in the Army, from when they'd snuck off together to Denver to the final days of the War. Emily couldn't always follow James's stories —false starts, interrupting himself to tell some side anecdote, sometimes laughing, sometimes speaking so quietly he was barely audible, his fists clenched—but she watched her parents' reactions, her own nerves wound tight.

Would they get angry? Explode at James? Vent their grief at him?

Instead, they sat silently, emotions playing one after another in their gestures and expressions—pride, grief, muted horror. Her father wrote furiously, gripping his pencil with white-knuckled hands only to stop, stare into space for long minutes, and suddenly begin writing again. Her mother kept her eyes fixed on James, shook her head slowly, one hand laid across her chest below her throat, the other wrapped tightly in the skirt of her lavender morning dress. But there was one image in Emily's mind, clearer than anything before her eyes.

William.

The man her brother had become. He'd left when he was very much still a boy, fresh out of high school.

"A lot of the guys I knew gave up on the future, but never William." James smiled, clearly caught up in some memory. "I think he would have gone to school again if he'd had the choice, like you wanted. When I couldn't imagine surviving the next offensive, he was making plans to become a journalist. He wanted to tell everyone about the War when I just wanted to forget it."

William? A journalist? He'd never mentioned that to her.

Emily looked over at James, squeezed his hand tighter.

Thank God he survived!

Here was someone who'd known William up to the end, someone who'd seen him become a man. James was a precious thread, a link to something she'd only glimpsed in letters and the few times she'd met her brother in France. As the picture of William, the man, coalesced, Emily couldn't help but imagine some future she would never know.

She saw her brother in a suit, seated behind a typewriter, typing furiously away. She could see him on the street, loitering next to policemen, angling for a view of the latest crime, the newest scandal, notepad in hand. She imagined him coming home to a wife, maybe children. And there Emily was in her own fantasy, older, sitting across from him, discussing current events, ribbing him for how he'd never taken the papers seriously when they were kids.

It was a bright, beautiful, terrible dream.

James let go of Emily's hand, and her fantasy evaporated. He got to his feet, walked the few short steps over to where her parents were seated, and stood in front of them.

"I would give anything to have that moment again and choose differently. If I could have taken the bullets myself, I'd have done it. If I could have been under that shell instead…" He knelt down, wincing as he bent his bad knee. "I can't possibly ask for your forgiveness, but I can tell you how terribly sorry I am. Please believe me. He deserved so much more than he got. It shouldn't have been him."

Silence filled the room. Emily almost couldn't breathe, her chest tight. Her parents looked down at the young man in front of them, their expressions strained. Her mother was crying, and Emily realized with a start that her father was, too.

Her own eyes were dry, as always.

At long last, her father wiped away his tears. "I understand now why you didn't want that parade. From what you've said, it was hardly appropriate. You are not the hero in the newspaper."

James looked at the floor, nodding. "No, I'm not."

Emily gaped at her father, anger rising in her throat. She was about to say something when he continued speaking.

"All the same, I owe you a debt of gratitude. What you've told us today…" He looked at his wife. "You have no idea how much this eases our minds. It's clear to me how much you and William cared for each other, and how much his death wounded you. In a strange way, I think we feel…" He trailed off.

James looked up, waiting.

But it was Emily's mother who spoke next, holding her husband's gaze. "William loved you as a brother, and he gave everything for you. You will be our son now, too."

She held out her hand.

Emily's heart pounded, her emotions at war, joy and grief wrapped together. She couldn't speak, could only watch as James stared at her mother's hand.

Whatever she had expected, this was not it.

But would James accept their compassion? Emily knew his feelings, knew he didn't feel he deserved it.

The clock ticked. Outside, Brianna laughed, caught up in childish play.

After an eternity, James took her mother's hand and nodded, though he didn't—or couldn't— say anything. They all held still for a moment, James kneeling in front of her parents, who both looked at him with softened expressions, compassion that made Emily's heart swell into her throat.

Finally, her mother stood. "I expect you to tell us your future plans over dinner, Mr. Garrison."

James exhaled as if he'd been holding his breath, and Emily could swear he looked bigger somehow, lighter. He turned and met her gaze, a smile on his face. "As a matter of fact, I have an interesting idea."

JAMES ANNOUNCED his intention to go to college the next day. "And when I'm done, I want to work in newspapers. Someone has to tell the truth."

The Garrisons had been almost beside themselves at the sudden change in their son's demeanor and his decision to stay in the United States.

"My son, a college man!" Mr. Garrison clapped James on the back. "Now you're making sense."

His mother beamed at him. "We're so proud. It's time to put the past behind you and embrace your life."

"I'll give it a try." James accepted his father's handshake with a smile.

Emily saw him often that fall, spending their days studying together in the library. It was almost like friendship, and for the moment, she was content to put more intense emotions aside to focus on their shared task.

As the Rocky Mountain winter approached, James completed his entrance examinations for the University of Colorado and submitted his application soon after. He didn't wait long for the reply.

"What will I possibly do around those kids?" James looked up from his acceptance letter, his grin only partially concealing his genuine worry.

Emily understood. How could anyone who had served in France spend time among innocent, untarnished youth and not feel alone? "There will be many other veterans there, I think."

She hoped that was true.

Emily would have felt jealous of James, his impending entrance into the world of higher education, had she not also completed the examinations for the women's school—and received a similarly rapid acceptance.

"William made it clear you ought to have a full education, and others have confirmed that opinion," her father had finally said, after sitting her down in the parlor. "I expect you to give this an effort equal to the headaches you've caused me over this issue. If you can do that, you have our support."

She had answered him with a hug, almost giddy with excitement.

Emily knew full well who the "others" were, knew James had spent no small amount of time emphasizing the support William had always felt for her educational ambitions. While it still annoyed her that her father had only changed his mind because of a male opinion, she was too happy to complain openly about it.

For the first time since she'd come home from the War, she'd felt a little like her old, untroubled self.

Of course, she could never be her old self again, but a victory over her father's obstinacy was still a victory.

It wasn't long, however, before world events clouded even the prospect of attending college, and Emily found herself at the Gould's house, heart sinking as she read the headlines.

"I can't believe this." She shook her head, rereading the same black-and-white words. The senate had voted to reject the Treaty of Versailles—and with it, any hope of America joining the League of Nations.

"Are they insane?" James threw the newspaper down on the coffee table. "Did they learn nothing?"

Emily folded her own paper, her emotions bleak. "I think instead they learned the wrong lessons."

He threw his hands in the air, a ragged edge to his voice. "How will we prevent another war if we don't participate in the League?"

Walt drummed his fingers on his thighs. "Maybe it's better to remove ourselves from these sorts of problems. Was it our war, after all?"

Emily didn't know what to say to that. Was the new world taking shape really worth the death of the old? There was fighting in Poland, Russia, the Balkans, and the Levant, and bitter, violent division within Germany. Hadn't President Wilson promised America would end all that with one, final Great War?

How long had Emily held on to that promise, come to rely on it through her darkest days in France? Then again, the Nineteenth Amendment was winning victory after victory in the ratification process. American women would have the vote, and with Prohibition soon to take effect, perhaps they'd no longer fear abuse and violence from drunken husbands. Progressivism had triumphed, at least at home.

Marion took Walt's hand. "We have to have faith. Things can still be better. It's too early to tell."

"Faith?" James raised his eyebrows, but didn't say anything else.

It seemed a foolish, naïve word. But then again, what was the alternative?

She heard again her own words, felt the shell of her conviction.

What you are fighting for here is going to matter to millions of people. It's the most important thing anyone on earth is doing.

Emily made her choice and straightened the paper on the table. "I'd rather hope than not."

WINTER BROUGHT the mixed joys of the holidays, the defiant celebration of a Christmas that would never again be complete. It also heralded a sharp diminishment in the amount of time she got to spend with James, for the rigors of school quickly followed the family obligations of the festive season.

At her first class, Emily scanned the room, the small crowd of young women looking back at her. She swallowed, her mouth dry. She picked a spot next to an older-looking girl in a light blue sweater.

While she waited for the professor to arrive, Emily arranged and re-arranged her books and notebooks on her desk. This was foolish. Stupid. How could she possibly expect to succeed when she'd been out of school for so long?

"Bored already?"

Emily turned and saw the blue-clad woman looking at her.

"Oh. No, not bored."

She nodded, seemed to understand. "I've been bored. If you ask me, this will be a great relief." Noticing Emily's perplexed expression, she added, "I nursed in France. I've been bored to death ever since I got home."

Emily held out her hand. "Emily Culver."

"Elizabeth Proctor."

And just like that, Emily knew she was going to make it.

Within a few weeks, she was totally engrossed in her studies, almost too busy and too content to regret the time she wasn't spending with James. Almost.

He stopped by occasionally to visit with her or do homework together, or to talk to Julius and Brianna—he seemed to take his responsibilities as an adopted Culver seriously—but they hadn't been alone and on a proper date in what felt like an age. More than that, he seemed different somehow. Less affectionate. Closed, even.

They both had classes to attend, homework to complete, essays to write. Surely, it was normal that they should see less of each other, and that their time should be focused on academics rather than romance.

Not that Emily didn't worry that something else could be happening. Could there be some barrier between them now? Some reason for him to pull away? Did he want some respite from her, for their emotions over William to heal?

"You are working yourself up over nothing," Elizabeth said one night, her voice hushed to avoid the librarian's ire. "Besides, you have more than enough to occupy your time without him."

Emily pressed on, her own worries circling in her head. "We fell in love during the worst time in our lives. What if being with me will always make him relive it?"

"Talk to him about it, or stop worrying."

"But what should I say to him?" Emily yawned, almost too tired to argue. After everything she and James had been through together, was it possible he could simply drift away? Or become nothing more than a friend?

"Focus." Elizabeth tapped her pencil on Emily's book. "You fought for this, remember?"

For years.

"I remember." Emily returned her attention to her book.

"HE PROPOSED YESTERDAY EVENING." Marion held out her

hand so Emily could examine her ring. "I am almost too happy to believe it. Can it be real?"

Emily put an exaggerated frown on her face, pretending to examine the stone. "It seems real to me!"

"You goose!" Alice snatched Marion's hand from Emily's views. "Marion, it's beautiful! I'm so happy for you, my dear."

Marion laughed and pulled back her hand to look at it herself. Her expression became more serious, and she worked the ring between the fingers of her other hand as she spoke. "I know life will never be as easy for him as it could be, but right now I don't care. I'll take it all to be with him. Is that foolish?"

Emily shook her head. "It's brave."

That night, she lay awake in bed, unable to sleep. If Walt and Marion could attempt a future together, couldn't she and James? Worrying and wondering would accomplish nothing. She resolved to talk to him soon. Tomorrow, if possible. It was the weekend, and she was caught up enough on her schoolwork to spare the time.

As it turned out, she didn't need to.

"Someone at the door!" Emily's mother glanced from the breakfast table toward the foyer.

Mrs. Rawlins appeared from the kitchen, coffee pot in hand.

"I'll get it." Emily strode to the door, covering a yawn with her hand. The sleepless night clung to her eyes, and she wished she'd had some of the coffee first. If this was Marion hoping to discuss wedding plans, she would need energy.

Emily opened the door and stared at—

"Good morning, James."

It was unusual for him to visit this early in the day.

He stood on the porch, bundled in a gray hat and a gray coat, hands clasped behind his back, a smile on his face. "Hello, Emily."

She took in the hopeful tone of his voice, the way he rocked on his feet.

He's nervous.

"Hello." Emily collected herself, not sure what to say. "Did you bring your Latin reading?"

"It's… It's a nice day out." He waved a hand around. "Chester and Maggie invited me to take a walk at the ranch. Would you care to join me?"

WHEN THEY ARRIVED at High Valley Ranch, the sun was bright and warm enough for James to remove his overcoat. He breathed in the fresh, cool air, trying to calm his nerves. It was one of those sunny, dry Colorado days that defied winter, blue skies over the dark green pine forests and golden, cured grass that hugged the mountains.

"It wouldn't do for you to visit the ranch without some refreshments." Aunt Maggie hugged James as he stepped down from his father's car.

"She's been torturing me all day with the smell of her cooking." Chester shook James's hand, turned to give Emily a peck on the cheek. "It's about time I actually had some of it."

James couldn't focus on lunch, his stomach in knots. He watched Emily sipping tea from her cup, a bright smile on her face as she laughed at Chester's jokes.

He had to do this. And if she rejected him?

At least then he'd know and wouldn't have to wonder.

At last, Chester and Maggie left them to their own devices.

"I think I'll go see the high meadow." James pointed off to the hills. "I can't say I've had much time for fresh air lately."

"Want to escape the books, huh?" Chester leaned back in his chair, winked. "The ground that way should be dry."

"Perfect." James stood. "Would you like to come, Emily?"

If she didn't, this whole plan would be for nothing.

"I've been buried in the books, too." Her chair scraped as she got to her feet. "Let's go for a walk."

They bundled back up and started off, their conversation coming in fits and starts, James's knee protesting the exertion like it always did. They talked about classes, agreed the weather really was exceptional today.

There were so many things he wanted to say to her, but where to begin?

You don't have long to figure that out.

"Here we are." James came to a stop and gestured around them. "Do you recognize it?"

Emily narrowed her eyes. "I don't think so."

"This is where William and I were shooting that day you came and found us, remember? It hasn't changed at all."

It all looked so familiar, and yet strange. The wide, grassy meadow, cured brown and gold. The humps of the mountains to the west, the distant, snowy high peaks beyond. The tree trunk, the one on which they'd set the tin cans, was still there, just a few feet away.

Looking at this place, it was as if nothing had happened. James wasn't sure if that was reassuring or disturbing. Maybe both. He half expected William to pop out from behind a tree, Chester's Krag rifle in his hand.

Emily's eyes widened, a hint of sadness in her expression. "Oh yes, I remember."

She looked at him, clearly waiting for him to say more.

James took a steadying breath. There was nothing for it. "This is the first place I can remember having feelings for you."

She knotted her brow. "James... We haven't acted like a real couple in months. Not really. And now you say..." She seemed to be searching for words. "I am not a toy to be picked up and dropped."

"I know." How could he explain? "When we were together this summer, there were so many times I hated myself for it. I didn't think I deserved to be with you after what I did. How could I be with William's sister and not hate myself for it?"

She crossed her arms over her chest. "You could have asked her rather than leave her in the cold."

"I needed to be sure of my own feelings. I needed to know I wouldn't sabotage a romance with you or hurt you again."

At the word *romance,* her eyebrows rose, but she said nothing.

He pressed on. "I'm sorry if I hurt you, but I had to settle myself."

She eyed him. "What did you decide?"

James gestured to the tree trunk and they both walked over to it. He sat, and she settled herself beside him. He faced her, gathering his courage. He saw the moment realization hit her. Her expression changed, and her eyes flew wide, her cheeks blushing.

"Emily," he began. "I—"

"James, I can't..." She interrupted him, stammering. "I can't marry you. Not now. I worked so hard to get to school that I have to finish. You understand, don't you?"

James stared at her. Is *that* what she thought this was about?

She's not far off.

If she wasn't interested in marriage, would she reject what he had to say?

He shook his head. "I wasn't asking you to marry me."

"Oh." Her blush deepened. "Well, then."

He resisted the urge to laugh, and gathered both her hands in his. "I was asking if you'd like to be together again.

Not married, at least not yet, but together. I love you, Emily, and..."

There were so many more things he wished he could say.

I need you. It hurts to be apart from you. You're the only one who understands.

It was trite, hollow, totally insufficient.

She squeezed his hands. "And I love you."

His heart expanded, filling his chest to the point of bursting. "You do?"

She leaned forward and kissed him.

James was giddy, drunk with happiness, but...

This is too good to be true.

He pulled away. "Are you certain? Nothing will ever change what happened with William. I'll always be the reason he—"

She put a finger to his lips, silencing him. "You'll always be the man my brother loved more than life. James, we are alive, and we're supposed to live now."

"Won't his death always lie between us? How can it ever go away?"

She cupped his face. "The War is part of who we are now. It will never go away. None of it will, but..." She trailed off, and tears gathered in her eyes. Her expression changed to one of surprise, and she raised a hand to the wetness on her cheek.

Confused, James squeezed the hand he still held tighter. "Emily?"

She met his gaze again and smiled. "But that," she said, "is what tears are for."

EPILOGUE

July 13, 1936
Douaumont Ossuary
Near Verdun, France

"I can't see! What are they saying?"

"It'll be over soon, Mary." Emily looked down at her daughter, who was teetering on her tiptoes, straining to look over the tall man standing in front of her.

William, standing between James and Clémentine, Cousin DeLisle's wife, looked around. "You wouldn't understand it anyway, Sis. It's all in French and German."

Mary crossed her arms, her young face the image of annoyance.

Mathilde, Henri and Clémentine's little girl, looked around, her thumb in her mouth, curious at the unfamiliar language of her parents' American relatives.

"I'll describe it for you." Emily returned her gaze to the scene in front of her. Lines of soldiers stood at attention. They weren't like the soldiers she remembered from the War, but gray-haired, their backs bent, their uniforms fitting tightly. French blue, German gray, Italian gray-green, a smattering of British and American khaki.

Hundreds of people—the families, civilians, minor functionaries—gathered around the sides. Beyond them, the honey-colored stone of the ossuary, shaped like an upsidedown T with a tall, central tower, caught the bright sunshine and reflected it on the faces of all the veterans in formation. Their expressions were closed, tight, as they eyed each other, former enemies united to begin a friendship.

In theory.

Henri had written to invite James and Emily to this reconciliation event in the spring. At first, they hadn't known how to react.

"If you want to go, maybe…" James had looked up from Henri's letter, shadows in his eyes. "I don't know if I can go back there. And how will I get away from work?"

Emily hadn't known what to say, her own emotions split. She'd read about the new American monuments and cemeteries in France, had heard about the walls carved with the names of the missing. William had no grave, but somehow the idea of seeing his name in a place of eternal rest felt like visiting him. She'd known how hard returning to France would be for James, though, and she had no desire to dwell on the War, either.

But the idea of participating in a ceremony to honor the dead and heal the hurts of the War had held a certain appeal.

Emily had tried her best to encourage her husband, something to make the decision easier for him. "Maybe you can cover the event for the paper? School won't be in session then."

As a professor of English and assistant dean of women students, Emily wasn't often able to leave town during the academic year.

"I'll think about it." James had folded Henri's letter and

tucked it into his desk, then taken her hand in his. "Do you think they're sincere about reconciliation?"

"It's a beautiful idea."

She looked over at the German war hero, the one named Von Brandis, who had captured one of the French forts near Verdun in 1916. He was gripping a flagpole, its red flag wrapped, a proud expression on his face. Could she ever feel friendship for him? And how could she describe this all to an eight-year-old, what it really meant?

Mary pulled on her hand. "Well?"

Emily dropped her voice to a whisper. "Two men are walking up to the front door. One French, one German. They're laying down a wreath together."

"A Christmas wreath?"

Emily had to keep herself from laughing. "No, a wreath to remember the soldiers."

"Like Uncle William?"

"Yes, sweetie, like him." She held her daughter's hand tighter. "Cousin DeLisle is holding a French flag. He's standing near the door, opposite Von Brandis. Now the two men are saying something."

"What?" Mary's voice made a couple adults nearby turn to look, their annoyance obvious. "What are they saying?"

"Take this." James turned around and held his cane out for William to take, the medals on his overcoat dangling. Emily and Cousin DeLisle had both insisted he wear them.

"To honor the occasion, if nothing else," Henri had written in his invitation. "Any man who faced what you did merits recognition."

Emily had squeezed James's shoulder as he'd read the letter, watched the war of emotion in his eyes.

"I can't stand there in uniform." He'd folded the letter, met her gaze. "You know I don't deserve—"

She'd interrupted him, kissing him on the forehead. "You don't have to."

She knew he still had his uniform tucked away, knew the mix of emotions he still felt about his service. Pride for his fellow soldiers, guilt he'd never completely forgotten. "Just this once, let others see what you endured."

James gave Emily a reassuring smile and moved to pick up their daughter. He grimaced as her weight came into his arms.

"Careful." Emily held out her hands to steady her husband. She didn't want him making his knee any worse than it had become.

James turned and faced the ceremony, Mary on his hip. He pointed to where the two men were standing. "They're making an oath to peace. 'Because those who rest here and elsewhere have gone to the peace of the dead only to establish the peace of the living, and because it would be sacrilege for us to allow what the dead abhor—"

Mrs. DeLisle leaned over, finishing James's sentence with a whisper. "'We swear to safeguard the peace which we owe to their sacrifices.'"

They repeated the oath again in German, Italian, and even English. Then a band struck up the French national anthem, and after a pause spent shifting their instruments in their hands, played the German one as well. Von Brandis straightened his posture and unfurled his flag. Emily couldn't help but stare at it, the black swastika in the center of a white circle over a blood-red field.

To safeguard peace...

She could see again the headline from only a few months ago, the chilling announcement that Germany had remilitarized the Rhineland, violating the Treaty of Versailles. James had come home late that evening, exhausted from editing that day's edition of the paper, tight-lipped.

"The League is doing nothing. Roosevelt is fishing in Florida."

They'd both lain awake that night, neither of them speaking.

Finally, she'd taken his hand in hers and held it. "They say Hitler has promised a non-aggression pact with France and Britain. We may be worrying for nothing."

"Maybe," had been his only reply.

The next day, they'd both agreed to accept Henri's invitation and go to France. They'd invited Marion and Walt to join, but they'd declined.

"It's not worth wrestling the kids onto a boat," Walt had said, their youngest child, Andrew, in his lap.

"Our thoughts will be with you." Marion had patted Emily on the shoulder, smiling. "We always pray for peace."

Emily stared at the German flag, trying to rein in her emotions. Was it naïve to think her former enemies wanted peace, too? Surely the fact that so many had come here was a positive sign. She searched the crowd on the German side, saw an older woman holding a handkerchief to her eyes, a worn black brassard around her arm.

How could anyone who lived through the World War wish to fight again? She glanced over at William, who was rocking on his feet, an interested expression on his face. He was still young, only eleven.

Not much longer until…

Emily pushed aside her fear, returned her gaze to the ceremony. Soldiers from both sides had crossed over, were shaking hands. DeLisle and Von Brandis were standing next to each other, hand in hand, their flags catching the breeze.

She was being too cynical. How could peace succeed if she always expected the worst from an entire people? She looked up at the single word, painted gold, over the ossuary's front door.

Pax.

Peace.

She had to hope. If for no other reason than to keep going.

"Looks like they're finished." James set Mary down, and accepted his cane back from his son, his complexion pale from the pain of standing with his daughter in his arms for so long.

The gathering dispersed, intermingled with the soldiers. William, Clémentine, and Mathilde led the group through the crowd while James limped behind. Emily stayed beside her husband, Mary's hand in hers.

"T'as été magnifique!" Mrs. DeLisle embraced her husband, hugging him and kissing him on both cheeks, one after the other.

"It was nothing." Henri waved a hand, speaking in his accented English, the many medals on his blue uniform sparkling. He hoisted Mathilde into his arms, then offered his hand to James.

James shook it. "Let's hope it does some good."

They all made their way around the ossuary, heading back toward where they'd left the cars.

"Daddy?" Mary looked up at James. "Why weren't you standing with the other soldiers?"

"I'm working for the paper." It wasn't the full truth, but it wasn't entirely a lie, either. He caught Emily's gaze and winked. "How can I cover the event if I participate in it?"

William was oblivious to his family's conversation, reading aloud from a small guidebook, his eyebrows rose. He looked a lot like James, but some of his features—his eyes, his nose—reminded Emily so much of her brother.

"'The monument's design represents a sword, driven into the ground to its hilt.'" The boy glanced at the building, then back to his book as he walked. "'It holds the remains of one hundred thirty thousand soldiers who died in the ten-month Battle of Verdun in 1916.'" He looked up, an expression of awe on his face. "A ten-month battle? That must have been extraordinary."

"You mean terrible." Emily shook her head.

What was it about war that so fascinated young people, boys in particular?

"Le pire." *The worst.* Clémentine nodded, her lips pursed. "My family lost two sons here. My brothers."

James and Henri shared a look.

"I'd like to show you something." James threaded his arm around his son's shoulders and steered him out of the group. "Henri, tu viens?"

"Certainement." Henri set Mathilde down and followed his cousin.

"Can I come?" Mary looked up at Emily.

"Stay with me, sweetie." She ignored her daughter's protests, watched as the men led her son over to the little glass windows running around the base of the building's back side. She knew what was in there, what William was about to see.

The view into the crypt, the heaps of bones, the vacant skulls, the jumbled mass of destroyed, decayed youth.

All the glory of war.

Emily and Clémentine reached the cars and helped Mary and Mathilde into their seats. When William appeared with James and Henri a few minutes later, he was pale, his eyes on the ground.

James met Emily's gaze, nodded. "Let's get some lunch in town."

William put a hand to his stomach, the mention of food a poor accompaniment to what he'd just seen.

Satisfied, Emily climbed into the car, careful not to crush

the bouquet of white flowers they'd left on the seat. "Yes, let's do."

She hated seeing her son absorb such a harsh lesson, but how else could they make him understand?

As the car sputtered to life and James followed Henri's vehicle away from the ossuary, she thought of her own brother, of a younger James, the foolish, youthful innocence that had led them to join the Army for adventure at a time when everyone should have known what was about to happen.

Better to teach her son here, now, than let him learn on a battlefield, like all the French and German boys in the ossuary had learned. She turned in her seat to look back at the monument, but it was already out of sight.

AFTER EATING an early lunch in Verdun, they drove north, passing through small, quiet villages, their walled gardens and neat, rain-washed buildings cozy in the warm sunshine. It was all so strange and unfamiliar to James, and he couldn't help but wonder if he was in the same place he'd seen so many years ago. The names were the same, but—

"Vauquois?" He leaned low over the steering wheel, trying to re-read the sign before they passed it. "Did that say Vauquois?"

"Yes." Emily pivoted in her seat, shading her eyes from the sun.

"Did you fight in this town?" William's head appeared in James's rear-view mirror, blocking the view of Henri's car on the road behind them.

"No." James shook his head, unable to stop himself from looking around, trying to take in the peaceful, tidy village around them. "No, we marched past it. Only it wasn't here then."

He could see again in his mind the little mounds of debris, the flattened, desolated spot, the young officer searching for a town that no longer existed.

"How can you remember it if it wasn't here?" Mary's innocent confusion warmed his heart.

"The Germans destroyed it." James returned his attention to the road.

"It's beautiful." Emily's hushed voice held a sort of awe, and he understood.

People were rebuilding. Slowly, but surely, the War was fading away.

They arrived at their destination in the late afternoon, winding their way uphill through the village of Romagne-sous-Montfaucon.

"Muse-Argonie American Cemetery." William read the words carved into the stone walls flanking the entry driveway.

"Meuse-Argonne." Emily corrected William's pronunciation.

The driveway ran along a low, flat area between two slopes. Young trees covered the slope to the left, scattering the sunlight into little gold medallions on the grass, and a stately white house stood at its top. The slope to the right…

James gripped the steering wheel harder. He knew without looking what the white blur in the corner of his eye really was. He parked the car next to a wide, circular reflecting pool, a small fountain in its center. A second later, Henri parked behind them. They all exited their vehicles, the usual fussing to get the smaller children down and out of the cars.

Emily turned to look up the white slope. "Oh…"

She put a hand to her mouth, reached for James.

He took her hand, gripped his cane with the other, drew a steadying breath, and faced the cemetery. It was bigger than he'd imagined. Large, rectangular plots flanked by young trees and filled with brilliant, white crosses in perfect rows. His gaze followed the central, tree-lined alley leading to a white stone building with the sun behind it.

The memorial chapel.

He shielded his eyes and saw its proud, classical façade and colonnade, its shaded, white stone tinged blue.

Emily started forward but stopped when James didn't move. She looked over at him, and squeezed his hand tighter. "We don't have to do this."

He swallowed, his mouth dry. "Yes, I do."

Without another word, the two families walked up the hill to the central alley. James looked to the side, reading the names and ranks as they passed, his knee aching like it always did these days. Had he known any of these men? Seen them die? His gaze came to rest on a headstone, its inscription different from the others, and he stopped.

Here Rests in Honored Glory
An American Soldier
Known Only to God.

His throat constricted, and he heard Emily's intake of breath. They all stared at it in silence for a moment.

"No one knows who is in there?" Mary tugged on James's overcoat, the little bouquet of flowers in her hand.

He tried to keep his voice even. "No one knows."

James left it at that. He didn't want to trouble his little girl with knowledge of what artillery could do.

William walked over to the stone and rested a hand on it, frowning. "Maybe our uncle is under one of these."

Almost certainly not.

"Maybe." Emily gently tugged William away from the headstone, and they continued walking.

It took longer than seemed possible to reach the chapel, its size and the immense scale of the cemetery making it seem closer than it really was.

"You see this?" Clémentine pointed.

James followed her gesture to read the inscription above the chapel.

In Memory of Those Who Died for Their Country.

"Euh, comment dire en anglais?" Clémentine placed a hand on Mathilde's shoulder and turned to her husband, speaking in French. James understood, but waited for Henri to translate for everyone else.

"Ah, yes." Henri nodded. "She says it's interesting they chose to say '*their* country' rather than simply, 'America.'"

Not understanding, James stared back at his cousin.

"You see," Henri continued. "These men died for France as well. We remember them, too."

James hadn't thought of that before. Had any of the men buried there?

The group started again, and soon they entered the chapel. James took off his hat, his head swiveling to study the space around them, the vaulted, white stone ceiling, the rows of brown mahogany chairs, the American eagle in the polished marble floor, the Allied flags gathered around the *livre d'or* in the rear alcove. Stained glass windows flanked the room, showing the insignia of the US Army divisions.

William looked between the two windows, then up at James. "Which one was yours?"

"That one." James pointed so his family could see. "The red number one on the khaki-colored shield."

"Let's have a moment of silence." Emily bent her head and closed her eyes.

James did the same, but his mind remained blank. This

place was so calm, so fine and beautiful. How could it possibly represent all the things he'd seen? It was completely at odds with the war he remembered.

After Mary and Mathilde started fidgeting, they returned outside and walked along the colonnade. They passed a large, multicolored map of the battle engraved in the stone and continued until the list began—the names of the missing, the men with no known grave.

Emily walked in front, and James stayed behind her. He knew she was searching.

She stopped in her tracks, and everyone gathered around her. She reached out, her hand trembling. She hesitated, and James saw the name carved into the wall.

CULVER William PVT 1ˢᵗ CL 26ᵗʰ INF 1ˢᵗ DIV NOV 6 1918
COLORADO

Emily pressed her hand to the stone, her breathing erratic. James knew without looking that she was crying. Mary and William looked at each other, alarmed. Their mother didn't cry often.

James stared at the name of his best friend, rooted to the spot. Just words, carved stone, but the memories… He fought to keep his composure, realized he was crying, too.

After a silent minute, Henri cleared his throat. "We'll give you a moment."

The DeLisle family turned and walked back along the colonnade and toward the cemetery.

James reached for his wife, stopped. Was it appropriate for him to comfort her? Wasn't it his fault, after all?

All the years later, he still lived with the guilt.

Emily answered his silent question by taking his hand in hers, the fingers of her other hand still on the wall of the missing. James gripped her tightly, leaned his cane against the wall, and reached out. His fingers touched the cold stone.

"Can I see Uncle William?" Mary's voice drew his attention.

"Of course, you can." James released his wife's hand and took his daughter into his arms. His knee protested the extra weight, but he held Mary up, her bouquet filling his head with the scent of flowers. She extended her little hand and placed it over the name, copying the adults. A second later, William was there placing his hand beside his mother.

James didn't know how long they stayed there, but it was Emily who finally broke the silence.

"The worst part is that he's still over here, whatever is left of him." She looked away from the wall and met her husband's gaze. "I'm sure all he wanted was to come home, and we couldn't even return the smallest piece of him."

"That's all any of us wanted." James set Mary down, biting his lip from the pain in his knee. "To come home. Would you like to leave the flowers, Mary?"

Mary nodded, her face the very image of seriousness, and she carefully laid the bouquet on the stone beneath William's name. They stayed a minute longer, the four of them gathered together. Then Emily turned, and James took up his cane.

"They all wanted to go home." Emily gestured at the crosses as they walked downhill back to the car. "I wonder if this place is a good thing after all, leaving them in France."

James nodded. "I'm not sure it's what any of us would have wanted."

"We can bring home here." William looked up at them, his lips pursed.

It seemed such a simple, childish idea, and yet…

Emily smiled, wiped her cheek. "Then we must come back again."

"Yes." James glanced back over his shoulder, back toward the name he knew was there. "We must."

~

"HOW MUCH LONGER?" Mary panted, gripped the stair rail.

"We're almost at the top." Emily reached out for her daughter. "You'll be glad you did it."

"The view is great!" William's voice reverberated down from above.

The boy had sprinted ahead of the group as soon as they'd arrived at the American Monument at Montfaucon, a tall, slender tower sculpted to look like a huge Greek column with lady liberty at its top, an observation platform at her feet.

"I'll bet I can get up there first!"

Henri had accepted William's challenge—though he hadn't tried hard, Emily noted—while the others followed behind.

To have that much energy again...

Emily imagined her younger self carrying supplies at the canteen, supporting the weight of wounded soldiers. How had she ever done all that? She looked past Mary at James, who lagged behind the others, wincing with every step.

"Hurry up, slowpokes!" William shouted again.

"Will someone remind that boy this is not a playground." James huffed, his discomfort clearly souring his mood.

Emily turned and continued up the staircase, Mary in tow. She stopped a couple more times to let Mary catch her breath and allow James to catch up. At last, the stairs ended on a small landing, a narrow doorway leading out onto the platform.

Mary let go of Emily's hand and ran to the low stone wall that ran around the circumference of the platform. "Oh!"

"Oh," Emily repeated, taken aback by the beauty of the view.

The French countryside stretched out below them, clumps of trees, rolling green hills, neat fields, little, buff-colored towns with slender church steeples pointing skyward. The sun was almost setting now, casting everything in orange-gold light.

Emily's throat grew tight, emotion constricting her chest. *This* is what William had died to save. *This* is what he and James had helped protect. *This* is what she'd suffered and worked to preserve. Many years had passed since she'd stopped repeating the same, tired justifications for the War, the hollow talking points of politicians. But if this place, this graceful countryside survived, had the War really been empty after all?

She searched for the idealism of her younger self. Was there just a shred of meaning in it all?

Emily heard heavy breathing and turned to see James emerge onto the platform, leaning on his cane, sweat on his forehead.

His gaze moved past her to the view, and his eyes opened wider. "That's… incredible."

"'The tower is the property of the American Battle Monuments commission.'" William was reading from his guidebook again. "It rests on land the use of which is granted to the United States in perpe… perpe.'" His brow knotted as he tried to work out the word.

"Perpetuity." Emily took James's hand and tugged him to stand beside her.

"Yes, perpetuity." William returned his attention to the book. "'The ABMC's guiding mission is to ensure, as its chairman, General John J. Pershing, who led America's armies in the World War, has said, that 'Time Shall Not Dim the Glory of Their Deeds.'"

James huffed. "What glory?"

Emily didn't think anyone else heard him, because they continued about their cheerful business. Henri and Clémentine pointed out features of the landscape to Mathilde, while William and Mary dashed around, trying to identify the landmarks identified in the guidebook. James just stared forward, gripping Emily's hand tightly.

After a few minutes, the children grew bored. Henri seemed to notice James's stone-faced silence, because he pointed toward the staircase. "I'll take them down. Meet you back at the cars?"

Emily smiled at him. "We won't be long."

In a moment, she and James were alone on the platform. A cool breeze rustled her hair. The light had faded to red now, painting the white stone of the monument a rich auburn.

"It's all happening again." James spoke so suddenly Emily jumped. He looked at her, frowning, and shook his head. "'The glory of their deeds?' You'd think they were talking about something good and beautiful. There was no glory in it. I didn't think they'd forget so soon."

"No, but..." Emily couldn't argue with that, but she wanted him to understand her thoughts, the realization she herself had just made. "Look at it, James."

She swept her arm over the landscape. She imagined free people living out their lives in peace, growing their crops, raising their children. She imagined a time when people who would live in the War's shadow would forget it entirely, benefitting from sacrifices they never knew. Certainly, other wars would come—how could they not, some day? —but somehow this would all survive, a heritage that couldn't be erased. How could she share this with James? How could she make him understand?

She tried again. "This is what you and William and all the

others did. *This* is the glory of it. Not fighting or bullets or generals. *This.* It's here because of you... because of us."

"It's a fine thought." He looked out at the landscape, the sunset painting him red. He raised her hand to his lips, kissed it. "At least I will always have you."

"Always."

They stayed there, hand in hand, until the sun had slipped below the horizon, and then took the long journey down the stairs, leaving the drowsy countryside behind to join the loved ones waiting for them below.

The American attitude toward the First World War is a paradoxical one. On the one hand, the average American, when asked about World War I, will confidently tell you that the United States showed the rest of the world how to fight, saved the Allies, and won the war almost single-handedly. On the other hand, if you ask this average American to name a single World War I battle in which Americans fought, he or she will draw a blank. While the contribution of the United States to the Allied victory of 1918 has become part of the American mythos, the Great War itself and the men and women who served and died in it have largely passed out of memory. In the United States, the Great War lies somewhere between hubris and ignorance, overshadowed by the larger World War it spawned.

It is my hope that this novel will inspire readers to learn more about the single most influential conflict in modern human history. The First World War wrecked empires, redrew maps, resurrected the dreams of national and ethnic identities, kindled new ideologies and galvanized old ones, changed the course of art and culture, and ignited tensions, jealousies, and hatreds around the world into wars and conflicts. It is difficult to look at a news headline today and not see some connection to that clash that shook the world a century ago. To better understand the Great War is to better understand both the 20th and 21st centuries, and our future.

The First World War also fundamentally changed the role and stature of the United States. An economically powerful but traditionally isolationist country with a small volunteer army found itself for the first time in the role of an international leader as the exhausted European empires collapsed and declined. While many Americans today may point to the Second World War as the origin of the US as a superpower, that story began a generation earlier. Only by studying the true beginnings of this story—the mistakes and missteps, the triumphs and tragedies—can we fully appreciate and understand the fullness of American history.

On the scale of the individual American soldiers, sailors, canteen workers, doctors, and nurses, the First World War was a unique and harrowing challenge. An unfortunate side effect of the assumption that US forces were always the best has been to obscure their real triumph. A small, unprepared US military rose within a short time to become the equal of the more experienced armies in the field and make a critical contribution to the final, decisive battles of the war. US troops learned these lessons the hard way, through bloody trial and error. Their courage and endurance during this hideous process makes their martial accomplishments all the more laudable.

Another side effect of the US mythos around World War I is the degree to which we have forgotten the sacrifices of our allies. US history classes, which often devote a fraction of the time to World War I that they grant to World War II, would do well to point out the staggering losses the Allied armies suffered before the US even joined the conflict. The US gave the Allies the final impetus to defeat Germany on the Western Front, but it was British, Commonwealth, and French soldiers who did most of the work to secure this terrible victory. In particular, the French contribution to the war and to training, equipping, and mentoring US forces was absolutely critical. French losses in both lives and property were beyond anything Americans today can imagine. Unfortunately, the full story of France in World War I has fallen victim to ignorance and, at times, the bizarre bigotry some Americans reserve for our oldest ally. It is a story that has yet to be fully told in English, and I challenge readers to discover it.

When I visited US World War I cemeteries in France, I vowed to the dead resting there that I would do something, anything to tell *their* story and make people remember them. Visit the Normandy American Cemetery at Omaha beach at almost any time of the year, and you will find it deservedly crowded with Americans paying their respects to the 9,385 heroes buried there. Visit the Meuse-Argonne American Cemetery, the eternal resting place of some 14,246 US soldiers, marines, and other personnel, and you may find, as I did, that you are the only American there, and perhaps the only one to have been there in days. If this novel motivates some few Americans to make the journey overseas to visit the men and women still resting there, it will have been a worthwhile endeavor.

During my lifetime, the last veterans of the Great War have passed away, and the War itself is fading from all living memory. Perhaps it is the tragedy of being forgotten, heaped on the mountain of tragedies that was World War I, that has always motivated my passion to study, understand, and educate others about this conflict. People like William, Emily, James, and Walter suffered death or emotional and physical traumas in the name of the Allied cause, many sincerely believing they were creating a better, more peaceful world. They came home to societies that had changed fundamentally in some ways but remained cruelly indifferent to what they had endured in others. The generation that fought the War to End War witnessed the horrors of the Second World War and the uncertain pall that fell over humanity with the coming of the Atomic Age. I have always felt that to forget these people now would be one final injustice against a generation that had its dreams and lifeblood torn away from it. In my characters, I hope to give these tortured souls some measure of repose and immortality. They live in our memories, and we shall not forget them.

Benjamin White-Patarino
    November 11, 2020

Photograph by Karina Puikkonen

Benjamin White-Patarino discovered a passion for military history as a small child and has lectured and written several articles about the topic, with a particular emphasis on the weapons and tactics of the First World War. After earning his undergraduate degree from Ithaca College, Benjamin taught English in France for two years before returning to the United States to obtain his master's degree from Colorado State University. In addition to writing, Benjamin enjoys gardening, hiking, and is a semi-professional competition target shooter and two-time state gold medalist. Benjamin lives and works in Colorful Colorado with his fiancée Courtney.

www.ingramcontent.com/pod-product-compliance
Lightning Source LLC
Chambersburg PA
CBHW031043110726

47900CB00003B/789